THE SHADOW GATE

MARGARET BALL

THE SHADOW GATE

Copyright © 1991 by Margaret Ball

The translation from the Anglo-Saxon Chronicle at the beginning of Chapter Two is taken from *The Lost Gods of England* by Brian Branston. Copyright © 1957, 1974 Thames and Hudson; reprinted by permission of the publisher.

The translation of Pope Urban's speech at the beginning of Chapter Four is from *A History of the Expedition to Jerusalem, 1095–1127* by Fulcher of Chartres, translated by Frances R. Ryan, published by the University of Tennessee Press in 1969.

The translations from Bernard Sylvestris at the beginnings of Chapters Seven and Nine are from the translation by Winthrop Wetherbee, published by Columbia University Press in 1973.

A Baen Books Original

Baen Publishing Enterprises
P.O. Box 1403
Riverdale, NY 10471

ISBN: 0-671-72032-5

Cover art by Tom Kidd

First printing, January 1991

Distributed by
SIMON & SCHUSTER
1230 Avenue of the Americas
New York, N.Y. 10020

Printed in the United States of America

"Up the airy mountain,
    Down the rushy glen,
We daren't go a hunting
    For fear of little men."
    —William Allingham,
    "The Fairies"

The book was lying open on the round table just inside the curve of the bay window, with light from the window dappling the picture of the forest glade and the little running stream; just as if it had been waiting for her. Lisa stared down at the picture and felt the calm of the scene soothing her raging headache. She could dimly hear the telephone ringing, steps outside and someone calling her name. *To hell with it,* she thought. *I don't have to go back. I can stay here as long as I want to.* Even as she thought the words, she knew that there was nowhere else in the world she would rather be than right here, looking at a picture that with every breath she took grew brighter and more vivid and somehow more real, much more real than any of the dingy furnishings around it. Lisa stared into the picture until she felt a dizzy blackness swirling about her, as if she were going to faint—no, as if she were being poured through a funnel, spiraling down and down in a black whirlpool, with nothing to cling to but the spot of brightness at the end of the funnel. She stared into the brightness, gripping her own hands so tightly that her fingernails cut into her palms, and gradually the point of light grew until it was the forest glade again; but with a difference. She was standing under the arch now, not looking through it; and when she took a step forward, the grass sighed under her feet; and when she knelt to drink at the stream, the water was as cool and clear and refreshing as she had always known it must be.

PROLOGUE

Thirtieth year of Queen Alianora—In this year the harvests failed, so that many poor folk, both mortals and elvenkind, had suffered but for the Queen's charity in giving of grain from the royal stores.

One hundredth year of Queen Alianora—The harvests having been poor these three years due to the inclement conditions, and the royal stores of grain being exhausted, the queen of her mercy remitted the third part of the tax due from every household within the royal demesne.

One hundred twenty-third year of the reign of Alianora called Queen of the Elvenkind—In this year departed the elven-loving Order of Saint Francis from these lands, the monastery, outbuildings, and serfs being now under the gentle and merciful rule of our own Order of Saint Durand, and may God blast with His fires all heretics and ill-disposed who resist the change.

One hundred fiftieth year of the reign of Alianora called Queen of the Elvenkind—In this year departed many of the lords of Elvenkind to join their cursed brothers the Jinni in Outremer, they saying that the land was too poor to sup-

1

port them, and now by the mercy of God may
we pray for better harvests that these soulless
ones are gone from the land, and may the rest
of their detestable sort follow them that the
curse on the land may be withdrawn!
—Extracts from the Chronicle
of Remigius Monastery

Alianora, Countess of Poitiers, Duchess of Aquitaine,
Regent of the Garronais and Queen of the Middle
Realm, held court in her palace at Poitiers.

In the hushed blue evening the stains and crumbling cracks in the palace walls were barely evident;
the flaws of age were softened, hidden in the hazy
sweet-scented air, swirled away by mists and illusion
until the casual observer saw only a vision of perfection rising above the encircling ring of the gardens:
white walls and slender white columns, spiral stair-
ways rising as sharply and sweetly as an *aubade*, high
pointed roofs shimmering with the iridescence of
seastone brought all the way from the sandy shores
of the Garronais.

A garden of sweet herbs and flowering trees encircled the palace, and beyond that, a wall of silence
and invisible forces warded it against the hubbub of
the dense-packed medieval city. In the streets of
Poitiers a carter swore at his oxen and lashed them
until they lurched forward and all but overturned his
stuck cart, a mason defying guild regulations by working past sunset swore even more vehemently when
the carter's load of quarried stone tumbled against
the back of the cart with danger of cracks and flaws, a
wine-shop keeper shouted the virtues of his wares to
calm the men's tempers and an impudent girl threatened to report them both to the burgesses of the city
if they didn't give her a sip from their cups.

Within the palace garden, a scant hundred feet

away, the Lords of Elfhame watched in appreciative silence and listened to the slow reluctant rustling of a rose unfurling its petals, brought from bud to full bloom in the course of one evening by the Lady Vielle's magic. Upstairs, those who were disinclined for such frivolous amusements paced a hall whose floors of pink-veined marble were worn smooth from many hundreds of years of such pacings, and discussed the future of the realm in low worried voices.

"Roses and moonlight!" burst out a thin golden-haired man when he heard the murmur of applause from the gardens. "Time was when the Lady Vielle's grandsire would have raised the winds and the waves to be his horses, and the court would have ridden from Poitiers to Outremer in one night's joyous adventure, with the water-horses foaming white beneath us and their haunches surging with the power of the tide. *That* was the High Magic! And now we toy with flowers while the Mortal Realms press in upon us daily."

His voice carried to the gardens below. "If *you* have the power to raise the water-horses, Lord Yrthan, be sure I shall ride one," Lady Vielle called up. "Until then . . . perhaps you would care to demonstrate your strength by turning my rose into a green growing tree?" Her sharp mocking laughter was echoed by the dancing notes of a lute played by the mortal jongleur who stood behind her.

Yrthan's right hand clenched and he made a quick casting gesture over the balcony. A shower of gray sparks flitted down upon the elvenkind assembled in the garden, sparkling and stinging where they landed. The petals of the rose turned gray, then black, and it drooped in Vielle's hand and gave off a stench of something long dead and rotting in stagnant water. With a little cry of dismay Vielle withdrew her hand, shaking the last of the gray sparks off her long fingers. She and her friends retreated to the shelter of the lower terrace, trailed after by the mortal jongleur with his lute.

Yrthan's companions wrinkled their noses at the foul smell that arose from the dead rose.

"I meant only to let it age, to make her see the petals falling," Yrthan murmured in apology, shaking his head. "The simplest magics go awry these days."

"And we're no more use than those children."

The High Lords of Elvenkind moved inside. In the garden, now that none of the elvenkind were watching, the walls of silence shook a little under the pressure of all the human noise outside, and a trace of a girl's tipsy song came through the rift. The rose was a bud on its bush as it had always been, freed of the illusions cast by Vielle and Yrthan, and with its inmost nature untouched by their weak magics.

And in the innermost chamber of the palace, a windowless room shrouded by silks woven by the Jinn of Outremer, Alianora d'Aquitaine wove her plans to restore the strength of Elfhame to its former glory.

In her three-hundredth year the Lady of the Middle Realm appeared untouched and smooth as a young girl. She was not as fair as most of the elvenkind; honey-brown hair streaked with gold fell loosely around a face gilded with the touch of the desert sun. That coloring was a memento of her first mortal marriage; riding on crusade to Outremer, barely tolerated by the good mortal clerics of the party for her friendship with the Jinn who guided them, she had been amused and delighted to discover that with enough sun, elven skin could change color just as that of mortals did. Pleased with the effect of this golden skin setting off her elven-pale eyes, she had maintained the tint for decades with only a little effort. It was not solely a matter of vanity; she liked to keep the conservative elder lords like Yrthan a little worried, to remind them that their liege lady was an unpredictable person with a strange taste for marrying mortals.

The man who attended her was one of the youngest in her realm; Berengar, Count of the Garronais, subject to the regency of Alianora until he attained his majority in some fifty years. In mortal years he was old enough to have ruled his own lands for two decades; as the Lords of Elvenkind counted time, a man of thirty-five was an impetuous youth, barely out of leading-strings and hardly to be trusted with control of any lands more extensive than his nursery garden.

Alianora, who had married two mortal kings, had a slightly different view of time and maturity. Her second husband had been no older than Berengar when they married, and a year later he had won the English crown. Of course, mortals were hastened towards maturity by their tragically short life-spans, like a flower forced to bud and bloom in a night by a trivial forcing-spell; still, there were circumstances in which a man like Berengar might be of more use to her than the counselors who usually surrounded her. Yrthan and his friends would have known that what she proposed was impossible, unwise, a defiance of the basic tenets of Elfhame and far too dangerous to be contemplated for a moment, lest what remained of their failing powers be destroyed in a moment. Berengar was young enough to attempt the impossible.

And besides, he was rich in the wealth that meant more to the elvenkind than any lands or gold. While Berengar still knelt, head bowed, before her, Alianora's glance strayed to the boy who knelt beside him. Kieran of Gwyneth, Berengar's fosterling.

It was part of the natural balance of things that the elvenkind, who lived for hundreds of years, should rarely bear children and should prize them above all things. Every elfin child grew up petted and cherished, surrounded by grave lords and great ladies who accounted it a rare honor to have their braids pulled or their backs commandeered for games of knights on horseback, loved and petted and brought gently into the way of the people. As they grew into their powers they were taught control of those powers and of their own emotions; people who could raise a storm or flatten a hayfield with an angry gesture had to learn very early not to make any gesture without thought for the consequences. And so the children were doubly cherished, once for their rarity and again for the freedom that their ignorance and relative weakness gave them. Alone among the elvenkind, the children cried and laughed, sang and raced and fought and gave way to the demands of the moment. Every elven child, before he began to reach the age at which his powers would become manifest, was a spoiled and petted darling, indulged in a way the mortalkind would judge sheer foolishness.

Every child but one. Kieran was the last child to be born to an elven couple in twenty years, and he had not been spoiled as was the birthright of every elven child. His parents had died untimely and he had been raised by a mortal couple, fishers on the Welsh coast. They brought him up overstrictly, fearing his elven powers and not knowing when or how they might become manifest. At ten, angry, confused by his developing powers, knowing that his mortal parents feared him and not understanding why, he had stowed away on a fishing boat to find his elven-kind in Brittany. Berengar had discovered him by chance, a boy of ten raging at the sea that would not obey him, desperate and angry and lost and starving, and had promptly claimed the boy as his fosterling.

Now, at twelve, Kieran was as steady and controlled as any elven child approaching his time of power, but without the legacy of love and laughter that should have been his. And the need for that control was debatable. *Once we raised the waves for our steeds and rode the air,* Alianora thought, unconsciously mirroring Yrthan's complaints. *Now most of our arts are illusion, and we know not what rides the clouds.* Even in this interior chamber, protected by walls and hangings and halls and gardens, from time to time she could hear the mortal clamor of her city of Poitiers breaking through the wards of silence that should have kept the High Queen's palace inviolate. Those noises raised echoes in her mind of the troubling rumors that had begun in the Middle Realm, and of some troubles that were more than rumor. It was said that those bound to darkness were free again; true, the Wild Hunt fed on mortal souls and not on the elvenkind, but the binding that held them had been of elven making, and it was a poor omen for the future should that centuries-old spell fail now.

It was also said that the lands of the Middle Realm shrank year by year, passing into the hands of mortal lords as the elvenkind lost their old power to control the tides and the seasons and the growing things in the land; and this Alianora knew was no rumor. And her best hope for renewing the strength of the Realm was in this impetuous elf-lad who knelt before her, a child raising a child, and both of them centuries too young to know anything about the catastrophe that had befallen their people before they were born.

"My lord Berengar." At the sound of Alianora's voice the young man looked up. "How much do you know about the Catastrophe?" Before he could speak, she waved him to his feet with an imperious gesture. "Oh, stand up, man. I did not have you brought here to play at games of court rituals. I apologize for having let you kneel so long—I was thinking, but that is no excuse."

"The Queen of Elfhame needs no excuse."

Fleetingly Alianora allowed herself to remember her second mortal husband. Henry Plantagenet would never have knelt so long in reverent silence; no, in the time she'd sat thinking here, he'd have tumbled her into bed between a quip and a jest, gotten another of their strange half-blood sons on her body and ridden away to conquer some place or set some new laws in force. The elvenkind paid a high price in silence and control for their powers and their long life. Could this grave young man, so proper, so restrained, really serve her need?

If not, their case was hopeless. "The Catastrophe, Berengar?" she prompted sharply.

The young man looked up at the pattern of intertwined knots carved around the ceiling. Fists on hips, his short cloak thrown back, he seemed to be searching for the answer in another world. "The Stones of Jura were once the seat of all power in Elfhame. Their magic flowed into the land, and we took it from the land. Lord Joffroi of Brittany thought to take their power into himself by the help of a wizard's apprentice who had stolen the secrets of mortal magecraft. The Lady Sybille, who was then the Queen of the Middle Realm, learned of his intention and confronted him within the circle of the Stones. No one knows what happened then, but that they both died—the apprentice, too, I suppose, but our accounts don't say what happened to the boy—and the power of the Stones was lost to Elfhame."

"No one *knows* even that much," Alianora corrected him, more sharply than she had intended. "What makes you think they both died there?"

Berengar looked confused, and more elven than before, when he'd seemed like a perfectly correct statue. "Why—why, so I had it from my tutor, and it is written so in the scrolls of the great library at Ys."

"Yes. So it is written," Alianora agreed. Too impatient to remain still longer, she rose and paced the length of the small chamber. "My lord Berengar, would you request your page to bring us some wine?"

"Kieran?" Berengar's hand ruffled the page's thick hair.

"At once, my lord."

"You are fortunate," Alianora said as the curtains closed behind the boy.

"I have had him for only two years, and next year he will go to the schools at Ys to learn the ways of his power."

"Even two years is more time to be a parent than most of our people are given now. Before the Catastrophe our children were born infrequently, but there were always enough to replenish the race. Now—" Alianora raised her empty hands before her. "You were the last child born before Kieran. And bringing his spirit into the world must have weakened his parents fatally, else they'd have warded themselves better against the storm that took them. The Realm is dying, Berengar. We must reverse the Catastrophe."

She turned away from Berengar and traced the image on a silken hanging with one long finger. As the cloth shivered and swayed beneath the pressure of her fingertip, the heavy folds moved and different parts of the large tapestry gleamed in the white light that emanated from the knot-carved stone: a lioness licking her cubs into shape, a gerfalcon stooping to his prey, a dragon breathing down cleansing fire upon a leprous knight. "I have spent many months in Ys, consulting with the far-seers and the memory-chanters there, and reading the scrolls of the Catastrophe. Where do you think the power of the Stones went, Berengar? Don't you remember the First Law?"

" 'Power is neither destroyed nor created. It flows and is guided; it is used and it is renewed,' " Berengar recited from memory. "But the Stones are different."

"Why?"

He made a helpless gesture. "Well—their power was destroyed."

"No. I have studied the Catastrophe longer, per-

haps, than any save the sages of Ys, and I myself
have more power to see beyond the Three Realms
than any elven sage in the schools." Alianora paused,
fingering the tapestry. "Berengar, I believe that the
power of the Stones was not destroyed, but sent into
another world. We know that such worlds exist; before the Catastrophe, our folk made Gates in the
places of power, and we visited back and forth freely.
Since then we have not dared to dissipate our remaining powers, for a Gate draws power more than
any illusion. And after all, most other worlds are
hardly places one would take any pleasure in visiting. They have no society worthy of the name—only
mortals, and perhaps a uisge or kelpie here and
there. The one to which I have traced Sybille's spirit
is worse than most."

"You have traced her?"

Alianora frowned and glanced where the silken
tapestries trembled. "Kieran is tactful," Berengar assured her. "He knew he was being sent away; he will
remain in the outer hall until I call him back. And no
one else will pass my page's guard."

"The power of the Stones, Berengar, is like a trail
of stars to those who know how to see. That star-
track leads through the paths of air and outside this
realm. I have followed it and I have seen the world,
even the place on that world where our power goes
and is wasted upon mortals with no strength to use
it." Alianora shuddered delicately. "It is a terrible
world, Berengar. Pray that we are not called upon to
follow Sybille's flight. My worst fear is that she will
have been driven mad by her sufferings there, surrounded by mortals and iron-demons and—"

"Iron-demons?"

"You will see." Alianora regarded him thoughtfully. "Even in that world, there have been some
mortals who sensed the existence of other realms.
One of them dreamed us, and painted his dreams. I

can use his dream-picture to open a Gate, and I can send dreams and callings to bring Sybille back, but I must have your permission."

"Mine? But, Lady—Of course," Berengar caught himself up in midsentence. "The Stonemaids of the Garronais?"

"We have lost so many of the places of power, as mortals infringed upon our lands and as we lost the strength to use them aright. The Stone Circle of Fontevrault is now within the grounds of a Durandine monastery, and there is a mill belonging to the Count of the Vexin over the Falls of Mathilde. The Jinn have reclaimed their own places in Spain and Outremer, and I would rather ask a Durandine brother for help than confess to a jinni how weak we are grown here in Elfhame; besides, they are inconveniently far away."

"There are two circles of standing stones upon the lands of Lord Yrthan."

"Who has his own ideas about the way to save Elfhame." An expression of distaste crossed Alianora's face. "I do not plan to marry again."

"N-no, my Lady. I mean, yes, my Lady." Berengar bent his knee briefly and remained with head bowed while Alianora outlined her plan to bring back Sybille and the power that had leaked out of the Middle Realm with her disappearance.

Some leagues away, in the Durandine monastery at Fontevrault, a circle of robed and hooded figures kept watch over a brass bowl filled with milky fluid. On the surface of the white liquid, shaken and trembling like figures in a dream, Alianora and Berengar appeared; the white fluid around them took on the semblance of silken tapestries, and their voices sounded like the tinny far-away calls of midnight demons. Behind the bowl, a monk skilled in mortal spells murmured ceaselessly and passed his hands over and above the milky potion, keeping the image faintly within view of the others assembled there.

All wore the anonymous gray robes of the order, with hoods pulled low over their faces to maintain the mask of anonymity and equality commanded by the Rule of Saint Durand; but only one man dared speak and interrupt the chanting magic that kept the image in place.

"Enough, I think," he said. "We know their plans. It remains only to keep our own watch and ward over the Gate, and to make sure that we, and not this elfling child-Lord, receive the Lady Sybille when she passes into this realm again."

"If only we could pass through ourselves, and take the lady in this strange world to which she has fled!" exclaimed another.

The first speaker swung towards him. Face and hands and feet were covered in the hooded robe of the Order, but the lines of his body expressed impatience enough. "And how should we know her there? She has doubtless changed her shape a dozen times by now. The spells we craft here may not work there, or may work differently; it is surer and safer to let the elven lords call her back, if we can but catch her on the moment of return."

He gestured back towards the image, wavering for a minute with his interruption, but now taking on new clarity as the brother who changed the spells warmed again to his task. "And even if we could know the lady by sight—would you really want to go *there*? No, my brother. Trust those older and wiser than you in the evil ways of the elvenkind. They do not risk themselves in that world; neither need we. We as well as they can send dreams and imaginations; we as well as they can find those in the other world who are close to us in spirit. I have found such a one, and with his help we will draw the lady

Sybille to us while this young elfling is easily distracted elsewhere."

As he spoke, Alianora was showing Berengar the starry trail of power leaking out of the elven realms, and the world at the other side of the Void to which that trail led. The assembled Durandine monks peered at the milky reflection of that image and shuddered with distaste—just as did Berengar, looking into the spellcast mirror behind the tapestries of Alianora's council chamber. Opposed as they might be in most matters, the elvenkind and the Durandine monks were agreed on one thing: far, far better to call Sybille back by spells and charms than to enter this terrible world in their own bodies! Demons with bodies of iron rushed about narrow tracks, screaming threats at one another and every so often colliding with cries of agony. Stone towers as high as the sky entrapped mortals who did not even know the purpose of their servitude in these monstrous keeps. And other mortals, careless of their weak fleshy bodies, actually descended to the narrow tracks ruled by the iron-demons and hurled themselves before them. . . .

CHAPTER ONE

"I saw a great star most splendid and beautiful, and with it an exceeding multitude of falling sparks which with the star followed southward. And they examined him upon his throne almost as something hostile, and turning from him, they sought rather the north. And suddenly they were all annihilated, being turned into black coals ... and cast into the abyss that I could see them no more."

—Hildegard of Bingen

Lisa could have sworn she'd looked before crossing the street; but the car seemed to come out of nowhere, burning rubber as the wheels screeched around the corner. A horn blared in her ear and the driver of the convertible yelled something as she threw herself out of the way. Her foot slipped on the wet asphalt and she skated forwards. The papers in her hands shot upwards and out, dancing in a vagrant breeze and mixing with a flock of the green and silver butterflies that frequented the garden across

14

the street. Lisa swore quietly and viciously, recovered her balance with one hand inches from the asphalt, and snatched at the papers whirling above the street. Somehow she retrieved them; the butterflies danced on their way; the blaring music from the car radio receded into the distance and Lisa made it across the street with her morning's work, if not her dignity, precariously salvaged.

"What are you doing, Lisa? Don't you know there's a bounty on pedestrians in Texas?" Judith Templeton called from the front steps of the New Age Psychic Research Center. Dressed for work in faded jeans and a Hot Tuna T-shirt, with her long blonde hair tied back with a shoestring, she looked like a time traveler on the deep, shady porch of the old house. "I knew the neighborhood would go to hell when they sold the Pennyfeather place to a fraternity. How did you manage to retrieve everything?"

"Just lucky, I guess." Lisa handed over her stack of Xeroxed papers and kept the originals to return to her own files. "Here you are, Dr. Templeton: copies of all Miss Penny's classes, contracts, and miscellaneous paperwork. Do you really think that's going to help you put the Center's business affairs onto a computer?"

"Probably not," Judith grinned. "The more I know about how my great-aunt has been running this place, the more confused I get. But the southern extended family is a wonderful and terrible thing. Dad would never forgive me if I didn't make one more try to rescue the Center before the creditors and the IRS descend on her."

"The what?"

"IRS. Internal Revenue Service." Judith glanced at Lisa and shook her head. "Come on, even you New Age types must occasionally have to interact with the real world. You *do* pay taxes on whatever minuscule salary Aunt Penny gives you, don't you, Lisa? I mean—oh, no. She does pay you? You're not kept here in peonage, or in enchanted servitude, or whatever?"

"I think," Lisa said, "you're trying to put off dealing with those papers. Let's go inside."

As always, when the heavy front door with its leaded-glass panels swung shut behind her, Lisa felt relieved to be insulated from the blaring world outside. The New Age Psychic Research Center, formerly the Harry James Templeton House, was located less than a block from the last street of windowless black office buildings and empty bank towers that had taken over Austin's downtown; but in mental and spiritual space it was a hundred years away from that world. Thick walls and overhanging eaves and good solid doors, built to keep out the Texas heat and sunlight, now toned down the roar of downtown traffic to a nearly inaudible murmur. The original hanging lamps with their stained-glass shades cast a gentle, multicolored light over the entrance hallway; soothing sounds of wind chimes and ocean waves came from the Harmonic Counseling Center in what had once been a formal dining room, and incense from the Afro-Jamaican Spiritual Fantasy Bookstore in the old library gave the cool air a hint of rose and jasmine.

For once there was no one waiting with a crisis demanding Lisa's attention, and the cabriole-legged mahogany table that she had commandeered for her desk was empty of messages. She hung her purse over the back of the chair, dropped Miss Penny's files in the top drawer of the table and wandered into the incense-scented darkness of the Spiritual Fantasy Bookstore. The curtain of hanging beads and bells tinkled pleasantly as she passed through it, and Mahluli arose from his armchair by the window.

"Can I help you—oh, it's you, Lisa. Come to look at the Nielsen pictures again? Be my guest."

"I'll be careful," Lisa promised.

"I know. I wish I could give you the book, but—"

Lisa shook her head. "Don't even think about it. I don't know how much you had to pay for a first edition with tipped-in plates of Kay Nielsen's illustrations, and if you tell me I'll just start worrying about your finances as well as Miss Penny's. Some day you'll sell the book to a wealthy collector."

"Who will put it behind *glass*, in a *climate-controlled* environment, and nobody will ever enjoy it again." Mahluli James Robertson O'Connor sighed and shook his beaded dreadlocks over his own prediction. "I ought to donate it to the Center—you wouldn't believe how many people have been dropping in to look at the pictures lately."

"I would," said Lisa. She picked up the old book and gently opened it to her favorite illustration. "They're very . . ." But the right word wouldn't come. "Soothing? Inspiring?"

Mahluli grinned. "Yeah. They sure are. Me, if I had to pick a word, I'd say *addictive*, the way you keep coming back to them—and the others, too. Go on, girl. Get a fix. I'll just tend to my business."

Lisa barely heard Mahluli's last gentle jab; her eyes were already fixed on the picture, and she was drinking in the feeling of strength and serenity it always gave her.

Compared with some of Nielsen's better-known illustrations, it was deceptively simple: a peaceful forest scene, a small creek running over boulders and shaded by tall trees, with a central grassy clearing framed by an arch of weathered gray stone. But the longer Lisa looked, the more enchanting detail and variety she saw in the picture. The arch of stone was freestanding, and around it the artist had painted a misty gray sky in which vague cloud-shapes seemed to dance; but beyond the arch, the forest floor was dappled with sunlight, and the green leaves of the trees formed a complex interlocking mosaic against a sky too brilliantly blue to be real. If she stared long enough, Lisa began to feel that she could actually see the sunlight dancing on the surface of the stream, and that the leaves overhead were stirring in an illusory breeze. With just a little more concentration, she would be able to hear the musical rippling of the water as it tumbled over those white boulders; somehow she knew that would be the sweetest sound in the world, one she had been longing to hear for untold ages . . .

"Lisa! Where are you?"

"Doesn't anybody know what's going on around this place?"

Lisa closed the book quickly and hurried back through the bead curtain. The tinkling of Mahluli's beads and bells was like an echo of the stream; the illusion of the picture clung to her, so strong that she found herself shaking her fingertips free of imaginary droplets of water. *I really must stop daydreaming during working hours.* She was almost relieved to turn back to the everyday crises and conflicts that were normal working conditions at the New Age Center.

"Lisa, you've let the storeroom run out of sea salt again," complained Ginevra of Ginevra's Crystal Healing and Meditation Room. "How am I supposed to cleanse my new crystals of their previous owners' karma?"

"Lisa, I need $4.59 out of petty cash *immediately*, and you've gone and left the box locked again!" That was Johnny Z., last name unknown, who sold T-shirts with inspirational messages out of what had once been the butler's pantry. "How do you expect me to give this lady her change if you keep the cash box locked?"

"I have an appointment with Miss Templeton," announced a heavyset man in a business suit. His dark hair was combed back with too much oil, and his black eyes looked over what he could see of the front rooms with an acquisitive gleam that made Lisa uncomfortable. *Real estate*, she thought automatically. *Developer*. "Doesn't anybody tend to business around here?"

Lisa unlocked the top drawer of her desk and took out a spiral-bound notebook. "Mr. Simmons?"

The dark man nodded. "Clifford J. Worthington Simmons III. Well, where is the old lady? I don't have time to waste."

"It is now ten minutes to eleven," Lisa said. "Your appointment is at eleven. If you'll please take a seat, Miss Templeton will be with you shortly." She stared at Clifford J. Worthington Simmons III, fighting down the desire to drop her eyes as she usually did when strangers looked so hard at her, until he backed away and took one of the striped Regency chairs against the wall.

"Hey, nice notebook," said Mahluli, who had come out of his bookstore room to see what all the fuss was about. He took the spiral-bound book out of Lisa's hand and looked closely at the cover design of unicorns dancing on a rainbow. "I don't stock anything like that. Where'd you get it? Whole Foods? Grok Books? How come you don't keep it on the desk?"

"I bought it at the stationery counter at Safeway, and I keep it locked away because otherwise someone like you would wander away with it and I wouldn't be able to keep track of Miss Penny's schedule," Lisa answered, twitching the notebook out of Mahluli's hand and dropping it back in the desk drawer. "And that's why the cash box is locked, too, Johnny—

because too many people have been taking money for change and not leaving me a note of what they took when. Here's your $4.59." Johnny reached for the money and Lisa held her hand back. "Uh-uh. You write a note first, remember?"

While Johnny Z. was scribbling his receipt, Lisa turned to Ginevra. "I'm sorry about the sea salt; we seem to have been using more than usual this month, and Whole Foods was closed this morning."

"It just cakes up so fast," Ginevra agreed. "There must be a lot of bad karma in the air these days."

"Mmm," Lisa agreed. "That does seem to happen whenever the humidity is over 90 percent, have you noticed? Anyway, I bought you a box of Morton's Kosher Coarse at Safeway. You can use that today, or wait till tomorrow and I'll pick up some more authentic salt at Whole Foods."

"Yes, but—"

Lisa glanced at her notebook again. "Don't you have a client waiting for consultation now? Amy Duval. Crystal healing and meditation to strengthen her spirit against a bad situation at the office, 10:45."

"Oh!" All at once the reception hall emptied. Ginevra disappeared in a flutter of hand-painted silk chiffon to placate her waiting client. At almost the same time Miss Penelope Templeton appeared at the door to the back hall, a small white-haired figure enveloped in voluminous white Indian cotton garments, and beckoned to the mysterious Clifford Simmons. Johnny Z. had taken his customer back to examine the T-shirt selection and Mahluli had returned to his reading in the Spiritual Fantasy Bookstore. Judith Templeton, leaning against the front door, raised her hands and applauded with great silent mimed claps.

"I don't know how you do it," she said, "but you begin to give me hope of reducing Aunt Penny's affairs to some sort of order. How *do* you cope with this mob? Are all the secrets of the universe in that notebook of yours?"

Lisa closed the unicorn notebook and slid it back into the top desk drawer. "Oh, well, it's not as bad as it seems," she said. "I was trained to be precise—to keep good records. . . ."

"Must have been one hell of a good secretarial school if it prepared you to deal with the likes of this crew," Judith said. "Where did you say you went to school?"

"Oh, here and there. UT's a pretty good school, isn't it? Do you teach there?"

Judith shook her head. "One year. Never again. If you think these people are nuts, you wouldn't believe what goes on in faculty meetings! I prefer working for myself. No pressure to publish, and I get an interesting variety of jobs. Mostly I help people to computerize their businesses—like this—only usually, of course, I get paid for it. And usually the level of chaos isn't quite this bad. It's a nuisance, though, having to straighten out all the records and business details before I can get down to playing with the computer." She eyed Lisa's immaculate desk. "I could do twice as many jobs if I had a good secretary. I don't suppose you—?"

"The family," Lisa pointed out, "would never forgive you if you stole Miss Penny's secretary-receptionist."

"No, I suppose not. But frankly, Lisa, after looking at the records you've brought me, I really don't think any amount of computer wizardry will shore up this business for long. You may be looking for a job sooner than you realize. Half her tenants are months behind on the rent—or I think they are; she doesn't give receipts most of the time, and she throws away cancelled checks because things that have passed through the bank give off bad vibrations. She's got unpaid bills all over town, threatening letters from all the utilities and an appointment in two days with an IRS agent who thinks he wants to take over the business in lieu of unpaid taxes."

"I know about the bills. We were hoping you could persuade some of the creditors to wait for their money. Now that you're going to make the Center so much more efficient—"

"I am not," said Judith, "a magician. You'd better get some of your crystal healers and spiritual fantasists working on Aunt Penny's case."

Lisa smiled faintly. "I expect they are already doing all they can. Unfortunately, none of it works."

Judith gave her a sharp glance. "No—of course not —but I didn't expect to hear *you* say that."

"Belief," Lisa said, "is not part of the job description. I answer the telephone, keep track of appointments, make copies of lost keys, keep the supply cabinet stocked—when I can—with sea salt and other necessities, and try to keep Johnny Z. and Miss Penny from taking small change out of the cash box without a receipt. I do not do windows, crystal healings, or bookkeeping."

"Just as well," Judith murmured. "That last task would break your heart. Here I am trying to set Aunt Penny up with a computer system to run her business, and I still haven't figured out whether all these people are tenants or business partners."

"Don't worry," Lisa said, "I don't think they know either. It all works somehow, though—"

"They are tenants," announced a deep and unpleasantly familiar voice from the door to the back hall. "I choose my own business partners."

Lisa's chair spun around, carrying her with it in a whirl of mouse-blonde hair and denim skirt. Judith looked up, startled, to see Clifford Simmons standing

in the doorway. For such a big man, he certainly had
come in quietly; there hadn't been so much as the
creak of an ancient floorboard to betray his presence.
And he was looking over the entry room and its
contents—the two women included—with a propri-
etorial stare that she disliked intensely. She slowly
straightened and folded her arms over her chest.
"And since when do *you* say how Aunt Penny runs
her business, mister?"

"Judith, dear." Miss Penelope Templeton was a
dithering gray presence in the hall behind Mr. Simmons's solid bulk. As he moved into the room with a
heavy tread, she fluttered in behind him. "It's not—
that is, you know the difficulties—well, the city
reassessed all the buildings on this block, and the
new property taxes—and there never seems to be
any *money*," she wailed, "and all the bills—"

Judith bent and hugged her great-aunt. "I know
you've had some problems, Aunt Penny. That's why
I'm here—to help straighten things out. And if you
need a loan, I'm sure Dad—"

Miss Penelope drew herself up to her full five feet
two inches. "I have never been a burden on my
family, Judith, and I do not intend to begin now.
Nor do I need money. Mr. Simmons has kindly
agreed to buy the business from me."

"What?"

"And all the stock," Clifford Simmons added, "furnishings, bookstore stock, crystals, incense, er—whatever. You needn't look so worried, girls. I'm going to
let Miss Penny keep right on running things just as
she always has; it's just that we both agreed she
needs a more experienced hand on the wheel. A
man's judgment, you know. I've had some business
experience. We'll get this place turned around in no
time. There may be a few minor changes in opera-
tions—we do need more emphasis on management

and planning—but nothing at all for you girls to worry about."

"I'm not worried," said Judith distantly. "I don't work for you. I was here as a favor to Aunt Penny." She looked at Lisa. "You might want to remember what I said earlier, Lisa." She didn't want to be so crass as to hire Lisa right out from under her new boss's nose; but the girl looked sick and white. No wonder. Having to work for Clifford J. Worthington Simmons III would make anybody sick. Lisa needed to be reminded that there were other jobs in the world, that she was a competent secretary, not a medieval serf.

"Well, well, girls, we'll straighten out all these little details as we go along." Clifford Simmons beamed at them and rubbed his palms together. "I'm sure you're both team players; that's all that really matters. Now, Judy, I'm sure you have some work to do on your computer; why don't you run along and—er—bug the program, or whatever, while I confer with Lizzie here about the mundane details of the changeover." He laid one hand on Lisa's shoulder. "You can begin by making an inventory of the bookstore stock while I look over your records. Where's that notebook I saw you going through earlier? And the rest of your files?"

A stray butterfly wandered in through the open window and fluttered right under Clifford Simmons's nose. He sneezed and flapped it away with his free hand, but the movement only seemed to attract more of the curious insects. They streamed through the window and made a dancing cloud about his head for a few seconds. While he was sneezing and shooing them away, Lisa pushed her chair away from him and put one hand protectively over the top desk drawer.

"Miss Penny's files are confidential until she tells

me otherwise," Lisa said, "and you'll have to discuss the inventory with your . . . tenants. They paid their own money for their stock and they are under the impression that the materials belong to them. You may have bought less than you think, Mr. Simmons."

"I'll start with the files you do keep, then." Clifford Simmons bent over her and tugged at the brass ring-handle of the top drawer. Nothing happened.

"Oh, dear," Lisa said, her voice dripping with sympathy, "it seems to be stuck again." Simmons used both hands to yank at the drawer and Lisa took the opportunity to stand up and put the desk between them. "These old pieces of furniture can be *so* annoying, can't they?"

"It's not stuck! It's locked!"

"Impossible," said Lisa with authority. "There's no key."

"You'll produce the key," Simmons said between his teeth. "Tomorrow. When I come back with my lawyer."

He stood abruptly and strode out of the house, slamming the heavy front door behind him. The three women stood in the entryway and stared at each other.

"Oh, dear," said Miss Penelope waveringly. "He seemed such a nice man when he was offering to buy the house and business. I never thought he would lose his temper like that. Have I made a terrible mistake, Judith?"

"Is the deal final?"

"I don't know. I signed some papers—but then he said something about having his lawyer look them over—and he was quite annoyed that Lisa doesn't have a notary's seal, in fact he said some very unpleasant things then too—"

Judith leaned over the mahogany desk and picked up the telephone.

"Who are you calling?"

"Nick, of course." Judith balanced the receiver in one hand and punched out a long sequence of numbers with the other. "Isn't it fortunate that my worthless little brother grew up to be a lawyer? You need more than computer expertise here, Aunt Penny. And speaking of expertise, where's Lisa?" Judith frowned into the phone. It wasn't a very big mystery, but she did wonder how a desk drawer that had been opening and closing perfectly smoothly all morning had become so thoroughly stuck just when Lisa didn't want to open it. And—surely that window had been closed when they came into the room? She hadn't really paid any attention. . . .

While she listened to the ringing at the other end of the wire, Judith absentmindedly jiggled the drawer with her free hand. No, not stuck. Locked. Clifford Simmons had been absolutely right.

And she'd been standing right there talking to Lisa, and never saw a sign of a key in her hand. "Must be going blind in my old age," Judith muttered. "I'll be wearing bifocals before I'm thirty." Which wasn't so far away, and that was another depressing thought—but then Nick answered the telephone, and she had to explain to him exactly why he should close a fledgling law office in Brownsville and drive to Austin immediately.

Lisa had quietly slipped out of the room while Judith was placing her call. Her head was throbbing and she was sick with worry. If Clifford Simmons owned the business, wouldn't he want to see her resume at some point? He'd want to straighten out the records, to pay her a regular salary by check, to list her Social Security number. And he'd probably think it was most unbusinesslike for her to live in two rooms at the top of the house.

Her safe haven was vanishing, and she needed to retreat to the only other peace she knew: the world of the picture.

"I'll explain later," she managed to say to Mahluli when he asked what all the shouting had been about. Mahluli had to be warned—all the tenants had to know about the change that was descending upon them—but first Lisa had to strengthen herself with another glance at the picture world.

It had changed since that morning, or else her own changed mood was causing her to read new meanings into the complex lines and swirls that indicated trees and stones and clouds. The shadows in the forest were more pronounced than the golden dapples of sunlight. The stream seemed stagnant, with greenish scum gathering along the banks. And the clouds that surrounded the arch were darker, with hints of blue-black thunderheads building in their midst. Lisa couldn't look at the forest; the border of clouds entrapped her and she stared at the vague swirling lines until her unblinking eyes burned. There were things out of a nightmare in those clouds, fearful shapes that she did not want to see clearly; she knew that as well as she knew anything.

There was no peace to be found in the picture today, and still it was an effort to tear her eyes from it. "Mahluli—" Lisa choked out.

He was at her side in an instant.

"What is it?"

"Close—the book?"

Instead he took the opened book from her hands, holding it up to let the light from the bay window fall on the picture. "Now look at that," he marveled. "Looks completely different by afternoon light, doesn't it? You'd almost think it was a different picture now. Fascinating . . ."

With the picture no longer before her eyes, Lisa could move again. She closed the book with a snap and ignored Mahluli's howl of protest at treating his prized first edition so roughly. "We don't have time for that now," she said. "We have to make plans. Get the others in here. I have to tell you what's happened. . . ."

The worst thing was that even while she explained the Simmons disaster to Mahluli and Ginevra and Johnny Z., even while the memory of the storm-scene chilled her inside, she still wanted to open the book and look at the picture again. The craving was a constant ache within her, and no amount of reminding herself of real problems in the real world could take her mind off the menacing storm clouds in that imaginary world.

CHAPTER TWO

Let no one be surprised at what we are about
to relate, for it was common gossip up and
down the countryside that after February 6th
many people both saw and heard a whole pack
of huntsmen in full cry. They straddled black
horses and black bucks while their hounds were
pitch black with staring hideous eyes. This was
seen in the very deer park of Peterborough
town, and in all the woods stretching from that
same spot as far as Stamford. All the night
monks heard them sounding and winding their
horns.

—Anglo-Saxon Chronicle, 1127 A.D.

A wind howled down out of the north and the
clouds of the summer thunderstorm swirled about
the circle of standing stones in the forest of the
Garronais, darkening the sky and sending drops of
rain pattering down on the stiff green needles of the
trees around the circle. Within the circle, and above
it, the sky remained clear and bright; sun sprinkled

the floor of green moss and played over the smooth gray surfaces of the Stonemaidens.

Just beyond that circle, where the path through the forest ended, a high pointed arch rose to mark the entrance to the circle. It was elven work, centuries old and uncountable centuries younger than the Stonemaidens themselves; stone raised and pierced and pointed like a palace of light, designed so that the first rays of the rising sun should pour through it and give the arch the illusion of being carved from light itself. Now, at noon, it was only an arch, and the boy who had been looking through it since dawn had long since felt his expectant wonder fade away into simple boredom. Even the vague distorted glimpse of another realm had ceased to hold his attention; most of the time there was only a gray haze to be seen, and the occasional views of a shadowy book-lined room had become dull through repetition. He had been hoping to see a dragon or a demon or something that might justify the loathing with which Berengar spoke of this other realm.

The lazy noontime heat baked into his bones, tempting him to slumber. He gave a bone-cracking yawn, sleepily hauled himself to his feet and went a few paces away to wash his face in the cold waters of the stream. Before he knelt, he glanced back over his shoulder to make sure that the one for whom he waited had not appeared; then, yawning again, he plunged his whole face into the bubbling cool water and blew a string of bubbles to startle the fishes.

It was in that moment of play and inattention that the thunderstorm closed in, clouds and rain and darkness moving preternaturally fast behind the driving lash of that northern wind. Kieran started up from the stream when he felt the pattering of raindrops on his back. Automatically one hand traced the pattern of warding, and the next raindrops were deflected by his personal shielding. He no longer felt the wet wind against his cheeks, but he could still hear the creaking of the trees around him and the high keening of the storm-wind in the sky above. If the storm grew a little heavier it would break through the light warding he had set; he was too young to have full use of his elven powers, and the task of guarding against wind and rain and falling branches all at once would be quite beyond him.

Beyond the arch, the circle defined by the leaning shapes of the Stonemaidens was bright and sunny. Kieran looked toward it with longing. If only he could take refuge there until the storm had passed! But he had been strictly warned against that. Now that the Gate had been prepared, any of the elvenkind entering the circle might find themselves drawn without warning into that other world that Alianora had shown his lord. Curiosity tempted Kieran, but—what if the tales of iron-demons and such were true?

His musings had distracted him from the gathering fury of the storm. As he'd expected, the wind and rain together were growing too strong for his shielding. Already fat drops of rain were splashing on the surface of his moonwoven cloak; soon enough even that elfmade stuff would be soaked through. Kieran drew the hood up over his head and told himself not to be a baby. A wetting wouldn't hurt him, not like stumbling into the world of the iron-demons would, and he wasn't a child to be terrified by the strange howling of the wind that drove the storm—

Howling, yes. But not of wind. Kieran's head jerked upwards and he froze for a moment as he listened to the long drawn-out cries that echoed on the wind, followed by the sound of a distant horn.

"The Wild Hunt!" he whispered. He knew the sound well enough, but it did not belong to the day. The Hunt rode on moonless nights when the storm-clouds were low in the sky: a dark shadow across the moon, the baying of ghostly hounds whose eyes glowed in transparent shadow-faces, an army of the dead out to capture new souls. Mortals feared Herluin, the One who Rides, and his army of the dead; their folk-tales reached back to the ancient days before elflords and churchlords had joined together to bind Herluin into the darkness, when his hounds could tear mortal flesh and his horn could call mortal souls out to run forever in the Wild Hunt. Of late there had been whispers that those days were coming back; strange tales came from the east, rumors of villages deserted and fields gone unharvested. None had yet been taken from the Garronais, but the silver horn of Herluin had been sounding all too often in moonless nights—and now the Hunt was out at noon, a noon that the summer storm was making almost as dark as night.

He should have guessed. A natural storm would have swept through the circle of the Stonemaidens as easily as through the rest of the forest. Only a spellcast wind would have been halted at the boundaries of the standing stones—as would the One Who Rides and the rest of his ghostly army, as would all created things not akin to the elvenkind or those they called to join them. Beyond the arch, Kieran would be safe from the ghost-hounds, if not from the iron-demons of the other world; and there was no question which he feared more. He took two steps forward, then stopped, trembling with the conflict between fear and duty.

He was of elven blood. What would the Hounds want with him? They hunted souls—and the Church had long since decreed that the elvenkind were without souls. The cold music of the silver horn frightened him, but at least he had no soul to lose to Herluin. But there were others who were not so safe. The village of St.-Remy was only a few miles distant, in the direct path of the storm. The villagers would have been bringing in their scanty harvest when the clouds rolled overhead; now they would be cursing the coming rain and working to save what they could before the storm flattened the fields, and thinking of little else. They had never known the Hunt to ride by day; it was a thing of the night. They would not be expecting it. Their mortal ears would not have the keenness to pick up the sounds of hounds and horn many leagues away, as Kieran's had done.

He might be able to get there in time to warn them. The Hunt might not pay any attention to him. The villagers of St.-Remy were under Berengar's protection, and Berengar was Kieran's lord and also his god, the elven lord who had rescued him from storm and starvation and his own impotent anger, who had given him a place in the world and had taught him how to make the most of his burgeoning elven powers.

There was no choice.

Kieran cast one last look at the safe sunlit world within the circle and then took to his heels, following the path beside the stream. Along the stream until it sank between cliffs to join the River Garron, then across Forty Thieves Field, Black Ewe Paddock, and between the two great oaks—he knew the way to St.-Remy as well as the way to his own chamber. As he ran, his lips formed the words for a speedspell he was not supposed to know yet, and his feet rose until he was just skimming the path, running on air and flying almost as fast as the oncoming storm.

At the first sight of clouds, the men in the fields worked even harder and faster than they had been doing. Stripped to the waist, sweating under the summer sun, they labored to bring in their harvest before rain flattened the fields, and while they worked they muttered prayers to avert the speeding thunderclouds. When the sky darkened, their women joined them in the last desperate attempt to save the grain. They worked beside the men, old wives and young girls, skirts kilted up above the knee, bodices tight to their bodies with sweat. Already drops of rain were mingling with the sweat that fell from the laborers, and the hot summer afternoon was chilled by the wind out of the north. The villagers shouted and cursed and prayed and panted, and no one heard anything out of the ordinary in the wind that whistled above them.

"Send for priest," Arn of the Bridge commanded his crippled daughter. Maud had been limping around the fields with dippers of cool water to slake the thirst of the able-bodied men. "Tell him to bring cross out o' church and hold it up. Maybe Our Lord will stand between us and the storm."

" 'A won't come," the girl reported a few moments later. " 'A's locked self in the church, praying, and shouted to me through the window-slit that us had best get within doors before the storm hits."

Arn took a long drink of water and spat dust and grime out, wiping his mouth with the back of his hand. "What's a wetting to us? It's t'winter's food I'm worried about. What'll us eat then if us hides inside while rain takes the crop?" It was a rhetorical question; before Maud could have answered, he had dropped the dipper back in her bucket and bent again to his task.

After a moment's thought, Maud set her bucket down by the edge of the field and followed behind her father, twisting the stalks of grain into sheaves so that he could spend all his time cutting. Let the men and women of the village walk over to the bucket themselves, if they wanted a drink; she and Arn were the only ones to bring in their share of the crop, and he couldn't spare her at a time like this. Nor could she spare herself. Over and over she bent to scoop up the stalks in her left arm, stood to bind them together with a twist of grass, stooped to set the completed sheaf upright where they could collect it when they gave up reaping for the day. The repeated motion turned the constant ache in her malformed hip into a living fire, but there was no time to think about that. Bend, stand, twist, stoop; bend, stand, twist, stoop. She followed behind Arn and tried to think of nothing else but the task in front of her nose.

She succeeded so well that she almost bumped that nose into Arn's broad back where he stood at the end of the row, sickle drooping in his hand. "What—?" Maud began. Then she saw the elf-boy where he had burst out of the forest. Chest heaving, he was down on one knee, red and sweating and scraped from falls like any mortal lad, and the silver-bright hair that framed his pointed face was dark with sweat. But he had still enough breath to gasp out a warning to the startled villagers.

"The Hunt is up! Get inside, for your souls!"

"Lord Berengar hunting?" Arn said slowly. "Nay, lad, on a day like this he'd be overwatching the harvesters on his demesne fields, wouldn't he?"

Kieran pointed up at the clouds racing by overhead. "Fools." All the customary scorn of the elvenkind for dull, slow, plodding mortals was in his voice; but there was also a note of fear that began to strike responsive sparks among the weary villagers. "Can't you *hear*? It's the Wild Hunt."

"Not by day!" protested a woman in the back of the gathering crowd.

"This is—a spellcast wind," Kieran panted. "I was at the Stonemaidens when it came—the storm couldn't get within the circle. Wind sent to bring the clouds down—make it dark—can the Hunt ride at noon, if a wizard turns noon to night?"

No one knew the answer to that. No one cared to know. For just then the silver sound of a hunting horn echoed through the sky, cold as ice and still as death. The villagers dropped their tools and left the sheaves of wheat standing in the fields.

It was only a few hundred yards to the nearest houses; by the time Kieran had got his breath back and stumbled to his feet, the first of the villagers were already safe. The horn sounded again, and this time it was accompanied by the long baying note of a hound sighting its quarry. The achingly sweet music of the horn robbed Kieran's legs of all strength; his knees were about to bend under him when a girl's hand pinched his arm and then dragged him upright again.

"Come *on*, elf-boy!" the girl sobbed. "You ran this far—you can come a little farther."

Kieran leaned on her and she staggered under his weight. He recognized her now: Maud, the bridge-keeper's crippled daughter. Not a girl. A woman of eighteen, but thin and wasted from the curse that had twisted her hip at birth. And not strong. He must lead her, not lean on her.

And there wasn't time. He could see the red eyes of the hounds now, glowing through the pale translucent gray of their shadow-bodies; and the horn's cold music never stopped; and all the others were within doors now, tumbling in helter-skelter and locking and barring doors and windows behind them. Maud couldn't run, and he was too tired, and the music took all the strength out of his soul; and maybe no one would dare to let them in if they did reach the shelter of the houses.

"You shouldn't have stayed," he said tiredly. With the hounds so close, now circling to cut them off from the village, his confidence that they would not hunt one of the elvenkind was leaking away from him. It was going to be hard enough to raise what little powers of illusion he possessed to defend himself; he resented having to defend this mortal woman too. "Why did you stay? You *know* you can't run; you should have gone at once."

"And leave you?"

She was pale now, and pressed close to him as if she thought his elvish body could give her mortal warmth and comfort. *Very frightened*, Kieran thought. So was he. The hounds were on the earth now, prowling round them in a diminishing circle. He could see the shapes of wheat-sheaves and houses and trees and the stone tower of the church through their ghostly bodies.

"Don't worry," Kieran told her. "They don't want me, not an elf, I've no soul for them to take; and I'll cover us both with illusion so that they won't dare to come near you either."

As he filled both hands with elflight and threw it outward to blaze in a ring about them, he hoped he had been telling the truth.

Near its rising place, the river Garron runs between the steep cliffs which it has carved out of the soft stone of the Garronais, and this narrow course forces the river into a continual splashing of ripples and rainbow-scented spray and sparkling little falls. Farther down, towards the coast, the land is lower and the riverbed fans out into a smooth, sluggish sheet of water and reeds creeping across the sands of the Garronais. But in the forested uplands where Berengar of the Garronais had his keep, the river splashed and sang to itself and threw up arcs of misty spray so that there was a perpetual glimmering of rainbows along the cliff edge. Shapes of towers and turrets and staircases arching into nowhere dazzled the eyes of unwary travelers who had heard, but not quite believed, the tales of the river-mirages of the Garronais.

These shimmering, evanescent images were the guardians of Berengar's keep. The real towers with their outer walls of iridescent seastone were concealed among a host of shifting, rainbow-colored illusions that looked sometimes like hills and trees, sometimes like barren gorges; the mist and spray that rose from the river were subtly enhanced by additional, illusory waterfalls; and a final spell of disquiet ensured that no traveler not of elven blood could stare for long into the misty illusions without feeling a vague discomfort, a fear without reason and a yearning to be somewhere else entirely.

And none of these safeguards, as Bishop Rotrou tactlessly pointed out, would be any protection at all against a band of mortal soldiers armed with iron weapons and guided by a Durandine mage.

"Or a renegade elf," Berengar politely agreed, "for we do quarrel among ourselves, and who knows but one of the elder lords might not offer his services to a mortal army bent upon my destruction? Fortunately, I have no enemies."

"I wish that were true," said Rotrou heavily.

The bishop of the scattered parishes of the Garronais was an old man in mortal terms, nearing his sixtieth year, but he was still strong enough to ride on his episcopal visitations and with a fist heavy enough to put the fear of God into any delinquent parish priest. Long years of mediating between the elven lords of the region and their mortal tenants had left lines on his heavy face and had drawn his thick black brows together in a permanent frown. Beneath eyes as bright and penetrating as ever, his jowls sagged tiredly and his broad shoulders were now slumped from the weariness of his long ride.

Berengar had known the bishop all his life, but the man's bounding energy and enthusiasm had concealed from him, until this visit, the changes brought by age. He signalled one of his mortal pages to pour more wine, and tried to conceal the pity he felt when he looked upon Rotrou's tired face. *When I first grew into my powers, he was a young man; and before I attain my majority, he'll be dead. No wonder mortals are short-tempered and impatient. So little time!*

"Do not trouble yourself on my account, my son," said Bishop Rotrou tranquilly. "I have all eternity to look forward to, while you have only your span of years on this earth—long though they may be compared with ours, still they are finite."

Berengar's hand shook a little, and the red wine of Burgundy that the page had just poured slopped over the edges of his carved wooden mazer. "I have heard that mortal magecraft had improved considerably in the last years," he said carefully, "but I did not know that it extended to the reading of thoughts. And is it not forbidden a loyal son of the Church to dabble in such matters?"

Rotrou's rolling, generous chuckle took years from his appearance. "My son, it takes no great skill in mind reading to know what a young man thinks when he looks upon one growing old. Add to that my knowledge of how you elvenkind pity us mortals our short lives, and you'll see that there was no magecraft involved. But, as I said, the pity is unnecessary; we are in better case than you."

"I am familiar with the Church's doctrine," said Berengar mildly. He, like most elves, had no wish to quarrel with the official decision of the Bishop of Paris—later confirmed by Pope Caritas—that the elvenkind had no souls and hence could not come under the jurisdiction of Holy Church. That decision had ended a wave of heretic-burnings and elf-murders that threatened to tear apart all the kingdoms where elvenkind and mortals shared the land. Berengar sipped his wine more carefully and watched Rotrou under slanted brows, trying to gauge what to say next. It had seemed to him that the bishop was delivering an oblique warning; could that be why he had gone out of his way to visit this keep?

"And," Berengar resumed at last, "I do not think that you came to me, a youth in your world and a child in my own, to discuss high doctrinal questions of Christian theology. I am, of course, delighted that you chose to break your journey here. . . ."

He let the sentence trail off, inviting some response from Rotrou.

The bishop sighed heavily and rubbed one hand over his face. "I am growing old, Berengar. It's a hard ride up from the coast."

Berengar pressed him to stay for the night with all the obligatory phrases of hospitality, all the while wondering how the resources of the keep could be stretched to feed the bishop and his extensive retinue. As the elvenkind lost their ability to ride the winds and move the rain clouds, harvests in this region and many others had grown thinner and poorer year after year. Berengar was lord of a hungry land, and on most nights he dined no better than his mortal peasants, on boiled grain with some milk and honey to lend it substance. Illusion, of course, could turn the meal into the semblance of roast peacocks and almond-sauced fish; but the elvenkind counted it poor hospitality to serve their guests illusory feasts. Magic should be used to enhance a noble reality, not to conceal poverty.

He was relieved when the bishop insisted that he must go on to the Durandine monastery of Remigius that very afternoon.

"It's near the boundaries of my lands," Berengar said, "not two miles, in fact, from my own village of St.-Remy. I'll ride with you that far, my lord."

Bishop Rotrou darted a sharp glance at Berengar. "But not, I take it, into the very monastery itself?"

"You know that the Durandine brothers have no love for my kind," Berengar replied. "And less for me, since I refused to sell them St.-Remy and the surrounding lands so that they could turn out the villagers and increase the empty territories about their monastery."

"Mmm." Bishop Rotrou nodded. "And has it occurred to you, Berengar, that the Durandines alone of our Christian orders are exempted from the prohibition against magecraft? I suspect that their stronger mages could even pierce the shield of illusions that guards this keep."

"Oh, I don't think the brothers are so eager for a little piece of pasture that they'd go to war against me." Berengar laughed, and hoped that he sounded as carefree as he pretended to be. "And if they did— well, my lord, we of the elvenkind have other kinds of illusion at our disposal, and other defenses besides illusion, if it comes to that. It has been a long time since any army of mortal men has cared to risk being transported to the sands of Outremer."

"It has also," said Rotrou, "been a long time since your grandsire performed that feat. Are the elvenkind still strong enough to work such wonders?"

Berengar laughed again. "Ask the men of your retinue, my lord, who had to ride here blindfolded and with elves leading their horses, because they could not abide the spells of aversion which surround my keep."

But he was devoutly grateful that Rotrou did not stay to test Berengar's own powers of illusion on the scanty meal of boiled grain and milk that awaited him below.

From Berengar's keep on the cliffs of the Garron to the hillside village of St.-Remy, the last outcropping of cultivable land before the forest and fields gave way to barren uplands, was a long hot ride for a summer afternoon, and no journey for an aging man who was already tired. Berengar felt guilty for his own selfish relief that Rotrou had chosen to continue on to the Durandine monastery, guilty for not urging him harder to stay, and relieved at the sight of clouds darkening the sky and the feel of a cool rain-scented wind blowing down from the north. At least the clouds would mitigate the heat of the day and make this last part of the journey easier on the old man.

"It looks like a storm brewing," observed Rotrou as they rode out at the head of his little train of guards and clerks and pack-mules with the bishop's formal vestments and his fur-lined cloak and his own linen sheets all following along in neat bundles. "Are you sure you wish to accompany me, my son? You'll hardly be able to return to your keep before dark."

"Then I'll beg a bed and a bite to eat from my villagers in St.-Remy," Berengar replied. "They'll be honored to serve their lord." He did not add that the villagers' coarse bread and sour cheese would be a more substantial meal than awaited him at home.

Rotrou shot him another of those puzzling sharp glances. "Will they indeed? I'm glad to know you have such good relations with your people. These Garronnais are a surly lot; I'd hardly have thought they would welcome a lord of their own race into their homes, much less one of the elvenkind."

"The folk of St.-Remy have reason to like the elvenkind," Berengar pointed out. "The Durandines are eager to get their land, and you know what follows wherever those new monks get land; they turn off the people and build walls to enclose their monasteries in solitude. While I hold this part of the Garronais, they shan't dispossess any of my people so." He did not mention his other reason for refusing the Durandine offers to buy his land. They would have taken not only the village of St.-Remy but much of the forest beyond it, including the glade where the Stonemaidens of the Garronais kept their silent watch. Berengar had been shocked by Alianora's cool summary of how many of the stone circles had passed out of elven hands; even when the present need for a Gate had passed, Berengar was determined not to let the Stonemaidens fall into mortal control.

"Yes. The Durandines are hard to refuse," Rotrou said neutrally. "Some people think they take too literally the commandment of their founder, to go forth and live in the desert."

Berengar's laugh was harsh enough to startle his gentle horse. "The English writer Walter Map said that wherever they go, they either find a desert or make one. Well, the barren section of uplands where they founded the monastery of Remigius is near enough to a desert; but I've no mind to see my own forest and my own villagers suffer such a fate."

"Harvests have been poor recently, have they not? What if your villagers began to leave the land?"

"That won't happen. They are very attached to their homes."

"Really? I'm gratified to hear it." Rotrou paused while their horses negotiated a tricky, narrow bit of path where the forest came down to the cliff edge. When the way broadened, he beckoned Berengar back to his side so that they could resume their desultory conversation. "And grateful, too," he went on as though there had been no pause, "for your taking so much time to escort an old man of another race to his destination. Surely you have duties elsewhere on your lands?"

Berengar glanced up the path. In a few miles it would divide, the straight way leading to the circle of the Stonemaidens and the leftward branch following the steep riverside cliffs to the village of St.-Remy. The stormclouds looked blacker up ahead; he hoped that Kieran wasn't getting a drenching.

"I trust my retainers," he said. When the messengers came to announce that Bishop Rotrou approached and requested guides to lead his retinue through the walls of illusion, Kieran had been overjoyed at the chance to take his lord's place watching at the stone circle. It would have been a gross discourtesy, as well as giving rise to some suspicion, if Berengar had failed to greet this old mortal friend personally. He had considered asking one of his elven knights to take the watch, but Alianora had been strict about the need for secrecy. Kieran seemed the safer choice. The boy had already guessed that something was afoot at the Stonemaidens; his loyalty was absolute and his young face would be a sweet greeting to the Lady Sybille, should she by chance pass through the Gate that very afternoon.

Only now, as he watched the deepening storm, Berengar reflected that Kieran's discretion was possibly not as absolute as his loyalty. The boy was too young to be able to ward off such a pelter of rain as was lashing the trees to the north. Might he be tempted to take shelter in a woodburner's hut? Berengar told himself that his fosterling was too fiercely loyal to forsake his post. He would probably glory in the chance of suffering a little under rain and hail. All the same, Berengar wished that he had not left his scrying-glass at the keep. Without that aid, and with the distraction of Rotrou's company, even his elven senses could not reach quite far enough to sense Kieran on guard at the Stonemaidens. He would have to make an excuse to separate from the party for a few minutes, to cast forward in trance.

As they neared the fork in the path, Berengar rode ahead of the bishop so that he could reach forth to Kieran in peace. His mare, well-trained against these moments of abstraction, picked her way gently along the broad trail until she reached the place where the path split into two. There she waited for the light mental pressure that was the elf-lord's equivalent of a rein against the neck. No guidance came; she lowered her head to the roadside and began noisily munching on the sweet grasses that grew out of the ditch. There were flowers, too: blue lady's-veil with the sweet white centers, and spicy golden dragonsbreath. Delicious! She abandoned all attempts to wake her master.

Wrapped in his trance of questing, Berengar was still distantly aware of the mare's pause and of everything else that was going on around him. One part of his mind tasted the sweet crunchiness of the lady's-veil and the spicy tang of the golden dragonsbreath, heard the bells on the rein of the bishop's fat white horse coming up behind him and the rustling and creaking and gossiping of the bishop's retinue. He could sense the feelings of those behind him, too, not as thoughts put into words, but more like something as tangible as the hard leather of a saddle or the cool wind rustling through the treetops. This questing talent was what gave the elvenkind the name of mind readers, though any who had experienced it knew that the sense was both less and more than the ability to read precise thoughts. It was more a perception of emotions, no more than any sensitive mortal could achieve by paying attention to those around him. Without really thinking about it, Berengar felt the mare's enjoyment of the tasty flowers, the tangle of complex issues and personalities that filled the bishop's mind, the weariness and amusement and boredom and peacefulness that variously occupied the members of his retinue.

He sensed, too, a hard sharp kernel of hatred for himself and all his kind, somewhere in the train behind him; and he flinched away from that without examining it more closely, for fear the hatred and his involuntary response would break the light trance of questing. That would be Hugh, the bishop's Durandine clerk, taught by his order and his own fears to hate the elvenkind as distinctly, unforgiveably, incurably *different.* It was a pity, thought Berengar, that so kindly a man as Bishop Rotrou should have a man like Hugh in his entourage. On the other hand, it was tactful of the bishop to bring his Durandine clerk on an episcopal visit to the Durandine monastery, to show the brothers that the members of their order who went into the world were treated as well as any other clerics. Doubtless that was why he had done it, trusting in Berengar to understand the reason without explanations.

And all this thinking was distracting him from the quest. Once again Berengar spread out his elven senses. Eyes closed, he imagined a gossamer web of delicate strands floating out through the forest, stretching ever wider and thinner until it encompassed all the land as far as the circle of standing stones where Kieran stood watch.

This time he did not allow himself to be distracted by the pungent mix of feelings from the approaching riders; yet still he could feel nothing, no other thinking presence, anywhere near the Stonemaidens. No elf, no mortal, not even a small demon or a nixie. The brightest flickers of consciousness in the vicinity came from the small fish in the stream; and they were like fireflies flickering in the darkness, where he had expected to find Kieran's consciousness burning as bright as a torch.

Berengar cast the net of his senses wider again and yet again. Nothing—no, there was something to the east! He sent tendrils of thought out that way and cried out in shock. Fire and agony and terror of death struck at the delicate web of questing, tearing and parting the net he had constructed. And behind that pain-filled terror was something worse, a cold consciousness that feasted on death and suffering. Berengar felt as if his mind were freezing and burning where he had contacted the alien sense. He reeled in the saddle and fell forward across his mare's neck, gratefully clutching the warm solid reality of her mane.

Coming out of quest-trance so quickly, and so wounded, was like fighting one's way up from a sea-floor where seaweeds tangled about the feet and watermaidens twined their white arms about his neck. Berengar ached with the need to reach the sunlit realm of the forest path where his body lay over the mare, he could see it and he strove upwards to it but reaching it was agonizingly slow. And when he broke through to the surface of reality, the bright colors and undampened sounds and sharp surfaces of the world struck his trance-sharpened senses like so many blows.

The bishop and his followers had come up with him; there were men on horseback ringing him round, looking down with stern disapproving mortal faces made expressionless by the metal helms that framed them. And one severe young face, framed in the dark hood of the Durandine order, held an expression of deep distaste.

"It would seem that the elfling has had a fit," said Hugh, the bishop's clerk, as though Berengar were still unconscious. "Such is the price of working his dark wizardry! My lord, best you leave him here; I warned you not to be contaminated by such a one."

"I'm sure you did," said Berengar before Bishop Rotrou could speak. "But it's I must leave you here, my lord, with my apologies." He would not speak of Kieran's puzzling disappearance from the circle of the Stonemaidens; Alianora had warned him most strictly against giving mortals, or even elflords of the opposition party, any hint of the gamble they risked there. His heart ached to ride for the Stonemaidens and search for his vanished fosterling. But he was lord of a wide land, and there was worse need elsewhere than at the Stonemaidens, and worse trouble afoot than any Kieran could have encountered at that peaceful stone circle.

"My son, you're in no case to ride on!" Bishop Rotrou cried out in protest as Berengar took up the silken threads that served as reins to his elf-trained mount. "I don't know what happened to you when you went on ahead of us just now, and I don't want to know." His fingers flickered in the sign of the cross. "But I do know that you need rest now. Do you return to your keep, and we will go on our way without your help."

"No, my lord," said Berengar mildly. "There's some evil afoot at St.-Remy, and I can reach there before you and your mortal guard—although I'll be glad to know you are coming up behind me, for I couldn't tell from my questing whether iron blades or elven wardings are wanted to cure this ill."

Or whether either will serve us, he added in his own mind, and he could tell from the look on Bishop Rotrou's heavy-jowled face that the good bishop was again reading his thoughts more accurately than any elf-lord could have sensed them.

"Go with God, then," said the bishop. He lifted his hand for a blessing as Berengar's mare sprang forward, obedient to the unspoken command and as light on her unshod hooves as elven powers could make her.

Hugh will give him hell for blessing a soulless elf, Berengar thought with wry amusement; and then he tried not to think at all, as the air rushed by his face and the trees beside the path whisked by at dizzying speed and the mare carried him forward to face the strange evil that had already wounded him, even when he did no more than brush it with the outermost tendrils of his thoughts.

CHAPTER THREE

These are articles disapproved as against theological truth and disapproved by the chancellor of Paris, Eudes, and the masters teaching theology at Paris, A.D. 1240, the second Sunday after the octave of the Nativity.

First, that the elvenkind, being rational and sublunary creatures like humankind, are also possessed of souls which it is the duty of the Church to save. This error we condemn, and we excommunicate those asserting and defending it, by authority of William bishop of Paris.

Second, that the divine essence is. . . .

Chartularium universitatis Parisiensis

The storm that had darkened the fringes of Berengar's lands had moved on by the time he reached St.-Remy, and at first the village looked as peaceful as any place might, with the harvest interrupted by a rain that beat the standing grain to the ground and a wind that tossed the garnered sheaves into hedge and ditch. The villagers were out again in the pale sunlight that followed the storm, squelching over muddy fields to salvage what they could after the disaster. One house had lost its thatch, and there were splashes of mud and broken branches about the churchyard to attest to the storm's fury, but all else seemed peaceful enough. Berengar drew in the mare to a walk and observed the scene from the shelter of the great trees at the edge of the clearing.

One woman, her arms full of broken sheaves and her gown dragging behind her in the mud, glanced up and saw Berengar and let out a cry that drew the other villagers. Her cheeks were stained with tears. She threw herself down beside his stirrup, clutching his leg and begging for something in a thick unintelligible dialect made worse by the sobs that choked her.

"Softly—softly, now!" Berengar dismounted clumsily, trying to shake himself free of the woman without kicking her. When he had both feet on the ground he patted her damp coif and tried to get her to slow down so that he could understand what was troubling her.

"Take me away!" she begged. "Please, m'lord, before they come back—"

Then her voice was drowned out by all the villagers arriving in a mass, shouting, crying, complaining in a cacophony that made Berengar's ears ring. Some babbled of hounds and hunters, some of their own people ridden down, others seemed to have some complaint about the priest, and mostly they just cried for help.

"Peace! Peace, friends!" Berengar shouted, waving one arm in a great commanding circle to sweep them into silence. "What happened here?" He saw the village priest standing at the back of the crowd. Good, at least there was one man with a little wit and learning to tell him a straight story. "You, Father—Simon, is it?"

The man advanced through a crowd that parted silently to let him pass. The peasants averted their faces and the woman who'd been gleaning broken sheaves drew aside her muddy gown as if the holy man's touch could defile it worse than the dirt that already stained the hem.

"I warned them, my lord." Father Simon bobbed his head obsequiously several times, tonsured pate shining in the pale rain-washed sunlight. "I tried to warn them, but they wouldn't heed me until it was too late. Luckily there were only two injured—"

"Warn—them—of—what?" said Berengar in a voice made dangerous by the control he forced upon it.

The priest swallowed and licked his lips nervously. "The Hunt, my lord—the Wild Hunt. Oh, aye, I know it's heresy to believe in such things—but, my lord, the great churchmen who decide what is heresy, they live in the cities, in fine stone towers with tiled roofs. You wouldn't find such a one as the Pope, or our own Bishop Rotrou for that matter, risking himself out in the forest on a day like this. But I heard them, my lord."

"We've all heard the Hunt," chimed in Arn of the Bridge, "but always at night it was, when honest Christian men and women are indoors where they should be. Now it's come in the day. How's us going to work the fields, m'lord, if the Hunt can savage us at high noon?" *What are you going to do about it?* his truculent tone demanded.

"Tell me," said Berengar, "exactly what happened, and then we will decide what to do about it. Are you sure it was the Wild Hunt? The thunderstorm—lightning—sometimes the sounds are frightening, more so when unexpected. . . ."

"I saw them," insisted Arn stubbornly.

"And I," piped up a boy at the fringe of the crowd.

"Riding behind their shadow-hounds, all in armor like . . ."

"Brigands?" Berengar suggested with dying hope.

"Skeletons in armor," Arn said firmly. "And the hounds like shadows on the grass. And they took one of us, m'lord. My own daughter, poor little Maud, couldn't run fast enough, poor crippled soul!"

Something in the man's tone rang false to Berengar. As he recalled, this Arn was a widower who'd beaten and badgered his wife to an exhausted death for the sin of having produced only one daughter, and that one crippled. Since then he complained unceasingly of the injustice of life that had saddled him with an ugly lame girl whom nobody would ever take off his hands. Now he was sniffling and wiping the back of one grimy hand across his face. Berengar was willing to wager that the grief was feigned. But there was some strong feeling there. Fear. The man was afraid; his hand shook and he kept glancing up at the sky as if expecting another attack.

"She could have taken shelter in the forest," Berengar suggested.

"No!" cried the woman who'd first approached him. "I saw them take her—rode down the elf-boy, they did, to get at her, and the poor lad throwing fire and light at them with all his strength to the last—"

She stopped and shrank back, fist pressed against her mouth.

"Kieran?" said Berengar in a voice he no longer recognized as his own. "Kieran here, and wounded, and none of you thought to tell me? Where is he?"

Arn of the Bridge glanced towards a shabby hut at the edge of the fields, and Berengar pushed past the man and covered the muddy distance in a few strides.

The door hung open on torn leather hinges; inside the windowless hut Berengar could just see Kieran's limp form laid on the bare ground. He touched the opal in the hilt of his bronze knife and the elflight blazed forth, a rainbow of colors and dancing lights.

Kieran's silvergilt hair was muddy with blood and his face was pale and cold as ice. Berengar felt a squeezing pain deep in his chest; then Kieran's head moved slightly, he mumbled something unintelligible and his eyes flew open.

"My lord! My lord—"

"Be still, lad. Don't try to get up," Berengar commanded. He knelt beside his fosterling and felt along the bloody locks of hair with the lightest touch he could summon. There was a nasty welt rising on Kieran's head, and a long gash in his scalp had bled copiously enough to terrify Berengar for a moment, but it seemed no worse a knock than any mortal boy might have taken on the tilting grounds. He felt his own breath returning, strong and sweet with life, with each breath that Kieran took; and only now, when he began to feel safe, could he acknowledge the hurt he would have taken if the boy had been lost.

"You mad brat," he said with the beginnings of a smile, "did you think to hold off an army of the dead with nothing but your two fists full of elflight, and you not full come into your powers yet? Next time save your strength to call me or my castle guard, child."

"I should have done that," Kieran acknowledged. "All I could think of was that the village should be warned, and they're all mortals, my lord—no one could have heard my call. I ran here as fast as I could . . ." His face screwed up with the effort of holding back tears.

"Rest easy, brat." Berengar tousled his hair, carefully staying away from the rising lump on the boy's forehead. "I'm not one to fault you for thinking first of your duty; only, next time, think whether you can do that duty best by yourself, or by calling for help."

"I failed," Kieran said.

"The villagers seem hale enough to me," Berengar remarked. "Cowards, and hysterical, and probably lying their heads off, but what can you expect of mortals?"

Kieran's head shifted from side to side. "They took Maud."

"Who? Oh—the bridgekeeper's girl?"

"I promised to protect her," Kieran whispered painfully, "and I failed—and now Herluin has her soul."

"I think," Berengar said, "you had better tell me exactly what happened."

As the whispered tale went on, Berengar's face set in grim, un-elven lines. At the sad conclusion, when Kieran related how Herluin's ice-shod horse had over-ridden him and knocked the sense out of him long enough to stop the flicker of elflight, while the army of the dead behind Herluin dived in and surrounded Maud, Berengar stood abruptly and lifted Kieran in his arms.

"I can walk, my lord!"

"Not now. I don't want you falling and knocking another such dent in the other side of your head," Berengar said easily. Beyond all else, he wanted to get Kieran out of that filthy hut, and both of them away from the villagers who'd left Maud and his foster son to face the Wild Hunt alone. If he didn't have Kieran's weight in his arms, he might not be able to resist the temptation to call down elf-fire on the village as he left; if it wouldn't have made a mockery of Kieran's sacrifice, he might test on these villagers just how much reality he could add to an elven illusion.

And the boy was no weight, besides; lighter and frailer than Berengar would have thought, and cold to the touch. Had he taken another wound that he wasn't speaking of? "You'll ride before me back to the keep," Berengar said. There Idaine, who had been his nurse and his father's, could try to warm the boy with her healing spells.

Kieran twisted in Berengar's arms. "No! The Stonemaidens, my lord! Who's watching for the lady Sybille? If she comes through the Gate now, with nobody to guide her . . ."

"*Hush.*" As he stepped through the low door of the hut, Berengar saw the bright sparkle of Bishop Rotrou's gold-bordered riding cloak; the bishop's train had caught up with them. And of all mortal men, the bishop's Durandine clerk Hugh was surely the last whom Berengar would wish to get a hint of the elven quest for Sybille. The Durandines had a name for attracting the few mortal men who had any skill in magecraft; it was inconceivable, of course, that mortal spells could compare with elven powers, even weakened as the Elder Race was now, but still there was no need to have the Durandines alerted and possibly weaving counterspells.

"God's grace to you, my lord Berengar," Rotrou greeted him calmly, "and to your fosterling. I trust the boy is undamaged?"

"He took a hard knock on his hard head," Berengar replied, "but I think it is nothing that will not heal with rest and quiet. The girl, though—"

Rotrou's quick frown warned him not to go on. "Yes. The villagers tell wild tales. Doubtless the child fled into the forest when the brigands came."

"Brigands? *Brigands*?" Kieran was twisted half upright in Berengar's arms. "My lord, it was the Wild Hunt. I saw them with these eyes."

"The Wild Hunt has no power to do physical harm," Rotrou countered, "nor may Herluin ride abroad by daylight. He was bound to darkness before your father's father lived, child—yes, even more than three elven life-spans ago! Now let us have no more of this talk, upsetting the village to no purpose."

"I know what I saw," Kieran muttered obstinately.

Rotrou smiled and ruffled the boy's bright hair.
"But do you know, young master, that if I believed
your tale of the Wild Hunt, I would stand in danger
of being arraigned for heresy? The Council of Clermont
decided that the Wild Hunt was a peasant superstition, the rite of binding performed on Herluin no
more than a show to persuade the country people to
give up their pagan sacrifices. And our best theolo-
gians have proved conclusively that demons have no
power to harm good Christians in this life, save by
tempting them to sin. A bishop of the Church must
not seem to believe in what the Church has decreed
nonexistent, must he? But to calm your fears—" He
turned to his clerk. "Brother Hugh, did you not
reach the rank of exorcist in the minor orders before
you joined the Durandines? I shall trust in you,
then, to ward all here from this ghostly Hunt."

"I pray for mortals," Hugh said. "The elfling will
have to take his own chances with his own kind."

Kieran smiled sweetly at Brother Hugh's thin, tense
face. "If the Hunt takes me, little brother of Saint
Durand, your council of churchmen may have to
rethink their decrees. For the peasants say the Hunt
wants only souls. What use do you think my soulless
elfin body will be to them?"

"Enough, Kieran! The Hunt takes no one who is
under my protection," said Berengar.

"Or mine." Rotrou stepped forward, holding up
the heavy silver cross that he wore as a pectoral.

Kieran's smile was so sweet that it hurt Berengar
to look upon his face. "You are too good to an elfling,
my lord of the church. But I have seen the Hunt,
and you have not. They have Maud now, and if they
ride again I do not think that your pretty toys will
stop them."

"Do not blaspheme," said Rotrou evenly. He inclined his head to Berengar. "It grows late, and we
must be on our way to the Remigius. God keep your

people, Count Berengar—since my clerk will doubtless accuse me of heresy if I pray God's blessing on
your princely self!" Smiling gently, he raised his
hand and sketched a cross between them. The deep
color of the ruby on his right forefinger caught fire
with the afternoon sun and dazzled Berengar with a
dash of brilliant red light.

That night Berengar sat up over Kieran's bed,
watching Idaine as she called a warm golden healing
light to flow between her wrinkled palms and bathe
the cold wound on the boy's head. Three times the
light washed over the edges of the wound, and each
time when Idaine relaxed her efforts the flesh was
torn and bruised as before. On the third attempt
Kieran cried out incoherently and tried to twist away
from the healing light. "It hurts, my lord—it hurts
me so!"

Idaine sighed and lowered her hands. The fierce
concentration left her face, and for a moment she
looked as old as any mortal woman feeling the weight
of her years. "I know not what it is," she told Berengar.
"Iron leaves a raw edge to the flesh like this, and
iron-wounds resist our healcraft; but if he had been
struck by an iron horseshoe, the wound should be
hot to the touch, not cold like this. It is growing
worse; when you brought him home, it was only the
wound itself that felt cold, now it is the whole side of
his head and his neck. And I know not why the
healing light should pain him, except . . ."

"Except?" Berengar prompted gently.

"Whatever made this wound," Idaine said reluctantly, "must be inimical to all life and growth and
healing. And some of its essence must have passed
into the wound itself, maybe even into the child—"

"*No.*" Berengar gripped Idaine's wrist and turned
her bodily away from the bed. "There is nothing
wrong with Kieran—nothing but a blow on the head

—he will recover in his own good time!" He paused, fighting for control. "You may leave us. I will watch by the boy's side until he is better."

Two miles from the village, in the Remigius monastery, others also kept vigil. Indifferent to day or night, the Durandines held a chapter meeting whenever there was business to discuss or news to impart. Tonight a single task consumed them.

"The village of St.-Remy must wait," their leader decreed. "We will offer the villagers shelter and succor in good time, should they fear another attack; but tonight is our chance to capture the lady Sybille. The boy's words made it plain enough that he had been charged to watch at the Stonemaidens. And his foolish lord took the child home to tend his wounds, instead of returning to his guard duty! If she can be brought through tonight, my friends, we shall never have a better chance of taking her. Join with me now in sending our will to that weak fool in the other world. He has delayed long enough—he shall bring her to us now, with no more excuses, or else she shall bring herself. They cannot both resist our will."

The bowl of white fluid over which the monks bent their heads quivered slightly and showed the world of the iron-demons again. In that world it was still early in the day, and the sight of the great metal demons that rushed about their narrow paths made several of the younger monks shudder and cross themselves in thanks that they had not been forced to live in such a terrible world. The image in the bowl shivered, almost dissolved; the leader of the Durandines bent a stern glance on the weaker novices and all returned to their whispered chant. Now the image steadied to show a single street, a house, an antechamber within that house and a thin, fair-haired girl speaking to a small black demon that perched on her shoulder.

CHAPTER FOUR

Let those who have been accustomed unjustly
to wage private warfare against the faithful now
go against the infidels and end with victory
this war which should have been begun long
ago. Let those who, for a long time, have been
robbers, now become knights. Let those who
have been fighting against their brothers and
relatives now fight in a proper way against the
barbarians. Let those who have been serving
as mercenaries for small pay now obtain the
eternal reward. Behold! on this side will be
the sorrowful and poor, on that, the rich; on
this side, the enemies of the Lord, on that,
his friends. Let those who go not put off the
journey. . . .

—Speech of Pope Urban before the First Crusade

"Yes, eight-thirty tonight. I'll be here at eight to
open the house, but Dr. Templeton and her brother
will be chairing the meeting. You can come? Good."
Lisa hung up the phone and made another neat,

precise check mark against one of the names written
in her unicorn notebook. Things were going well;
only ten o'clock in the morning, Clifford Simmons
hadn't shown up yet with his threats and his personal
lawyer, and more than half the people she'd called
had agreed to come to the emergency meeting that
night. It would be an ill-assorted group; Judith had
instructed her to contact anybody who might possibly be interested in keeping the New Age Center
going. Everybody who'd ever taken a class at the
center was on the list, together with the members of
Miss Penelope's Thursday morning bridge group,
the managers of Whole Foods and Grok Books, and
the entire staff of the Friends of Jung Spiritual De-
velopment School on 43rd Street.

And she'd only worked her way halfway down the
first column of names. Lisa sighed and reached for
the telephone again, wishing she weren't so painfully
shy. Normal people could telephone complete strangers and demand to break into their evening plans
without blushing in embarrassment. Normal people
didn't find their palms sweating and their temples
throbbing with the effort of sounding cool and businesslike while making their demands. Normal people
sat at their desks and did their jobs instead of hiding
in the smoky darkness of Mahluli's bookshop and
staring at the pictures in an old children's book—

Lisa set down the telephone again, closed her eyes
and took three slow, deep breaths, in and out, the
way Ginevra had taught her when she first came to
the Center for counseling. *Stop that!* she commanded
herself. *You're doing fine. Really. You're doing just
fine.* Three more breaths; feel the breathing from the
chest, from the diaphragm, from the energy centers
of your body. What else had Ginevra told her in
those first confusing days? *Don't worry about "normal" people. Everybody has their own problems.
The guy you're talking to is probably just as nervous*

as you are, honey, only you don't see it because you're too wrapped up in your own worries.

Lisa smiled and opened her eyes while continuing the deep, rhythmic breathing. Ginevra's wisdom was one part New Age theories to nine parts middle-aged Texas housewife, but she would never know that what people came to her for was just that salty common sense and not the magic she thought she worked with her crystals.

And there was no need to go back into the Spiritual Fantasy Bookstore for another look at that picture. In fact, considering how upsetting it had been last time, Lisa told herself, she was better off not ever looking at it again. Maybe Mahluli was right; it was like a drug to her, and the effects were getting worse even as it grew more addictive. Certainly the dry-mouthed craving she felt whenever she thought of going into the bookstore was like withdrawal symptoms, or what Lisa imagined withdrawal symptoms must feel like.

She took one more deep, calming breath and put her hand on the telephone again, then hurriedly snatched it back at the sound of a heavy step on the front porch. Even before he opened the door, Lisa knew who it was: Clifford J. Worthington Simmons. The Third.

He was alone, though. *What about the lawyer?* Lisa wondered, and thanked her good luck that she hadn't been on the phone when Clifford walked in. Before he was through the door, she had closed her notebook and slid it into the top desk drawer in one easy, unobtrusive motion.

"Ah, Lizzie." He was beaming; he leaned across the desk and shook her hand, pumping up and down and holding on fractionally too long.

Very friendly. His lawyer must have advised him not to antagonize us until the deal goes through.

Fine. Let's stall until Judith's brother gets here to tell us what our options are.

"Good morning, Mr. Simmons," Lisa said in her best neutral-pleasant-receptionist manner. "What can I do for you today?"

"Oh, nothing in particular." Clifford hitched himself up on the corner of the desk; it gave a warning creak and he hastily abandoned his casual pose. "I just thought it might be a good idea to drop in, gab a bit, touch base with everybody here. I'd like to get to know all the folks on my team a little better, make sure we're all going to pull together to make this outfit a winner. Since you're not doing anything, we might as well start now." He leaned over the desk again, this time taking both her hands and directing an intense stare. "I want to know all about you, Lizzie—who you are, where you're coming from, what you do here. I could tell, yesterday, that you're the grease on the wheels that makes this outfit keep spinning around smoothly. Now I want to know the real Lizzie, the girl behind that competent mask."

Lisa could not withdraw her hands from his damp grasp without fighting him. "To begin with," she said, "my name is Lisa, not Lizzie."

"Ah—right. Well, can't blame me for a little mistake, can you? Especially since I haven't seen your resume yet. In fact, I haven't seen anybody's paperwork. Why don't you get it out for me now and I'll just have a little glance over the papers, get filled in on your background and all that?"

"I'm sorry, Mr. Simmons. All the papers you want are in that desk drawer. Remember? The one that's stuck."

"Oh. Well. You'll just have to fill me in as we go along, then, won't you? And how about getting a locksmith out to work on that drawer?" Clifford's warm, friendly smile was getting a little crinkled around the edges. "You know, Lizzie—Lisa—not to criticize, I know I'm very much the new boy on the block around here, but it does seem to me you might have gotten on that little detail yesterday. A good team player does what's needed without waiting to be asked." Another of the deep, intense, penetrating looks. "You *are* a team player, aren't you, Lisa?"

Lisa dropped her eyes and hated herself for doing so. Clifford's unblinking stare made her feel undressed —no, worse; as though he were trying to read her innermost secrets. *Come on, honey, why would the man care about your innermost secrets?* Lisa could almost hear how Ginevra would laugh at her and dispense a little spiritual advice in her Texas twang. *He's got his own karma to work through, just like all of us. You stay centered and don't let the bastard get you down.*

"You know, Lisa, I can sense things about people," Clifford announced.

"You can?" Lisa stared at the man's clasped hands. Big strong fingers dusted with dark hairs, one knuckle broken at some time, ostentatious gold ring set with an opal—that was strange, she would have expected a diamond. A large one.

"And right now I can sense that you are a deeply troubled young woman, with no understanding of your own place in the universe. You are far from home, aren't you, Lisa? Very, very far from home. And you've been lonely for such a long time. I can help you."

If she didn't look at the man, his warm, slow voice was actually rather soothing. "Just rest for a minute, Lisa, rest and look at the pretty ring. That's right . . ." Cliff's voice faded, then came back stronger than before. "Look here, this is pretty too. This is what you wanted, isn't it?"

Lisa nodded slowly. She felt as if she were slipping into the lazy, sun-warmed waves of the Gulf coast, rocking back and forth. The twisting, flashing blue and green lights of Clifford's opal ring were like water, like the ocean—no, cool, like a forest stream with green trees shading it and an arch of ancient gray stones framing it. If she put out her hand she would feel the sunlight on her skin; if she walked through that arch, she could wade in the little stream and drink the water. Cool and fresh and tingling against her throat—Lisa could almost taste it now. Clifford's voice was a droning buzz far away at the back of her head; nothing was real now except the thirst she felt for the water of that little stream.

"Why, Mister Simmons, I declare, what a pleasure to see you here again!"

The picture disappeared in a thunderclap and Lisa cried out in pain. The light of another world danced briefly around inside her head, shattered in a shower of bright rainbow shards and disappeared, leaving her in a tiny room too full of people. Clifford Simmons had forgotten her and was reaching out for the book that Judith had snapped shut and taken away from him in one brisk movement.

"Give that back!"

"Why?" Judith looked too innocent to be real. "I recognize this book; it's from Mahluli's stock. And it's quite valuable. I'm sure you and Lisa enjoyed looking at the pretty pictures, but I really don't think you ought to take rare books out of the shop without Mahluli's permission, do you?" She whisked through the bead curtains before the bookshop room and was back in a minute, patting her heavy briefcase and looking meaningfully at Lisa. "And I'm going to have to borrow Lisa for a little while; she promised to help me enter this data into the computer, and I can't do any more work until she's finished the data entry phase."

Lisa rather thought Clifford Simmons began to protest, but Judith just kept talking over his burbles while she took Lisa by the arm and urged her out of the room. "You know how it is with software," she called back over her shoulder, "you have to have some test inputs to validate the algorithms before you can formalize the alphanumerical verification routines for the security sets—and I'm sure you, as a businessman, know how important that is!"

The hall door closed behind them with a satisfying thud and Judith gave a little sigh of relief. "Horrible man. I hope we can foil him tonight—goodness, what an old-fashioned word, but he is rather an old-fashioned villain, isn't he? I want to see him twirl his mustache and groan, 'Curses, foiled again!' when we block his purchase of the Center. Ginevra?" she called at the door to the Crystal Reading Room. "That Simmons man is snooping around in the reception area, and I need Lisa. Could you possibly go out there and keep an eye on him? Maybe you could give him a free crystal reading to keep him busy?"

"My pleasure," said Ginevra with a grim smile.

As they continued back to the little room that Judith had commandeered for her computer work, she kept up her cheerful babble. "I realize you still have to call a bunch of people for the meeting tonight, but you can't very well do that while dear Clifford is hovering over your desk, can you? We'll just have to wait until he gets bored and goes away. Oh, and did you call anybody on the Texas Historical Landmarks committee? I should think this house is easily old enough and elegant enough to get landmark status, and if Clifford wants it so he can tear it down for condominiums, that'll put a spoke in his wheel. Of course it takes months, but maybe we can get a restraining order or something—Nick will know how to do that, lawyers are real good at slowing things down, have you noticed? Here, take the chair, you look kind of shaky."

Lisa thankfully sank down on the gray swivel stool before the computer and stared at the blank screen before her while Judith took a seat on a box of printouts. "What exactly did you want me to do?" she asked. "I'm afraid I couldn't understand what you were telling Mr. Simmons."

"Nobody on this earth could have," said Judith with the impish grin that made her look thirteen instead of nearly thirty, "it was cybercrud. GIGO. Nonsense," she translated finally as Lisa only looked more confused. "Don't you know *anything* about the real world? I thought everybody had to learn about computers in school these days. Don't worry, Lisa, I don't want you to do anything. I just don't approve of sexual harassment, so I thought I'd break up the scene before Clifford did something you'd have to sue him over. What was he doing, trying to get you to go out with him? Or did he just want to sneak a kiss behind the water cooler?"

"Oh." Lisa's memories of the scene were rather confused. "Was that what he was trying to do?"

"Sure looked like it when I came in," Judith said cheerfully. "And he tried to back me into a dark corner yesterday, with some line about being able to sense that I was confused and didn't know where my home was, or some such gobbledegook. Hah! *I* know perfectly well where I live, and I'm not about to tell him; he'll have to think of some better line than that. And he's got to keep his paws off Mahluli's stock, too, or Nick will sue him for everything he's got when we're through with this other little problem."

Lisa spun around to face Judith and nearly fell off the stool. "The Kay Nielsen book! I don't know how he got it—I thought I was watching him the whole time, honestly—"

"Don't feel bad," Judith said. "Dear Cliff was probably a pickpocket before he became a real estate developer. Natural affinity, don't you think?"

"But we left him alone in there, he'll go back— maybe he wants to steal it—"

"Ginevra's watching, remember? And the book's in here." Judith carefully lifted the old book out of her briefcase, dislodging a sheaf of green-striped computer printout as she did so.

Lisa felt weak-kneed with relief. The thought of losing the Nielsen book had frightened her beyond all reason. It wasn't just the probable cost of a rare first edition; Mahluli could be repaid in time. But never to see it again—that would be a wrenching loss. Someday, she supposed, it would be sold, but she had managed not to think about that.

"It is a nice book, isn't it?" Judith mused, idly flipping through the pages. "Ordinarily I don't care much about rare books and all that—I'd rather have a paperback that I can stick in my hip pocket and read without worrying about cracking the spine—but this, oh, I don't know, it feels different. Maybe it's that old binding. Just makes you want to hold it. And the pictures are . . ."

Her voice trailed off as she stared down at the blue and green forest scene, Lisa's favorite of the many illustrations.

"Hypnotic," Lisa said. She reached out to close the book, carefully averting her gaze from that enchanted glade where the stream ran forever clear and pure. "Mahluli said addictive, like drugs, but I don't think that's quite right, do you?"

Judith shook her head briskly as if clearing away imaginary clouds. "They're *something*, anyway. I don't know just what, and I'm not sure I want to know. I'll leave that spiritual jazz to you—ssh. I think the Team Player is about to visit us. Are you ready yet to tell him to go to hell, or—oh, all right; use the old staircase door. I think you'd better have a few assertiveness training classes before you meet Dear Clifford again."

"A few what?"

Judith sighed. "One of these days I really must bring you into the twentieth century."

"Don't bother," Lisa said. "It's a nice place to visit, but I wouldn't want to live there." She slipped through the back staircase door as Cliff knocked, silently blessing the eccentric makers of eccentric old houses who'd put doors and closets and servants' staircases everywhere.

The only trouble was, the back staircase had been used as a storage room for so long that Lisa didn't think she could get up the stairs without dislodging something. She would just have to wait amid the clutter until Cliff went away.

At least she could make a place to sit down. Two dozen copies of *Mysteries of Ancient Egypt* were piled on a stack of white terry robes that had been left behind when the Women's Self Defense and Meditation Clinic vacated the basement. Lisa carefully moved the books and sat down on the pile of robes, transmitting a mental thank-you to the two girls who'd run the clinic. Like most of Miss Penny's tenants, they were lavish in offers of free classes to make up for unpaid rent; the difference was that they'd actually had a skill worth teaching, and Lisa had thoroughly enjoyed the series of classes she took before they went out of business entirely. Now the robes—left behind in lieu of the last two months' rent—were gathering dust, and the basement was occupied by an acupuncture clinic whose offers of free treatment Lisa determinedly turned down.

Lisa leaned back and dislodged a stack of cardboard boxes containing flyers for some long-defunct program. She dived to catch the slithering pile and almost succeeded; the noises were limited to one scarcely audible squeak of alarm, one thump as her elbow collided with the staircase wall and the rustle of the last set of flyers skating down the stairs.

"What was that?" Clifford's heavy voice demanded.

"Mice, I expect," Judith said calmly. "The house is riddled with them, hadn't you noticed? Ever since the foundation shifted and left those cracks in the walls we've had mice and scorpions coming in. You can hear the mice squeaking in the attic if you listen. Aunt Penny would like to get it fixed, of course, but she's never been able to raise the money—and there's the plumbing leak, too; you know those pretty green butterflies we have all over the place? The inspector said they're attracted to leaking sewage and the city will be serving us a notice about it soon. Of course if you buy the place you'll be able to get all those little things fixed; the work shouldn't cost more than fifty or sixty thousand."

"Ah, well, a few little repairs should be no problem," said Clifford. "I was really looking for Lisa."

"Poor girl, she wasn't feeling at all well," said Judith. "You can see that she wasn't able to do anything for me either." There was a pause, presumably while Judith pointed out the blank computer screen. "I told her that she'd better go home and rest."

"Where does she live? I—as it happens, I was just on my way out. I'd be happy to give her a ride."

"Oh, not far from here, I think, and anyway she's already gone. But if you're leaving now—so soon? do let me show you out; Aunt Penny will be so sorry she couldn't chat with you today, but you know how it is . . ."

Judith's loud, cheerful voice faded away into the long hall, and Lisa crept out of her dusty hiding place. A moment later she heard the thud of the heavy front door swinging shut, and then Judith returned, dusting her hands with the air of a housewife who's just disposed of a dead lizard. "We really ought to change the locks," she said as she came in, "Clifford is worse than an army of mice. Anyway, having just announced he was leaving, he had no alternative but to get into his car and drive away while I stood on the front porch and watched him out. It would be a BMW, wouldn't you know?"

"What would be what?"

"His car. It's a yuppiemobile," Judith translated. "I know you don't drive, Lisa, but haven't you ever noticed those large steel boxes on wheels that roll around our streets? Like the one that almost killed you this morning? A BMW is a very expensive variety of the same, suitable for men who wear gold pinkie rings. And I think we've established that he wants the house so he can tear it down, not so that he can take over the Center. Anybody who wanted to buy this place for honest purposes would have turned white when I fed him that line about the mice in the attic and the sewage leak in the foundation, don't you think?"

"You nearly convinced me," Lisa told her, "and I *know* there aren't mice in the attic—I live up there."

"My God," Judith said, "I was right. You really are a medieval serf. No wonder Aunt Penny can always count on you to open up the house for late classes; you can't get away from this place."

"I like it here," Lisa said.

Judith sighed. "Yes, I know, but—oh, never mind; I'll have to put off saving your soul until we've saved Aunt Penny's house and business. It's about time you got here, Nicholas. I never would have guessed you could take twenty-four hours getting from Brownsville to Austin."

Lisa spun round. She hadn't heard the front door opening and closing or the steps coming down the hall. The man who stood in the doorway was as large as Clifford Simmons, but he must have been incredibly light-footed to have moved with such silence through the creaky old house. And he didn't look a thing like Judith. He wore a dark suit, impeccably businesslike and anonymous, instead of faded jeans and a black and silver Grateful Dead T-shirt; his hair was black instead of bright yellow, combed neatly instead of frizzing out around an inadequate ponytail holder; and his cold blue eyes looked through and past Lisa in a way that made her feel as if she wasn't really there at all.

"Neither would I," Nick said. "I had a few small items of business to take care of for my Brownsville clients before I could leave."

Judith squealed in pretended delight and threw her arms round Nick. "Oh, my little brother has some real live clients! At last! I can't believe it!"

A little of the frosty look came out of Nick's eyes and he bent to kiss his sister on the top of her frizzy ponytail. "Do you think by the time we're sixty you will be able to stop patronizing me?"

Judith pretended to think. "Depends. You going to be a real grown-up by then?"

"Look," Nick said indignantly. He spun round, arms extended, and Lisa ducked out of the way. "I'm wearing a real suit. I have real clients. I'm a real lawyer. And if you didn't believe in my capabilities, why didn't you hire some local shyster and save me the trip?"

"I prefer my own personal shyster," Judith said, "the local lawyers won't work for free. And I never said you weren't a smart kid. Now sit down and let me explain the problem."

"Is this a general meeting?" Nick asked, looking at Lisa. "Or is this young lady part of the problem?"

"Oh, I'm sorry. I haven't introduced you. Lisa, you must have guessed that this is my rotten kid brother. Nick, Lisa is the mainstay of the Center and the prop of Miss Penny's declining years. She keeps all the Center's vital data in a magical unicorn notebook, and if you offend her, she'll look cross-eyed at her desk drawer and the notebook will automatically lock itself away and the telephone will stop working."

"Very impressive," Nick drawled. "I gather that means she's supposed to be sitting at the front desk, keeping suspicious characters from prowling through the building. Right now anybody could walk in. And the telephone has been ringing for some time."

Lisa mumbled an apology and escaped the tiny room before Judith could draw her into the council of war. Judith might tease her about acting like a medieval serf, but Nick obviously thought she was one and ought to know her place better. Clearly it was beneath him to discuss the Center's legal affairs with a mere secretary. "Obnoxious, arrogant, presuming son-of-a-*bitch*," she chanted to herself on the way down the hall to the reception room.

Ginevra's curly head popped out of the Crystal Healing Room. "If you're looking for that Mr. Simmons, honey, he's gone home with a bad headache—and good riddance!"

"Sometimes," Lisa said darkly, "the cure is worse than the disease." She dashed into the reception room and grabbed the phone just as it quit ringing, said a few more good twentieth-century words that would have cheered Judith to hear, and settled back down to her list of phone calls.

Clifford Simmons slowly navigated his gleaming BMW down the Austin streets and cursed every dangling live oak limb or carelessly parked pickup that threatened to mar the shining perfection of his paint job. He hated this untidy snarl of streets west of the Capitol, with their old-fashioned houses and untidy lawns and ill-assorted clutter of people. The new office buildings downtown were more to his taste, gleaming black glass and polished pink granite and smooth hard edges. A pity they were mostly empty in the current recession—or perhaps not such a pity; his own imposing office was nearly rent-free, the owners of the building were so grateful for any tenants to make the place look occupied.

He wanted to be back in that office now, comforting his soul with the sweep of his kidney-shaped mahogany desk and the polished chrome desk set and the cube of smokey black glass that most people took for a paperweight. All the symbols of success, and concealed among them, real power that the fools he dealt with never recognized. He *could* sense things about people, could make them do and say what he wanted, could gently push men and events the way he wanted them to go. Ever since he could remember, even back when he'd been a rawboned farm boy named Clay Simcik, Cliff had known about the power. His mother gave him extra cookies when he'd earned a scolding; his teachers smiled and passed him up to the next class without bothering about little details like his abysmal reading scores. Even now Cliff had trouble reading the long legal documents that crossed his desk. So what? If you're powerful enough, you can always hire somebody to do your reading. Why bother with deciphering chickenscratches, when you can get what the scratches mean by looking deep into someone's eyes and pushing his soul the way you desire?

Nothing mattered but that, the rush of power he felt when somebody gave in against their own inner resistance. Easy ones like his old lady schoolteachers were no fun; he could never be sure they weren't really passing him out of pity or misguided kindness. The only time he really knew and believed in his own powers was when he could make somebody do something they really didn't want to.

Cliff paused in the snarl of traffic on Fifth Street, enjoying his own memories and oblivious to the backed-up cars that blocked his way. There'd been that old man, the dean, who didn't understand why Cliff had ever been admitted to college and didn't think he should be allowed to graduate . . . until Cliff *looked* at him. There'd been girls, too, but they were too easy, wanting to be submerged in his superior will. Except for one—he still remembered her, that snippy redhead who'd laughed out loud when he asked her out. Cliff smiled, remembering how it had been when he finally got her alone and made her look into his eyes. After that the memories faded into a blur, so many faces, so many eyes, shamed, beseeching, begging. Years went by, wheedling and dealing and telling fine stories that didn't even feel like lies, only slight rearrangements of the truth to make a more fitting background for him: his father's played-out forty acres turned into a plantation, the red brick schoolhouse transformed into a private academy for the sons of the southern gentry. Loading himself with the trappings of success, German cars and English tailored suits. And always this gnawing need to exercise his power one more time, to prove to himself again and again that he really was someone special, set apart from common people by his rare talent.

Each time it was less of a rush, more commonplace. Each year he doubted his own early memories, wondered if he'd been fooling himself. Maybe he was just a fast-talking wheeler-dealer like the men he played cards with, a poor boy making it by his own hard work and pretending it was due to a touch of magic.

Until a few weeks ago, when the glass paperweight began talking to him.

Cliff grinned at the red-faced, honking drivers around him. Why hurry? The traffic jam would break up soon, he'd be back in his office with the cube, and this headache that was plaguing him would go away. Meanwhile, it was funny to think how people would call him crazy if he told them that his paperweight told him what to do.

It was true, though. From the first time he'd seen
the swirling images form, vague and indistinct against
the smoky glass, Cliff had known he was seeing
truly. It was all as he'd known it must be, somewhere, someday: the circle of hooded figures, a secret society of some sort dedicated to finding and
fostering just such arcane powers as he possessed.
Finally his striving had come to their attention, and
now, if he could just prove himself, he would be
admitted into the inner circle. Cliff had always known
in his heart that there must be some sort of secret
circle running things. Probably these men were the
real power in the country; the President and the
legislatures and the banks were their puppets, dancing to their tune. And if he served them well, he
would be one of them—one of the secret masters!
Cliff's heart pounded and his hands grew sweaty on
the wheel. The traffic was moving forward again. In a
few minutes he'd be at his office. Then he could call
to his masters and tell them what he had done. It
hadn't been complete success, but he had made progress. Definite progress. He thought they ought to be
pleased.

The instructions themselves hadn't been that definite. The Masters—that was what he called them in
his own mind—the Masters did not speak in words,
rather in feelings that manifested themselves like
vague pressures on the inside of his head, pictures
that formed and vanished in the swirl of dark glass.
The Templeton house had been clear in those pictures; finding out where it was had been his first,
easiest task. Then there was the book—also clear,
opened to show that stupid painting of some trees
and some broken stones—and a command that was
like a swelling in his brain. He was to bring the girl
and the picture together. What girl? The girl in the
house. But there are people all over the house! Cliff
had protested after his first visit there. Couldn't they

show him a picture of the girl, the way they had shown him the other things?

No. It is your task to find her.

But how would he know which one?

There was an impression of a dry laugh. *That is your task. Look for the one without a past.*

And a fat lot of help that was, Cliff thought sourly as he turned into the parking garage under his building. When you were dealing with a bunch of overage hippies and weird stuck-up college professors, you could just about say that *none* of them had a past! That Templeton woman was adopted and didn't even bother to make a secret of it, acted just as uppity as if she had been a real member of the family instead of some girl's bastard baby left at an agency. The witch who ran the Crystal Healing place was rumored to have spent ten doped-out years in the Haight between the failure of her marriage and her present life as Ginevra the Crystal Healer—although you could hardly call her a girl. And the mousy little secretary had no resume, at least none that he'd been able to discover in Miss Penny's mixed-up files, and she kept her own drawers locked and looked so scared that you knew there had to be a secret somewhere in her past.

And they all responded powerfully to the picture. It could be any one of them—or none; perhaps it was one of the flaked-out dames who came for classes in astrology and yoga and deep breathing and whatever other garbage the Center was purveying this month. Oh, well. He'd go back and try again, once he got over this headache. It would be better when he was in his own office.

It wasn't better. It grew worse; from a pressure in his skull to a rhythmic pounding interspersed with flashes of light. And for some reason, looking into the cube only made it worse. Maybe this, too, was a test from the Masters. Cliff held the cube in both hands, squinting against the office lights that hurt his eyes now, and concentrated as strongly as he could on calling up the images that filled the glass.

The cube responded almost at once, and he felt a rush of exultation that almost overrode the headache. Clouds swirled and coalesced, tiny lights sparkled inside the cube, and the image of a single man, hood drawn down over his face, became clear.

Find the woman. Why do you delay?

It wasn't exactly like words inside his head; more like a pulling and a sense of impatience. But the only way he could communicate back was with words. Stammering a little, Cliff tried to explain the difficulties he'd encountered and the progress he'd made. He had access to the house, he'd made the old woman who owned the place sign it over to him for practically nothing; now he could come and go at will.

Find the woman.

He tried to explain that he hadn't quite identified her yet; it was harder than they thought, there were so many people wandering in and out and most of them seemed to react to the picture. Even the men. But now that he practically owned the place—and the deal should be final tomorrow—he could take his time about identifying the right person. . . .

Fool. You have no time. It must be done now.

The sense of impatience grew, swelling into a crescendo of pain that made his previous headache seem like nothing.

"You don't understand!" Cliff howled at the glass cube. "I'm doing the best I can—the best anybody could!"

Useless.

On that last, chilling declaration the cube went black, and though Cliff shook it and held it close to his face he could not cause the image to return.

"You all right, mister?"

Some idiot in a dark blue uniform was at the door. "Who are *you*?" Cliff snapped. "Go away. I'm busy."

"Security, Mr. Simmons," the uniformed man said cheerfully. "Sorry to disturb you. Thought I heard sounds of an altercation in here." He glanced around the office. "I see you're alone, though?"

"Telephone call," Cliff said. "I—guess I lost my temper for a moment. You know how it is."

"Sure," said the security man with a grin. "In my business you see all kinds of kooks. Well, if everything's okey-dokey, I'll be on my way." He saluted, waved, grinned and winked.

Only after he left did Cliff realize that he'd been trying to cradle his black glass paperweight on the telephone stand.

At least his headache was gone.

And he could make plans. The Masters might be annoyed with him, might be punishing him by withdrawal, but surely they wouldn't be gone forever. If he could still serve them, they would forgive him and let him into the inner circle. They had to. In his brief communications with the Masters, Cliff had glimpsed powers far beyond anything he'd aspired to, strength and control that made his ability to influence people seem like a child's first game with blocks. He had to have that. They couldn't show it and then deny it to him. It wasn't fair.

Somehow he would prove his worthiness to them.

The circle of men gathered in the chapter house of the Remegius monastery sighed and relaxed as one man when their leader wiped his hand across the scrying-glass and broke the delicate threads binding their minds to the other world. All of them together, concentrating totally, could barely achieve the link required; and it was still frail, flawed, incomplete.

"The man is useless," the leader repeated his condemnation. "And our time is too short."

Berengar's worry over his fosterling, distracting him from the task of watching the Gate, was an unexpected boon but one that would not last forever. By morning he would surely have remembered his duty, and he or one of his household knights would resume the guard over the Stonemaidens.

"We will call to Sybille directly," the leader decreed, "following the trail she left between the worlds." He too was tired; it was an exhausting game, this fishing for one soul in the teeming, confusing world where Sybille fled. For a moment he remembered his boyhood, lying on his stomach beside a clear cold stream and reaching one hand in with infinite care until the stupid fish swam right into his fingers. The water was deceptive, angles and distances were all wrong; all you could trust was the feel of the fins and scales against your hand.

"We will feel our way to her," he said, and smiled in grim amusement. "The elvenkind are already calling to the lady; let us join our voices to theirs. Think of it as an act of charity, to aid these our brothers in their quest."

The brothers of Saint Durand laughed obediently at the dry jest, stretched and drank water and knelt in prayer for a few moments, then re-formed the circle and sent forth the combined strength of their minds to bring the Lady Sybille home.

Through the afternoon Lisa's headache grew worse. She felt irrationally convinced that if only she could slip into Mahluli's bookstore for a moment, to spend a few quiet minutes leafing through the old book of fairytales with the Kay Nielsen illustrations, she would be able to regain her sense of balance. But somehow there never was a minute when she could get away. If it wasn't the telephone ringing with somebody who wanted to return her call and ask about the emergency meeting, it was Johnny Z. with a report of bad auras in the T-shirt store or the Chinese acupuncturist complaining that all his needles had mysteriously blunted themselves overnight.

"It's as if there were a curse on this house," Lisa told Ginevra when the fourth person in a row reported that the upstairs toilets were flushing themselves incessantly.

"Probably it's haunted," Ginevra said. "Did you get my sea salt yet?"

"No!" Lisa took a deep breath and told herself to be calm. It wasn't Ginevra's fault that her head was throbbing in time to the flushing of the toilets. "I'm sorry, but you see how it's been. I honestly haven't had a moment to get away."

"I know, honey. I was just thinking that I could do a crystal reading on the whole house. If sea salt absorbs the bad karma on crystals, maybe if we sprinkled it through the house—" Ginevra paused and looked Lisa over carefully, her green eyes narrowing to slits in her concentration. "But I don't think that's it. Do you?"

"No," Lisa confessed. The phone rang again and she picked it up with one hand while continuing to jot down notes from the preceding call. "New Age Center for—yes, Mrs. Harrison. I'm delighted to hear you'll be able to attend tonight. Yes, there's a threat to close down the Center; I'm sorry, but I'm not supposed to go into the details at this time. Dr. Templeton will—Good. Eight-thirty. Yes, by all means bring your husband if you think his engineering expertise will be helpful; we'd be very happy to see him." She put down the telephone with a sigh. "Mr. Stringfellow Harrison," she reported, "has twenty years' experience building bridges for underdeveloped countries. Do you think we could use a good bridge-builder?"

"Maybe he can fix the plumbing," Ginevra suggested. "But I think it would help more if you calmed down, Lisa, honey."

Lisa bit back a question as to just how Ginevra thought anybody could stay calm in this madhouse, and why it should be her fault they were having so many problems when everybody else was just as edgy. Ginevra might have a point. The assorted tenants-cum-partners of the New Age Center were sensitive souls, attuned to the subtle harmonies of the universe and easily upset by disturbances in the psychic fabric—at least, that was how they saw themselves. She, Lisa, was supposed to be the sensible receptionist who didn't believe any of this psychic mumbo-jumbo and who kept calm through any emergency.

And her head hurt, and she was afraid of Cliff Simmmons, and everybody else in the Center had wandered through Mahluli's bookstore that afternoon to fondle the Nielsen book since Judith brought it back—and she had been stuck at her desk for *too long*.

The telephone rang again.

"New Age Center for Psychic Research—can you hold?"

Calmly and sensibly, as if there were no other possible action, Lisa pushed the red hold button on the telephone, left the lights blinking and her notes for the meeting open on her desk, stood up and went through the swinging bead curtain into the smoky incense-scented darkness of Mahluli's bookstore.

Mahluli wasn't there; but the book was lying open on the round table just inside the curve of the bay window, with light from the window dappling the picture of the forest glade and the little running stream; just as if it had been waiting for her. Lisa stared down at the picture and felt the calm of the scene soothing her raging headache. She could dimly

hear the telephone ringing, steps outside and someone calling her name. *To hell with it*, she thought.
*I don't have to go back. I can stay here as long as I
want to.* Even as she thought the words, she knew
that there was nowhere else in the world she would
rather be than right here, looking at a picture that
with every breath she took grew brighter and more
vivid and somehow more real, much more real than
any of the dingy furnishings around it. Lisa stared
into the picture until she felt a dizzy blackness swirling about her, as if she were going to faint—no, as if
she were being poured through a funnel, spiraling
down and down in a black whirlpool, with nothing to
cling to but the spot of brightness at the end of the
funnel. She stared into the brightness, gripping her
own hands so tightly that her fingernails cut into her
palms, and gradually the point of light grew until it
was the forest glade again; but with a difference. She
was standing under the arch now, not looking through
it; and when she took a step forward, the grass
sighed under her feet; and when she knelt to drink at
the stream, the water was as cool and clear and
refreshing as she had always known it must be.

CHAPTER FIVE

They stole little Bridget For seven years long,
When she came back again Her friends were
all gone. They came and took her lightly back
Between the night and morrow, They thought
that she was fast asleep, But she was dead of
sorrow.

—William Allingham, "The Fairies"

Her face still wet with the water of the stream,
Lisa stood and stretched lazily and took a deep breath
of the resin-scented air. It felt fresh and cool, with a
scent of early morning; she looked at the long shadow
she cast on the grass and nodded. It was earlier here
than in the world she had left. *It's real*, she told
herself. *I'm not imagining this*. Water and grass, sun
and shade caressed her and made her welcome. She
looked back over her shoulder at the arch through
which she had passed to come to the stream. It was
taller and more ornate than she remembered from
the picture, a fantastic construction of springing shafts
and up-curved keystones and pierced narrow walls.

Beyond the arch she could just see a hint of Mahluli's dusty, shadowy bookshop, like a semi-transparent picture laid over the reality of grass and stones and wavering slightly in the breeze. Far clearer was the reality of this world: not the dark book-lined room where she had been standing, but a circle of great stones, weathered and worn and covered with moss, leaning towards one another like women with their arms outstretched to enclose and protect the clearing.

I wonder if I can get back? But it didn't, just then, seem to matter very much. Her headache was gone, there were no ringing bells or complaining people waiting for her to attend to them, and she felt too lazily peaceful and relaxed to worry very much about anything. It must be right for her to be here, or the picture wouldn't have brought her. In a little while she would leave the clearing, perhaps to follow the path she saw beside the stream; there was no hurry about that or anything else.

A flicker of gray caught her eye; she turned, felt alarm too late, started to run far, far too late to evade the gray-robed man who sprang from the trees and gripped her wrist. Who was he? She had never seen him before, but his narrow face blazed with an intensely personal hatred.

Lisa jerked and twisted uselessly under his hand. "Let *go*," she panted. "You're *hurting* me!"

He laughed at that. It was a very unpleasant laugh, and Lisa knew that he didn't mind hurting her and that she'd been a fool to act as though he would.

"It's time you learned to fear mortal men, my fine elf-lady!" he said when he had finished laughing. "What ails you—cannot you call up your spells while I keep you so busy? Shall I lay my knife-blade on you and see how that touch distracts you?"

"You're crazy," Lisa said. "Let me go."

The man laughed unpleasantly. "What, catch an
elf-queen and let her go again? I'm not such a fool!"

The language he spoke was not English, but a
lilting tongue that reminded Lisa of French. Lisa
found that she could understand him without diffi-
culty. And although she was still thinking in English,
the sounds that came out of her mouth sounded like
the madman's language.

None of which did her any good. She might as
well have been speaking English—or Greek, for that
matter—for all he understood of what she was saying.

"I've done nothing to hurt you," Lisa appealed to
him.

"No, nor shall you!"

He *was* mad. He reached into his robe with his
free hand. *To get the knife*, Lisa thought. *I can't let
him get the knife.* The world around her seemed to
freeze; she had time between heartbeats to think
everything out very clearly. This madman wanted to
hurt her, and he had a knife, and he was bigger than
she was and arguing with him was going to do absolutely no good. She had just this moment while he
was distracted and a little off balance, fumbling in his
robes, to get away.

She could hear Nadine, the older of the two girls
who had run the self-defense clinic in the basement,
speaking as if she were there now. "I can't teach you
to fight in a few free lessons after work. All I could
teach you would just be enough to get you in trouble. But I can show you a couple of ways to break a
man's hold when he's bothering you. After you've
done that, you'd better run and scream bloody mur-
der—you'll never be a fighter."

He was still reaching inside his robe when Lisa
made her move. The fingers of the hand on her arm
were splayed out; she grabbed the little finger and
twisted backwards with all her might. There was a
crunching noise that made her sick; the hooded man

screamed, thin and high like a snared rabbit, and nursed his injured hand. Lisa scooted around him and ran for the open arch and the shadowy image of the bookshop. She never even saw the two men who tripped her up and sat on her. There was a crushing weight on her back, and her left foot was agonizingly twisted under the weight of another man, and she heard the one she had hurt talking about how he'd like to mark her with his knife blade before they delivered her.

"Stand up," one of her captors said, and getting off her, he hauled her to her feet. "You're not hurt, my lady. Not yet." He whipped thin lengths of cord about her wrists and ankles while she was still too stunned from the fall to resist. "Please notice that these cords are braided about an iron wire," he advised her, "so your pagan cantrips will avail you naught, Sybille. But if you do not struggle and abrade the cords, the iron will not touch your flesh. Despite Brother Hugh's careless remarks, we do not wish you injured unnecessarily."

"Good," Lisa said. "At least we're in agreement about something. Where are you taking me? And why?" She was not entirely sure that she wanted to know the answers. "And by the way," she went on hastily, "if you think you're kidnapping somebody named Sybille, may I point out that you've got the wrong person? I'm not even from this *world.*"

They ignored everything she said and went on wrapping bits of iron-reinforced cord about her person, waving crosses in the air around her, and chanting bits of prayers. Lisa recognized some of the words.

"What are you, anyway? Monks? What order? Look, if you'll just take me to your abbot, I can—"

"You shall face the head of our Order in good time, elf-maiden," said the man who'd grabbed her first, "and I think you will be more minded to confess the truth then than you are now. In time we must all follow the one path."

"Oh, cut it out! You sound like an old war movie— and not a very good one. What is this routine? 'Ve haf vays of making you talk?'" But they probably did, and Lisa was beginning to feel sick. Perhaps she was going to faint. Certainly something seemed to be going wrong with her vision; the glade seemed blurry now, wavering as if everything were under water.

"I hope I broke your finger," Lisa said. The clouds were coming lower, brushing the treetops, turning into fantastic shapes even as she watched.

"What's that?" Unable to point, she jerked her chin towards one of the worst looking shapes. The tall man who was binding her turned, cried out and threw up his hands against the dragon-shaped darkness with its smouldering heart. The dark shape engulfed him and its scaled tail lashed around towards Lisa and her other captors. The two men threw themselves down as a screeching fireball passed overhead. There was a roaring from the forest like a pride of starving lions, and a horse screamed somewhere. Thunder came rolling down on them from all sides, and in the midst of the thunder was a silver-haired man on a white horse. His cloak and the horse's saddle and reins glowed like moonlight, and he came riding through the cloud-shapes as if they weren't there and lifted Lisa with one arm to sit on the saddle before him.

With her arms and ankles bound she couldn't help herself balance; she was completely dependent on the arm that encircled her. She couldn't even put a hand before her face to protect herself from the branches and leaves that whisked by. She closed her eyes tightly and buried her face against the rider's chest and tried not to think about what would happen if he let her fall. She could smell the resinous trees all around her, and the trickle of the stream was muted by distance. They were deep in the forest now, moving too fast and too quietly and too smoothly; she could have sworn the horse's feet weren't touching the ground.

She opened her eyes a slit and peeked, and wished she hadn't. The silvery horse was galloping at least a foot above the surface of the path, and the rider had his eyes closed and was murmuring something in words that rhymed and rang and whispered through the air like a wind out of nowhere. Lisa closed her own eyes again. If she was about to break her neck, she didn't want to see it coming.

After a long time—too long—their pace slowed and the rider allowed his horse to touch the ground. Lisa could tell from the small bumps and jolts that they were going slowly now, the horse ambling along as if it was too tired to even think about galloping again.

"You can look now, my lady." The man's voice was light, amused, with a hint of silvery chimes in the undertones. He sounded happy and secure and completely in control of the situation; Lisa felt herself responding to that certainty, wanting to trust her rescuer. She resented and fought the feeling. But she did open her eyes again and look around her.

They were riding along a narrow, rocky path misted with rainbows. On one side of the path a steep hill rose into the sky, covered with dark green trees that were not quite pines or firs or spruce, but something in between all the conifers of Earth. Their springy needles made a dark green and brown carpet with a resinous scent that made Lisa think of winter and snow and Christmas.

To the other side the path fell away into nothingness, a space of rainbows in the mist with the sound of falling water on rocks a long way below. And before them a yawning gorge opened directly through the path. Lisa gasped as the horse stepped daintily out onto emptiness.

"I had not thought a Queen of Elfhame would be surprised by my poor illusions," the man who held her said, as calmly as if they were still on the solid path.

"Illusions?"

He waved one hand, and the gorge shimmered until Lisa could just see the path beneath them, like a double-exposed photograph.

"Oh!" Then, "*What* did you call me?" She resolved not to look down or ahead any more. It was too unsettling. Had the flying also been an illusion?

"Sybille, Lady of Elfhame, well met and well come to your realm again," the man said. He sounded almost as if he were singing: the formal cadences and intonations of his speech reminded Lisa of the words with which he had sent his horse flying above the path, whisking through air and illusion. "I am Berengar, Count of the Garronais, charged with guarding my lady's safe path through the Gate at the Stonemaidens. I crave your pardon that I was delayed in greeting you. I—we have been in some anxiety about my foster-son, who has taken a hurt that even Idaine can't heal him of." He sounded more human now that the formal phrases of greeting were done with. "I watched by his bed last night and sent one of my knights to take the guard of the Gate. It wasn't until your passing woke the Gate to full life that I quested forth in trance and found no trace of Garins. I came as quickly as I could—and glad am I to see my lady has taken no hurt from those foul Durandines—"

He sounded harassed and apologetic and almost human by now. "It's all right," Lisa said, "truly it is, they didn't hurt me, but I'm not who you think I am. This Sybille or whoever. My name is Lisa, and I'm not a queen of anywhere."

Berengar looked pained. "My lady has suffered many perilous adventures in the world of the iron-demons, doubtless, but here it is not necessary to hide. My keep is safe enough against such little mortal schemers as the Brothers of Saint Durand."

"Your keep," Lisa repeated, looking around her at rocks and trees and the mist above the river.

"Even here."

There was music, and sunshine striking rays of prismatic color through the rainbows, and people cheering. The horse stopped; the rider lifted her to the ground and Lisa stared in amazement. Trees and hill had melted away like a dream, leaving behind a construction of lacy towers and walls, arches and bridges, carved balconies and spiraling bridges. The peaks of the towers matched the jagged outlines of the rocky hill and the curving sweep of the farthest wall replaced the downward curve of the tree-covered slope.

Before the castle stood a little group of men and women, tall and slender and silver-haired like the rider who'd brought her here, and dressed in trailing long-sleeved robes of peacock hues. Iridescent flashes of blue and green and purple, singing rainbows of fire-colors and floating bubbles of scented flower colors dazzled Lisa's eyes. *How can a color have scent, or sound?*

She didn't have time to think out an answer to the puzzle; the slender silver-haired people were all kneeling as the rider lifted her from the horse, and then he knelt too.

"My Lady Sybille," he addressed her, looking up with almond-shaped greenish eyes whose slant was not quite Oriental, not even quite human. "My lady, welcome back to Elfhame. Be pleased to receive our gratitude and our homage that you have returned to save your people."

The courtly speech and the circle of kneeling people made Lisa feel as if she were acting in a play. Something equally gracious was called for in response.

But she didn't know her lines. She was tired and frightened and hungry, and all this shimmering glamour was only another net around her, prettier than the chains she'd first been threatened with but perhaps even more dangerous.

"What did you call me?" she asked for the second time.

"Sybille?"

Lisa shook her head. "I *told* you. That's not my name."

Now this Berengar looked bewildered. "I mean it," Lisa insisted, "you've got the wrong person. I gather you were expecting somebody named Sybille to appear out of thin air and solve all your problems? You'd better go back and look again. I'm not a Queen of Elfhame, my name isn't Sybille, and I have problems of my own." Beginning with the need to find her way back to the circle of standing stones where she'd entered this world. Berengar's rescue might have saved her from an immediate threat, but he had also carried her too far away from her only way home. As for what would happen when she got there, whether she'd be able to return to the safe smoky darkness of Mahluli's bookshop, she would just have to worry about that when the time came.

"You are confused," said Berengar gently, "by your journey between the worlds, and perhaps by your sufferings in the world of the iron-demons. We will speak again when you have rested, my lady."

He managed to rise and bow and swirl his cape about him in one fluid movement, more graceful than any dancer. He offered her his arm, and Lisa was too tired and confused to do more than take it. *We can sort things out later.*

She was relieved to find that the interior of Berengar's home was less confusing than the rainbow-hued, constantly shifting exterior. Here, though the furnishings and architecture were unfamiliar, at least the soft carpets on which she walked stayed on the floor and the carved window-lattices of scented wood revealed the same view each time she looked out. Berengar escorted her to a suite of rooms overlooking the river gorge and left her in the charge of two giggling and distinctly human-looking girls who hovered around her like nervous butterflies.

"What would my lady desire?"

"A Coke and a Big Mac?" Instantly Lisa regretted the words; the younger girl's lip trembled and she looked ready to cry because she couldn't instantly understand and fulfill the request. "Food." How long had it been since she'd eaten? She had been too nervous to bother with breakfast that morning—and then, Lisa thought on the edge of hysterical laughter, then her worst problem had been a slimy real-estate developer threatening her job! "And—is there somewhere I could wash?"

There was a deep tub made of something that gave the impression of being light as wood, but was as hard and shining as polished stone. Lisa sank into it and tried not to think about where the scented water that filled the tub came from; she had a feeling that the girls who waited on her probably had to carry it up more steps than she wanted to think about. *I'll worry about that later.* There was an appallingly long list of things being shoved into the back of her mind to deal with later; her head ached at the thought.

While she was soaking in the tub, the girls fluttered about the room and whispered to one another and whisked things in and out of cupboards. Lisa didn't much mind what they did, once they'd been made to understand that she didn't want anybody to scrub her back; and she was tired enough to be glad of the wide linen towel they held out to wrap her in when she stepped out of the water, weary enough to sit back and relax while her tangled wet hair was combed into a mass of damp mousy-blonde ringlets.

Even the discovery that her dirty clothes had been taken away somewhere—to be washed?—didn't trouble her, as the girls smilingly brought out an assortment of dresses from a carved wooden chest. She was quite prepared to let this Count Berengar give her a dress; it looked as if he could afford it. The only problem was that she wasn't sure what would be appropriate attire for a common mortal being entertained in an elven count's castle. This notion that she was a lost queen of Elfhame was bad enough; she didn't want to seem to be dressing the part.

With that in mind, each dress the girls offered her seemed less suitable than the previous one—longer, more flowing and bejeweled, more bedraped with gossamer and glitter. Lisa settled on what looked like a simple green shift and was dismayed to find that it changed when she put it on, clinging to her body here and developing long trailing skirts there and sparkling with a scatter of diamond-like stones that certainly hadn't been there when she chose the dress.

The food arrived as a collection of covered wooden bowls on a round tray of hammered copper, and with the food came the silver-haired man who had swept her out of the forest and into this dream-world.

"I trust you are feeling refreshed, my lady? I apologize for disturbing you again so soon, but we have little time." He seated himself cross-legged on a silk cushion. The girl who'd brought the food set down her copper tray on a low wooden tripod before Berengar and backed out of the room.

"That's perfectly all right." Lisa decided it would not compromise her position to sit down opposite Berengar. She felt silly standing over him, and anyway, the food smelled delicious. "I'm eager to settle this myself. I'd like to go home as soon as possible."

"Home? But—oh, you mean Poitiers?"

"Home," Lisa repeated. "The—the world I came from. I want to go back."

"My lady," said Berengar, "you *are* home, and this is our day of rejoicing. Long and arduous has the search been, but there can be no doubt of the results. We followed the trail you left among the stars, and beyond them, into the world of the iron-demons. We have been calling to your spirit along that trail, that you might be drawn back to the world of your birth. Only the one who passed from Elfhame into the world of the iron-demons might return by that track, and so you see that you must be the Lady Sybille, Queen of Elfhame before that Lady Alianora who now reigns in Poitiers."

"I see," Lisa said slowly, "that you're convinced of that. But—you're mistaken, really you are. If I were this Sybil-whosis, I'd know it. And besides—" She shook her head. "Look at me. Do I *look* like one of your people? Silver hair, slanting green eyes?" She tugged on one lock of light mousy hair and held it out, as much to reassure herself that she hadn't been transformed as to convince Berengar.

"Our features and coloration vary, as do those of mortals," the Count of the Garronais informed her, "and the ruling line in Poitiers is generally darker than we of the Garronais, who have preserved the pure elven blood. Your family has some ties with the Jinn of Outremer. And, too, there have been rumors of mortal blood in the line, some generations past, which might help to explain the Lady Alianora's strange taste for coupling with mortals. She herself is more golden than silver in complexion, although I must admit the resemblance between you is not so striking as I might have expected. Alianora," Berengar said, "is radiantly beautiful. I had thought that you would have shown some of that same glory."

"You sure know how to sweet-talk a lady, Count Berengar." Lisa picked up an applelike fruit from the tray between them and bit into it, crunching as loudly and uncouthly as she could manage.

"Excuse me? I am afraid I do not understand."

"It's not important. What we've agreed on," Lisa said, "is that I don't *look* like a fairy princess, I don't *act* like a fairy princess, and I don't *think* I'm a fairy princess. The weight of evidence, Count Berengar, suggests that I am not your fairy godmother. Your wizards slipped up."

"Impossible," Berengar protested. "Our sending brought you; you must be the Lady."

"Wait a minute. It's my turn to explain some things. This call that you sent out—it was supposed to make your Lady Sybille look at a picture in a book, right?"

Berengar nodded and Lisa kept on talking before he could get a word in. "Well, your aim was slightly off. You may have been calling Sybille, but just about everybody in range heard you. *Everybody* in the house where I lived felt this compulsion to look at the picture. We *all* noticed something funny about it, something hypnotic. I just happened to be the one who looked longest and got drawn into your trap, that's all. Your Sybille is probably still back there."

"That's impossible. If you weren't Sybille, you could not have passed the Gate."

"But I did, and I'm here, and I'm not Sybille," Lisa pointed out.

Berengar rose to his feet with that fluid, graceful motion that Lisa envied whenever she saw it. "We seem to have reached an impasse. Perhaps a night's sleep will help to restore your memory."

Lisa had no intention of sleeping; she had too much thinking to do. Her dream-world, the paradise of the picture, had become an appallingly real trap and she intended to spend the quiet hours of the night figuring out a way to escape it. There must be some way to convince this charming madman that she wasn't his long-lost queen!

She fell asleep on that thought, and woke to the

dawn with an answer as good as any she might have achieved if she'd spent the night in planning.

"Dumb," Lisa addressed herself aloud, hitting her forehead with the heel of her hand. She pushed aside the shimmering walls of sea-green silk that enclosed the bed and ran to the window, too excited to stand still. "Dumb, dumb, *dumb*. If I had any more brains I'd be a half-wit. Why didn't I think of it immediately?"

"Please?"

The two girls who'd waited on her the night before, tucking her in between silky sheets on a bed that felt like goose down and rustled like straw, had reappeared on Lisa's first word. This morning they were determined to clothe her in the state suitable to a Queen of Elfhame. Lisa submitted to being layered in blue and crimson silks, their hems weighted with threads of gold and their wide sleeves lined with something that glowed of itself like the clouds in the morning sky. Tiny golden bells were the fastenings on the gown, and more little bells decorated the edge of the wide cloth-of-gold belt that was the finishing touch.

"Mirror, mirror!" one of the girls cried aloud when they had done, and the window through which Lisa had been watching the dawn shimmered, clouded over and became a perfect reflection of the room in which she stood. A shiver ran down her back, involuntary as the reaction to a screech owl's hoot, and she felt the fine hairs on the back of her neck prickling. *This is not my world. This isn't real. I don't like it.* Until that moment, she had not realized how much she loved solid ground and houses that stayed the same shape from one day to the next and people who knew her as just-Lisa-the-receptionist and didn't expect her to perform any magic tricks more demanding than organizing Miss Penny's tenants.

The more this elven magic hummed about her,

the more cloddish and down-to-earth and ordinary Lisa felt by contrast. Well, she wouldn't show them that she was afraid; and she wouldn't make a fool of herself by trying to act like an elven lady, either. She stood stolidly in front of the magical mirror, hands clasped to stop her fingers from trembling, and pretended to care about the reflection she saw there. The doll-like figure in blue and crimson, tinkling and sparkling with every breath, wasn't the Lisa she knew. Was nothing to do with her really. Was only an— illusion, like the rest of Berengar's works.

"Not bad," she said. "But the sleeves are too long. And all those jingling bells make me nervous. Could you possibly cut off a few—"

Before she'd finished speaking, the bells had stilled their jangling music. The sleeves of the dress shrank before her eyes, gathering their fullness into narrow cuffs about her wrists. Lisa lifted one of the bells that dangled from her girdle and inspected it. There was no way it could ring; clapper and bell were one solid piece of gilt metal, nothing more than a decorative button.

One of her handmaids gave a sharp sigh. "I wish *I* could do that," she murmured.

Lisa shook her head slowly. "I didn't do anything. The dress did it of itself."

"But on your command."

"You made the mirror appear . . ."

"Oh, that's just one of my lord's magics," the girl explained. "Think you, how much bother would it be if we had to disturb one of you high elf-lords and ladies every time we wished a can of water heated or a window closed! So he's made those things to answer anybody's voice. But these things . . ." Her fingers caressed the softness of Lisa's gathered sleeve. "These be more, more . . ."

"Personal?"

"Yes, just so!"

"Then you couldn't make it . . . ?"

"Bells! Be as you were, ring again!" the girl commanded.

The gilt buttons remained buttons.

"You see?"

"I . . . see. You may go now," Lisa said. Being surrounded with elven magic was bad enough; being credited with the ability to work it was somehow worse, entangling her in the nets of Berengar's belief.

As the girls slipped through the door-tapestry, the one who'd spoken to Lisa elbowed her silent helper. "You see? She is *so* elven, even if she do look common as us."

Lisa shook her head again. Thank goodness she had realized a simple way to convince Berengar of his mistake; much longer among the illusions of his palace, and she'd be in danger of losing her own grip on reality, ready to believe in the dressed-up doll-princess they had made of her.

She was so eager to end the masquerade that when Berengar burst into the room, she did not even give him time to greet her.

"It's about time you showed up! Listen, Berengar— I mean, my lord Count—whatever—it's time we settled this matter once and for all. Bring me something made of iron."

"Surely you jest."

"I think that's my line," said Lisa. "No, I'm serious. Isn't it true that the elvenkind can't touch iron?"

"You should know that as well as any of us, my lady."

Lisa gritted her teeth. "I keep *telling* you I'm not your Lady Sybille."

"How else should you know our weakness?"

"It's fairly well documented," Lisa said carefully, "even in my world, all the stories about your sort agree on that point. So if I can handle iron unharmed, wouldn't you agree that I am not Sybille?"

"It would . . . be troubling," Berengar agreed.

"Good. Bring on the metals."

"You demand a test which you know I cannot fulfill."

"Translation?"

"My lady," Berengar said. He sounded slow and deliberately patient, as if he were speaking to a child —or to a woman too shocked to acknowledge her own identity. "My lady, I know not what may have been the custom in your day, but I can assure you that it is *not* the custom of the present lords of elvenkind to keep a deadly poison by them."

"Oh!" Lisa thought for a moment. "Well, never mind. It should be obvious anyway. You keep talking about the 'iron- demons' in my world; if I'd been Sybille, I could never have survived in a world full of iron and steel machinery, could I now?"

Berengar frowned; the expression made him look almost human. "My lady, I am not trained in the subtle logic of the schools of Paris; I have not the wisdom of the sages of Ys. You have survived to return among us, for which I rejoice; the matter of your exile and the curious manner of your survival will doubtless furnish many a romance and epic in days to come, when it shall please you to unfold the tale. Now, if you will give over your jesting and logic-chopping, we have other matters afoot this day."

"I don't," Lisa said. "I appreciate that you want to find Sybille, but I'm *not* Sybille, and I want to go home." Another method of proving her case struck her. "Look, haven't any of you people ever *met* this Sybille? I realize we're pretty far out in the sticks here, but if you can just show me to anybody who knows the lady, I'm sure they'll tell you at once—"

Berengar's eyes were icy green as the northern seas in winter. "I do not have time for foolish jests this morning, my lady, and you have delayed me long enough already. Come with me." He grasped her wrist and hurried her out of the room, down long echoing corridors and spiraling stairs, until Lisa was thoroughly lost.

"What—where?" she gasped at Berengar's side, but he paid her no heed. The breakneck pace he set did not ease until they were in the courtyard where she'd been received the previous evening. A groom was waiting with two horses.

"You can ride?"

"Yes, but—"

"Good." Berengar grasped her by the waist and lifted her; automatically Lisa settled herself in the saddle. For a moment her skirts were in the way, and she pushed them aside irritably; even as her fingers touched the fabric, the crimson dress re-shaped itself into a divided skirt, and the delicate fabric shrank in upon itself until its very texture was heavier and more suited for riding through the woods. "We'll have to go air-footed."

"If you mean that—flying trick you did yesterday, I don't know how—and I don't particularly want to, thank you! I said I could *ride*; you didn't ask me about flying."

"You have no choice," Berengar said, almost mildly, but the anger was still there in his eyes. "If you refuse to help, my lady, then I have enough strength to guide both our steeds. But you *shall* ride out with me this day, and you *shall* see what devastation you have brought to our lands. The Hounds have come again to St.-Remy; I felt Herluin's cold mind touching the fringes of my land at dawn, and I must go to the villagers now to make sure that none are harmed. My own fosterling has left the keep, foolish boy, and I cannot even stay to search for him till I have seen to my people—and in the midst of all this, you delay me with jests and babble!" He gathered the reins of Lisa's mount into his own hand, raised his other hand and spoke three words that she could not quite make out, and the walls of the courtyard dissolved into mist.

"I brought nothing but myself to your land," Lisa told him, "and I'll be only too happy to take myself away again, if you'd only cooperate! Just let me meet some people who know Sybille, that's all I ask. They'll tell you—"

The ground fell away beneath her, and her voice seemed to fall out of her throat. They were moving with the same speed as yesterday, but this time there was no arm about her to keep her safe; there was nothing but her own wobbly knees clutching the sides of an impossibly tall, sleek horse that rushed through wind and sun as though it were no more than a current of air itself. The soft square of gilded and embossed leather on which she sat was no more than a token saddle, nothing like the high Western saddles people used on the ranches around Austin, with no saddlehorn for a frightened girl to hang on to. Lisa set her teeth and her knees and determined to endure the ride without begging Berengar to let her down again.

This time they did not go through the forest, but along the clifftop edge of the river—the Garron?—that sparkled below Lisa's left hand in a continuous, musical shower of crystalline droplets. Despite her resolve not to look down, the soft rainbow colors of the mist-filled gorge and the hints of glittering waterfalls kept drawing her eyes. White rocks plunging down to meet silver water, deep green walls of resinous long-needled trees, rainbow clouds of misty spray glowing with the morning sun: she was seduced by the beauty of it, remembering against her will the first sense of peace and serenity and homecoming which this world had given her.

And, after all, she had not fallen yet; possibly, Lisa dared to think, she would not.

Berengar kept their horses skimming just over the

rocky path. They moved much faster, this way, than if they had had to touch the ground; but she did notice that he still followed the tortuous bends of the cliffside path.

"Why don't you go straight through the air to—wherever you're going?" she shouted.

Berengar looked over his shoulder at her. "Don't ask stupid questions. You know well enough I haven't the power to raise us so high, so long; and you know why."

"I don't!" Lisa protested.

"No? Well, I suppose it *is* possible . . . "

Lisa heaved an exaggerated sigh of relief. "At last! A sign of rationality! Don't tell me you are ready to quit pretending I'm your fairy godmother?"

Berengar's jaw set in an expression that Lisa would have called mulish, if she'd seen it on a mortal man. "You were brought back along your own path through the stars; you must be Sybille, and the sooner you stop teasing me the better off we'll all be. No, I meant that it is possible you don't understand what damage you have done to the Middle Realm. In your day, no doubt we could ride the clouds instead of skimming along barely above the surface of earth."

"And exactly what is Sybille supposed to have done?"

"Look around you!"

The high wooded hills that had bordered the cliffside path were falling away here, opening onto gently rolling pastures that should have been rich farmland. But the grass was thin and sparse, the low walls of piled stones that separated the fields were tumbling down in neglect, and thorny weeds choked every corner. In one field a woman in a patched, earth-colored gown was hacking at a pile of roots. She raised her head as they rode by and stared at them with the dull, glazed look of someone who has been tired and hungry for so long that she cannot remember any other life.

"It looks miserable," Lisa conceded. "But you're the Count of the Garronais, remember? Why blame me if your people are hungry?"

"This was some of the richest land in Elfhame," Berengar informed her, "in the days when we could bring the rains in spring and shelter the growing crop from ocean storms. Now it is—as you see."

"And it is, of course, my fault that the rains don't come when you want them!"

"Yes." Lisa could see no motion of Berengar's to guide his horse, but both horses turned aside from the river bank and went skimming across a storm-flattened field, still a few inches above the surface of the ground. In places their hooves brushed a standing stalk of golden grass and left it swaying, but pounding rains—or other things—had laid most of the crop to the ground. A wide muddy swath had been trampled through the rotting hay, as if people had run through here in terror—why did she think of fear and pain? It seemed to cry up at her from the earth. With an effort Lisa looked away from the puddled field. It was no easier watching Berengar. He looked as if he hated her. No, Lisa reminded herself. Not her. Sybille.

"When you broke the power of the Stones and fled our world, you broke the secret heart of the realm. Year by year our strength has leached away, until it is all I can do to cloak my keep in illusion and send a few more illusions to discourage the mortal lords who prowl the borders of my lands."

"Gee, that's rough," Lisa said coldly. A stone spire rose on the horizon, with a group of thatched huts huddled around it. Something like a sobbing scream threaded through the air; she couldn't have heard anyone in the village cry out at this distance, she was imagining things. Berengar's unjust condemnation was getting her spirits down. "You might even have to work for a living some day, just like a common human being. My heart bleeds for you."

"Unless you can find some way to reverse the process you started," Berengar told her, "you will suffer the same fate. You are not in your world of refuge now, my lady. You are back here with your people whom you abandoned. And what will you do, when the lands of elvenkind are all taken by mortals, when the Durandines are yapping at the Church to have us all burned, when those who would have defended you are facing mortal iron with no elven powers to protect us? If," he added in a low, troubled voice, "if we are lucky enough to go down before the armies of the mortals, that is. Time was, I'd have laughed at any man who called death by cold iron a clean death—but that was before I heard Herluin's horn. They say he hunts only mortal souls; but he wounded my foster-son, and Kieran—"

"The boy who's missing?"

"Yes. He has been strange since he took the blow; cold in body and wandering in his mind. He must have stolen out of the keep during the night; I knew it not until I felt the passing of the Hunt, and then there was no time. I pray we may find him well when we return—and that all is well with the villagers, too. May their God have mercy on any who were caught out of doors last night!"

"And I suppose whatever disaster you're hinting at is also my fault?"

"Judge for yourself." There was just one long, low wall of stones between them and the village now; Berengar broke off speaking for a moment, sang one long phrase in a descending minor melody, and the horses rose into the air and effortlessly cleared the wall. "You are remembering your day, when the Hounds were no more than ghostly voices heard in the dark of the moon. Once they would not have dared to come among us. Now they have flesh and blood, bones and teeth and claws, and—they have begun to hunt in the daytime. No one will be safe now, Sybille, unless you halt what your folly began. These lands will be a desert, fit for nothing but to sell to the Durandines."

"I *wish*," Lisa snapped, "that you would quit calling me by somebody else's name! How many times do I have to tell you that I'm not your Sybille? Are you afraid to let me meet somebody who knows what she looks like?"

At a gesture of Berengar's hand, the horses paused and sank to the ground, delicately picking their way over stubble and puddles as they approached the houses grouped around the village church. The sobbing wail rose again, too clear for Lisa to tell herself she had imagined it.

"The jest grows old," Berengar snapped without looking back at her, "and I've no time to play your games, my lady. Even Yrthan is not old enough to remember the days before the Catastrophe. The elven lords of your day are gone, Sybille; they wearied of this failing realm and rode west into the sea before I was born."

"I think you are confused," Lisa said slowly. "It can't have been that long since—"

"Now you pretend not to know the length of your own exile." Berengar looked back with a sour smile. "Very well—I will play the game. You have been away from the Realm for seven hundred and seventy-four years, my lady, and those who might have known you have long since passed out of Elfhame. You will search in the sunset and the sea-foam for your friends of the court; only their children remain to guard the death of the Realm that you brought upon us. And now," he said with cold courtesy, "will you excuse me? I have my people to tend; and you, if you're not willing to help, will stay back and look at what you have brought upon us in your careless folly."

They rode between two leaning, mud-walled houses and a crying, dirty child came stumbling forward to hold their horses. Lisa's breath caught in her throat at the smell of blood. The market square looked as if a battle had passed over it; she saw torn and bloody rags, mud churned by running feet and red-brown smears on the small stone building in the middle of the village. But there were no bodies; no people at all, save the child who had come to greet them.

"Where are the others?" Berengar demanded.

"In t'church—those as is left . . . " The boy jerked his head towards the small gray stone building that was the center of the village. His throat worked convulsively to hold back sobs.

Berengar dismounted and threw the reins of his horse to the boy. Behind him, Lisa slid off her own mount, somewhat less gracefully, and leaned against the mud-walled house behind her. She stared at the devastated market square, the church, the huddle of houses, like a tourist taking in the first sight of a foreign land.

Except that tourists always go home again, and I can't . . . I never can . . .

The wall she leaned on was sticky. Lisa brought one hand away from the wall and saw her palm imprinted with a smear of drying blood.

CHAPTER SIX

Vos exorciso, Larve, Fauni, Manes, Nymphe,
Sirene, Hamadryades, Satyri, Incubi, Penates.
    ut cito abeatis,
    chaos in colatis,
    ne vas corrumpatis
    christianitatis.

—Ms. of Benedictbeuern

(I exorcise you, ghosts and gods, fauns and
dryads, nymphs and satyrs, nightmares, sirens,
shades and spirits, you shall vanish into Chaos,
you shall not corrupt Christendom.)

As he entered the church, Berengar knew that the
girl was hanging back, but he hadn't time to force
her inside just now. Let her look at the emptiness
left by the Hounds; later would be time enough to
make her understand what had caused it, after he
had heard the tales of the surviving villagers and had
sorted them into some kind of sense. *So you haven't
the stomach to face what you have done, my lady?*

Well enough—perhaps this will shock you into doing your duty, Berengar thought with grim satisfaction.

After that, for some crowded minutes, he thought no more of Sybille; he had enough to do in soothing the frightened peasants who clutched at him and cried out their stories of loss. There were pitifully few of them; no more than a third of his people remained.

This time the Wild Hunt had come just before dawn, when all were safe inside. At first the villagers, wakened by the shrill music of the hounds, had clutched one another and hidden in their rustling straw beds. They told each other that the Hunt was only passing overhead as it had used to do on winter nights in the dark of the moon. Only those who were foolish enough to go outside, who encountered the Hunt and didn't have the wit to draw a circle around themselves and call on the Blessed Virgin, would be taken; those inside were safe enough.

Only this time, the Hunt had not passed. The Hounds circled the village, baying from all quarters at once, until it seemed they would never stop and dawn would never come. There was something in that mad music that the villagers talking to Berengar could not explain and would never understand—something that made them want to run and run, as if safety were only to be found out in the woods.

Nearly all the families had the same sad end to their story. Someone within had broken under the sound of the incessant baying, had run outside and been pulled down by the Hounds. Everyone agreed that the first to go had been Arn the bridge-keeper, crying that he heard his lost daughter calling him to join her. Then parents went to save their children, husbands to save wives, babies ran to catch up with their mothers, and the Hounds feasted. And when the Hunt left, the bodies of their victims, living and dead, were carried along with them to ride the darkness with Herluin forever.

The blacksmith's family was whole; he'd barred the door and plugged his ears with clay and stood before his own door with an iron hammer, telling his panicky wife and children and his old father that he would knock down anyone who tried to leave the safety of the hut behind the forge. Two other households had come safe through the night by similar measures. Apart from these, not one family was safe and entire. Some had been destroyed utterly; others, perhaps less lucky, had left one or two to mourn the rest. There were babies too young to crawl and old people too weak to walk without help and a very few pious, determined souls who had stayed on their knees reciting prayers while their families ran out into the black night without them.

The Hunt had passed at dawn, and with the brightening of the sky the remaining villagers had crept together in the church to take what comfort they could from the stone walls, blessed as they had been by a priest who'd left them to face the Hunt alone.

"What's that?" Berengar queried sharply. "Father Simon gone?"

"Went to the Remigius yesterday, and 'a hasn't been back," said one.

"No, nor won't," another said. "He's feared to stay here."

"No shame to him. *I'm* feared. My lord, you'll take us with you? He said you'd take care of us."

"Who—Father Simon?"

"No—the elf-boy. Young Master Kieran."

"He was here? You saw him?" Berengar questioned sharply.

A confused babble of voices told the usual conflicting tales. One said that Kieran had been in the village just after the Hunt left; another contradicted him and claimed to have heard Herluin's silver horn after Kieran called to the peasants. They argued among themselves for a while about whether the elf-boy could have passed unscathed through the departing Hunt. All agreed that Kieran had told them to stay within doors until dawn, and one little girl claimed to have seen him through a chink in her father's hut—"All silver he was, my lord, and beautiful as—as an elflord!"

Berengar took what comfort he could from the stories. Kieran had been here; he was not here now; and he would not be free to search for his fosterling until this matter of the villagers had been settled. What was he to do with this handful of shocked, wary peasants? Could he take them into his keep and feed them for the winter, then settle them on new lands in the spring? If they were afraid to work their own fields and finish taking in their own harvest, he would be hard pressed to find enough food for them all this winter. Nor could he guarantee their safety in any other part of his lands.

"My lord, you'll not leave us here?" pressed the blacksmith. "Take us with you. The Hunt won't trouble your keep. For the sake of our souls, my lord—"

"If there's need to save souls," said a deep voice from the church porch, "then turn to Mother Church, not to the temporal powers. The good monks of the Remigius offer shelter to all in peril of their souls."

Berengar felt the little church grow smaller as Bishop Rotrou entered, resplendent in gold-banded cloak and bejeweled rings. The bishop's broad shoulders and burly arms bespoke his youth in the days when a churchman was expected to take up arms to defend his own; his pose assumed an authority over this church, these people, that Berengar was not ready to give him.

"St.-Remy is my village," he said. "With respect, it's for me to make disposition of these folk. I have other lands—"

"Can you promise that those lands will be safe from whatever assailed these good people last night?"

Berengar chose his words carefully. "If what attacked this village is mortal or elven, Bishop, then I am as well able to defend my people as anyone else. If you say that what passed at dawn was the Wild Hunt, then do you not commit a heresy against the decision of your own church councils?"

"I do not need to know what it is," the bishop replied, "to know that these, my people, are afraid, and that you have not kept the wolf from my sheep. This visitation may be a sign of Our Lord's displeasure at the vast landholdings of the elven lords and the temporal power they have achieved in Christendom."

"If so," Berengar murmured, "it seems strange that Our Lord didn't get displeased a few hundred years earlier, when the elvenkind were indeed a power in the land. Is your God a craven who dares strike only the weak, Bishop?"

The bishop's face was grim. "Do not presume on our friendship by blaspheming, Count Berengar. My duty to these mortal souls comes before friendship. Let us leave theological wranglings, and let me ask you only this—can you protect them? Can you promise them safety from the terror that comes by night?"

"Can you?"

"I can," the bishop said. "No land belonging to Mother Church has been molested by this new evil, no monk in any enclosed house has heard the passage of these unknown beasts. Come to the Remigius, my children, and you will be safe." He opened his arms to welcome the peasants of St.-Remy.

A few of the villagers, mostly those without kinfolk remaining alive, trailed dispiritedly across the floor to stand by Bishop Rotrou. The rest hung back, looking sidewise at Berengar, then at the bishop, then down at the floor.

"According to the Council of Clermont, the Church may not interfere with the temporalities of elven lands," Berengar reminded the bishop.

"But according to the Treaty of Jura," Bishop Rotrou said, "I may not be prevented from bringing the Word of God to mortal souls, even when they are bound to the lands of an elven lord."

Berengar shrugged. "You may speak as long as you like, my lord bishop, and any whom you persuade to follow you may do so. I will remain to make sure that none of my people are coerced into leaving their lands and their livelihoods against their will." He wondered if he was being unreasonably stubborn. Hadn't he just thought that he would be hard pressed to feed and house these people over the winter? He should be glad that the monks of the Remigius, through Bishop Rotrou, were willing to take them off his hands. But the Durandine monks hated Berengar and all his kind. And from the tales he'd heard of the harsh life inside the monasteries, he'd wager they were not overfond of their own kind either. Berengar was not at all sure that the villagers who took shelter at the Remigius would be allowed to return to his lands in the spring; and once they were in the Durandine enclosure, his status as their erstwhile lord would give him little power to defend them. Their lands would go untilled, the village would be empty, and in a year or so the Durandine order would renew their offer to buy the village and the surrounding lands—and another piece of Elfhame would be gone forever.

No, it was worth standing through the bishop's impromptu sermon, if that was what it took to assure his people of his care and concern for them and to make sure those gray-robed monks of the Durandines took none against their will. Even if it meant that he had to delay hunting through the forest for Kieran.

But it did just cross his mind, as Bishop Rotrou

launched into the fourth subheading of his exposition
of the text "Come unto me," that Sybille was lucky
to have stayed outside, where she didn't have to
listen to all this mortal superstition.

At that moment Lisa was wishing very much that
she could be inside the church, claiming whatever
protection Berengar might be willing to give her—
whoever he thought she was.

The file of gray-robed monks had crossed the bridge
while she was still staring at nothing, trying to make
sense of the shocks that had landed her in this strange
land. They were between her and the church before
she recognized the need to get away from them—so
many hooded men, all in the long gray robes of those
who'd attacked her yesterday! And a thin-lipped clerk
who'd been following the bishop into the church
turned and came towards her, and she recognized
the one whose finger she'd broken the day before.
He moved instantly and quickly when Lisa tried to
sidle around him. His arm shot out to trap her against
the wall; thin, bony fingers fell on her shoulder and
he brought his stiff, righteous face close to hers. He
had bad breath.

"Here she is, my brothers—Sybille, and ours, while
the elflord is busy within!"

Lisa's scream of protest was cut off by a bony hand
over her mouth. "God's blessing on thy quick wits,
Brother Hugh," she heard someone call through the
roaring in her ears. Was she going to faint? *Not now.*
Kicking and screaming would be more useful. Lisa
kicked backwards and entangled her feet in Hugh's
robes; screamed into his palm and felt nausea rising
in her throat. She couldn't *breathe.* And he was
lifting her up, stronger than he looked, no, somebody else—hands all over her, carrying her towards
the monks—don't waste energy hating them; get away.

The line of men parted and closed about her,
forming into a tight circle of rough gray robes and

faces shadowed under their deep hoods. Lisa could
no longer see the church; the monks pressed close
about her, She began to understand that she might
be gone from here, gagged by Hugh's long dirty
fingers and hidden by the circle of monks, before
ever Rotrou and Berengar emerged from the church
and noticed that she was missing.

Hugh was whispering in her ear now, broken glee-
ful phrases about iron and cells and chains. "Your
warding doesn't work now, does it, elf-maiden? Powerful evil spells you soulless elvenkind have, but not
if we keep you too busy to concentrate on them. I'll
see that you don't have leisure to call on your demons, elf-maiden. You shall follow the one true path
now, whether you have a soul to save or no." While
he whispered, his free hand poked and pinched at
random over her body. Lisa repressed a shiver of
disgust. She was better off now; he'd lowered her to
her feet as though assuming she'd have no choice but
to walk with the moving circle of men. And while he
was fondling her, he wasn't holding her so tightly.
She might be able to break loose—but what good
would that do, with all these others around her?

If she struggled more, they might tie her up or
worse. Lisa let Hugh push her before him and plodded as slowly as she dared in the direction he indicated. The Durandine monks formed a solid wall of
gray all around her; she couldn't even see where
they were going, but the rushing sound of the Garron was louder and louder in her ears. Did they
mean to throw her over the cliff? Surely not; Hugh
had said something about taking her to the Remigius.
He was still talking about that, making sarcastic promises about the fine entertainment of iron-barred cells
and iron chains that awaited her there.

Lisa had a feeling that she would be better off if
she did throw herself over the cliff before this madman and his friends got her into their monastery.

Oh, sure, Berengar and Rotrou would eventually notice that she and half the Durandine monks and the bishop's psychotic clerk had disappeared. And even if this Berengar wasn't terribly bright, he and a bishop ought to be able to figure out where they had all gone. But how long would it take them to catch up, and where would she be by then?

They were nearly at the bridge before Lisa saw her chance. The monks had to re-form their circle to escort her over the narrow bridge, where there was barely room for two men to walk side by side. And they hadn't quite planned that movement. While they were milling around, Lisa caught a glimpse of a very unmonastic short sword dangling from the girdle of one monk. He seemed to be the leader of the group; at any rate he was brusquely shoving some monks on ahead and motioning others to stay behind. And he was too busy directing traffic to watch Lisa.

Hugh had given up pinching in favor of fondling, and he was breathing hard. Lisa bit down hard on the hand that covered her mouth; he yelped and let go for a moment, and she dived for the handle of the short sword.

It came out of the scabbard like a knife out of butter, so smooth and easy that she could hardly believe it. Lisa slashed out wildly in a great swinging half-circle and felt the blade connect with something that jarred her arm to the elbow. There was blood on the ground, and the monks closest to her had tumbled over their own feet to got out of her way, and the one who had reached to retrieve his sword was nursing one bloody arm in the wide sleeve of his habit.

Lisa remembered the counsel of the girls who'd given her those few self-defense lessons. "Don't pick up a knife or a gun unless you know how to use it; he'll just take it away from you."

She didn't know how to use *anything*; it was just plain dumb luck that had brought her this far. Lisa threw the sword at a monk who was starting towards her, turned and ran.

There were gray robes before the church, and she had no breath to call to Berengar. But there was an unguarded, narrow way between two of the houses that leaned into the shadow of the church. Lisa skidded on mud, jumped over a pile of brush and kicked a gate open. Behind the rickety fence was something that smelled distinctly like a pigsty. As she skimmed through a series of puddles that stank even worse than the rest of the village, she heard the grunting of the disturbed sow behind her, and then a cry of dismay from one of the monks. From the sounds, Lisa rather thought that he'd tripped over the sow. She didn't take time to look. Ahead of her, the path led into a forest, deep and glimmering with green-filtered light, where she could surely lose herself until the Durandines gave up the search.

CHAPTER SEVEN

The angels are His creation, whom He has so
ordered that by a system of unbroken continuity
the highest are linked with the intermediate
and they in turn with the lowest. His are the
animate powers of the firmament, the celestial
fires, rational creatures of a kind neither destroyed
by death nor altered by passion.

—Bernard Sylvestris, *Cosmographia*

Losing herself, Lisa concluded some hours later,
had been the easy part. Finding her way back to
civilization might just not be so easy. And it was
getting dark already.

In the first moments of her panic-stricken flight
she'd had no thought beyond getting as far away as
possible from the Durandine monks and the bishop's
crazy clerk. There'd been no time to mark her trail
or to think about how she would find her way back to
the village. She couldn't even remember much of
those first minutes; just branches slashing her face, a
deep narrow stream that twisted and curled diaboli-

cally so that she had to jump it innumerable times, glades of moss-covered ancient trees like pillars and crackling leaves underfoot that threatened to betray her. Behind her she heard the shouts of the Durandines and the steps of heavy men pounding through the forest after her.

Even with the momentary lead she'd gained, Lisa could hardly believe that she'd gotten away. She certainly hadn't done anything very clever. In books, people who were being pursued through a forest had any number of options. They could run through a stream to hide their footprints, or climb up into an oak tree until the pursuit passed, or startle a fox that would take off in the opposite direction and mislead their trackers.

Lisa had just run. She'd jumped the stream without thinking about it, she hadn't had time to climb a tree even if one with appropriately spaced branches had presented itself, and the only living thing she'd encountered had been a squirrel that was much too small to delude the monks into following its trail instead of hers.

But she was small and thin, and her elven-made gown had obligingly turned itself into a snug tunic and leggings of rusty red, and she had been able to wriggle through thorny bushes and sneak under low-lying branches while the big, healthy men behind her were catching their robes in the thorns and banging their heads on the branches. Hugh, the bishop's clerk, had been the only one of them who was small enough and dressed appropriately for a chase through the woods; and somehow Lisa didn't think Hugh spent a lot of time in the woods. He had the smell of sour brown ink and burnt candle-ends and much-scraped parchment about him.

"Not that I've spent much time in the woods myself," she said aloud, for the comfort of her own voice, "but it looks as if I'm going to now."

She was leaning with her back against a stone outcropping that shot into the sky in jagged peaks. It came out of a tree-covered hill that was quite real and solid and definitely not an illusion concealing one of the elvenkind's secret castles. Lisa was quite sure of that. Some time ago she had realized that the only sounds she heard were the noises of her own passage; when she stopped running, she heard nothing but her own breath rasping in her aching throat. She'd lost the pursuers; unfortunately, she had also quite thoroughly lost herself, and night was coming on. Since then she'd been up and down the hill twice, trying every trick she could think of to walk through illusions and spells and into a hidden elven castle. She'd even gone so far as to knock on a few likely-looking stones and beg for entrance.

Nothing worked, and why should it? Reluctantly Lisa concluded that this particular hill was just a hill. The forest was just a forest. And the rough high stone against which she leaned was as much of a shelter as she was likely to find for the night—unless the trail that curved around it led somewhere.

Lisa blinked and squinted along the trail in the fading light. A moment ago, when she came sliding and panting down the cliff side for the second time, she would have sworn there was nothing around her but leaves and trees and those nasty little thorny vines that tangled around everywhere at ankle height. Now, as the golden light of afternoon gave way to a blue twilight, she could see a distinct trail leading around the stony hill.

What had concealed it from her before? A trick of the light? Or elven magic? Lisa shook her head and wiped her sweating forehead with the back of her hand. As long as she could see the trail now, it didn't really matter. All that mattered was deciding which direction was more likely to lead to a village where she could get shelter for the night—and as she had absolutely no idea where she was and no basis for the decision, *that* didn't matter very much either.

A cloud passed over the sun, leaving the forest dim and full of secret rustling shadows. Lisa shivered. She'd better get moving, one way or the other. If only she had some clue to help her decide!

A moment later, as the cloudy darkness deepened about her, she had some help. A long, eerie howling echoed through the forest, a strange music that sent new shivers running up and down Lisa's spine. She had never heard anything like that before. It was beautiful and frightening and it made her bones feel as if they were turning to water and dripping away.

Then the long music of the howling died away, to be replaced by the excited baying of hounds that had caught the scent of their quarry, and three silvery notes from a hunting horn picked up the hounds' excitement and relayed it through the forest. And Lisa found herself running without ever having made the decision to do so.

This chase was far worse than the last one. At least the Durandine monks had had to stumble over the same rough ground Lisa faced, fighting the same thorny vines and low branches clawing at their faces and habits. But these hunters swept through the sky like the night wind, and the hounds bayed at her heels before she had run a hundred paces. The clouds were so thick and dark now that Lisa could not tell whether the sun had actually set or not; she ran through a blue dimness, tripping and gasping and almost falling and catching hold of anything before her to help her along, not caring about skinned palms and knees and her chest burning for air. Once only she risked a glance behind her. The silvery gray shapes of hounds and hunters glimmered like a veil against the night air, riding the currents above and between the trees. A black shadow of a horse with burning eyes swooped down through the empty air over the path, and Lisa saw a thin girl with disheveled hair and hands tangled in the horse's mane. She sat awkwardly, as though one hip wouldn't turn out properly, and her open mouth and eyes were full of the black shadow-stuff that made the horse; but Lisa knew that those empty eyes saw her.

Behind that one came others, some ugly with wounds and rotting flesh, some fair and silver-haired as the lords of Elfhame, some no more than skeletons in rusty armor; and beside them, in the empty night air above the path, loped long gray shapes with open mouths and teeth that gleamed like candle flames.

Lisa left the path and plunged into the dark forest of evergreens that had replaced the oaks and beeches near St.-Remy, into a pine-scented darkness where the trees grew too close and tight together for anything, mortal or elven or demon, to plunge through those sharp-needled branches. She could still hear the silver horn sounding far above her, but it didn't paralyze her now: the piercing music was like long sharp knives behind her, forcing her to run on and on until she sobbed for breath and the ground opened before her and she tumbled into a pool of ice that sucked the air from her lungs.

The Remigius monastery was a scene of controlled confusion that evening. Fires burned late in the kitchen, where half a dozen monks ladled thin cabbage soup into pots and bowls and mugs and fed the exhausted villagers of St.-Remy as well as they might. In the scriptorium, three clerks labored over a parchment conveying the lands of St.-Remy to the keeping of the Durandine order; they had been advised that the cursed elf-lord would soon comply, now that more than half the remaining villagers had sought sanctuary in the monastery. And in the chapter-

house, a circle of hooded men stared into a brass
bowl.

The white liquid in the bowl shivered and transformed itself as they watched, suggesting leaves
trembling in a forest, branches broken and trees
shaking in an unearthly wind. Like a shadow of white
on cream, the form of a girl shaped itself among the
trees. She ran through briars and branches, skidded
down a long smooth slope covered with slippery
brown needles and plunged into an icy pool; little
droplets raised themselves from the surface of the
bowl where the girl's image struck the water.

"She is close to the Stonemaidens," one of the
brothers of Saint Durand commented. "What if she
finds the way back?"

"All the better," said a raspy, unpleasant voice.
One of the slighter of the monks pushed his hood
back for a moment, revealing a pimply, thin-lipped
face. "She cannot be Sybille."

"But you yourself said—"

"I was *wrong*," snapped Hugh, the bishop's clerk.
"Yes, this is the girl who came through the Gate; she
admitted it when I questioned her. But she is—not—
Sybille. You saw her handle our brother's sword.
Would one of the elvenkind have come so close to
cold iron? Her common looks might be illusion, but
no illusion would keep the metal of that sword from
burning an elf-maid's fair flesh. She is mortal—and
that fool Berengar never thought to give her the test
of iron!"

"She touched only the hilt—"

"Which is bound with iron clasps," interposed the
monk from whom Lisa had taken the sword, "against
the thieving fingers of the elvenkind. She held it in
her hands and swung it well. If she had been a
soulless elfling, her palms would have been burned
to the bone. Our brother is right. The girl is mortal."

"And it is my intention," said a third hooded man,

whose stature and bearing proclaimed him the unofficial leader of the circle, "that she shall find the Stonemaidens again. Even now the Hunt drives her towards the circle."

"And back to her own world?"

"You mean to lose her, after all our labor!"

"What if—"

The tall monk held up his hand for silence. "Peace, my little brothers. Remember that we are not without friends in that other world. I have seen to it that we shall not lose her. This girl may not be the one we seek, but if she had not been close to Sybille she would not have heard the call. If she can pass the Gate again, she will lead us to Sybille.

"And remember," he added as the monks murmured among themselves, "where one mortal has crossed the Gate, others may follow. If Sybille resists our sending, we shall have to take her by force once that girl has led us to her."

"God and Saint Durand protect us," whispered one monk, "are we to go into that place of demons now?"

"If necessary, my little brother, Saint Durand will give you the courage. Even there, you will follow the one path to the Light. May we all keep to the one path!"

The brothers bowed their heads and murmured the ritual blessing. As they looked away from the brass bowl, the milky fluid settled into peace again.

As they were filing out of the chapter-house, the liquid in the bowl shivered violently, and for one instant there was a dancing haze of red-gold flames above the white pool; but the monks, heads bowed, knowing that the charm on the scrying-bowl had been released, did not see this.

The chaos at the Remigius was mirrored in the world of iron-demons and mortals that frightened the monks and elves alike. In the street where the New Age Psychic Research Center stood, the warring breeds of iron-demons fought and snarled among themselves over the few coveted treasures still available. Lisa had very efficiently arranged for over a hundred friends of the Center to attend that night's emergency meeting; but since she didn't drive, she had not thought about the parking problem. There was a pre-Halloween toga-and-costume party at the fraternity house on the northwest corner of the block; the travel agent whose office occupied the old house on the southeast corner was holding an open house with exotically costumed young ladies handing out travel brochures and drinks to anyone they could lure in; and in the center of the block, one long black car after another deposited the frail old ladies of Miss Penny's bridge group and created a traffic jam that backed up, on occasion, as far as Sixth Street.

"I wish Lisa would get here!" Judith Templeton yanked at her long yellow hair for the tenth time. "She promised to be here early and arrange everything. Instead we've got everything happening at once and no help. No extra chairs in the meeting room, no handout for people to read and get an idea of the problem, and police all over the place this afternoon about those damn books of Mahluli's."

"Can't blame Mahluli for getting burgled," Nick pointed out.

"No, but I wish he hadn't noticed the missing books until after this meeting," Judith said frankly. "I've got enough to worry about tonight, especially with Lisa's disappearance."

"The perfect secretary," Nick drawled. He leaned back against the wall and drummed his fingers on the molded plaster. "Tell me, sister, this *is* the paragon of a secretary-receptionist you've been raving about? The one you were going to hire for your own business if Aunt Penny's circus folded its tents? The one who disappeared in the middle of the day and hasn't been heard from since?"

"Spare me the sarcasm," Judith suggested. "Do something useful instead."

"Like what?"

Before Judith could answer, Ginnie rushed in, pink-cheeked with the excitement of bearing bad news. "Judith, are you aware that the cars from our people are blocking the fraternity driveway?"

Judith smiled. "That's the first *good* news I've heard all day."

"Are you also aware that they've called the police?"

"Tell my lawyer." Judith placed one hand behind Nick's arched back and shoved him towards the door. "There you go, little brother. Useful tasks. Get out there and mediate between the frat rats and the cops. Or if you can't do that, direct traffic. And stop being sarcastic about Lisa."

"Lisa wouldn't just disappear like this," Ginnie agreed. "It's not like her."

"Why not?" Nick was elegantly draped around the doorframe now, bonelessly graceful in his dark suit. "I gather that's how she started here. Judith and Aunt Penny have filled my ears with the saga of how this wonderful girl just suddenly appeared for counseling, saw the disorganization in this place, attacked the chaos and became the receptionist-cum-office-manager while she was waiting for an interview."

"We do not," Judith told him, "require any more sarcasm."

"I was just trying to point out," Nick said in hurt tones, "that you ladies are reposing an inordinate amount of trust in someone who, by your own account, came out of nowhere, doesn't seem fully conversant with modern American life, turned white when the new owner mentioned the need for resumes and personnel files, and disappeared without warning the next day—immediately after a burglary."

"Exactly what are you implying? Damn you, Nick, you've barely met Lisa. I *know* her, and I know Aunt Penny could never have lasted this long without her, and I also know she would never do anything criminal!"

"Oh, she may not be actually criminal," Nick allowed generously, "at least not in the popular sense of the term. But I'm reasonably sure she is an illegal alien, and in the context of the burglary and her disappearance I think it's very interesting that whoever broke into Mahluli's bookshop knew exactly where he keeps his rare and valuable books. And I'd be willing to bet money that you'll never see her again."

Judith stuck one hand into her jeans pocket and withdrew it with a crumpled wad of bills. She extended the pile of money to Nicholas, straight-armed, palm up. "Count that and match it, little brother," she snapped. "Whatever I have says that Lisa will be back by tomorrow—unless something really bad has happened to her."

It was only water; only a cold, swift-running stream whose bank had been covered by a deceptive loose carpet of the thick brown needles that fell from the conifers. And it was only—once she spluttered and splashed to her feet—only as deep as her knees.

And by some miracle, her last terrified burst of speed seemed to have lost the beasts that hunted the air. Lisa started to squeeze the water out of her tunic, then shook her head slowly as the tunic itself pulsed on her body, contracting and releasing until the individual fibers had squeezed themselves dry. The leggings that now formed the lower portion of her costume kept on working furiously, but the stream kept her soaked from feet to knees.

"It's all right," Lisa told her elf-made dress. "I

don't think you can do much about the parts that are under water."

As if it had understood her, the costume quit its anxious vibrating. Lisa listened closely, but she heard nothing but the splash of water and the sleepy, rustling sounds of a forest at night. Where was the Hunt? Had they swept past her while she lay in the pool? Wading through water was supposed to deceive real hunting hounds who followed a scent along the land; perhaps being completely under the water, even for a few spluttering, choking seconds, had served to screen her from beings who moved as fast as the wind.

Lisa devoutly hoped that was the case. But just in case the Hunt returned, she decided to stay where she was for a while. Dusk had given way to the total darkness of night; if she waded along the stream, she might fall again into some hidden pool deep enough, with currents strong enough, to pose a real danger. And if she tried to clamber up the slippery, needle-covered slope of the crumbling bank, she might not be able to find this pool of refuge again in case the Hunt returned.

And in any case, she had no idea of where to go from here.

Perhaps daylight would offer a solution.

"Oh, dear," Lisa sighed aloud, "I *am* cold. If only I could see something, maybe I could find a nice rock to sit on." And maybe, if she were entirely out of the water, and if she mentioned being cold a few more times, her elf-woven dress would take the hint and turn itself into a nice fur cloak. *Or better yet*, Lisa thought with an ache of homesickness in her throat, *a nice thick down coat from Land's End or Eddie Bauer, one of those toys for yuppies with zippers and snaps and a hood and hidden pockets. Maybe it could even manage a sandwich and an apple in one of the pockets.*

At the moment, keeping her top half warm and dry seemed to be the most the elf-dress could manage. Oh, well; even in the dark she could feel about for a rock or a nice dry ledge to perch on. Lisa bent and passed her hands over the surface of the water around her. She had a sense of a solid mass to her right, probably the high bank down which she'd tumbled; perhaps there would be some place to sit there. She sloshed cautiously towards the hint of darkness upon darkness, waving one hand before her just at water level. Her fingers encountered a frizz of roots descending into the swift-running water, a boulder—unfortunately completely submerged—a strong heavy root extending right into the water, a tangle of smaller hair-like roots waving and knotting about that base, something soft—

Something soft, and moving, and unnaturally warm beneath that cold stream water. Lisa's fingers jerked back and she yelped in surprise, not just at the touch of warm living flesh but also at the cry she heard at the same moment.

Help me, please help me.

Where had it come from? Lisa stood erect, straining her ears. Was the Hunt returning, driving some other poor soul through this forest?

She heard nothing but the trickling of the stream over rocks and the sighing of the wind in the trees.

But the voice had been clear, and shrill with desperation, and very close.

Was it possible—? Lisa scowled into the darkness. "I have enough troubles already," she informed the night. "If anybody needs help here, it's me!"

All the same, she bent and reached under the sunken root again, fighting a shiver of fear and distaste. Tendrils of tiny roots brushed her wrist and wrapped about her fingers. She'd imagined the whole thing; there was nothing here, and if she had touched anything, it was a slimy fish or a frog or some other

water-creature long since gone and probably much
more frightened than she was—

*Oh, you came back! Please don't leave me here
alone.*

Not exactly flesh; it was more like touching feathers, warm soft feathers with a thin skin of air between them and the water. And the touch on her
mind was feather-light too, as though the—thing—
knew it had frightened her before.

"Don't worry," Lisa said, "I won't leave you."
Cold and frightened though she was, she could tell
that the thing under her hands was much worse off.
It was shaped for air and light and movement, and
now it was slowly growing still under the water.
Dying. And she knew, too—the information came
into her mind seasoned with a touch of inaudible
laughter—that there'd been no need to speak aloud;
as long as they were touching like this, she had only
to shape the words in her mind for the underwater
thing to pick them up.

"I understand," Lisa said, "but if you don't mind,
today has been strange enough already. I feel more
comfortable talking aloud. Then I can at least pretend you hear me. Now. What sort of help did you
have in mind?" She hoped it wasn't anything very
difficult. She was tired and hungry and lost and
soaked to the knees, and she couldn't see her hand
in front of her face. She was not exactly equipped for
serious rescue missions. Maybe, she thought without
much hope, maybe she'd guessed wrong; maybe this
thing didn't really want her to get down under the
water and untangle all the tight knotty roots that
were wrapped in and out of its feathery substance.

Free me.

It felt like an impatient shove inside her head,
forcing her fingers down until she could feel how the
hair-fine tendrils of roots wrapped around the feathery creature, in some places so tight that they cut

into its—not flesh, exactly, but—"That must hurt," Lisa said.

It does. That is not important. Free me! The tone was imperious now, like a toddler demanding its juice and cookies *now*.

"All right, all right, I'm working on it," Lisa grumbled. The roots were so tightly snarled together that it was like untying knots in wet cord. Under water. Without being able to see what she was doing. But no individual root was that strong; slowly, with infinite care, she separated the tiny root strands and broke each one.

"I just hope this plant isn't telepathic too," she muttered, "I'd hate to think what it would say about what I'm doing to its life-support system. It probably —ah!"

The last knot of roots fell away under her fingers. There was a fluttering of feathery warmth against her palms; then the thing she'd been working to free burst out of the water in a blaze of flames that sent Lisa reeling back, one arm up over her face. She tripped over a stone and sat down with a splash in the center of the shallow pool.

Don't do that. You splashed me!

"My humble apologies," said Lisa. "You—er— startled me." She got up slowly, squinting against the brilliance of the light that glowed from the feather-thing—not a bird, she couldn't call it a bird, but not anything else she had seen outside the borders of some fantastically illuminated manuscripts. It was slender as her wrist and almost as long as her arm, with long sweeping wings that curved to twice the length of its body. The head was rounded and almost human, if you discounted the feathered crest; at least so Lisa thought, but she could not be sure of the thing's features while it moved so quickly and gave off such a glow of delight. Freed of the roots and the water, it swooped about her head in dizzying arcs and spirals of light, shooting off tiny sparks that danced over the surface of the pool and then, as if repelled by the water, returned to their source.

"Er—feather-thing—do you think it's quite a good idea to go making such a fireworks display?"

What?

"The lights," Lisa translated. "I don't know if you noticed, being under water and all that, but there are some rather unpleasant creatures hunting the forest tonight."

The Wild Hunt. Yes, I know them. They startled me into the water. I am not afraid of Herluin and his followers; but I was not expecting them to be so strong in this world. And while I was observing them, the nixy-reeds twined their fingers around me. The feather-thing dimmed itself to a soft golden glow and sank down until it was hovering over the pool, just at the height of Lisa's head. Now she could see a thin pointed face with wild up-slanting eyes— not human, but not elven either; something entirely outside her experience.

Of course I am outside your experience. It sounded rather smug. *We are not supposed to show ourselves to mortals, except those who are very holy or in danger from demons.*

"Well, I certainly don't qualify on the first count," Lisa said, "but for the second—are the Wild Hunt demons?"

Not exactly. They are of this earth. But they should not be so strong; I do not know what has gone wrong here. Of course, it had been a few hundred years since I last visited. Many things have changed. It is not important; they are gone for the moment. I owe you a life, mortal.

"I wish you wouldn't call me that. My name is Lisa."

And I am Zahariel, one of the angels of light, and not a 'feather-thing.'

"An angel?"

Are all mortals as slow as you, Lisa-mortal? Yes, an angel. Zahariel's feathers rippled with sparks of red and magenta light. *And I owe you a life. Tell me quickly how I may pay my debt, so that I may go home again.*

"Home," Lisa said slowly. "I—could you possibly take me home again?"

Not to my realm. Sublunary creatures cannot survive there. Zahariel's eyes shone blue-green and its head tilted to one side. *Of course, once you are dead —if you qualify—*

"That's quite all right," Lisa said. "I didn't mean your home, but mine. I—well, you see, I don't come from here."

Of course not. No mortals live in this forest—oh. I see. Lisa felt as if feathery tendrils were stirring through her memories. *Another world? One absolutely without angels or demons? How fascinating! And you came through the Stonemaidens—I had not realized that the elvenkind retained enough power to open a Gate. I wonder if it is still open? I should like to explore this barren world.*

"Me, too," Lisa said. "All I want is to get back there—but you see, the monks tried to make me— and then Berengar took me to his keep, and I can't find my way back—and—" She stifled a sob and wiped one hand across her eyes.

You cannot find the Stonemaidens? Zahariel's mindtouch conveyed astonishment and delicate laughter. *Why, follow your feet up the stream.*

Lisa looked down at the dancing ripples of reflected fire and the blackness of the stream beyond Zahariel's light. "This stream? This is the one?" It seemed too good to be true.

Upstream.

"Of course. Away from the river." Did one kiss an angel? Probably not. Lisa looked upstream into inky blackness and cold, gurgling water, took hold of her courage with both hands and nodded to Zahariel.

"Well, if that's the way, I'd better be going. I only hope I can get back through again—are you sure the Gate works both ways?"

It always did before. And if it fails, we will think of something else.

"We?"

I will light your way. It is the least I can do—and not enough to repay my debt.

"More than enough," Lisa told it. She felt surprisingly lighter of heart at the promise of a companion through the forest. Zahariel's fiery presence warmed more than just her body.

The journey to the Stonemaidens was not as simple as Zahariel had made it seem—that is, it might have been simple for an angel of light who could hover above the water and glide between the branches, but for Lisa's tired and thoroughly mortal body it was a long, chilly, exhausting trek over slippery boulders and through treacherous underwater sands. The stream wound and curved, banks overhung the edges with curtains of those grasping, slender roots that Zahariel called nixy-reeds, wet stones turned under Lisa's feet and true underwater things scuttled past her ankles. More than once she was tempted to leave the stream and strike out through the forest, with Zahariel to light the way and make sure she didn't lose the path; but whenever she set foot on the bank, something deterred her. Once it was as simple as a slide of water-soaked clay that proved impossible to climb, and more than once it was as subtle and as terrifying as the faint echo of a silver horn winding through the forest.

The Hunt does not sleep yet. Do not leave the stream, Zahariel warned once, unnecessarily. His golden glow had dimmed to the merest hint of a shimmer, hardly more than the reflection of what light might have come from the cloud-covered moon, and his uneasiness wrapped about Lisa like a damp cloak.

She waded on.

Towards the end Zahariel kept telling her they were nearly there, and she needed his reassurance. The hunting sounds, once so faint they had been all but swallowed up in the night air, were closer now. How close, Lisa could not judge, but she kept looking up and behind her, and she was never totally reassured to see nothing but trees and sky. The hounds bayed now from one side of the stream, now from the other; she felt as if they were being hunted into a trap.

But it was no trap. They rounded a corner and Zahariel's light blazed out to show the dark sentinel shapes of the Stonemaidens, weathered pillars against the night sky. Lisa caught her breath with hope and longing and sudden fear at the sight of the remembered arch, so near now. She could not see what lay beyond it. What if she went through it and found herself still on the circle of mossy turf guarded by the Stonemaidens?

Oh, beautiful and strange! Zahariel crooned to himself. *So many lights burning in the sky!*

The only light in this world was Zahariel himself. "Can you see—is the Gate still open?" Lisa whispered.

"Oh, yes, yes, open and beautiful, your world— and dangerous. Your people truly do not know angels. How is this?

Before Lisa could snap that she wasn't in the mood for a philosophical discussion, the hounds bayed again —directly behind them, this time, and the eerie music of their cry was carried on a chill wind that whistled about her face.

Go now. Quickly! They cannot follow you through the Gate.

"Come with me?"

I dare not. Zahariel sounded shaky but regretful. *It is too strange, your world. They have no angels. What would they make of me?*

"You can't stay here!" And Lisa did not have the courage to stay and plead with it. The wind whipped her loose hair about her face and plastered her elven-made garments to her wet body, and the cries of the hunters sounded in the night sky.

Child, I am an angel. They startled me before, but only because I was surprised to find Herluin so strong in the world. Do you really think they can harm me?

Zahariel's feathery form shivered and expanded like an explosion of fireworks in the night sky, until the arch of his wings filled the sky and the light of his face cast long black shadows from each of the standing stones. *Run!* he commanded. In that golden light, Lisa ran from the shelter of the stream, across slippery needles and crackling leaves and smooth turf, through the arch and onto the hard smoothness of a polished tile floor. She looked back to call to Zahariel, but the arch dwindled as she looked until it was only a painted page in an open book.

"It's about time you came home," said Clifford Simmons. "I have been waiting a long time."

CHAPTER EIGHT

A la fontana del vergier,
on l'erb' es verta
jostal gravier,
a l'ombra d'un fust domesgier,
en aiziment de blancas flors
e de novelh chant costumier,
trobey sola, ses companhier,
selha que no vol mon solatz.

—Marcabru

(By the fountain in the garden, where the grass
grows green down to the edge of the water, in
the shadow of a orchard tree, adorned with white
flowers and singing the new songs of the new
season—there I found her all alone, this girl who
does not want my company)

For just one breath, while the Gate dwindled behind her and she knew that she had made the crossing, Lisa had felt safe. She had expected to return to
Mahluli's shadowy bookshop, hung about with dusty
velvet curtains and redolent of eastern scents and old

leather bindings. Instead she was in a hard, shiny room of glass and polished tile and shining chrome. The blue-white glare of the fluorescent office lights bounced gaily off all the bright smooth machine-made surfaces and hurt her eyes. After the wooded glades and weathered stones of that other world, everything here seemed too new, too bright, too slick and sharp-cornered.

Clifford Simmons was sitting behind a large desk of polished wood, toying with a smoky glass paper-weight. Lisa couldn't imagine what he used it for; there were no papers on the desk. Before him, the book of fairy tales with the Nielsen illustrations lay open on the dark polished wood of the desk; behind him, opened curtains showed the Austin skyline—empty office buildings sparked by random pinpoints of lit windows—through a sheet of dark glass. A blinking red light that seemed to hang in the sky puzzled Lisa for a moment, until she realized that it was the reflection of the coffee machine that stood on a cabinet beside her. She could feel the heat from the hot plate and smell the acrid odor of coffee that had been brewing for hours into an acid black glue. Clifford Simmons was telling the truth; he had been waiting for a long time.

"I—I don't understand," Lisa said slowly. "What are you doing with Mahluli's book?"

"It's not his now," Clifford told her with obvious satisfaction. "It's mine. And so are you."

"Oh, no." Lisa shook her head and started to back away; she could see the door behind her reflected in the window glass, a faintly transparent image super-imposed on the view of Austin by night.

"Don't be in such a hurry," Clifford said. "You don't want to go anywhere dressed like that, do you? And surely you want an explanation of the odd things that have been happening to you."

Lisa paused and looked down uncertainly. Her

elf-dress was still in the form it had assumed for her journey through the woods, dark crimson leggings and a loose tunic ornamented with a great deal of gold embroidery. *Blue jeans and a T-shirt, please!* she thought without any real hope of success.

The dress remained unchanged; it felt like dead cloth—like all the clothes she'd ever worn in this world; Lisa hadn't realized until now how still and unnatural that could seem.

And she did want to know whatever Clifford knew.

"I mean you no harm," he said, coming around the desk with both hands outstretched. "There's no reason to be afraid of me. I will take care of you, Lisa."

His voice was warm and steady and comforting. As long as she didn't look at his intent dark eyes, Lisa felt better. So she very sensibly watched the sparkling blue and green lights in his opal ring instead, and let the warm caressing voice wash over her. She did need comfort; she did long to stop running and fighting and protesting. Being taken care of should be all she wanted; why did she feel this small, protesting, niggling doubt? She didn't want to doubt Clifford. She wanted to relax and enjoy being safe at home again.

"Just sit down, there's a good girl." He guided her to a soft, low chair beside the coffee machine. "You must be tired after all your travels. Would you like a cup of coffee? No? Just sit back and relax, then." The lights inside the opal danced and sang to her as his hands moved.

Lisa felt so sleepy she could hardly keep her eyes open. It had been a punishingly long day. But it wouldn't be polite to fall asleep in Clifford Simmons' office; and she wanted to be safe at home, in her own little room on the top floor of the Center.

"I would like to go home now."

"In a moment—in a moment. I have to explain everything to you first, Lisa, to make sure that you are on our side. There are powerful forces at work in this world."

"I know that," said Lisa. Why did Clifford feel it necessary to explain this to her? She was the one who'd been whipping back and forth between the worlds. She could explain a thing or two to him, if she had the energy. But it was too much trouble to talk.

"Those forces must not belong to those who would use them ill, or to the ignorant who would misuse them. Don't you agree, Lisa? You would not give a loaded gun to a baby, would you? Only those who are wise should be entrusted with the power."

Lisa nodded slowly, following the soothing motions of Clifford's hand with the opal ring. Everything he said was so right, how could she argue?

"There is someone in this world who does not belong here," Clifford crooned, "someone who holds too much power, someone who could be very dangerous to us all. You will take me to Sybille, Lisa."

"Can't," Lisa murmured. She felt warm and soft and safe and she wished that she could make Clifford happy by doing what he wanted, especially when everything he said was wise and true like this. But why did people keep nagging her about Sybille? She wanted to be nice, she wanted to help, and they kept asking the impossible. Lisa felt very sorry for herself.

"You must." Clifford's voice hardened. "There is no more time to delay your choice, Lisa; you are either with us or against us. You do not wish to stand against us, do you?"

Slowly, slowly, Lisa's head moved from side to side. Of course she didn't want to set herself up against Clifford. She just wanted to be nice and have people like her. Clifford liked her; that was nice. If she didn't help him find Sybille, would he stop liking her? That would be so sad. Two big tears squeezed out of Lisa's eyes and trickled down her cheeks. She thought about wiping them away, but her hands were so heavy; it was easier to leave them lying relaxed in her lap.

"Of course you don't." Clifford's voice was warmly approving. "You're a good girl, Lisa, and you want to follow the one true path, don't you?"

Someone else had spoken of the one true path to her recently. Who was it? Hugh—the bishop's clerk! Lisa's body tensed as she remembered his hands poking and fondling while he whispered threats to her. The other Durandine monks liked that phrase, too. Was Clifford a Durandine? How could that be? Lisa tensed involuntarily, remembering leather-bound wires about her wrists and cruel hands pinching her.

"You're worried about something, Lisa. Don't worry. I want you to relax now. You don't have to think any more. I'm going to take good care of you."

Not if he was a friend of the Durandine monks, he wasn't. Lisa forced herself to look up at Clifford's face. His voice was still going on and on, steady and soothing as the rolling of waves, but his face was tense and he was staring through her as if he didn't really see her—like Hugh—as if she were a tool he didn't want to pick up. She had to get away from him. If only he would stop talking! His voice was like warm honey running through her limbs, making her soft and boneless.

Think about something else, Lisa told herself. She tried to concentrate on something, anything, to keep the soporific effect of Cliff's voice at bay: the office buildings she could see through the window, the reflected red light of the coffee machine, the stain on one corner of the heavy drapes.

"I'm very sleepy," she murmured, and it was easy to keep her voice slow and relaxed. "I don't want to go to sleep before we find Sybille. I'll have some coffee now."

"Yes, that's a good idea. You don't want to go to sleep yet; you want to help me and the Masters. You're a good girl, a very good girl . . ."

His voice kept rolling over her as she stood and

languorously ambled over to the coffee machine. She picked up the carafe, half-full of hot black coffee that had long since simmered down to a corrosive acidic potion, and held it steady in her left hand while she placed her right palm down on the hot plate.

It was too hot, much too hot; no wonder the coffee had boiled down! Lisa had leaned down with all her weight; now she jerked her hand away and felt skin tearing, lost her balance for a moment and almost dropped the carafe. The burning pain tore through her, shooting up to her shoulder and bringing instant tears to her eyes—and clearing her head. Clifford's soothing voice was only background noise now compared to the screaming of her open hand.

"What are you doing?" Clifford sounded worried. "Lisa, dear girl, have you hurt yourself?"

Lisa whirled and threw the carafe of hot black coffee straight in his face. She heard glass breaking; Cliff screamed and both hands fumbled at his eyes. Broken glasses, broken coffee carafe, scalding coffee and splinters of glass everywhere—Lisa was at the door before Cliff could move to go after her, and she was even clever enough to open it with her unhurt left hand. He was scrambling after her now, half-blind without those heavy black-rimmed glasses, but she was in the hall already. Somebody cried, "Stop!"

Lisa kept running. But, unbelievably, Cliff Simmons didn't. She made it to the end of the hall with no one after her. Elevator? No, too dangerous to wait. Stairs—ah! The red Exit sign. Lisa went down gray metal steps four at a time, slipping on the turns and banging her burnt hand against the wall to steady herself and screaming inside her head at the pain that she didn't have breath to acknowledge out loud. She hadn't imagined it would hurt so much, she'd only wanted to clear her head. There must be something wrong with the coffee maker. Fire hazard. Somebody ought to do something about that. People ought to be more careful what they kept in their offices . . . magic books and overheating coffee machines. She wasn't making much sense, was she? Didn't matter. She didn't have to think now, only run. Three flights down, then a brown-painted metal fire door with a red handle. As Lisa pushed at the red handle, bells began ringing over her head, and when she burst out onto the street there were people staring at her and at the building with the ringing fire alarm. She didn't care. The night air was crisp and cold to clear her head, and the sidewalks were solid under her feet, and she knew where she was now: at the edge of downtown Austin, only six blocks from the New Age Center.

And she felt as if the Wild Hunt were baying over her shoulder. Knowing it was ridiculous and a waste of time, promising herself that Zahariel had been right and that the Hunt could not come through the Gate, Lisa still responded to the prickling sensation between her shoulder blades. When she should have been running, she stopped on the sidewalk and looked back over her shoulder at the office building. There was only one lighted window on the third floor; that must be Clifford Simmons' office. As Lisa looked up, she saw the gray curtains moving to block out her view of that room.

Gray curtains.

The heavy, expensive draperies in Clifford Simmons' office had been red.

They still were; she could see them framing the window. The sweep of gray she'd seen had been something else; something like a hooded robe with long sleeves and long skirts.

Lisa did not really think that Clifford Simmons was up in his office putting on a Durandine monk's habit. She didn't think anything at all; she just ran. And not straight down Congress to Eighth, as she'd planned, but through an alley she'd never explored before and across a parking lot and over a fence and through a

nice thick hedge of oleanders. And as she ran, she
decided that angels were too literal in their speech.
Zahariel had said that the Wild Hunt could not pass
the Gate; he hadn't made any guarantees about normal, living people.

"Fool! To have had her in your power, and let her
slip away so easily! Blessed Saint Durand, what sins
have I committed, that I must be punished by having chanced upon such a useless tool as you!"

Clifford Simmons was already distraught enough
from having had hot coffee thrown in his face and his
glasses broken. Everything was going wrong; nothing
was as he planned it. First Lisa had scared the dick-
ens out of him, coming out of nowhere like that.
He'd thought the Masters wanted him to steal
Mahluli's book so that Lisa would come to get it
back. They'd never said anything about her coming
out of the picture like—like—well, never mind. Cliff
prided himself on his presence of mind. His mission
had been to establish control over Lisa's mind, and
he couldn't do that if he gobbled and pointed and
demanded to know how she'd worked that trick; so
he acted as if nothing unusual had happened, and
almost believed it himself.

She'd almost been his; he still didn't know what
had gone wrong. Without his glasses he couldn't
think properly. It had seemed as though these new
arrivals had also come through the picture; it must
be some sort of trick, of course, but he hadn't been
able to see exactly how they worked it. And now—!
The men in the office with him wore the gray hooded
robes of the Masters, but they spoke to him as one
would speak to an incompetent servant, not to a
respected junior member of their organization.

"I can still get her," he promised.

"Do you know where she's going?" Without waiting for an answer, the leader grabbed him by the

shoulder and pushed him towards the door. "Show us. Quickly, you fool! We must not lose her now."

At least he had said *we*. Stumbling half-blind down the hall, his face burning where the scalding coffee had hit, Cliff Simmons took comfort in that. He was not yet excluded from the circle of the Masters. He could still prove himself.

That hedge of oleanders framing the parking lot was the last good bit of cover for several blocks. There was nothing but bare concrete sidewalks and streets and smooth-sided office buildings. Lisa looked over her shoulder, thought she saw a flicker of gray robes, and ran.

"There she is!"

Sobbing with exhaustion, Lisa turned to the right and ran across 15th Street in the face of a red light. Cars slammed on their brakes and rubber screeched and a red-faced man leaned out of the high window of his pickup and shouted curses at her. A moment later, just as the traffic started moving again, a line of blue-green lights flashed into being after Lisa and two men in long gray robes charged across the intersection.

It was a bad night for the iron-demons. The driver of the pickup truck was slow to brake, staring at the shower of blue-green sparks that laid a dancing trail ahead of the two loonies in gray. He nearly ran over the second robed nut before he stamped on his brakes and skidded across a puddle and wrenched at the wheel to pull his car out of the way of the telephone pole that was rushing towards him. Across the street, a Chevrolet dodged out of the way of the runaway pickup and collided with a Mazda. A Porsche hit the two cars with a crunch of destroyed fenders. The driver of the pickup evaded the pole but his truck jumped the curb on the far side of the street and landed on a fire hydrant with a gentle crunch. Water spurted into the sky and drenched him as he jumped out of the truck, fists swinging, ready to punch out the two idiots who'd forced him into a wreck.

They were out of reach, and there were flashing lights all around him and men in dark blue uniforms who wanted to know how he'd started the traffic pileup.

"Brother Alured, what do you suppose 'gawdamn doped-out punk freak' means?"

"Some incantation of this world, no doubt. Don't interrupt!" Brother Alured went on chanting the finding-spell as he ran. It had been crafted for Sybille, following the trail of magic she'd left behind when she fled into this world, but for some reason it seemed to work well enough on the thoroughly mortal girl whom they were following—perhaps because, as their master had said, she was closely linked to Sybille? No matter; their task was only to follow, and to be grateful that their magic worked at all in this horrifying world. The shower of blue-green sparks that followed them was a distracting side effect, but at least the spell still worked, although it seemed faint and weak compared to the way it operated at home. And Brother Eric was not making the task any easier with his constant interruptions and naive curiosity about the world around them. It was a strange and frightening world, this, with its light-angels perched on every pole and its iron-demons clashing in their terrible wars. Even now, the fool of a novice who'd been sent to help him was lingering to watch the new blue and red light-angels who flashed over the bodies of the iron-demons.

"Their wars are none of our concern, Brother Eric. Now *run*, or we shall lose her, spell or no!" That incompetent red-faced native who'd been their tool in this world claimed he knew where the girl was going and could take them there, but Alured was not ready to trust himself to an iron-demon under the uncertain control of this untrained half-mage. If the native mage reached the girl's destination before she did, well and good; if he didn't intercept her, Alured was quite prepared to follow her on foot until they discovered where Sybille was hiding.

"Let me get this straight, buddy," said the first policeman patiently. "You saw three aliens land in the street? That's what made you spin your truck around into the fire hydrant?"

"Aliens, crazies, *I* dunno," muttered the pickup truck driver. "Three of them, dressed funny, and there was this, like, rainbow connecting them."

"Right," said the policeman with heavy irony. "Rainbows. In the middle of the night. And aliens. You must be a friend of Whitley Strieber's or something. Tell you what—after you tell it to the judge, maybe you can write a book about it."

"Just ask the others," the pickup driver pleaded. "They was here too. They had to've seen it."

The driver of the Porsche said he hadn't seen anything but two cars locking bumper grills ten feet in front of him. The driver of the Mazda said all he remembered seeing was a Chevrolet coming at him like the wrath of God and it was a surprise to him he wasn't dead. And the driver of the Chevrolet, who had been making a rapid mental rundown of the unusual chemicals he had ingested recently, denied seeing anything at all but a pickup truck out of control. By the time they got around to taking down his story, he almost believed it himself.

Despite parking squabbles, absence of chairs, and a general air of total confusion that made Nick realize he might have underestimated the value of Lisa's usual services, the emergency meeting at the New Age Center had gone off quite well—at least, the results had been promising. The meeting itself had been as confusing, irritating and downright maddening as anything else Nick's aunt got herself involved in. Trailing strands of bluish knitting that kept getting tangled in her necklace of power crystals, Aunt Penny had made a confused speech that somehow left everyone sure that a great danger confronted the Center in the person of Clifford Simmons and that only their immediate help could save this valuable spiritual resource for Austin. Exactly what kind of danger Simmons posed, and what kind of help was required, varied depending on who was speaking in the vibrant question-and-answer period after Aunt Penny's speech. The ladies of her bridge group had targeted Simmons as a developer who would probably tear down the Templeton house to make room for a glass-walled office building; the group from the Jung Foundation thought he was a deeply troubled soul who should take creative art therapy until he had worked out his irrational urges to seize power; and there was a third group in one corner, including Mahluli and Johnny Z. and some street people whom Nick would rather not meet, who muttered dark stories linking Kennedy's assassination and the prevalence of demon-worshippers and this Simmons person.

On the whole, Nick told Judith afterwards, he rather thought the arthritic, blue-haired ladies of the bridge group were the best bet. They might be wrong about Simmons' plans for the building, but they had enough contacts in the city government to ensure that one enthusiastic young lawyer could delay the purchase and remodeling of the Templeton house almost indefinitely. And best of all, they were willing to contribute to the cause. Nick wouldn't starve while his partner in Brownsville handled the practice. He might even be able to hire a secretary to help him bury Clifford Simmons under paperwork.

"You won't need to hire a secretary," Judith said. "Lisa will help you with all that when she gets back."

Nick sighed ostentatiously, drummed his fingers on the steering wheel of Judith's battered Volkswagon, and very markedly did not contradict her assumption that Lisa would return at any moment. The cozy glow of victory faded away; they traversed the winding roads to Judith's home in an icy silence one degree short of becoming the kind of quarrel both would regret.

They were almost home when Judith broke the silence with a cry of dismay. "My notes from the meeting!" She pawed through her big leather handbag frantically. "Oh, no. I remember now. I had everything in my hands when Mrs. Basingstoke stopped to write out a check to the New Age Center Defense Fund, and I put my things down on Lisa's desk there in the front hall. I must have left the notes there."

"No problem," Nick said, "I'm too tired to go over the notes now anyway. We'll pick them up in the morning." He pulled into Judith's usual parking place and switched off the ignition with a sigh of relief. It was a long drive from downtown Austin to Judith's home, and the last few miles of winding, semi-paved road were no fun at all in the dark.

"No. No, we can't do that. Remember the burglary? Whoever broke in and stole Mahluli's books might come back. I've got the sign-up sheet for all the people at the meeting, with their names and addresses, and how much each one contributed or pledged, and the list of things we might do to stop Simmons—"

"As I recall," Nick said, "that list went from Ginevra's idea of waggling crystals in unison to Johnny Z.'s suggestion that we find a demon of our own to combat him."

"Yes, but in between were some things we're really going to do," Judith pointed out. "Legal stuff."

"So?"

"So I'll bet money that the first burglary had something to do with that Simmons man. So if he finds that list we're in trouble. Right now he thinks we're a bunch of aimless nuts who can't do anything but flutter and meditate and pray about whatever he plans to do. If he finds out we've got contributors and a defense fund and a hotshot young lawyer on our side he might speed up his own plans and take over the Center before we can get started."

Nick sighed. "All right. For the flattery, I'll do it." He reached across Judith and opened the passenger door. "I'm tired, but you look worse. Go in and get some rest. Better yet, fix me something to eat. I'll be starving by the time I get back."

Judith stared. "Flattery?"

"You called me a hotshot young lawyer," Nick reminded her. "It's the first indication I've had that you thought I had actually grown up into a reasonably competent adult. I'm quite willing to make the miserable round trip between here and downtown again if there's another compliment like that waiting at the end of the trip."

"You're competent," Judith said at once. "Also brilliant, clean, reverent, and kind to—"

"Enough, enough. I'm going."

The dark, winding road that led back to town gave Nick more than enough time to mull over the day's events. He was actually glad of the peace and quiet and privacy. Having to make the long drive twice more was a small price to pay for the chance to sort out his thoughts.

This psychic-psychotic center that Aunt Penny had started was hopeless as a business venture, of course. All the same, Nick had to admit that the people she'd collected were rather more stimulating than the clients he met in Brownsville. And they seemed to be genuinely nice, most of them, and not out to con people so much as to convince themselves that their mystical magic worked.

All but that pretty little secretary, the one who'd

vanished in the middle of the action. Nick shook his head. Why was Judith worried about a few papers left lying around, when that girl with no background and no references was running around Austin with the keys to everything at the Center in her purse? His sister kept insisting that this Lisa wouldn't betray them, that something terrible had happened to her, but that was ridiculous. There wasn't any gang of maniacs going around Austin snatching secretaries away from their office desks; the girl had clearly got up and walked out of her own accord. Without bothering to tell any of the people who were counting on her. And with the keys to her desk and Mahluli's bookshop and the front door of the Center.

She'd disappeared on the very day that a lawyer appeared to help the Center stop Clifford Simmon's attempt to buy the place, and just before somebody stole the most valuable books out of Mahluli's store— somebody who had known just where to look.

Nick could imagine a very clever—or very desperate—lawyer arguing before a jury that all these things were pure coincidences. He couldn't imagine a jury fatheaded enough to accept that many coincidences. The simplest explanation was usually the best. This Lisa was an illegal alien; that explained her dismay when the Center was about to be bought by somebody who would want to see her papers and who would pay her by check instead of with room and board and petty cash. The fact that she'd been willing to settle for a minuscule cash salary suggested that she'd been filling her pockets some other way, either by skimming off the tenants' rent and fiddling the books, or maybe by a whole series of petty thefts—these people were so disorganized, you could probably walk off with half their inventory and they'd never notice.

She was probably taking money under the table from Clifford Simmons to set up Aunt Penny, a dithery old lady who could easily be persuaded to sell that valuable property for a song in the belief that Simmons really would let her continue running the Center as always. Only when Aunt Penny turned out to have some defenders, and one of them a lawyer who might find out about her other little games, Lisa had decided to disappear. Most likely she'd simply walked out with Mahluli's rare books, breaking the window to make it seem like an outside job; one last good haul to keep her in luxury until she found another set of innocents to fleece.

And she'd completely fooled both Aunt Penny and Judith. They would be badly hurt when they were finally forced to realize that Lisa had lied to them and deserted them and ripped off Mahluli's books as a parting gesture.

Nick vowed to himself that when this business with the Center was taken care of, he would personally get the INS on Lisa's trail and see to it that she was deported back to wherever she came from.

Nick's musings occupied him, pleasantly or unpleasantly, so deeply that he reached his destination without really being aware of how long and dull the drive had been. It was, he noted thankfully, much easier to park now. The street in front of the New Age Center was all but empty now. The travel agency had long since closed and the students at the fraternity party were mostly upstairs, to judge from the shrieks and giggles Nick heard coming from the white-pillared building. The only sign of activity came from two students in authentic-looking Dracula costumes who chased each other around the lawn of the fraternity house with cries of, "Plagiarism!"

The two parking spaces right in front of the Center were occupied by a single gleaming black BMW, carelessly parked at an angle with its polished hood slanting up to the curb and its shining tail sticking out into the street. Nick cursed the drunken kids in the fraternity under his breath, pulled up as close behind the BMW as he dared and reflected that it would serve the driver right if one of his fraternity brothers came roaring down the street and left a few scratches on that perfect paint job. Oh, well, none of his business; all he meant to do was retrieve Judith's lists, stick around for a few days to put legal spokes in Cliff Simmons' juggernaut wheels, then return to the peaceful business of building up his fledgling law practice in Brownsville.

Whistling softly under his breath, Nick started up the steps to the Center's front porch, then slowed. Something moved in the bushes, and the moonlight showed a glimpse of a glittering scarf. Fancy dress suggested the fraternity party next door, but that didn't make sense; the students didn't need to hide in Aunt Penny's bushes when they had the whole upstairs of the fraternity house to cavort in. And this house had already been robbed once today . . . Nick's steps slowed even more and he patted his pockets, talking out loud to himself for the benefit of the listener in the bushes.

"Now where did I put that key? Could have sworn —ah!" On the last word he vaulted over the porch railing and came down with a crackling of bushes, on top of a slight figure in some kind of sparkling, shiny costume.

It was only a girl, and a small one at that. Nick's reflexes betrayed him; instead of throttling his catch as he'd planned, he lifted his weight off her and started to apologize. She twisted from beneath him, lithe as a cat, and was almost on her feet before he grabbed one hand and brought her down to his level again. She gasped and made a queer whining sound in her throat, but she didn't scream. Not exactly an innocent bystander.

"Don't go so fast," Nick said under his breath. Gripping her hand tight, he forced a way through the bushes and dragged the girl after him. "I want to know who you are and what you're—"

It seemed to be his night for unfinished sentences. The moonlight shone down clearly enough to answer his first question at once. The girl's face was dirty and streaked with tears, her hair was snarled with twigs and she was wearing some kind of fancy-dress tunic and pants unlike anything Nick had ever seen before, but she was unmistakably the missing secretary from the Center.

"Well, well," Nick said slowly. "So much for that. Now we know who's been sneaking outside the Center, and maybe I can make a fair guess why. Want to tell me about it?"

"Please let go of my hand," Lisa whispered. "You hurt me."

"Tough. I don't want you running again."

"*Really*! Here. Hold the other one." She thrust a grubby left hand at him and Nick belatedly realized that something felt wrong about the hot skin under his fingers. Maybe she had scraped her palm while she was skulking under the bushes, or when he jumped her just now. He shifted his grip and started to apologize, then decided that might not be such a good idea. There was no need to make it absolutely clear to the girl that he didn't like to hurt people.

"Now. Want to tell me why you're hiding here?"

"I wanted to go home." She was still whispering. "I live here. On the top floor. But—" The shudder seemed real enough, but who could tell what was truth and what was lies with this girl? "I don't know how, but they were here first."

"They," Nick repeated, slowly, raising one eyebrow. "Friends of yours?"

"No. People I—very much do not wish to see. They want—oh, it is useless! You would not believe me."

"Try me," Nick suggested.

Lisa shook her head. "It doesn't matter. I was wrong to come here; I think I have brought some great trouble on your aunt's house. But perhaps, if I leave now, they will follow me."

She sounded so drained, so hopeless, that Nick felt sorry for her in spite of himself. "Where will you go?"

"It doesn't matter. There is no place for me in this world." She said it matter-of-factly, without self-pity; that was what made her certainty so unbearable. Nick told himself that the girl was a stranger, untrustworthy, that she'd just admitted her guilt. It didn't help. He could feel her despair as if it were a black weight pressing on his own mind. You didn't leave people in that kind of mood to wander the streets on their own, to walk into the river or jump off the freeway.

"Well, I'm certainly not leaving you here to make more mischief for Aunt Penny," he told her. "I have to get some papers—you come inside with me, and don't try anything, I'll be watching you every minute. Then I'll take you—"

"No. Don't go inside, don't you understand anything, you stupid man? They are waiting for us—for me!" She struck at him with her free hand; the blow stung Nick's face, but Lisa was the one who doubled over and gasped, making that strange whining sound like someone who wants to scream but doesn't dare.

"*Now* what's the matter?"

"Nothing. I hurt my hand. I forgot—"

Nick sat down on the steps and took Lisa's wrist, very gently now, and raised her right hand into the moonlight. Even in that cool silvery light, her palm looked terrible: puffy and hot, with blistered skin rising off the surface and more blisters oozing where he'd grabbed her.

"Who did this to you?" All his theories were spinning madly, reformulating themselves as he spoke. Lisa's lack of papers made her a perfect victim for anybody who wanted a collaborator inside the house; perhaps she'd been blackmailed into acting as she did, tortured when she wouldn't go along any more. No wonder she was scared! Nick felt in some dim recess of his mind that he too ought to be scared of Lisa's erstwhile partners, but he was too angry for any other emotion to surface. Who would hurt a girl like this, just to buy an old house or get hold of some rare books?

"It was—an accident," Lisa said. "I mean, I—I burned myself, that's all."

"No, you didn't," Nick contradicted her flatly. "You'd have to—" Somebody would have had to hold her hand flat down against a hot plate or a stove, and pushing hard, to burn the whole palm like that. The thought made him sick. Grown men didn't get sick in the streets. Nick gritted his teeth and thought hard about other things. "Lisa, this burn is too bad to have been an accident. You'd better think of a better story before we get to the hospital."

"No." She was tense against his hand, not trying to get away, but every muscle taut.

"But you have to—" Nick sighed. Of course. No papers, probably a false name; she'd be terrified of going near places where they wanted drivers' licenses, social security numbers, health insurance cards. "All right. I'll take you to Judith's place; she can clean up that hand and bandage it, and maybe if you're real lucky the blisters won't get infected." And she'd give him hell for not picking up her notes from the meeting, but that was just too bad. He couldn't drag Lisa inside the house while she was so hysterical about it, and he didn't dare leave her here for fear she'd vanish again before he had a chance to find out exactly what was going on. Between keeping Lisa safe and getting a look at the bastards who'd tortured her, Nick reluctantly chose to keep Lisa and let the others get away—for now.

CHAPTER NINE

In the flowering bosom of the earth there lies
a region upon which the sun, still mild at its
first rising, shines lovingly; for its fire is in its
first age, and has no power to harm. There a
tempered heat and a favoring climate impreg-
nate the soil with flowers and rich greenery.
This little retreat harbors the scents, produces
the species, contains the riches and delights of
all regions of the world. In this soil ginger grows,
and the taller galbanum; sweet thyme, with its
companion valerian; acanthus, graced with the
token of a perpetual blossom, and nard, redolent of the pleasing ointment which it bears.
The crocus pales beside the purple hyacinth,
and the scent of mace competes with the shoots
of cassia. Amid the flourishing wilderness strays
a winding stream, continually shifting its course;
rippling over the roots of trees and agitated by
pebbles, the swift water is borne murmuring
along.

—Bernard Sylvestris, *Cosmographia*

Lisa had expected that Dr. Judith Templeton, computer expert, would live in surroundings that looked, well, computer-like. Lots of white floors and walls, expensive gadgets with lights and switches to perform every chore from dimming the lights to starting the morning coffee, a constant hiss of air conditioning keeping the atmosphere in chilly purity.

The reality was considerably messier and much more comforting. On the drive out to Lake Travis, Nick had told her that Judith lived on a houseboat.

"That's good," Lisa said, remembering that the "lakes" around Austin were actually wide, damned-up sections of the Colorado River.

"Why?"

"Technically, Lake Travis is running water." If the Hounds did manage to pass the Gate, that might be some slight measure of protection.

"You do need a bath," Nick said, "but Judith has adequate facilities on the houseboat. You won't need to go swimming."

Lisa was too tired to explain. Besides, what was the use? Nick wouldn't believe her anyway. Nobody would. This long car ride and Judith's houseboat were only temporary refuges, a chance to rest through the night while she tried to think what to do next.

When they reached the sheltered bay where Judith lived, Lisa stared in disbelief at the dark island of wood outlined by the car headlights. "That's a boat?" It looked more like a conglomeration of fishermen's shacks and Japanese moon-watching platforms, with a small castle in the center. Her unbelieving eyes passed over terraces and turrets, raised decks and dangling curtains of vines. Warm light glowed through a stained-glass window somewhere in the center of the castle section, and a candle in a glass bowl hung over the deck.

"Started off that way. Technically, I guess it still is. She's added on a bit over the years, but it still floats. I wouldn't want to try taking it out of the bay, though." Nick stepped on the plank that connected boat to shore and held out his hand. "Coming aboard? It's actually quite comfortable inside—and you need to have that hand looked at."

Judith was waiting in a low-ceilinged, lamp-lit room whose wooden walls were lined with narrow shelves holding row after row of brightly covered paperback books. A rainbow-colored hammock from the Yucatan swung in one corner, a low frame supported a mattress covered with a scrap quilt in several hundred shades of red and pink, and the floor was scattered with big soft pillows whose woven covers repeated the glowing reds and pinks of the quilt. On this October night when an unseasonably early norther was sweeping its cold breath through the streets, the room was everything Lisa could have dreamed of as a refuge; soft, glowing, warm, with wooden walls and running water between her and the outside world.

Judith and Nick were talking at one another at such a rate that Lisa could barely keep up with the conversation. Nick seemed to be telling Judith a garbled version of how he'd found her, while Judith simultaneously exclaimed over Lisa's reappearance, claimed to Nick that she'd won some bet or other, fussed at him for not bringing her papers back and brought out a first-aid kit to dress Lisa's burned hand.

"This might hurt a little," said Judith, "but don't worry, I got a merit badge for first aid in Girl Scouts and you never forget these skills; it's just like riding a bicycle."

For some time after that, the throbbing ache of Lisa's hand woke into a dark fire that swirled up through her elbow and shoulder and into her head, and she could not concentrate on anything except not screaming and not throwing up and not jerking her hand away from Judith's painfully careful ministrations.

Eventually the black and scarlet flames around her head receded and she began to notice her surroundings again. Her throbbing hand was completely covered with strips of white gauze, she was holding a mug of something hot and sweet-smelling in her other hand, and Judith was looking at her with the bright-eyed expectancy of one who expects to be Told Everything.

"Maybe you didn't fall off that bicycle," Lisa murmured, "but I nearly did . . . Could I lie down for a while?"

"You're going to have a nice bath and go to bed," Judith said, "*after* you've told us what happened to you."

"I'm so tired . . ."

It wasn't going to work. "Lisa, you *must* tell us. Don't you understand? You could be in danger! Before any of us go to sleep, we have to decide what to do next, and we can't do that if we don't have all the facts." Judith guided her to a low chair stuffed with woven pillows. "Here, sit back and drink your tea while you talk."

The tea was warm and brown and smoky. "Lapsang Souchong," Nick said, making a face. "I don't suppose you have any instant coffee?"

"Spare me!" Judith gave a theatrical shudder. Nick mentioned food snobs. Judith mentioned certain people who tried to prove how grown-up they were by torturing their bodies, and hadn't Nick learned anything from the time he tried to smoke a cigar?

Lisa smiled and listened to the comfortable, homey bickering and slowly felt the tension in her tired body dissolving. The softly lit room, the sense of water surrounding them, Judith's calm competence— all were easing her back into the plain, workday world where she belonged. It would be nice, she thought, to have a family that bickered and argued and remembered embarrassing stories from one's childhood. Better not to think about that. They were waiting to hear her story now.

Unfortunately, her story was wild enough already; it wouldn't improve from being told in such cozy surroundings. Lisa brought the hot stoneware mug to her lips again and glanced over the rim to the two faces watching her: Judith, strong and sure of herself and imagining that she was ready to hear anything Lisa could tell her; Nick, lounging against a wall of paperback books with his arms folded and one eyebrow raised. *I haven't even begun, and he already thinks I'm lying.* The thought made it possible for her to start. Nick was hopeless, there was no point in worrying about convincing his buttoned-down lawyer's mind, so she didn't need to worry about him. All she needed to worry about was the danger that Judith, too, would think she was lying, and that she'd lose the one friend she trusted in this world—and that didn't bear thinking about, so Lisa took one scalding-hot gulp of the tea in her mug and began before she could think herself into paralysis.

"You know that book of Mahluli's, the one with the Kay Nielsen plates?"

"It was stolen today."

Lisa nodded. "Uh-huh. I know."

Nick gave a sardonic chuckle. "I just bet you do."

Judith looked at him and he shut up.

"Never mind that now. I'll explain later how I know it was stolen and who has it now. I want to do this in order, or I'll never get it all straight. You know that one picture that everybody kept looking at, the one of the forest and the arch of stone and the little stream?"

Judith nodded. "Yes. I think it must have been one of Nielsen's best works—it was so real, you almost thought you could step into that forest and drink from the stream."

"I did."

Mercifully, Nick held his peace as Lisa explained how she'd looked too long at the picture and had found herself being drawn into its world, immediately to be attacked on all sides by people who insisted she was someone else entirely.

"But what did they want?" Judith demanded.

"Their world was—dying, I think." Lisa wrapped both arms around herself and shivered, trying not to remember barren fields and stony uplands and the infinite weariness in the face of the peasant woman who'd stared at her; refusing to remember blood on a church wall and the call of a silver horn. "They thought the magic was leaking out of it somehow— they thought Sybille had come into our world and somehow had brought the magic with her—they thought I could fix everything. At least, that's what the elvenlord—Berengar—wanted. The Gray Monks, the Durandines, I don't know exactly what they had in mind. They're a new sect, new since—well, since Sybille's time, anyway. They hate the elvenkind, that's all I learned." But Hugh's whispered promises had been sickeningly explicit.

"I think you know more than you're saying," Judith prompted.

"What I know or guessed about the Durandines," Lisa said passionately, "believe me, Judith, you don't want to hear! And they had followed me back into this world—I saw them in Cliff's office, after I got away, and they were waiting for me in the Center, too,—"

"Shh!" Nick's upraised hand stopped her. He was leaning forward, head bent towards the stained glass window, listening intently. In the silence that followed his command Lisa heard the thud of a car door, shuffling footsteps and a loud braying laugh.

"It's just my neighbors," Judith said with resignation. "There's another boat around the curve of the shore, you can't see it from here, but you can hear them coming and going."

"Par-ty animal!" A voice sang through the night. "Where's that beer?"

"Coming right up, Captain!" Girlish giggles followed the promise. "Anything else coming up, Captain?"

Nick made a face. "Nice neighbors. I thought you liked this place because it was so quiet."

"The people who own the boat don't use it very often," Judith said. "And they're older than they sound—late forties, I'd guess."

"What good is that?"

"They sound like college kids, and their sense of humor is definitely on the frat-rat level, but they go to sleep a lot earlier," Judith explained.

"I see." Nick gave one swift nod and dismissed the case of the next-door party animals. Lisa could see his face hardening as he turned back to her. She felt like a witness on the stand, facing a hostile attorney. *I bet he's good in court. Probably terrifies little old ladies into contradicting themselves all over the place.*

"I didn't quite understand what you were saying before we were so rudely interrupted," Nick said. "In the course of my researches today I had occasion to get Clifford Simmons' office address. I thought it was Suite 303 in the XCorp Building."

Lisa nodded. "I didn't see the number. But it was on the third floor."

"I would have thought," said Nick mildly, "it might be difficult to see into a third-floor window from the street level."

Lisa sighed and brushed a tangle of brown hair out of her eyes. "It was dark outside. His lights were on. And I didn't claim I had a full view of everything in the room. I didn't need to. I saw someone in a Durandine habit."

"Which is?"

"A long gray robe. Hood. Full sleeves."

"Halloween costume," Nick suggested.

"I don't think Clifford Simmons was preparing to go trick or treating." Lisa gave Nick a long, level stare. "And I thought you were the one who didn't believe in coincidences. If I'm being chased by people in gray monks' habits, isn't it quite a coincidence that somebody in a long gray robe should show up in the office of the man who was trying to hypnotize me?"

"*If* you are being pursued," Nick agreed with a smile that made Lisa want to push his teeth down his throat. "Go on, then. We have another little point to clear up. Would you care to explain how you knew they were waiting for you at the Center? As I recall, you were outside, and the blinds were closed. Or can you see through blinds and curtains, as well as through third-floor windows?"

"I can't," Lisa said miserably. "I just—knew, that's all."

"You seem to *just know* a lot." Nick's smile would have looked great in a courtroom where he was preparing to pounce on a perjured witness.

She had thought she was prepared for his disbelief, but it hurt worse than she'd expected; maybe because he'd seemed, earlier, as if he cared what happened to her. Lisa sat quietly and took a deep breath, as Ginevra had taught her, and managed not to say the first things that popped into her head. A car door slammed outside, and the people on the neighboring boat were laughing. Beyond that little puddle of noise, the lake would be still and quiet, smooth black water and white limestone cliffs and a sky full of stars. Lisa stayed in that quietness for a moment. When she felt calm again, she looked up at Nick. "It's your choice. Either you believe what I'm telling you, or you don't; I'm too tired to care, and there's no way I could prove that I'm telling the truth."

"Lisa's right," Judith said. She moved quietly to stand behind Lisa, long firm fingers moving gently on Lisa's shoulders, calming her and soothing aching muscles and sending an unspoken message of trust. "There is no point in exercising your skills at cross-examination on her. She is my friend, and she is in trouble, and I trust her."

"Judith. Even you can't believe the fantasy she's been spinning . . ." Nick's voice trailed off and he stared past Lisa's head, at one of the walls lined with brightly colored paperback books.

"She tells a consistent story," Judith said, "and there are precedents. Simon Tregarth found a door into another world—"

"Judith, *Witch World* is a novel! A work of *fiction*! Granted, Andre Norton is a good writer, but—"

"Holger was just a soldier in our world, but in the Middle World he became a great hero—"

"*Three Hearts and Three Lions*," Nick interpolated. "Poul Anderson."

Lisa looked up at Judith's shining face, then back at Nick. "Novels? You're talking about *books*? This is real, don't you understand?"

"I understand," Judith said quietly. "I am afraid Nick has forgotten."

"I've outgrown that adolescent phase," Nick corrected. "I can't help it if you're still devouring science fiction and escaping reality, Judith, but I've moved on to adult interests."

"But don't you remember, in *The Last Unicorn*—"

"Another fantasy novel, Judith? Peter Beagle is a good writer too, but he's not exactly a reporter for the *Wall Street Journal*."

Judith's hands tightened on Lisa's shoulders. "Ah, yes, Nick. The rising young lawyer's favorite reading. Remember what Ursula LeGuin said? 'The ultimate escapist reading is that masterpiece of total unreality, the daily stock market report.' "

"Clever, very clever, but beside the point. I'll agree that Lisa's little story is the stuff of a fantasy novel, but does that make it real?"

"Nick." Judith's voice was low and urgent. "Do you remember the night we asked Aslan to let us into Narnia?"

"We were *children*. I don't play those games any more. And besides . . . we didn't get into Narnia, did we?"

"Not then. But now, perhaps we have a chance." Judith swung round to kneel on the floor before Lisa. She took Lisa's unburnt hand and gently chafed the cold fingers. "I believe you, Lisa. At least, I—I choose to believe you. Maybe I'm being a fool, but I'd rather look ridiculous than miss a chance of going through this Gate of yours. Will you take me there?"

"It—Clifford Simmons has the book now," Lisa said slowly, "and I don't know exactly how the Gate works, or whether it will work for anybody else. And —that world is in terrible trouble, Judith; there are worse things there than I told you. I don't think you really want to go there."

Nick laughed under his breath. "Of course. These people always make some excuse when the time comes to prove the objective reality of their pretty stories."

It was hopeless. Why had she even tried? Judith wanted to believe her, but Nick would hammer and hammer away at her with all his rational arguments, with his cold refusal to accept anything he hadn't seen with his own eyes and touched with his own hands, until his sister gave up. She would still be loyal to Lisa, she would still call her friend, but she would start looking sorry for her and talking about delusions and professional help. Lisa didn't want to stay and watch that happen.

"I'm sorry," she said at last. "Judith, the world where I went is not Narnia, and anyway I can't take you there. Nick, I can't prove to you that I'm telling the truth; I don't think there is any proof you'd accept, anyway. Thank you for the tea, Judith, and for bandaging my hand. But I think I'd better go now."

"Don't be ridiculous, you're tired, you need to sleep—"

"Where will you go?" Nick's cool question cut cleanly across Judith's protestations. "And how will you get there?"

"Does it matter?"

"It does to me," Judith said.

"You're not going anywhere until I am assured that you're not going to make any more trouble for the Center," Nick told her. "You've caused Judith and Aunt Penny enough grief already."

"My keys are in my purse," Lisa told him. "It's in the bottom drawer of my desk. If you think I've copied them, you can change the locks tomorrow. I won't be back. Will you take my word for that, or do you want me to sign something?"

"Lisa, stop talking like this!" Judith took her hand. "You'll stay with me tonight, and tomorrow you'll come to the Center. We need you there. And together, all of us, we'll find some way to solve whatever trouble you've gotten into."

Whatever trouble you've gotten into. The temptation to lean on Judith and her other friends at the Center, calm Mahluli and salty Ginevra and dancing Johnny Z., was strong and sweet as honey in her mouth. But it was impossible. Already, Lisa thought, Judith's momentary will to believe was losing strength. By morning she'd have convinced herself that Nick was right, that Lisa was either suffering from delusions or lying to conceal what she'd really been doing.

And in any case, she had no right to drag Judith

and the others into her personal troubles. All this time, while she told her story and Nick cross-examined her and the couple in the next boat enjoyed their raucous party, there'd been a quiet insistent fear building in the back of Lisa's mind. Every time a car door slammed outside or a laugh rang through the night, the fear leapt inside her.

"No. I—I told you, I can't stay here. It isn't safe." Lisa backed towards the door as she spoke, and Judith made no move to stop her. It was Nick who moved between her and the door.

"You're running from something, aren't you?"

Lisa bit back the urge to say *I just told you so!* and only nodded.

"You can't go on running forever."

"I know. It's been too long already." Through the open door she could see the gray mists that rose off the water, soft and shapeless in the glow of the candle that hung over the outside deck. Wasn't there any place where she could go where she would bring no more trouble on anyone? She had been running so long—longer than she knew. Perhaps it was time to stop running. She could just walk into the water . . .

"No," Nick said sharply, as if he could see the picture in her head. "No, I won't let you. You're in trouble; all right, I'm a lawyer, I can help. I don't even mind that you've lied to us. All my clients start out by lying."

A car's headlights blazed across the houseboat like a low-flying meteor and abruptly went out. A door slammed. Nick did not bother to turn around, but Lisa, looking past him to the candlelit deck, saw two men coming towards the plank. Their robes were the same color as the gray mist, and the hoods were drawn low over their faces.

She wanted to scream a warning, but an invisible hand had caught her throat. Nick saw her eyes widen, though, and he glanced round and swore under his breath. He pushed Lisa behind him and stepped out onto the deck. "Gentlemen, you're trespassing," he said quietly. "You want the next boat over, around the rocks—that's where the party is."

They kept coming as if they hadn't heard him. On the last word Nick brought his fist around in a wild swinging punch that landed in the middle of the first gray robe, or would have if the man had been solid. As it was, his hand went right through a gray mist, and he fell forward on the edge of the deck. The first man dissolved while the one behind him, who was quite real, leapt on board and kicked Nick in the head.

"Thank you for leading us to her," he said to Lisa, and then, with a nod into the darkness, "and thank you, Brother Alured, for the illusion-spell."

"*What* do you clowns think you're doing?" Judith erupted onto the deck, swinging an empty bottle in one hand, and a semicircle of gray-clad men formed around her. She swung at the wrong one; the bottle went through dissolving mist, and while she was off balance a cloak fell over her head and the real monk wrapped her up like a package.

"That's the one," he said with satisfaction. "Fair-haired, beautiful as the day, and as nasty a temper as the rest of her kind. How could we ever have mistaken that little mouse for Sybille?"

His nod dismissed Lisa as something of no importance. Inside the cloak, Judith wriggled and hit out and the monk nearly dropped her. "Give me a hand, Brother," he panted, "she's a fighter, the Lady Sybille is."

The monk called Alured came stepping daintily over the gangplank, lips moving in a soundless chant, and waved his white hands at the squirming blanket. Judith got one leg free and kicked him in the shin.

"God's fingerbone!" Brother Alured cried, and Lisa found herself able to move again when his chant stopped. She threw herself on Alured and grabbed at his hand, trying to pry his little finger back. It was the only trick she knew, and this time it didn't work; both his white hands were clenched into fists, and one of them went into her jaw with a crack that left her sick and dizzy, with blackness and points of light swirling about her.

When she could see and hear again, the sound of a car's engine was dying away in the distance. Her jaw ached worse than her burnt hand. Nick was stirring and groaning softly. And Judith was gone.

"Can you sit up—no, better not—" She was too late to stop Nick. He pushed himself up too quickly, turned green and clapped one hand over his mouth.

"Where are you going?" Lisa followed his staggering motion through the door. Nick lunged towards the deck railing and managed—just—to throw up into the quiet waters of Lake Travis instead of over Judith's houseboat.

"Common effect of head blows," he mumbled, turning back towards her. "Moving too soon. Plenty of clients told me—never realized how powerful, though."

"What a strange thing for your clients to talk about. Hadn't you better sit down?"

Nick's greenish pallor looked even worse in the moonlight, and the grin he attempted didn't help. "What do you think I'm doing, company law? Most of my clients are pleading to charges of drunk and disorderly in the town square. Guilty, too," he added after a moment of tenderly massaging the back of his head. "I think I may've been insufficiently sympathetic." His voice was clearing with every sentence, and he was standing quite straight now.

"Are you feeling all right now?"

"What a question."

"I mean, can you drive?"

"Why?"

He must have been unconscious during those last minutes. Lisa hated herself for what she was about to do to him. Nick didn't need to go charging off into the night on a rescue errand; he needed to sit down and recover from shock. So did she, for that matter. But they didn't have time. Somehow, in the next few minutes, she had to convince Nick of the truth of her story, get back to Austin, and either stop the Durandines before they took Judith through it or else go after her into the world of the elvenkind.

"Nick, they took Judith. We have to go after her."

"*What?*"

Before she could answer, he was moving. First to look inside the houseboat, taking in the empty disorder of Judith's living room; then he had Lisa by the wrist and was half dragging her across the plank to the shore. "And you know where? Of course," he said as if to himself, "I remember now. Just before I went out, they were thanking you for your part in the job."

"I did lead them here," Lisa said miserably. "But I didn't mean to—I never thought—I was running from them, Nick, not working with them, don't you remember?"

"I remember that was your story, yes." Nick opened the door of Judith's ancient VW and pushed her towards the car. "Get in. You can direct me as we head back to town."

"Nick, we can't—"

"*Get in*, damn you! I haven't time to play word games now."

"Nick. This car isn't going anywhere."

"What?"

Lisa pointed at the tires. The moon gave enough light to show that all four had been slashed. The VW was sitting with its axles resting on a ledge of Lake Travis limestone.

"Telephone," Nick said. He towed Lisa back inside. Her wrist was beginning to ache.

"You don't have to keep dragging me around like a sack of barley," she told him when they were inside again. "I'm as interested in finding Judith as you are."

Nick merely grunted and kept jiggling the receiver of the antique black telephone mounted on the wall. After a few minutes he shook his head and hung it up, very gently. "Wires cut, I suppose," he said. "They planned well, didn't they? We're isolated here and they'll have plenty of time to do whatever they want with Judith. What is it they want with her, Lisa?"

"They seem to think she is Sybille, though I don't know why, except that I came to her—they must realize, since I took the sword, that I'm not elven. So perhaps they think the magic made a slight mistake, drawing me into their world because I was close to Sybille, and that whoever I went to here would be her," Lisa said. The syntax was no more scrambled than her thoughts; but this felt right. No matter what she did, she couldn't shake the conviction of those in the elven world that she had some close tie to Sybille. "They will be taking her back to their world, and then—" Her mouth felt dry. That madman Hugh would be waiting for Judith there in the Remigius, with the iron-barred cell and the other torments he'd hinted at. And Judith, who knew nothing of that world, wouldn't even know what lies to tell to stop Hugh from torturing her. "Cold iron won't hurt her, she's not elven," she said slowly, thinking aloud, "but they may not stop at that."

"They didn't with you." Nick picked up Lisa's bandaged hand and turned it over, staring at the strips of white gauze that criss-crossed the palm as if he'd never seen anything like it before. He looked as if he wanted to cry. She suspected he was imagining Judith's long brown fingers blistered like that.

"Nick, I did that myself. But—" She had been

about to say that he was partially right, that she had burned her own hand to save herself from whatever worse things the Durandines had in mind for her, but he stopped her with one hand across her lips.

"Please, Lisa," Nick said. His voice shook a little. "I really can't bear to listen to that story again. It was all right to indulge in a little fantasy when you were just trying to conceal your own part in this mess—whatever it is—but this is serious. I know you've been hurt, I know you're scared, I know you are afraid or ashamed to tell me what you've gotten yourself into—but, Lisa, we don't have any more time to tell funny stories about ghouls and goblins. Don't you understand? I can't let you play games while my sister needs our help."

"But—you saw them yourself," Lisa said when he moved his hand. She was on the verge of tears; she didn't know how to convince him of the truth if his own eyes would not serve, or what she would do if he persisted in thinking her a liar. "They were wearing the Durandine habit."

Nick sighed. "Lisa, anybody can put on fancy dress if they want to, especially with all the costume parties around Halloween, and those robes are great disguises. They don't prove a thing."

"But—"

"Look at you," Nick went on as if she hadn't spoken. "I don't know where you got that outfit, but it's definitely not something you see on the street in downtown Austin every day. Surely you're not going to tell me that just because you're rather strangely dressed, you come from another world, are you? Lisa, my great-aunt's receptionist, the girl at the front desk?" Nick smiled down at her and Lisa felt her face growing hot. *Change shape!* she silently commanded the elven dress. *Grow. Glitter. Do something to show this patronizing bastard how stupid his assumptions are!*

The dress retained its form without even a flicker of shape-changing along the seams. And Lisa felt all the angrier for being so helpless. The Durandines' magic had carried over to this world; why hadn't hers?

"All right," she said at last. "I'll tell you the truth."

"And about time!"

"Those men," Lisa began, feeling her way, "they—they know something about me that I didn't want everybody at the Center to know."

"That you're an illegal alien?"

Lisa gasped and Nick gave her another smug lawyer-smile. "I guessed that ages ago. Why else would you be afraid to let Cliff Simmons look at the personnel files, work for Aunt Penny for a pittance in cash and a free room instead of insisting on a real paycheck, run away when a lawyer shows up? Typical pattern. You're really not a very good liar, Lisa."

That's all you know. "They wanted me to do something for them, and I was afraid not to—"

"What was it? Are they using the Center for drugs? It would be a natural place for a dealer, all those burnt-out hippie types wandering in and out, that explains Simmons' interest," Nick thought aloud, and Lisa nodded.

It went on like that. She had only to say a few words and Nick would jump in with his own version of what had happened and she would agree. If she hadn't been sick with fear for Judith, Lisa would have thoroughly enjoyed herself. As it was, she hurried Nick through a confused story in which drug dealers, gang wars, smuggling of illegal aliens and massive bribery of the police force all figured in peculiar and contradictory roles. It didn't really matter what she said; he was ready to believe anything but the bare truth of the elvenworld, and all she had to do was to make sure that the story led him to the right conclusion.

"Then they must be holding Judith in the XCorp Building," Nick said at long last, "until the boss—what did you say his name was?"

"Hugh." Brother Hugh of the Order of Saint Durand, to be precise; clerk to Bishop Rotrou, a man of little importance in the outside world, but every time Lisa had seen them with the Durandines he had been acting as their leader. Berengar had told her that the head of the Durandine order was chosen by secret ballot, that not even all the Durandine brothers knew their leader's identity; they met hooded and cloaked for their chapter meetings, and obeyed the one who showed the symbols of authority. Hugh had been careful to preserve his humble anonymous position in the outside world, but Lisa had heard him snapping out orders to the other monks.

And all that, if she explained it to Nick, would be dismissed as more of her "wild fantasies." Leave it at that, then; his name was Hugh, as common a name in this world as in the one mortals shared with elvenkind.

"They'll be holding Judith until Hugh shows up," Nick mused. "And we daren't inform the police, because they've been bribed, is that right?"

Mentally apologizing to the Austin police force, Lisa nodded.

"So we have to get there before Hugh does," Nick concluded. "All right. Come *on.*"

For the third time that night Lisa was dragged across the plank at top speed. "Nick, your tires are still slashed!"

"I know," Nick said. "We're going to visit the neighbors. With any luck, your drug-running friends didn't know there was another boat around the corner."

There was even a narrow path through a screen of junipers and stunted live oaks. And on the other side of the trees, Nick's pocket flashlight illuminated a large cream-colored car.

"Are you going to ask them to drive us into town?"

"Don't have time. Besides, I don't know them. They might not want to lend their car to a couple of bedraggled strangers." Nick stooped and passed his hand under the body of the car.

"Are you going to hot-wire it? Isn't that illegal?"

"Nup," Nick grunted in a strained half-whisper. He made his way slowly around the car, still stooping to feel the underside. "Can't hot-wire these modern cars. They've all got steering wheel locks. No, I'm looking for the spare keys. Lot of people put a car key in a little metal box with a magnet on it and hide it cleverly under the car, so when they lock themselves out they can get in easily. It's the first thing a car thief looks for these days. Wonderful, the things I learn from my clients. Unfortunately, they—"

The window on the driver's side was open. Lisa reached in and felt along the steering wheel column. "Would these be what you're looking for?"

Nick wouldn't need to find the spare keys. Captain Party Animal had left his keys in the ignition.

CHAPTER TEN

But besides these gross absurdities, all their plays be neither right tragedies nor right comedies: mingling kings and clowns, not because the matter so carrieth it, but thrust in clowns by head and shoulders, to play a part in majestical matters, with neither decency nor discretion.

—Sir Philip Sidney

At this late hour, the streets of downtown Austin were dark and empty. To the north, the pinkish dome of the Capitol reflected a faint glow from the lights set around the building; further north, the tower in the center of the University of Texas campus was illuminated with orange floodlights to celebrate some athletic victory. The tall office buildings that lined the downtown streets were walls of black glass and stone picked out with random squares of yellow where a janitor was cleaning or where somebody had forgotten to turn out his office lights.

One of these squares of yellow was on the third floor of the XCorp Building, the black steel monolith

of empty suites and unrented offices. More lights
flared across an entire floor higher up, but Lisa and
Nick paid no attention to them.

"He's not being subtle about it, is he?" Nick muttered. "I wonder if it's a trap."

"If it were a trap," Lisa pointed out, "I'd think
they would have made it easier to come after them,
don't you? What is the penalty for car theft?"

Nick's grin was distinctly lopsided. "Less than for
breaking and entering—ah, but we won't have to do
that!"

The lobby was dark, but the double glass doors
were unlocked, and no alarm sounded as Nick pushed
on the metal bar that opened the right-hand door.
He glided into the lobby sidewise, as quietly as if he
had been in his stocking feet, and Lisa followed him.

"Careless janitors they've got here," Nick whispered. "Leaving the doors open, turning on all the
lights on the floor where they're working. After I'm
disbarred maybe I'll apply for a job as head of security for XCorp."

The light whisper moved ahead of Lisa as Nick slid
along the north wall of the lobby. "Where's the
stairwell?"

"Down this hall. . . ."

A beam of light pierced the shadows and Lisa
swallowed the end of her sentence. Nick froze where
he stood and Lisa tried to shrink into the narrow
crack between the hall door and the wall while two
sets of heavy footsteps came toward her, paused . . .

"Don't see anybody here. Maybe something tripped
the door alarm by accident."

"Better check it out anyway."

"Okay, okay. You take the north hall, I'll take the
south."

While the guards talked, Lisa felt fingers on her
wrist. She followed the light tug and Nick drew her
down the hall with agonizing slowness, pausing ev-

ery few steps. She could see nothing in the darkness, but every time he paused she heard very faint metallic clicks.

"Hurry," she breathed. "One of them is coming down this . . ."

"I know." Nick moved a few feet down the hall and stopped again. This time he breathed out a long satisfied sigh. "Door's unlocked," he reported. "Wait . . ."

There was a circle of light shining on the glass doors through which they had come. Lisa died several times while Nick slowly turned the knob and eased the office door open. They were inside, the door not yet shut, when she heard the guard walking down the hall. The inside of the office was black as a broom closet, but she could feel every agonizing centimeter of progress as Nick closed the door without a single betraying click.

Outside, there were rattling noises. The guard was trying the doors of the offices as he came along. "Lock it," she whispered into the blackness.

Nick pushed the button just as the guard rattled another knob, masking the slight click of the lock catching. A moment later the darkness of the office was sliced by a thin line of light and the door Nick had just locked rattled with the guard's testing.

"That's funny," a voice mused, and then, "Jerry? You got the master?"

Footsteps retreated up the hall, then paused. Nick cursed under his breath. "He must have seen that the deadbolt wasn't locked. Damn! We'll have to run—"

Lisa caught his hand. "No. They'll be sure to catch us—and Judith—"

"But if we stay here—"

Three minutes later the first security guard returned with the master key, opened the door and shone his flashlight into an obviously empty office.

"Careless. Why do these folks insist on deadbolts

if they won't use them? Probably doesn't even carry the key," he grumbled. "Serve him right if he can't get in tomorrow." He closed the door and a key scraped in the lock and the unused deadbolt clicked home.

Nick, crouching uncomfortably in the crawl space above the ceiling, sneezed explosively into his cupped hand and used several words Lisa had never heard before.

"Do you learn a lot of—er—colloquial Spanish from your clients in Brownsville?"

If there had been light to see by, she felt sure Nick's glare would have shriveled her. "Lisa, this is no time for making light conversation! Don't you understand? He's locked us in. We can't get out of here."

"Of course we can," Lisa whispered back, "only not through that door. We'll have to go over the partitions to the next office and let ourselves out that way. Nothing to it." She lifted the asbestos ceiling panel away from the metal grid on which they crouched and slipped down to stand on the desk beneath the hole.

Some sweaty and dusty maneuvering followed; Lisa skinned her knee on a raw edge of one of the metal grids, Nick banged his head on a low partition, and they left a trail of asbestos dust behind them. But eventually they were in the next office over.

The deadbolt was locked.

"We'll try the next one?" Lisa suggested.

Three offices later, they found a door they could open.

They were at the stairwell when someone shouted behind them. Nick let the heavy metal door swing shut, grabbed Lisa by the wrist, and raced up two flights of stairs.

The third-floor stairwell door was locked, and somebody was opening the door they'd come through two flights below.

They kept going up the narrow metal stairs. There was a stabbing pain in Lisa's side and her legs felt like soft melted marshmallows, but if she didn't keep up with Nick she felt sure he would just tow her up the stairs by one arm.

The fourth-floor door was also locked.

By the time they reached the top of the last flight, Lisa's legs felt like marshmallows with hot wires running through them. *Please let this door be open.*

Nick put his hand on the door and it swung open before he even leaned on it. Lisa stumbled into a blaze of golden lights and almost collapsed onto the broad shelving bosom of a woman in green satin.

Gasping in shock and exhaustion, she stammered out an apology while she took in the scene. Women in long dresses and men in suits milled around a large hallway opening onto a room full of folding chairs. "I—I'm sorry we're late." It looked like some kind of party; something half official, to judge from the institutional surroundings. The large woman was half smiling, looking uncertain. Maybe she didn't know all the expected guests. Nick looked smooth enough for any occasion, bless his conservative stuffy soul and his expensive dark suit; if only her dress had remained in its court form, all gauzy overskirts and dangling golden bells, perhaps they'd have been able to blend in with the crowd. They might as well try it anyway, there wasn't time for anything else, Lisa could hear the steps coming up the stairwell behind them.

"So sorry," she breathed, "unavoidably detained—looking forward so much to this occasion, dear Mrs., um . . ." Lisa mumbled a few unidentifiable syllables.

"I don't believe we have met before." The woman's expression was setting into what looked like habitual lines of frowning discontent. In a moment she would call the guards to throw them out; in a moment the guards would be there anyway. Lisa glanced about the room. Where could they hide? Was there another way out of here?

On one side of the hall was a card table laden with jugs of wine and plastic glasses; on the other side, another card table held bowls of potato chips and some greenish paste in a small cup. Most of the people in the hallway were clustered around the wine table. Maybe they could go under the wine table—no, not with everybody watching.

"Of course we have not met, dear lady." Nick clicked his heels, bowed, and kissed the woman's pudgy hand. "The pleasure is entirely mine, and a long awaited one. Had I but known what delightful company was in store for me . . ."

Lisa wondered how long he could blather on like that without saying anything.

"Oh!" said the woman in green satin. "You must be Dr. Przhevalsky?"

Nick bowed again and murmured something non-committal.

"Aileen, dear, here's Dr. Przhevalsky at last! Now we can begin!" the woman called to her friend.

Nick bowed and kissed Aileen's hand as well. "Please accept my heartfelt apologies for keeping you waiting, Mrs.—Mrs.—"

"Oh, how silly of me," their hostess giggled. "I'm such a little featherhead, that's what Alvin always says, I *quite* forgot to introduce myself. I'm Josephine Burrell." She paused with an arch smile. "Yes, *those* Burrells—the Burrell Foundation for the Arts," she prompted as Nick said nothing and Lisa concentrated on catching her breath. She heard the stairwell door opening behind her but did not dare to look round.

"I am honored indeed," said Nick. "Would you be so kind as to introduce me to your friends?"

"Yoo-hoo! Aileen! Darby! Everybody, here is Dr. Georgy Przhevalsky, our speaker for the evening! And, ah, er—"

Mrs. Burrell looked at Lisa and shook her head slightly. Clearly her plans for the evening, whatever they had been, did not include a speaker who showed up in company with a bedraggled young woman in some kind of foreign costume.

"My invaluable secretary and assistant, Miss Thistlebottom," Nick said into the silence.

"Miss, er, Thwistlebott," Mrs. Burrell mumbled before turning her attention back to Nick. She laid a pudgy hand on his arm and smiled brilliantly at the people around them. "*Such* a pity that Dr. Przhevalsky was unavoidably detained, but as you see he has made every effort to get here before the end of our little meeting, and perhaps now he would favor us with a few words on the subject you're all anxious to hear about."

As she escorted Nick towards the room full of chairs, Lisa glanced behind them. The two security guards were still standing at the stairwell door, looking worried. A man in evening clothes detached himself from the group near the wine table and went over to speak to them. Lisa caught a few murmured words. "Guest of the evening—late—unfamiliar with customs of this country—"

"Russian?" said one of the guards.

"Spies," said the other. Both guards looked happy, as though a boring evening had been unexpectedly spiced up.

The man in evening clothes raised both hands and murmured comforting phrases. Lisa hung back, as close to them as she dared, and gathered some useful information about Dr. Georgy Przhevalsky and what he was supposed to be doing here.

Nick was taking his sweet time getting to the front of the room, stopping and shaking hands with people and exchanging bland social chitchat while Josephine Burrell tried to nudge him toward the speaker's podium. Lisa slithered through the crowd and managed to worm herself between Nick and Mrs. Burrell. "Forgive me, please, but Dr. Przhevalsky and I always go over his notes before a speech," she announced firmly. She lifted Mrs. Burrell's hand from Nick's coat sleeve and gave her a wide, square, nononsense smile. "I know you will understand. These great men are so absentminded—it is our privilege to nourish and support their greatness, is it not?"

While Josephine Burrell was preening herself, Lisa pushed Nick into a corner where some heavy drapes partially shielded them from the gathering audience. He was looking rather shaky. "Are you sick?" she whispered. "Or did you drink some of the wine cooler? You look positively *green*."

Nick shook his head. "It's you," he said in a strangled half-whisper.

"Me! I've just been finding out some things you needed to know," Lisa said indignantly. "You ought to be grateful to me, instead of whining because I happened to leave your side for a moment. Anyway, you didn't need my help to flirt with that overstuffed satin whale."

Nick shook his head again. "Your, um, your dress. Pants. Whatever it is. What did you *do*?"

Lisa looked down and swallowed hard. It seemed the elf-dress responded better to need than to direct commands. Her gauzy overskirts were back, the tunic's neckline had crept down to frame her neck and shoulders with a border of gold-veined scarlet leaves, and little chains of golden bells swayed from a low, broad girdle.

"We don't have time to go into that now," she said, and wondered what she would say when they did have time. "You're about to make a speech— want to know who you are?"

Nick nodded. His blue eyes were slightly glazed over, but he did seem to be making a serious effort to focus on her.

"Okay. Your name is Georgy Przhevalsky. You're originally Russian, but you left the country last year and now you're a professor of cartography at Texas Tech," she said rapidly, "but that's not why you are here. You're also an amateur dramatist and these people have just been watching one of your plays at the Zachary Scott Theatre Center. I don't know why the reception in your honor is being held here instead of at Zach Scott, but they're expecting you to say a few words explaining your play. I gather," she added, "most of them find your work terribly obscure."

"Not nearly as obscure as I find it," Nick whispered it. "Did they happen to say what the play was about?"

Lisa shook her head. She hadn't been able to get any clue as to the nature of Dr. Przhevalsky's dramatic work. "I don't think anybody understood it well enough to say."

"Oh, well, if they don't know, how will they be able to call me a liar?" Nick squeezed her arm. "Keep up the good work, Thistlebottom. Yes, Mrs. Burrell, I was just coming—I quite agree with you, we must not keep these good people waiting." A hand over Mrs. Burrell's be-ringed fingers, a warm smile that illuminated Nick's eyes and made Mrs. Burrell flush. "*May* I call you Josephine? Although we have just met, I feel very close in spirit to one who so obviously appreciates the deeper meaning of my work. In fact, Josephine," he went on briskly, now steering Mrs. Burrell into the lecture room instead of being led by her, "I would so much like to hear your interpretation of this play. Perhaps I could persuade you to say a few words before my talk begins—as a sort of introduction? It would help me so much to understand what parts of my meaning I have succeeded in communicating to American audiences. Of course you, with your obvious taste and insight, would hardly represent the *average* American playgoer, but perhaps as a patroness of the theatre . . ."

Lisa dropped behind them, gagging slightly, and missed the rest of Nick's speech. It must have been persuasive, for by the time she'd found her chair at the very front of the lecture room Mrs. Burrell was holding the microphone and Nick was standing slightly behind her. She dropped into her chair with a sigh of relief as Mrs. Burrell started talking.

The first few minutes were entirely predictable; gushing references to their "honored guest," and how honored they felt that he could join the Group for the Improvement of Austin Theatre following the presentation of his celebrated but obscure work, "Four is Five."

"Dr. Przhevalsky has asked me to begin by giving my own impressions of his work as staged at the Zachary Scott Theatre Center," Mrs. Burrell said, "but as you know, I myself was not privileged to attend this evening, being too involved with the organizational problems of our little group. Therefore I can only wait, like the rest of you, for Dr. Przhevalsky's dazzling interpretation of what I understand to have been a very—very—meaningful experience for those who were so privileged." She stepped away from the podium and gestured to Nick. "Dr. Przhevalsky?"

Nick looked about as sick as Lisa felt. One hand fluttered at his chest; she wondered if he meant to fake a heart attack. That would certainly get them out of this room, but then they'd have EMS to deal with, ambulances, paramedics—and meanwhile, what was happening to Judith? They had been delayed too long already. And the applause that followed Josephine Burrell's introduction was fading away into scattered handclaps.

Nick stepped up to the microphone with all the alacrity of a man walking into the dentist's office. "Ladies and gentlemen," he began in a heavy accent that Lisa supposed he meant to sound Russian, "or—no—let me call you friends. Dear friends. For though I have never met you before, I feel a deep and true spirit of kinship with all lovers of the arts, and especially with those of you who have been so kind as to come to meet me tonight, at such a late hour and at such personal inconvenience. Neffer before haf I been so touched by the magnificent soul of the American people!" Nick spread his arms wide and brought them in to thump both fists on his chests. "This people, of whom the warm heart, the generosity, the impulsive and intuitive goodness are so well known throughout the civilized world, who haff giffen me a welcome so warm and so unforgettable . . ."

He went on in that vein for longer than Lisa could have dreamed possible, but eventually he had to pause for breath, and three hands shot into the air.

"Mr. Haskins!" Josephine Burrell pointed at the nearest questioner and Mr. Haskins, a skinny, bespectacled man with adolescent zits and middle-aged receding hairline, stood up. "Dr. Przhevalsky, would you care to comment on how your academic work in cartography has affected your developmentas a dramatist?"

Nick looked pained. "Please! My friend, we are here to discuss Art—Spirit—the Universal Truths! Is this a time to drag our spirits down to the petty level of maps and labels?"

"No!" roared a sizeable portion of the audience.

"I only thought," struggled on the valiant Haskins, "that the spirit of despair which informs your more recent works might relate to the fact that your cartographic work has been superseded in favor of the

Zoraster algorithm, which is so markedly superior—"

"A true artist always knows despair!" Nick roared. "But a true artist neffer, neffer gives in! My friend, if you find despair in my works, it comes from the rotting worms within your own soul! My work is intended to affirm the glories of the human spirit and its triumph over adversity—"

"But what about the scene where the kindergarten is destroyed by a nuclear accident?" someone called out without waiting to be recognized by Mrs. Burrell.

"And the three paralyzed veterans with AIDS—"

"And the dead blackbird! *What* do you make of the dead blackbird in the pie?"

"Chernobyl—"

"AIDS—"

"A clearly ironic reference to the false naivete of American capitalist society as expressed in the nursery rhyme—"

The playgoers shouted their conflicting theories at each other, all but ignoring Nick. He looked over the seething room with a benign smile. Just as Lisa was beginning to hope that they could sneak out unobserved while the lovers of literature battled, a new element erupted into the room. These latecomers were dressed in jeans and sweaters rather than sequined evening gowns and tuxedos, and the young man at the head of the group carried a megaphone which amplified his words so that he could easily drown out the art lovers.

"PRZHEVALSKY, COLLABORATIONIST SWINE! WHAT ABOUT LEONID LYONSKY?"

Nick looked staggered by the sheer volume of the shouted question, as well as by the silence that fell over the embattled lecture room.

"What *about* him?"

Lisa shook her head sadly. Up to now Nick's performance had been all but flawless. Now she subtracted two points for brusqueness, and a third for letting the audience see that he was confused.

"IT WILL DO YOU NO GOOD TO PRETEND IGNORANCE," the young man with the megaphone shouted.

"We have copies of your speeches!" screeched a girl behind him, jumping up and down and brandishing a sheaf of smudged typewritten papers.

"You made a deal! You denounced him to get your own visa!" cried another.

"Quiet, please! Everybody be quiet! This is a serious discourtesy to our distinguished speaker!" Mrs. Burrell pleaded unheard through the tumult. She turned to Lisa, wringing her hands. "Oh, I knew this would happen! They were going to stage a riot outside the theatre when Dr. Przhevalsky appeared, so we moved the meeting here."

Well, Lisa thought, that explained that. And the tumult in the lecture room was certainly a good excuse for her and Nick to slip away. "Can you get us out of here?" she whispered to Mrs. Burrell while the young man with the megaphone shouted more accusations.

Mrs. Burrell glanced at Nick, now surrounded by protestors, and waved her hands feebly. "Create a diversion," Lisa suggested. "Faint. Have a heart attack. Shout—"

Come to think of it, there was no reason why she should depend upon Mrs. Burrell to do the heavy work. "Fire!" Lisa shouted.

"Yes, fire the bastard!" the girl carrying the papers agreed enthusiastically.

"No, I mean the room's on fire!"

"Where?" The girl peered through glasses set with thick lenses. "I don't see any fire. You must be mistaken. Say, aren't you with *him*?"

"Certainly not," Lisa replied with dignity. It occurred to her that while Nick was wasting time arguing with the rioters, she could get away on her own. With all this commotion going on, the security guards would never notice one girl slipping down to the third-floor offices. She edged towards the door while the other girl followed.

"I saw you outside, before the speech started. You're his assistant or something. Louie!" she yelled over the heads of the crowd. "This one's trying to get away!" She grabbed Lisa's wrist.

"Don't be ridiculous," Lisa said. "I never saw Dr. Przhevalsky before in my life." She jerked free and stumbled backwards towards the door. Something soft and warm blocked her way.

"That, at least, is true."

Lisa turned to face a short, balding man with gray eyebrows and a pointed gray beard. Behind him stood the two security guards she and Nick had evaded earlier, and behind them—

Oh, no! Lisa's heart sank and she barely took in the man's next words.

"I," he announced, "am Dr. Georgy Przhevalsky, and I have never seen this young lady who claims to be my assistant. And *who* is that man on the stage?"

"Who, indeed," said Cliff Simmons, stepping forth between the two security guards. He was pale and his hands were shaking and there was a strip of masking tape holding his glasses together, but he managed to get out his prepared speech in one long desperate breath. "This young woman used to work as the receptionist for a business I've just bought. This afternoon she quit without notice and took a box of extremely valuable rare books with her."

"I did not," Lisa gasped. "You stole the books! And I can prove—"

Cliff's brows went up and he favored Lisa with the sort of smile one gives to slightly retarded children. He was back in his element now, growing more confident by the minute. She wished she had another coffeepot to throw at him. "Stole my own inventory? You'll have to do better than that." He turned back towards the guards. "Fortunately, I had already removed some of the most valuable books to my own office for safekeeping. No doubt she and her accomplice broke in tonight hoping to complete their haul."

"Sounds likely," the first guard agreed while the second waded through the crowd, swinging his arms to clear a path and yelling for silence. He didn't get it, but most of the rioters and all of the art lovers trampled each other to get out of the way of a man in uniform with a purpose. Only the young man with the megaphone remained to block his path. "YOU WON'T RESCUE PRZHEVALSKY THAT EASILY!"

"Keep yer pants on, son," the guard said, sweeping the boy out of his way as easily as Lisa would swat a fly. "I ain't rescuing him. I'm taking him in."

The other guard took a firm grip on Lisa's elbow. While they were being hustled out of the lecture room, Nick pointed out in vain that the security guards were not police officers, that he had never *said* he was Przhevalsky, and that he could think of any number of ways to sue them for this high-handed action.

"And while you're harassing us," Lisa joined in, "you're letting the real criminals escape—as usual. This man and his friends kidnapped my boss and they're holding her prisoner downstairs." She had very little hope that Judith and the Durandines were still there. But the picture might be. And if she could get to the picture—She wondered what these two security guards would make of the world behind that gate.

The man holding Lisa snorted and kindly advised her to think of a better story.

"Fire hazard," Lisa said.

"What?" Suddenly she had the guards' full attention.

"In Simmons's office. The coffee maker is overheating and I think the wiring's shot. Look, I got burned when I tried to use it earlier." Lisa held up her bandaged hand.

"Ah, so now you admit you were there!" one guard pounced on her words.

"Yeah? Thought I smelled something funny," said the other man thoughtfully.

"How's the insurance on the building?"

"Never mind the insurance. I don't want to try and evacuate all those screaming maniacs." The second guard jerked his head back towards the lecture room, where the real Dr. Przhevalsky was disappearing under waves of rioters and theatre lovers shouting contradictory slogans. "Might as well check it out on our way down. You got your key, Mr. Simmons?"

"Yes, but—"

"Think you could have accidentally left the coffee maker on? Think there's any problem with the wiring?"

Cliff Simmons shrugged elegantly. "I hadn't noticed anything, no, but if you gentlemen wish to assure yourselves that everything is all right in my office you certainly may do so. At the same time," he added with a slight smile, "you might want to look under the desk and behind the draperies in case I'm concealing any prisoners."

The guards guffawed. Nick's face fell. Lisa knew what he was thinking; if Simmons wasn't worried, then Judith must have been transported somewhere else already. She wished she could tell him not to worry, that they could follow her and the Durandines, but she didn't want to remind Cliff of the book. If only it was still there!

Clifford Simmons unlocked his office with a flourish and stood back to let the guards enter first. Since each of them was holding a prisoner, Nick and Lisa had to go in with them.

The room was empty. Someone had cleaned up

the broken glass and spilled coffee. But the rug still squelched gently, the hot plate of the coffee maker sizzled away the last few drops of spilled coffee, and—peering around the guard who held Nick, Lisa saw with a leap of her heart that the Nielsen book was still open on Cliff Simmons's immaculate desk. If only she could distract the guards long enough to get to it!

"Ought to've turned that thing off when you left, Mr. Simmons, sir," one of the guards reproved Cliff. He let go of Nick to lumber over to the coffee maker. When he flicked the switch a blue spark leapt out to bite him. "Short somewhere there. And getting it wet didn't help, sir. Better replace it. Tell you what, I'll take this one out to the stairs now, save you the trouble."

The other guard let go of Lisa to step out of his way. She grabbed Nick's hand and dove towards the desk, concentrating on the picture in the open book. Trees and a stone arch and a stream trickling—it was just paper, it wasn't going to work—

"Stop her!" Cliff Simmons's voice sounded shrill behind her. "She's going to get away, you have to, have to burble bubble gurgle gurgle splash . . ."

The stream was louder now than his voice, and the sky under the arch was very blue. Lisa fell into the picture, dizzy and whirling as before, conscious of nothing but that she mustn't let go of Nick's hand. The circle of green turf swam up to meet her and she fell hard on her burnt hand and the red flames of pain ran up her arm and blazed up all around her. There was a sound as if the sky was being torn in two, and a flash of darkness more intense than any light, and then she was sitting on the grass and Nick was tumbling down beside her.

Clutched in his free hand was a crumpled piece of paper. As he hit the ground he let go of the paper and it floated down between them.

It was the picture from the Nielsen book, one end

of the passageway between the worlds. Somehow he had torn it out as they passed through the picture, closing the gate against those behind them.

In this world it was late afternoon; the sun slanted golden through the trees, the blue sky overhead was clear and bright. There was no hint of the October night that Lisa had just seen through Clifford Simmons's office windows, no sign of any passage remaining to the world from which they had come.

Lisa stood up slowly, ignoring the protests from bruised legs and throbbing hand, and walked through the ancient carved arch and back again. On both sides she felt nothing but the springing turf under her feet, saw nothing but forest and sky and a circle of green grass guarded by standing stones, heard nothing but the murmur of the brook.

The Gate was well and truly closed, and she and Nick—and Judith—were on the wrong side of it.

CHAPTER ELEVEN

Caritas, servant of the servants of God, to his cherished bishops in France and Poitiers:

It has recently come to our ears that certain vile and detestable heresies have been revived from ancient burial and spread by credulous folk who thereby undermine the faith of others.

Bishops and their officials must labor with all their strength to uproot thoroughly from their parishes the pernicious belief in demons and phantasms of demons, commonly called the Wild Hunt or the Hunt of Herluin, and that these demons riding in the hours of night have the power to draw the dead, and the souls of the living, after them. For whoever believes that anything except God can have power over souls, or can make the dead to rise, is beyond doubt an infidel; and whoever states this belief or offers prayers to demons on this account or makes (o vile and horrible sin) sacrifices of animals or humans, he shall be excommunicate.

Given at the Lateran, the ides of April, the fourth year of our pontificate.

The village of St.-Remy, perched between the forest and the barren cliffs of the river, had never had very much in material assets: a few houses, a few fields cut into a crazy patchwork of strips and triangles as marriages and inheritances divided and rejoined the peasants' holdings, and a church with one reluctant and ill-paid priest who constantly complained of the hardships of doing service in an elflord's realm.

Now it had even less. The priest had refused to return to a place so clearly marked as godless; he preferred to stay in the Christian lands on the other side of the river, under the protection of the Durandines at the Remigius monastery. The good brothers had offered the sanctuary of their house to any of the villagers who chose to stay. Some had accepted the offer; most, after the terror of the Wild Hunt's visitation wore off, returned to tend their fields. In that autumn when five years of poor crops had sent too many families begging their way along the roads, any fate seemed better than being landless—even the chance that the Hunt might return again.

"You're fools," the priest had chided those who returned. "The Huntsman will have the soul from your body. 'Tis God's visitation on those who choose to till elf-owned lands."

Serlo, the unofficial leader of the returning villagers, summed up their feelings when he commented, "Hunt might come again, or might not. But there'll be no food for winter unless us finishes the harvest, and hunger will have soul from body as certain as Huntsman will."

In daylight his words made brave sense. But each afternoon, as the shadows lengthened, the few villagers who'd returned to keep a claim to their lands felt the chill of the Hunt striking into their souls and wondered whether they should not, after all, have accepted the monks' offer of sanctuary at the Remigius.

It was not much of a life, being an unpaid lay-brother or sister of the Durandines: hard work and cold food, husbands and wives separated, children sent away as oblates to some distant monastery so that family ties should not distract them from serving the Order. But it was life, and life never seemed more sweet than on those bright afternoons of late summer when the air was already crisp with fall and the blue shadows reminded them of ghostly hounds and hunters. They tended to leave work early, gathering in worried knots in the square before the church and telling one another tales that did little to relieve their fears.

"Anybody seen Walo today?" one man asked.

"He went into forest with the pigs."

The old wife Letselina crossed herself. "God send he comes back before dark. Wouldn't send one o' mine into forest these days."

"What then? Let pigs starve?" Serlo demanded.

There was no answer to that, so Letselina changed the subject. "If us stays here, should have some guard against them coming back."

"Priest couldn't stop them. Neither could Lord Berengar."

"There was a way. In the old days." Letselina glanced around and lowered her voice, though everybody in the square was gathered around her. "My granny's gran told her how it used to be, back before they bound the Huntsman—and she had the tales from her gran, and on back to the Dark time. Didn't your mothers tell you to stay inside on Hallows Eve?"

Serlo spat in the dust. "Us all stays inside, all nights alike."

"In the Dark Time it used to be just one night in the year," Letselina said, "because folk paid the Huntsman proper respect in those days."

Serlo grunted and spat again. "I know what you mean. And we're not having it here. Pagan ways."

The men and women gathered around them looked

uneasily about, no man meeting his neighbor's eyes for more than a second.

"Aye, you know too—all of you!" Serlo challenged them. "All right. If you're all afraid to say it, and you too, you old witch, I'll say the words for it. Letselina wants us to tie somebody in the woods for a gift to the Hounds, like the old songs from the Dark Time tell. Pagan ways. Church'd excommunicate anybody as tried it now, old woman!"

"Church can't stop t'Hunt any more," one man mumbled. "Priest run away, didn't un?"

"Maybe she's right. If us showed proper respect—"

"Could be no harm would come to 'un."

"If Walo doesn't come back afore dark—"

"He will." Serlo straightened his back and stared around the circle of white faces, staring each one down in turn. "And who's to be our woods-gift, then? Well? Come on, speak up, don't be shy. I remember the old tales, too. And for a woods-gift to be fair and acceptable to the Huntsman, he had to come of his own will, or be chosen by the Huntsman."

"Like Walo, if'n he doesn't come back."

"He'll come back," Serlo repeated. "So tell me now. You're all so fast to mumble over the old tales and the old ways, now who wants to prove them? Who wants to give himself to the Huntsman so that the rest of the village can live free? Well?"

He waited barely a moment before exploding into a short barking laugh. "Thought as much. All right. Let's get back to work—and if you spread any more of your poison, old witch, I can tell you who t'Huntsman will choose next!"

The threat should have cowed Letselina. Instead she was looking past Serlo, grinning in triumph. Serlo spun and saw his only son, Walo, emerging from the forest with the pigs trotting before him.

Dangling from Walo's muscular arm was a thin, ragged boy whose eyes were rolled up in terror.

"Look what I found on the path, Da," Walo cried. "It's that cutpurse who took our coins at the Remigius fair last year. Calls himself a peddler now, but I'd know that gallows face anywhere. Thought it wouldn't be fair to take all the fun of thrashing him for myself, so I brought 'un back to let you have a turn."

"Like you said, Serlo," Letselina whispered, "sometimes the Huntsman chooses his woods-gift."

They were scared; that was what frightened Giles worse than anything. He hadn't been seriously worried at first, not until they'd started to drag him into the forest and he'd seen how it scared them to go in there. A thrashing was one thing; he'd been beaten before and lived. But the big one, the one they called Serlo, hadn't laid a finger on him. Nor had he stopped the others from surrounding him, pushing and prodding and kicking and forcing him back along the forest path down which Walo had just dragged him.

"I'm sorry, lad," he'd said quietly. "Even a thief doesn't deserve this. But I can't stop them. They're scared, y'see?" And he wouldn't meet Giles' eyes, as though he, not the boy, had been the one in the wrong.

"Come on, you," growled one of the men, lifting Giles by his shirt and almost strangling him.

"I'll leave quietly!" he promised. "Gentle sirs, there's no need for this—I'm an honest peddler, Giles of the Vine, ask anyone in the Rue de Fouarre in Paris, I'm not one to stay where I'm not wanted—"

"Honest peddler? An' where's your wares?"

"My pack is where *he* left it, when he knocked me down without reason and hauled me into your village," said Giles, jerking his chin towards Walo. It was difficult to be offended and righteous when you were being hauled by the neck of your shirt towards an unknown fate, but Giles managed it.

"He had a pack," Walo acknowledged. "Prob'ly full of other men's goods." He aimed a casual kick at Giles as he spoke.

"Not so! I'm no thief!"

"Just a lightfingers and a cutpurse," Walo growled. "Make your home in Paris, do you, and come all the way into Poitiers to steal from poor honest men?"

Giles' indignant denials were drowned out by a chorus of accusations from the other villagers. It seemed that by now, Haimo and Alcuin and half a dozen others distinctly remembered having their knives stolen or their purses cut at the Remigius fair, and the rest had complaints of stolen chickens and missing pigs and three-legged stools that had unaccountably wandered off.

"Good sirs and ladies, you wrong me," Giles protested. "I've not been in this part of the world since the Remigius fair, so how could I have taken a ham and a chicken and a stool just last month?"

"Ah, so you admit you were there!"

Giles prudently shut his mouth and refused to speak again until they reached their destination: a great spreading oak, older than the village by centuries, that dominated a bend in the forest path. Two of the men, he saw now, carried ropes. It seemed a strange place for a hanging.

"Here's as good a place as any," Haimo decreed, "no need to go too far from the village. Want Huntsman to know who made the offering, don't we?"

As if in mocking answer, the cold music of a silver horn rang through the treetops. And suddenly the villagers' fear, their muttered hints and talk of a "gift," all made sense to Giles. He'd never heard that music before, and an hour earlier he would have laughed at those who stayed within doors at night for fear of some old wives' tales. Peasants might huddle inside their smoky huts and tell over old stories, but a free-living man who made his living on the road had to be used to sleeping in a ditch when night fell.

But he hadn't guessed, from the tales, how that music could run like cold fire through nerves and muscle and solid bone, so that all you wanted to do was run from it—run until your legs shook and your chest ached, and still run mindless to the world's end. Giles could no more stop himself from struggling to get free and run than he could have stopped breathing. He lashed out wildly to break free of the men who held him, kicked and scratched like a girl and butted his head against something solid that rang like the great bell in the church of Our Lady in Paris. He went down into the blackness under that ringing sound and struggled awake, a few minutes later, to a fire in his head and a stabbing pain in his right wrist and the sound of Haimo boasting how he'd knocked the thief unconscious with two good blows of his staff.

There was no more fight left in him; he was so sick and dizzy that Walo had to hold him up while the others lashed him to the tree. The stupid oafs of peasants were pale and sweating with terror, but they worked stolidly at their task, wrapping his body round with the cords that he'd thought were meant to hang him. If only it were that! Giles prayed for the horn to sound again in the hope that the peasants would be frightened away before they'd finished tying him; then the knots were jerked tight, nearly cutting into his skin over the ribs, and he prayed that the horn would never sound again. If he heard that music again, unable as he was to run or even to move, he thought he would surely go mad.

"Get the hands too," Walo decreed when the others would have run for shelter, leaving Giles free to pick at whatever knots he could reach. "Be in the nature of a thief's skill to undo knots."

Someone behind the tree grabbed both his wrists and forced them around the trunk, and Giles screamed on a thin high note that hurt his own ears. "Ah, mercy! You've broken my hand—you've broken my hand already, don't hurt me more!" White-hot stabs, like heated blades, ran from wrist to shoulder and back again; it wasn't hard to weep and beg and scream when they tried to bind his right hand.

"Oh, all right, just the left hand," Walo decreed. "I doubt he'll pick at those knots with a broken hand. Gently, Haimo, no need to hurt him more than we must." He reached out to pat Giles on the shoulder; Giles flinched away from the gesture before recognizing its intent. "You see, lad, we're not—even though you did take my purse—"

"Did *not*," Giles protested, and got a mouthful of knuckles for his trouble.

"Cutpurse and thief though you be," Walo went on as though nothing had happened, "we don't mean to hurt you more'n needful. This village been harried by the Wild Hunt twice in three days, y'see? We can't have it again. Letselina says it's because we don't pay Huntsman his dues. So—you're the woods-gift. If he takes you, maybe he'll spare the village. I don't know if it makes you feel better, to know you could be saving the rest of us?"

After a pause he shrugged and said, "Well, anyway. If he don't take you, I'll be back in the morning to cut you free, and we'll consider all debts canceled. I won't even thrash you for taking my purse. Or give you over to our lord's justice. Last the night, and you're a free man."

He waited again for Giles to show some sign of gratitude for this offer, then gave a heavy sigh and turned. "Come on, then. Us better be getting on before it comes on dark."

They walked, with dignity, until a bend in the path carried them out of Giles' sight; then he heard them running, crashing through vines and over ditches in their breathless haste to get back to the safety of the cleared land around St.-Remy. He would have laughed, if there'd been any impulse to merriment left in him.

For some time he hung against the ropes that bound him, too limp with fear and pain to think or notice the passing of time. Slowly it came to him that he had not heard the Huntsman's call since the peasants departed. How long had it been? The trees around him blocked any view of the sun, but he fancied the shadows were deeper and colder than they had been when he was bound to the tree.

Perhaps, after all, the Huntsman would not take him. What had Walo said? "Last out the night, and you're a free man." Giles' lips curved in a mirthless grin. He was not minded to trust the peasants' gratitude—or the Huntsman's mercy. His chances both of lasting out the night and of finding himself free in the morning would be immeasurably improved if he could somehow wriggle free of these bonds.

Clever of him, to talk them into leaving one hand free. Giles strained to reach the knots until sweat broke out on his forehead. The stupid louts weren't so dull after all; they'd taken care that all the knots were on the other side of his body. And when his fingertips at last brushed the edges of the nearest knot, there was no strength in them. When he yelped and cried about his broken hand he'd been putting it on a bit to impress the oafs, never thinking he had more than a sprain to swell up his wrist. But something was not working right, there in the clever junction of fingertips and thumb. All his old skill and delicacy of touch was there, but he could put no strength behind it to ease the tight ropes.

Giles told himself bracingly not to worry. When Haimo had first hit him the hand had been nothing but a blazing center of pain and he'd been unable to feel anything with it. Now the nerves had recovered; in time, so would the strength.

The only question was, would he recover before dark? Giles could not keep from thinking about that darkness, and the sweat dampened his palm and made his fingers slick until he cursed the ropes and the peasants and his own hand under his breath. Suddenly a noise deep in the forest made him stop in mid-curse, suddenly erect and taut under the ropes that held him fast, with a cold chill of fear wrapping him round like a winding-sheet. What was that? He strained his ears for the sound of the Huntsman's death-music, was rewarded by distinctly human voices raised in argument, and fell slack against his bonds as he spied the gray robes of a pair of monks coming along the path. Gray robes meant Durandines, not an order Giles favored for begging—even the Cistercians were more generous—but at least they were men of God. Merciful men, good men, lettered men, not subject to the superstitions of the peasants; men who would not approve any sacrifice but that which Our Lord had made long ago.

"Good masters, of your mercy—" Giles cried out.

The two monks halted and turned towards him.

"What's that?" called a man coming up the trail behind the two he'd first seen.

"Some boy, being punished belike—"

"Set upon by robbers!" Giles interrupted before the monks could pursue this thought. Almost without forethought or calculation the story poured out of his mouth, how he had been trudging towards the next village when two great hulking men leapt upon him from the bushes, took his peddler's pack and bound him here that he might not raise the hue and cry against them.

He was hardly well begun on the pitiful tale when the main body of the travelers caught up with the two monks who'd paused to listen to him. Four more men in long gray hooded robes surrounded a lady in some strange outlandish costume. The fair sweet shape of her breasts was outlined under a tight, white tunic emblazoned with cabalistic symbols—Giles saw an orange circle and a horned shape like a demon with a cow's head. Below the tunic she wore heavy blue hosen that ran from ankle to waist and outlined her body most indecently. Her yellow hair fell loose over her shoulders and her eyes were wild and lost-looking, and the men on either side of her held her arms tightly as if they feared she would run from them at any moment.

"Move on," snapped the man who'd first called out. He was thinner and slighter than the others but they seemed to defer to him. "We've no time to waste on him."

"At least cut me loose!" Giles cried.

A decisive shake of the gray-hooded head was his only answer. "No time. If you're not honest, you'd likely delay us. If you are—well, I'll tell the villagers at St.-Remy of your plight; they can come and free you if they choose."

Giles sagged down on the ropes that bound his body. He could not believe that help had come so close, only to be refused. "No!" This time he told the truth, or near as made no difference: how the villagers had mistaken him for a thief they'd seen last year and had bound him to this tree for a woods-gift to the Huntsman. Surely these good men of religion would not leave him here as a living sacrifice? Couldn't they see how dark it was getting? Hadn't they heard that silvery music snaking through the afternoon air?

But the men were marching on now, dragging the lady with them. They passed right by Giles' tree, and in the depths of his misery he stared at the lady and felt a moment of sorrow for her condition— better though it was than his own. Poor mad lady, with those wide staring eyes in her white face, her hair disordered and her costume so indecent that she might as well be naked. No doubt she was some great lord's wife, and these men were taking her to their monastery to be cured of her madness. She was as lovely as the picture of the Blessed Virgin in colored glass in the great church at Paris, and if she had her wits about her she would likely be as sweet and merciful as Our Lady.

"I think you would help me," he said sadly, "if only you were in your senses."

Her eyes rolled up in her head when he spoke and she dropped, limp as a stone going down into deep water, all but dragging down the two men who held her.

"*Now* what?" demanded the thin-lipped leader, striding back as he spoke.

"She's fainted."

"Weak, these elvenkind."

Giles stared almost greedily at the lady's white face. An elf-queen! He'd heard tales of such folk, but there were few of them to be seen in Paris; they were not well liked in the north. But aye, she was every bit as fair as he'd imagined the elvenkind would be. Surely she knew some magic that would free him! She hadn't fainted; these monks might be fooled, but Giles, who knew every beggar and shammer and fake cripple in Paris, could tell that she was peeping through her long eyelashes and following the arguments of the men above her.

"Water," she murmured weakly as they began to discuss making a litter on which to drag or carry her. "Please—I am so faint—if I might have a little water, I think I could go on better."

One of the monks went to the stream to get water, while the two who'd been guarding the lady lifted her to her feet and propped her against the trunk of the tree, just inches from Giles, ignoring him as if he were no more than a protrusion in the rough bark.

She moved her head and moaned for air, and they moved back but stood watching her still, close enough to grab her if she tried to run.

Judith found it easy enough to pretend that she was on the verge of fainting. It wasn't far from the truth: it would have been a great relief to let herself collapse onto the ground. But fainting was a luxury she couldn't afford.

In her nearly thirty years of privileged middle-class academic life, no one had ever laid hands on Judith Templeton to force her into doing anything she didn't want to do. She'd started college too late for the sit-ins and demonstrations of the sixties; the closest her life had ever come to violence was the time one of her computer science professors had told another one that anybody who programmed in BASIC was risking terminal brain damage.

Hitting the men who invaded her houseboat with an empty bottle had seemed like a good idea at the time, the sort of thing people did all the time on television, but somehow it hadn't worked out right in real life. The man she swung at had seemed to vanish before her eyes. Judith's academic training had taught her that when something peculiar like that happened, you stopped right where you were and studied the evidence very closely until you understood what was going on.

She'd been rubbing her eyes and trying to believe the evidence of her senses when the blanket went over her head and arms. For a few minutes life was nothing but a series of raw uninterpreted sensations: jostling, bruising, the swaying as the men carried her off the boat, sick fear that they meant to throw her into the water to drown in this blanket all tangled in the limestone ledges. It was almost a relief to be pushed into the back seat of a car; that, at least, was something familiar. She wriggled about and got the blanket off her head—it smelled terrible, like a wet sheep—and recognized Cliff Simmons's shiny dark head. She'd been about to tell him off when one of the men in gray saw that she had her head free and said something urgently to the other one, who'd begun chanting in a language she did not know. Suddenly Judith felt very tired, too tired to do anything but lie back against the car seat and watch languidly as Cliff Simmons maneuvered his BMW over the rocky road back to Austin. The ruts and rocks and overhanging branches weren't doing his fancy car any good, and that made Judith happy, only she couldn't quite remember why she didn't like Simmons.

She'd been so tired that she protested mildly when the car stopped and they wanted her to get out and climb stairs. But for some reason all three men were quite insistent about it, and it didn't seem worth the effort of arguing with them.

Just as Lisa had said, the book with the Kay Nielsen illustrations was lying open on Clifford Simmons's desk. While the men in gray robes argued with Simmons, Judith stared at the picture and wondered mildly what had possessed Lisa to spin such a tale about walking through the picture into another world, and why she had ever believed it. It was the kind of story that sounded quite wonderful in the lamplit warmth of the houseboat, and quite improbable here with the blue-white glare of fluorescent office lights starkly illuminating every expensive modern furnishing.

All the same, there were other things to support Lisa's story; the dark puddle of spilled coffee seeping into the carpet, for one, and the glitter of broken glass here and there where somebody had failed to pick up all the shards from the carafe. From the cloudy place where her will and consciousness rested Judith tried to pay attention to those things, because for some reason it was important, now, to know whether Lisa had been telling the truth; she couldn't remember just why.

Then the short argument finished with one of the monks telling Cliff Simmons, "You will remain behind, to stop those who might follow. Never fear; my master will know how to value your services." He and his companion took Judith's arms and walked towards the desk, chanting steadily, and the picture in the book grew larger and brighter as they chanted, and Judith felt the center of her body lifting and swooping as if she were in an elevator going down too fast and she knew exactly why it had been important that Lisa was telling the truth after all.

CHAPTER TWELVE

Amors de terra lonhdana, Per vos totz lo cors
mi dol; E non puesc trobar mezina Si non au
vostre reclam Ab atraic d'amor doussana Dinz
vergier o sotz cortina Ab dezirada companha.

—Jaufre Rudel

(Love from a distant land, my whole heart aches
for you; and I cannot find a cure unless I go
at your call following sweet love into the garden
or behind the curtain with the one I long for.)

It was very bright and clear and crisp, this strange
world with its circle of gray stones like guardians
around Judith and her captors. They had all fallen
onto the bright green grass, and for a moment the
breath was knocked out of the man who'd been chanting and blessed silence reigned. If only she weren't
so frightened, Judith thought, she would have felt
more awake and alive than she had ever been in her
life. All her senses were sharp and clear and the
beauty of the world around her was so vibrant and

joyful that she could hardly bear it. A bird's wings flashed overhead, a trill of music danced in the sunlit air, the resinous scent of the forest outside the circle of stones mingled with the fresh living smell of green growing things within the circle. Everything was beautiful, from the lofty arch of carved stone before her to the sharp flintlike chip that dug into her right leg where she knelt on the grass.

Well, perhaps the chip of stone was not absolutely beautiful. Judith reached down absently and extracted it from the turf: a small sharp-edged crescent of gray stone, half buried in the springing grass, with one sharp point up to catch her when she fell on it. The tall standing stone to her left had a matching crescent-shaped scar where the chip had been knocked loose, probably ages ago; the scarred place was half-covered over with moss. But the broken edge of the stone chip was still sharp. How long did it take stone to weather to an ageless smoothness? Longer than it took moss to grow, clearly. Judith thought about that, very slowly and carefully, while the men who had brought her here picked themselves up and dusted themselves off. As long as she could concentrate on something as comfortably academic as the different aging rates of stone and moss, she could avoid thinking about anything else—like what these men wanted of her, and why they had brought her here, and where in the world or out of it she might be, and whether she could ever get home again, and—

It all rushed in on Judith at once, and she felt sick and dizzy. She moaned slightly; one of the men in gray turned at the sound and hauled her to her feet. Before she could get her balance he pushed her ahead of him with a hard thrust that sent her between two of the standing stones. She felt as if a cloud of buzzing gnats encircled her head immediately. Another man was waiting there to catch her, a sour-faced ugly fellow who grabbed her arm and twisted it against the direction of her stumbling fall; the pain brought Judith up with a gasp. She looked back at the arch through which she had come and saw, shimmering like a veil over the grass and stones, the image of Clifford Simmons' office in the XCorp Building. If she could just get back through that arch, would she tumble between the worlds again and find herself safe?

The man who'd shoved her through the arch followed and took Judith's other arm. "That's better," he said. "Cursed elven stones! She almost recovered her will, Brother Alured; maintain the chant, if you don't wish to deal with Lady Sybille and the Stone-maidens together."

"One day," said the man who'd twisted her arm, "one day all these devil's circles will fall, and there will be no more elven magic to trouble our land."

"*Deo volente*," murmured the other one, "but in the meantime, Brother Hugh, let us have the lady away from the Stones before she remembers how to use her power." He looked Judith contemptuously up and down. "If she remembers anything at all. She was easy enough to take; I hope she may not have lost her wits in that terrible world."

"I will help her remember," said the one called Hugh with a smile that made Judith feel very cold inside. He had a pimply chin, and his teeth were crooked, and he was quite young. Judith told herself that she had no need to be afraid of some pimple-faced adolescent. Her inner self was not convinced. How old had Billy the Kid been?

The other man began his low-voiced monotonous chant again. The words swirled and spiraled in Judith's head and she began to feel the gray misty clouds replacing the sharp, joyful clarity she'd known when she first fell into this world. She hated this vague confused feeling, and she hated being power-less even worse. They were dragging her down the path that led away from the arch, and she couldn't even fight them. Judith's whole body tensed in rejec-tion; her hands squeezed into fists and the two sharp points of the crescent chip stung her palm and it seemed to her that the gray clouds receded just a little, just enough to let her keep some of her own will and understanding through the fog of the chant. Not enough for her to fight her way free of these men, but at least she could think her own thoughts while her body stumbled between her captors.

How had she acted before, when she'd been sur-prised and unable to fight against this—whatever it was—some form of hypnotism? Judith unobtrusively slid her right hand into the pocket of her jeans while she concentrated on making her face blank, eyes wide and empty, moving passively where these men wanted her to go. That was the hardest part. No one had ever laid hands on Judith against her will; civi-lized people didn't do that sort of thing. She hated to feel them touching her, wanted to pull away and scream and shout and hurt them.

And if she did any of those things, they would know that this chant of Alured's was no longer fog-ging her brain as it was supposed to do, and what would they do then? Judith found that she wanted very much to live. She wanted it even more than she wanted to keep the pride that was screaming inside her. She let her head loll slightly to one side and made them support her down the path away from the circle of stones, and as they made their slow progress she did her best to mark trees and stones and the direction of the sun and anything else that might help her find her way back to this place.

It shouldn't be too hard. The path turned and

twisted, and she didn't dare let them see how intently she was watching her surroundings, and but for one thing she would have been hopelessly lost before they'd gone half a mile. But—praise the Blessed Virgin!—however the path turned, it always came back to follow the gurgling stream to their right.

Judith frowned. Praise the Blessed Virgin, indeed! That wasn't the way she usually thought. Something strange was happening to her in this place.

She stumbled over a tree root that lay slanting across the path, bubbling out of dust like a creature of earth rising into the air, and the monk called Alured jerked her by the right arm to get her over the obstacle without loss of time. For a moment Judith lost hold of the chip of rock she'd taken away from the circle, and Alured's steady chant sounded like sea-surf in her ears and the terrible gray hopeless feeling swept over her like inexorable waves. She plunged her hand deep in her pocket again and as soon as the tips of her fingers brushed the stone, she felt safe again.

And that's a laugh! she thought with the part of her mind that remained free of Alured's enchantment. Here she was in a different world, maybe a different universe, kidnapped by these total strangers, but everything was all right as long as she could hold that sharp-edged crescent of gray stone.

All the same, it did make her feel better. Judith trudged on between her captors, trying simultaneously to look blankly witless and to keep note of their surroundings, and the effort of concentration this required slowly drew her into a trance-like state in which she hardly felt tired or sleepy or afraid; all she was really conscious of was the sharp reality of the stone in her hand and the ever-changing, ever-same flow of trees and brown needles and blue sky and gurgling water.

And then they rounded a corner and Judith drew
in her breath in shock. There was a skinny black-
haired boy ahead of them, tied cruelly tight to a tree
and with marks of tears on his face. He begged the
monks to let him go; Judith half listened to the story
that spilled out of him and could hardly make any
sense of it. Peddlers and robbers and the hue and
cry, and then talk of a Hunt—she could tell by the
way he spoke that the word would have been capital-
ized if he were writing—and a woods-gift, whatever
that was. It meant nothing to her, but the boy's
terror was palpable. And whatever was really going
on, someone had been too rough with him before
they left him tied to that tree. He looked about
thirteen, pale and grimy and painfully thin, with
dirty black hair falling over his face and obscuring a
dark flush along one cheekbone that would probably
develop into a bruise by tomorrow. And he was
terrified.

She couldn't believe it when the monks took her
arms again and set off without freeing the child.
What kind of cruel world was this, beyond the beauty
she'd seen initially? Judith dug her heels in against
the pull of Brother Alured's hands and the rock chip
in her own hand stung her palm painfully, almost
like a warning: don't fight, they think you're hypno-
tized, don't make them think they have to tie you up
like that.

So she fainted.

It wasn't a very good faint, she wasn't an actress,
but the stumbling fall seemed to've been good enough
to deceive the monks who, Judith decided, probably
had little to do with women and rather expected
them to faint on the slightest provocation. They even
propped her up against the tree the kid was tied to.

"I wish I could help," she whispered while they
were fetching water for her, barely moving her lips,
"but they won't let me go either."

The boy's eyes widened and he strained against his bonds for a moment. "You're not mad!"

"No. But—" There was hardly time to explain how she came to be here, even if she'd understood it herself. "Their prisoner."

"Get me free, and I'll help you."

"How?"

"Can you get a knife?"

A double handful of cold water splashed into Judith's face. She jerked back reflexively and the thin-lipped monk they called Hugh, the one who'd been waiting for them on this side, laughed. "No talking, *my lady*," he said with a derisive bow, "and we'd best be on our way here. This beggar brat is none of your concern—you'd do better to worry about your own fate."

No doubt he was right. And as Brother Alured resumed the monotonous chant, Judith's fingers groped for the sharp curved bit of rock that had mysteriously given her comfort and strength so far. It cost her very nearly all her strength to give it up now; but it was the nearest thing to a knife she had. Just before they jerked her away from the tree to resume the long march, she managed to brush her hand across the fingers of Giles' free hand, transferring the crescent chip to him.

Once she'd given it up, the dull music of Alured's chant filled her head, sapping strength and will and sense together. Judith fought back in the only way she knew and was relieved to find that she could barely hold the gray mists away with her own counterchants. While the monks chanted and Judith's body stumbled on along the forest path, she reviewed inside her head the programs she'd used to get Aunt Penny's tangled finances into a computer. She had meant to write a manual for Lisa, so that she could learn the system without Judith standing over her, but had never gotten around to it. Now she organized the pages and the corresponding flow of data in her head. The concentration required kept her safely in there with the data flow diagrams, far away from the distant buzzing of Alured's chant: this world of complex symbols, Judith thought, was its own sort of magic. She even spotted two potential problems, ways that Lisa or somebody else could tie up the system by entering the wrong data, and made a mental note to fix those bugs when—if—she got back.

She was mildly irritated when a sharp cry interrupted Alured's chanting and her own thoughts. The monk who'd been holding her left arm let go suddenly, flailing his arms about his face as if he were having a fit. There was a humming sound all around them, almost like some kind of machine, and dark specks in the air—

A red-hot needle sank into Judith's bare arm, and a cloud of bees whirled before her eyes. She yelped just like the first monk and began beating the air in front of her, frantic to keep the buzzing, stinging things away from her eyes. Something grabbed her wrist and she twisted, ducked, and looked straight into Giles the peddler's green eyes.

"Come *on*, will you!" he snapped "Bees won't stay forever." And he set off straight into the green depths of the forest, tugging Judith with him.

The stream would have been shelter against the bees, but not against the monks. They had only been confused for a moment; now Judith could hear their heavy steps crashing through the underbrush at the edge of the path. She and Giles splashed through the stream and clambered up the moist clay bank on the far side. He was slowing; Judith snapped at him to hurry up and then saw that he wasn't using one hand. She grabbed his arm and hoisted him bodily over the lip of the bank—*so light; did nobody ever give him a decent meal?*—and they scrambled on, breathless, while shouts and splashes echoed behind them. Something whirred past Judith's ear and buried itself harmlessly in the dead leaves and brown pine needles before them. The boy scooped it up in passing and laughed his thanks to the stupid monk who'd thrown his knife, as if this were all a game.

"Fool! We want her alive!" the one called Hugh shouted in a thin high voice behind them. "If you were any kind of mage, Brother Alured, you'd whistle a wind out of the north to becloud the sky . . ." The rest of his words were lost in the laboring of Judith's own tormented lungs. She barely heard Brother Alured shouting back, "Are you mad? They grow stronger each . . ."

The words made no sense. But it sounded as if nobody would be throwing knives at them again. They wanted her alive. For what? Judith found that she could, after all, run a little faster up the slippery, leaf-covered slope. Her chest burned with gasping for air and her legs hurt, but they were almost at the top of the long slow rise. Giles was slowing again. She hauled him along with her and put on one last desperate burst of speed.

To no avail. Just over the crest of the hill, a wall of boulders blocked their way: great gray rounded stones rising out of the brown leaves, lichen-covered and immovable. Alone, Judith might possibly have scrambled over the obstacle before the monks caught up with her; but the boy was exhausted, and with only one hand he could not be expected to climb. Judith sighed and bent to pick up a broken branch. The monks were only a few feet away now; she noticed with grim amusement that Brother Hugh, who'd been so free with his hands and threats when he thought her spelled into helplessness, was hanging back behind the other two now. She hefted the branch experimentally and saw that Giles, beside her, was caressing the hilt of the monk's knife as if it were a long-lost friend.

"I hope you know how to use that thing," Judith said, "for I don't."

He gave her a sidelong glance. "Of course not, my lady. I'll take care it doesn't touch you. Just don't get in my way."

"Alured, calm them!" called Brother Hugh, still keeping well back. Judith swung the broken branch back over her head and whacked Alured in the mouth with it before he had gathered breath for his gray mind-dulling chant.

After that, for a few hectic minutes, there was no time for conversation on either side. Judith swung her branch valiantly and without much skill; but the monks had not much skill in fighting either, and their long robes impeded them, and Giles darted about with his knife, menacing and pricking and keeping them from getting close enough to grab anybody. As Judith got her breath back, she found to her shock that she was almost enjoying herself. Her lips had drawn back in a tight hard grin and she laughed aloud every time she got in a good blow on one of her attackers.

But it was a game that could only have one ending. To protect their backs, they had to stay against the wall of boulders. Judith saw, out of the corner of her eye, that Brother Hugh was slipping off to the left while the other two kept her and the boy pinned against the rocks.

"*Stop him!*" she cried to Giles, and his left hand blurred in a movement too swift to follow. A glittering arc of metal pierced the air; Hugh cried out and sat down abruptly, clutching his shoulder and looking more surprised than hurt.

And now there were only two against two. But the odds were hardly equal. Giles was tired, and now he didn't have a knife, and Judith could tell that her

own desperate swings of the branch were getting too
wild to do much good. She could hardly put any
strength behind the branch now, her arms ached so.
One of the monks darted under her guard and grabbed
the boy by his bad hand. He screamed on a thin high
note that hurt Judith's ears. She brought her branch
down square on the monk's wrist and there was a
loud cracking sound. He staggered back, holding his
wrist. But it was the branch that had broken. Judith
scooped up a rock from the base of the wall and
threw it at his face. She missed, but he backed off
anyway.

"Come and get it," she taunted. There were more
loose rocks ready to hand, nice small round ones.
Why hadn't she thought of this before? "What's the
matter, surely you big strong men—aren't afraid—of
a woman and a wounded kid—*are* you?" Each phrase
was punctuated by a well-aimed rock, driving the
monks back almost to the low crest of the slope. As
long as she could keep this up—

But, of course, she couldn't. She reached for another rock and felt only the smooth curve of the
great boulder behind her. As she scanned the ground
from left to right, looking for another little cairn of
throwing rocks, the monks began moving closer like
great gray prowling cats.

"Get behind me," she ordered Giles. Not that she'd
be much protection for him, when the monks made
their final rush; but it seemed they wanted her
alive, while they didn't care whether or not they
killed him. Maybe she could slow them down—maybe—

"Oh, hell," Judith sighed. There was no real point
in prolonging the fight; there was nobody to rescue
them. The rational thing would be to give in now
and save her strength. But if she did that, she had a
nasty feeling the boy would be left dead. He'd come
back and thrown a honeycomb full of bees at the
monks to save her, when he could have run the

other way and saved his own skin. She lifted a medium-sized boulder with both hands and heaved it weakly at the monks. By sheer good luck it landed on Brother Alured's sandaled foot and he gave a pained yelp that interrupted his chant. "Can you scramble over the wall if I give you a boost?" she asked Giles.

"Are you going to cast an illusion? My lady?"

"I'm not going to cast anything," Judith said, "unless you can find me some more nice round rocks. No, forget that." The two monks had backed off again while Alured nursed his bruised foot, but now they were advancing again. "Just get over the wall. Maybe I can keep them busy long enough for you to get away—and if you know anybody who might help us, you could send them to look for me."

"But if you'd just use your *magic*—" Giles protested.

Judith opened her mouth to tell Giles to stop gibbering and get away while he still had a chance, but between one breath and the next a shimmering cloud of rainbow-stuff formed between her and the gray semicircle of her attackers. She heard them crying out and retreating, but she couldn't see anything. No. There was something large and scaled, with teeth as long as Judith's arm, rearing out of the mist; and more things thrashing beyond it, with long spiked tails and clawed legs. Judith couldn't quite see the things clearly. She did not want to. Beside her, the boy was gazing openmouthed, his eyes shining as if he'd just seen their salvation.

"*Don't look!*" Judith said sharply. Her knees were shaking and she had to lean back against the stone wall. Just now, to judge from the roars and screams and crunching noises she heard, the—*things*—were attacking the monks. But any minute, one of them would look this way. Could they get over the wall, or would those beasts notice them scrambling up the rocks and pick them off like fruit from a tree?

She was afraid to risk it. Maybe, if they kept very still in the shadow of the rocks, they could escape notice. She reached for Giles and held him against her. He was so thin, hardly more than a bundle of bones covered with grubby skin.

"If we don't move," she whispered, "maybe they won't notice us."

There was a crashing noise very close at hand, and Judith squeezed Giles tightly and shut her own eyes.

"My lady, I beg pardon if I have affrighted you," said a light, young voice, quite unlike the voices of the monks.

Judith opened her eyes and stared at the liquid brown eye and white muzzle of a sweating horse. "No," she said wildly. "Mad monks, human sacrifices, and dragons are quite enough for one day. I don't do talking horses. Go away." Maybe she was dead already, or being munched up by one of the dragons, and in shock and hallucinating.

"Up here," the voice said with a ripple of laughter. "On the horse."

Judith looked again and saw soft leather boots, thigh-high and covered with an intricate tracery of gold leaves and vines. Above that, a loose coat as blue as the summer sky, with more vines curling and twining about every seam, so real they seemed to be moving and growing as she watched. And above that, a man with eyes as blue as the coat looked down with amusement crinkling his lids.

"Berengar, Count of the Garronais," he introduced himself casually. "Can you mount?" he asked. "I fear we haven't long before they see through my illusion."

Even as he spoke, Judith heard Brother Alured's gravelly voice begin the strange words of his incantation again. The rainbow mists dulled to gray, then thinned until Judith could see the three monks through the translucent shadowy shapes of the dragons.

"Cowards!" Hugh was back on his feet, and in one

hand he was waving one of the long thin knives the monks all carried. He was unsteady, and the blade wavered in wild circles, but he looked mad enough to run straight in among them. "Take the elf-lord, or we'll lose everything!"

Berengar spat out a short phrase that sounded like acid in the mouth. The mists thickened and swirled about the three of them and tongues of flame shot out towards the monks. Two of them hesitated, but Hugh ran on as though he could not even see the fire, holding his blade before him. In the moments when Berengar could have dodged the blow, he bent from his saddle to grasp Judith's arm. He hauled her up before him; she felt as though her arm had been pulled right off; in slow motion she saw the wicked sharp blade coming at the two of them, then Berengar's arm slashed down across the path of the knife and deflected the monk's aim. The horse snarled and snapped at the monk and he fell back, but there was blood on his knife now. Berengar hissed with pain and his left arm hung useless at his side. And he was using his other arm to hold Judith, not to control the horse. She got her left leg over the horse's back in a desperate scramble and clamped on with both knees. "Take the reins," she cried. "I can keep on!" She didn't know whether she could or not, but if Berengar didn't get them out of there it wouldn't make any difference. The monk was coming at them again, and the flames of Berengar's illusion were pale as milk now. "Wait!" she cried as the horse wheeled. "Giles!"

There was another clumsy scramble that ended with Giles across Judith's lap, and Berengar speaking words she had never heard that rang like bells, and a dazzling of broken lights about them and a wind from nowhere. She heard Alured's chant dying away behind them, and a shout of frustrated rage and hatred from the leader, and she should have been afraid but instead she laughed for joy to be riding this wind into the heart of the storm. There was a white horse under her and a rescued child in her arms and a man with the face of a young god carrying her into unknown adventures. *This is what I was born for*. The thought came from nowhere and she laughed again. But already the rushing wind was dying, the horse's hooves struck ordinary leaf-covered dirt, the sparkling mist of light and crystals that had surrounded them was fading into the calm blue twilight of any autumn day.

"I am sorry," said the man who'd rescued her and Giles. "I think I cannot carry us any farther just now." His voice sounded very tired, as if he had been bearing the three of them up with no more than the force of his will. "Perhaps, my lady, if you would lend your strength to mine?"

"I—what do you want me to do?"

Berengar sighed. "No matter. We must dismount now; Fleurdevent is tired too. And we must consider what to do next."

Giles slid off first, landing on the ground with a thump that hardly dimmed his grin. Ever since the illusory dragons had appeared, he'd been as happy as a kid in a candy store. Judith couldn't blame him; she'd felt the same way herself for a few brief, exhilarating moments. Her own ungraceful landing knocked most of that feeling out of her. She didn't quite land on her bottom, like Giles, but it was a near thing. Berengar, she noted, moved with a fluid grace, like water shimmering over rocks. Only his left arm was stiff and awkward.

"You're hurt!" She remembered the monk running towards him, the blade extended awkwardly, and Berengar knocking it out of the way. "Let me see."

"It's not important." But Judith could see that Berengar was white around the lips, and that his face was tense with the effort of holding back pain.

"If you're badly hurt," Judith said, careful now not

to offend his pride, "the boy and I will have no one to defend us. And—I don't know who you are, or where you came from, but we did need your help, and we are grateful. So will—you—let me tend that cut?"

Berengar laughed, unexpectedly; a silver ringing sound, as magical as the horn she had heard earlier, but joyful music rather than the cold frightening notes of the horn. "Spoken like a true Queen of Elfhame. This time I think I have found the right lady." He extended his arm as he spoke, and Judith carefully drew aside the cut edges of the blue sleeve. Her breath caught in her throat at the sight of what lay beneath. Instead of the clean cut she'd expected to see, there was a long festering wound that looked as if it had been untreated for a week. The edges of the raw flesh were seared and bubbled as if the blade had been red-hot, and the skin peeled away in patches from the jagged line of the cut.

I will not be sick. I will not be sick.

"I don't understand," she said when she could speak again. "I thought you were wounded just now, in the fight."

Berengar nodded. "Even so."

"But—was the knife poisoned, do you think?" She knew of no poison that could destroy skin and flesh as this had done, but it was the best explanation she could think of. Maybe some kind of acid?

Berengar gave her a strange look. "It was iron. What need of any other poison?"

Judith shook her head in bewilderment.

"Will you work your healing skills, my lady? In this age we have lost the art to cure such wounds, but perhaps you know the old arts."

"Well," Judith said as lightly as she could, "Girl Scout training didn't exactly cover major surgery, but I'll do what I can."

There was a brook nearby, but what little she'd

seen of this world did not incline her to trust the water. It looked like a seriously pre-industrial culture; she had visions of pigs and offal heaps and villages upstream tossing whatever they didn't want into the convenient disposal system. She ripped Berengar's own ruined sleeve into pieces and bound them about the wound. At least it would stay clean, and maybe the wrapping would help the raw edges to draw together.

Both Berengar and Giles looked rather disappointed when she finished. "Is that all?" Giles demanded.

"What do you want? I'm not a surgeon!" She turned to Berengar. "But you'd better have that wound looked at when we get—er, that is, where are we going?"

"That," said Berengar, "was the next question I wished to raise. It is not wise to linger in these woods after nightfall."

"I heard the Hunt—" Giles started, but Berengar hushed him with a wave of his hand.

"It is also," he said quietly, "not wise to call upon those who may be listening. Now. We are too far from my keep for Fleurdevent to bear us all three there, unless the elf-wind could somehow be called to our aid again." He and Giles both looked at Judith. When she said nothing, he continued.

"The village of St.-Remy was the closest shelter to the place where I found you, but we have traveled some distance from there already. In any case, it is too close to the monastery of the Remigius to be a safe place for us tonight. I've no wish to involve my peasants in a war with the Durandines—and I fear that they do mean to force us of Elfhame to open war —but that is another matter, to be considered in peace. All that matters now is that we cannot seek shelter at St.-Remy."

"Not to mention," Giles put in, ostentatiously rubbing the rope-marks that lingered on his bare arms, "that it's the home of the peasant oafs who tied me to a tree for a woods-gift for—the ones we don't name."

Berengar's blue eyes lit with anger. "Is it so? I shall have a word with these serfs of mine, and I think Bishop Rotrou will have somewhat to say also. They could be excommunicate for such a deed! When we have found shelter for the night, you must tell us the tale of your adventures." He bowed ceremoniously to Judith. "I fear there is only one safe place close enough for us to reach before nightfall—the Stonemaidens." He looked at Judith as if expecting her to approve his suggestion.

The Stonemaidens. The monk Hugh had used that name. "That was where we came into this world," Judith said. "Won't they be looking for us there?"

Berengar's smile was grim. "I think . . . not tonight. Even the Brothers of the Order of Durand will not brave the forest tonight, I think. No, they will have taken shelter at the village, or perchance returned to the Remigius monastery. My concern was for you, my lady. Shall you object to spending the night in the open?"

"You're in charge," Judith said. "I don't know this world."

Berengar sighed. "You still insist upon that? Truly you are fair enough to be Sybille, and the Durandines fought mightily to keep you as their prize. But if you are not ready to trust me—"

"I'm trusting you," Judith pointed out, "with my life. Which you just saved, I think. But I'm not your missing elf-queen, any more than Lisa was."

Berengar looked startled, and drew breath to speak, but Judith didn't give him a chance. "And really, Berengar, after hearing Lisa's story, I do think you people need to exercise a little more discrimination. You can't just keep collecting fair-haired young women out of our world in the hope that one of them will turn out to be Sybille."

"Lisa came to us," Berengar said, "we didn't take her. And it was the Durandine monks, not my people, who forced you against your will into this world. But—I take your point." He sighed again. "It is very complicated, is it not? I am not used to thinking this hard."

"Apparently," said Judith, "nobody in this world is. For goodness' sake, let's find a place to rest for the night, and you can tell me all about it—I have a feeling Lisa only told me half the story, if that. If we go over the evidence carefully maybe we can think of some better way to find Sybille."

Berengar laughed quietly to himself. "If you are indeed not Sybille, you might pass for her in a pinch. No one outside of the ruling house of Poitiers has given me so many orders in so short a space of time. Perhaps—"

He broke off and they all listened, frozen, to a sliver of bright music that cut through the upper air. Three notes of a silver horn, no more, but it was enough to remind Judith that she was in a strange and deadly place. The effect on Giles was even worse. He leapt to Berengar's side and tried to climb him like a frightened child, as if the only safety in the world was to be found in the person of this tall elf-lord. "Did you hear that, didn't you *hear* that?" he demanded, almost stuttering in his fright. "Why are you two standing around *talking*? Come *on*! We have to—have to—"

Berengar gently detached the boy's clinging grip but kept one thin grubby hand in his. "Softly, softly, little peddler. If you knew anything of hunting, you should know that the running quarry is soonest sighted. Let you get up on Fleurdevent with the lady—he is rested enough to bear you a short way— and I will walk beside and guide you. We have time enough to reach the Stonemaidens before sunset, and I dare promise you that even the Huntsman will not profane that circle."

"I can walk too," Judith said quickly.

Berengar looked surprised but approving. "So? Good, we will make better speed if Fleurdevent does not have too much to bear. I would not have thought to ask it of you; most gently bred ladies would not set foot to ground in our wildwood. Though I must admit," he said, looking her over with a glance of even warmer approval, "that you are dressed more sensibly for the exercise than most of our ladies. If you are indeed not of the elf-kind, who molded that robe so closely to your shape?"

Judith felt her cheeks growing warm. Nobody in Texas thought twice about seeing a woman in tight jeans. But from the way Berengar was looking at her, she could guess that this world ran more to loose, enveloping robes and flowing draperies.

The really unsettling thing was that in other circumstances, if she hadn't been quite so tired and frightened, Judith thought she might have quite enjoyed Berengar's attention. How Nick would have teased her! *Collecting another one, sister? Don't you have enough on your mind already?*

She had, of course. "Er—we have, ah, mages who make a specialty of such work," she said finally. "Hadn't we better be getting on?"

They paced slowly down the broad path, one on each side of the white horse, occasionally talking across the horse while Giles sat proud and straight with his knees gripping the saddle tightly. Judith thought that perhaps he was pretending to be a knight. Fair enough, if it took his mind off their problems. She herself was pretending that nothing unusual had happened, that it was the commonest thing in the world to be walking at dusk through an enchanted wood. In particular, she was pretending that she was not listening tensely for a certain cold music that she had now heard twice in her life and that she knew she would never forget.

Berengar's light conversation helped the pretense to become reality. They were only exchanging desultory comments, but somehow each one gave her something new to think about and opened up a new understanding of the world into which she had tumbled that afternoon.

"I gather that we seem slow and stupid to you," he said once. "But . . . things do not change very quickly here, and the elvenkind are accustomed to having some centuries in which to think over each new thing. Your impatience makes me believe that you are, indeed, mortal. It is part of the terrible beauty of your kind; why you are so dangerous to us, even when you do not bear iron."

"Our legends," said Judith, "say that you are dangerous to us, not the other way around."

"My experience, brief though it is, suggests otherwise." Berengar gave her a long steady look across the white back of his horse. It was too dim in this deep part of the wood for Judith to read his expression. She knew what she would have thought about his comments and glances, in her own world; but here? *Don't get distracted!* she commanded herself. *You have to remember the main point of your situation.*

And which main point was that? That she was lost in an alien world, with no idea how to get home, with a bunch of mad monks chasing her and something worse hinted at by the silvery hunting music she had heard, strolling through the woods with a handsome but slightly dim elf-lord and a grubby little street urchin? "I take it back," Judith muttered to herself. "Let's go for the distraction."

"Your pardon?"

"Nothing. I was talking to myself." Judith flashed

Berengar her best smile. "Tell me more about the charms of your world."

"Would that they could charm you, fair stranger! Alas, my enchantments fail me, and I shall need to call upon the Great Khan of the Eastern Horde to lend me his skystone, the one that gave him mastery over half the mortal world, only to protect me from one mortal woman . . ."

He went on in that vein of nonsense for some time, and Judith was grateful to him for it; he kept her laughing, and surprised, and altogether too busy fending off his nonsensical flirtation to think about what kind of hunters could worry an elf-lord with Berengar's powers.

She was almost sorry when she glimpsed an open space through the trees, and Berengar announced that they had reached their destination. Then a bend in the path gave her a clear view of the place he had called the Stonemaidens, and her heart skipped. Yes, this was it—the place where she had come into this world—but something was terribly wrong. The wavering image of the office in the XCorp building was gone; she looked through the arch and saw only the green turf, the standing stones at the back of the circle and the forest behind them.

"Who has broken the Gate?" Berengar demanded. Fleurdevent halted abruptly and Giles slid forward, down the horse's neck, to land on the ground with his usual undignified thump.

Giles ignored their doubts and fairly hurled himself forward, through the arch and into the protected circle of green turf. Nothing happened; no shimmer of air disturbed and worlds drawn too close for a moment, no breath of the space between the worlds. He was still there on the other side.

A long cold musical note shrilled in the darkening sky and Judith found herself on the far side of the arch, within the circle of standing stones, before she had quite decided to risk it. The bright clarity she had sensed here before was still strong, but something was missing. It was like a power plant that had been turned off, full of potential but with nothing going on now.

Berengar followed more slowly, with Fleurdevent pacing behind him. Once they were all inside, the white horse lost its air of nervous tension, lowered its head and began placidly cropping the grass as if it were in any common meadow.

"What's wrong?" Judith asked. She did not want to ask the next question, and she did not have to. Berengar answered of himself.

"The circle will still protect us; can't you sense the power in the stones? But the gate between the worlds has been closed. Who has been here?"

Judith shook her head in bewilderment. Her one hope of getting home again had rested in finding her way back to this place. Now Berengar was telling her that it would not work, that she couldn't go home the way she had come. But—perhaps it was not the same place, after all? She didn't know these woods, let alone this world. They had come here by a different path; the monks had taken her along the banks of a stream, not straight through the woods.

Judith determinedly ignored the faint gurgling of a stream nearby and prowled the circle of stones, looking for some sign that this was not the place where she had entered this world. Instead she found the proof she'd been desperately hoping not to see, and with it, something that made her feel dizzy with fear and hope.

The crescent-shaped chip in the stone was there where it had been that afternoon. And below it, something small and hard twinkled among the close-set blades of grass.

"Look!" She picked up her find and showed it to Berengar. He flinched away.

"An evil thing."

"What? Oh—iron? Sorry." Judith's hand closed around the small object. "I forgot. You see, I know this particular thing. It's my brother's pocketknife, the one he always uses to slit open letters. Nick must have been here. I knew he would come for me!"

"Then where," Berengar asked, "where is he now?"

Around them, the woods were dark and empty and silent. And no matter how often Judith called Nick's name, nothing answered her but the icy notes of a silver horn.

CHAPTER THIRTEEN

You have all heard of my lady Sybille, the fairest of all the queens of Elfhame. Now the lord Joffroi of Brittany was courting her, but she would not receive him as her true lover despite all the love and honor that he did as her faithful knight; so in his anger he turned his hand against the lady and all of Elfhame, saying that when he was king of Elfhame and she a supplicant, he would show her more tenderness than she had given him. Therefore he conspired with a mortal wizard's apprentice to do great treason against the realm. And this song shows how the lady Sybille gave her life to save the realm, but was too late to keep the powers of the realm from departing the land; wherefore may all ladies mortal and elven remember to give more mercy to their knights who love and honor them than did Sybille to the lord Joffroi!

—Troubadour's preface to the *lai*
of Joffroi and Sybille

Nick and Lisa had left the circle of stones long before Judith returned with Berengar and Giles. If they had followed the broad path that led to the village of St.-Remy, and beyond that to the Remegius monastery, the two parties would have met in the forest. Unfortunately, both Nick and Lisa were far too intelligent to go charging into a stronghold of their enemies with no help and no definite plan.

At first they didn't go anywhere; Lisa knelt on the springy green turf beside Nick and tried to persuade him to open his eyes.

"Mmmph," Nick mumbled. He had drawn his knees up and wrapped his arms about his head. Everything he said was muffled. "Go away. This is not happening. I am not here."

"That," said Lisa, "is not logical. I thought you were a lawyer!"

Nick raised his head and gave her an exasperated look. "Precisely. I am a lawyer, not a damn hero of one of Judith's damn fantasy novels. I always thought those books were unrealistic, and I was right."

"How can you say that when you're *here*?" Lisa cried.

"Not unreal," Nick corrected her. "Unrealistic." He got up slowly and carefully and looked around him. "In those books Judith reads, the hero gets transported back into—oh, some alternate universe roughly compatible with medieval England—and he takes about three pages to say, 'Oh, here I am in an alternate universe, let's go slay some dragons.' I always thought any normal person would be more likely to curl up in the fetal position and refuse to move until all the impossible stuff went away."

"Then," Lisa said bracingly, "isn't it a good thing you're not normal!"

"I am also not the hero," Nick told her. "What you want is a knight in shining armor. I'm a struggling lawyer from a dusty little Texas town, and I want to go back there. Now."

"What about Judith?"

"Yes. Well. Judith." Nick spoke slowly, as if he were trying desperately to remember his past life. "Yes. Let's get Judith and—go back? Please?"

Lisa remembered all too well the way she had felt when she first crossed between the worlds. Nick needed time, and a practical problem to concentrate on—she had been, she supposed, lucky that she'd had some immediate problems to solve.

"I think they will have taken Judith to the Remigius —that's the nearest Durandine monastery."

"Will they be there by now?"

Lisa shook her head. "I don't know. We were delayed an awfully long time at XCorp. She might be."

"Time," Nick said. He stared up at the brilliant blue of the sky and tried out the word on his tongue several more times, as if he were tasting it for poison. "The sun was shining on the sea," he said in a conversational tone that made Lisa wonder if he'd decided to go mad rather than face the change in worlds, "shining with all his might; and this was odd, because it was the middle of the night."

"Oh—Lewis Carroll!" Lisa belatedly recognized the poem. "Nick, is this any time to quote poetry? If you've stopped being scared, can't you be serious for a moment?"

"I haven't stopped being terrified," Nick said. "I've just decided that the fetal position is too cramping for a long-term solution. And I am being quite serious. Last thing I recall—last *reasonable* thing," he corrected himself, "it was quite late at night. This looks like mid-afternoon. Have I somehow skipped eighteen hours, or what?"

"Oh!" Lisa felt physically ill. She had managed to

put this problem out of her mind for a little while. "Time seems to run differently between the worlds."

"*How* differently? How long has it been since Judith passed through here, can you tell?"

Lisa shook her head. "We were, what, half an hour behind them? I don't *think* such a short time span would be very much different. But I don't know," she said miserably. "I just don't know. All I know is that a few years in one world can be hundreds of years in the other."

"Mmm. Like the old legends—wander into a fairy hill and you're gone for seven years?"

"N-not necessarily." It could be a lot more than seven years. It could be, for all practical purposes, forever . . . To her horror, Lisa felt a lump rising in her throat, almost choking her. She turned away from Nick and stared into the dark green forest, fighting the urge to burst into tears. She had managed to keep calm for so long; couldn't she hold together a little longer?

Nick's hand was warm on her cheek, forcing her to turn back to face him. She blinked away the tears gathering in her eyes.

"Don't cry, Lisa," he said gently. "It's only an old story. It's not going to be that way. We are going to find Judith and get home again, and it's not going to take any seven years." He pressed a large white handkerchief into her hand.

Lisa blew her nose once and found that the urge to cry had passed. "Are you always so well equipped?"

"A lot of people cry in lawyers' offices," Nick said. "My office, anyway. Corporate law is probably much calmer. Me, I'm usually defending Arturo Ruis against seven simultaneous charges of drunk and disorderly and his sister is explaining what a good boy he always was. Now. About those dragons we're going to slay; do you have any idea how many of these—what did you call them? Durandines?—how many Durandines are at this monastery?"

Lisa tried to remember her glimpse of the Durandines that had accompanied Bishop Rotrou when he came to St.-Remy. "I saw, oh, maybe twenty at one time. But that was just the ones who came with the bishop; there may have been more at the monastery."

"Doesn't make much difference," Nick said. "As you've already seen, one lawyer isn't even a match for two monks, let alone twenty, or forty, or whatever we're up against this time. I'm afraid you and Judith didn't pick a very good hero to slay your dragons. I can't even handle a little thing like being transported to an imaginary world."

"Stop that," Lisa said, suddenly furious. "I will *not* have you putting yourself down because two evil men caught you off guard and used magic to overpower you. We cannot afford to have you indulge in the luxury of depression. You're doing much better than I did when I found myself in a different world; you talk about babbling, well, I literally did, I'm lucky I wasn't locked up in an insane asylum, and I didn't even have the excuse of surprise, I should have known what I was getting into. But now I don't have time to be upset about—about all that has been happening, and neither do you. I need you to use your brains. Nobody's expecting you to rescue Judith with your bare hands; we have to think of some way to get her out of there." *Quickly!* she added, but only to herself; there was no point in adding to Nick's burdens.

"Point taken," said Nick with a wry smile. "All right, I'm thinking, I'm thinking . . . Do you know how the monastery is laid out? Where they might be keeping Judith? Is there a women's section? Would she be alone? Is there any way we can reach her without alerting everybody in the monastery? Do they have walls? Guards?"

Lisa shook her head unhappily to all but the last two questions. "I'm sorry, I've never been there," she apologized, "but of course the buildings will be walled, and of course there'll be a gatekeeper and a watchman; only a fool would leave a rich place like a monastery unguarded."

Nick looked at her with more careful attention than he'd given anything since he first came into the elven world. Lisa felt hot and uncomfortable under his slow, measuring stare; it reminded her of the way he'd first watched her, when he suspected her of unknown crimes, before they became allies. *Were* they allies? She hadn't stopped to consider the question lately—and from the look of him, neither had Nick.

"You seem to know quite a lot about this world," he said finally. "*Of course? Only a fool?* How do you come to be so certain about the way things normally run here? I thought you were only here for a day."

"I am," Lisa said, "not entirely illiterate. It's a preindustrial, feudal culture. Apart from the elvenkind, it seems quite similar to your twelfth-century France, and I am assuming it operates much the same way."

"*My* twelfth-century France?"

"You said that was where we were," Lisa pointed out.

"My exact phrase, as I recall, was 'medieval England'."

"*Lawyers.*" Lisa glared at him. "Do you want to quibble over phrases, or do you want to *do* something?"

"I'd love to do something, I'm just trying to figure out what to do!" Nick snapped at her. "I thought we'd agreed that it would do no good for us to go charging in blindly. Or do you think it would cheer Judith up to have us locked in adjoining cells? This is my sister we're talking about, remember. I want to get her out of the Durandines' hands, and I'm willing to try anything within reason to do so. Now *do* you think you could apply your powers of reasoning to figuring out where, in a medieval universe complete with elves and dragons, we're going to get some help?"

"Count Berengar," Lisa said promptly, having come to the obvious solution while Nick was ranting at her. Now that he was recovered enough to be acting bad-tempered and lawyerly again, she felt calmer. "The elvenkind are no friends to the Durandines; I think Berengar will be glad of an excuse to give them some trouble. He can say that Judith is one of his serfs and that he wants her back. No, that won't work, they know she isn't from this world. Well, then, he can say—"She scowled at the silent stones around them.

"Let it wait," Nick advised her. "How do we find this Berengar?"

"His keep is on the river," Lisa said, "the Garron. If we follow this path along the stream to St.-Remy and then turn south along the river, we should come there. But St.-Remy is awfully close to the Remigius. And that way will take too long. Maybe . . . oh, I *wish* I knew this area better!" She stared at the green circle of woods outside the ring of stone. The broad track leading to the village was clear enough to see. There was another, narrower path that started off towards the south, in the general direction of Berengar's keep; but it turned and twisted and lost itself in the gloom of the forest.

"By virtue of your previous day's experience," Nick said, "you're the local expert. Which way do we go?"

Lisa pointed at the broad path along the banks of the stream. "The only sensible way to go is that way. We know where it leads, and the villagers may be able to give us directions."

"If," said Nick grimly, "they don't turn us in to the

monks as suspicious strangers. What about the other path?"

"I wish I could be sure. If it leads to Berengar's keep, it would be a much better way to take."

A flicker of light shimmered among the trees. "Look out!" Nick shouted. He dived for the ground and tried to pull Lisa with him as the fireball darted towards them, but she broke free and stood in the center of the circle of stones, hands clasped just below her breasts. The light grew into a glowing shape of fire that turned Lisa's long loose hair into a burning halo and made her tired face almost beautiful in the reflected radiance. While she watched and Nick slowly, shamefacedly got to his feet, the fireshape danced in and out between the tops of the standing stones, whizzed round the circle in a spiral and finally settled at the narrow opening of the second path.

"Zahariel! You weren't hurt?" Lisa rushed towards the fire-thing as if she were greeting an old and dear friend. Nick shook his head slowly and followed her. He was beginning to wish he had obeyed his first impulse and remained in the fetal position.

"I was so afraid the Hounds would take you too," Lisa babbled on. "Did you drive them away, then?"

The glowing shape dimmed from fiery red to a pale golden glow that shivered around the edges. Within the light Nick could now make out a slender body as long as his arm, topped by a small head with curling hair and dwarfed by the great feathery arcs of wings that swirled behind it like a train of light made palpable.

"The dragon, I take it, is on our side?" After his disgusting display of cowardice when they came through the Gate, Nick would be damned if he would show this—thing—how he felt about conversing with a transparent fire-shape.

"Nick, how can you be so rude!" Lisa snapped

over her shoulder. "Imagine calling Zahariel a dragon; it doesn't look at all like one. Haven't you ever *seen* a dragon?"

"No," Nick said, "and neither have you. What is it, then?"

"My friend," said Lisa. "It saved me from the Hounds—don't you remember, I'm sure I told you that part of the story. It—oh, don't be ridiculous, Zahariel."

Nick remarked that he hadn't heard the fire-thing say anything.

"You can't hear it? Oh . . . well, it said that it was still my debtor. It thinks I saved its life in the stream, and it says holding off the Hounds while I ran through the gate doesn't count as repayment because I would have made it anyway. Oh, and it says to tell you it is an angel of fire, not a dragon or a fire-thing, and it *does* wish the mortals in this world would stop calling it names. Who else has been calling you names, Zahariel? Oh, well, you should have known better than to go near the Remigius; those Durandine monks don't like any form of life they can't control. I'm not surprised they said the prayers against demons at you . . ." Lisa's voice trailed off and she cocked her head to one side, listening as intently as if she could really hear a voice inside the shape of fire. "It is? Good. Can you guide us? Yes, I *know* guiding us won't save a life and therefore doesn't constitute repayment of your debt. You could just do it as a favor to a friend. Oh, *thank* you, Zahariel!"

The fire-thing glowed and expanded into a brilliant sphere. "Watch out, Lisa!" Nick threw himself at her and knocked them both flat on the ground just as the burning sphere whizzed over them.

Lisa rolled over, spat out grass, and shoved Nick off her with a sharp elbow. "*What* do you think you're doing?" she demanded furiously.

"Uh—saving your life." But he didn't feel as certain of that as he had a minute ago. He pointed at the glowing sphere of light, now poised over the tip of the stone arch. "That thing was going to go right through you. Probably burn you to a crisp."

"No such thing. It wanted to share energies with us—and I need it, even if you don't." Lisa rose to her feet and Nick stood with her, feeling rather sheepish. It took all his will to stand there while the fire-thing approached, shimmered, surrounded them . . .

He forgot to breathe. It wasn't a burning fire; it was like being immersed in air that bubbled like champagne, like seeing the world in a light that showed every detail in loving and joyful clarity. For a long moment Nick felt as if he could understand and balance all the contradictory books and statutes and legal decisions he had crammed into his head, measure human justice against human need and weakness and find the perfect balance that always eluded him in practice. Then the sphere of cool fire shrank back to a translucent envelope about the feathery shape of Zahariel, and Nick felt all the understanding and wisdom and joy evading him again.

He looked at Lisa and saw that there were tears in her eyes, too. She held up her hand; the bandages were gone, and smooth new skin had replaced the puffy blisters Judith had treated.

"I—never felt anything like that," Nick said. It was the closest he could come to confessing how totally wrong he had been.

"Nor I." Lisa smiled, but her mouth was still tremulous. "I think I understand, now, why men and women lock themselves away from the world to pray. It would be worth giving up the world to come that close to God."

"God?"

Lisa looked at him reprovingly. "Zahariel *is* an angel," she pointed out. "Now we must go on." The angel rose before them, gliding smoothly up to the arch of branches that shaded the beginning of the narrow path. "It says it will guide us to Berengar's keep," she told Nick, "and a good thing too, because even if we had chosen the right way through the woods, I don't know what we would have done about the illusion-spells he sets about the place."

"The what?"

"You'll see when we get there," Lisa informed him impatiently. "Come on."

Zahariel was not the most reliable or steady of guides. The angel tended to become bored with the slow pace of its mortal companions and to take darting side-trips off to investigate anything interesting it saw along the way. In between side trips, it treated Nick and Lisa to a dazzling light show, whirling and dancing above their heads like a fiery winged acrobat —which was not, Nick thought, such a bad description. Both he and Lisa tripped and walked into briars and suffered a number of small cuts and scrapes before they learned to keep their eyes on the path, not on Zahariel.

"All it's really good for," Nick complained after he'd walked into a thorn bush while watching Zahariel change colors from fire-red to glowing aquamarine, "is to warn us if we stray too far in the wrong direction."

Lisa gave him a cool measuring glance. "And that's worth quite a lot, when we've got the maze of little paths in this forest to contend with."

"Yes. That's funny, don't you think?"

"Why? What did you expect, a freeway?"

"Well. That place where we came through—if it's a gateway to other worlds, I should think it would be rather important. And you claim this Berengar is an important man. Why isn't there at least a decent road between his house and the gateway?"

Lisa sighed. "Mortals don't usually go to the Places

of Power, they can't use them. And elvenkind don't need a road."

"You do seem to know a lot about this world . . ."

"And another point," Lisa interrupted him, "it's not a gateway between the worlds. Not any more. Thanks to you."

"*Me*? I'm an innocent bystander!"

"I bet a lot of your clients say that, too. If you didn't mean to close the gateway, why did you tear the picture out of the book as we passed through?"

Nick looked bewildered. Lisa stopped in front of him, reached into his jacket pocket and pulled out the crumpled page from the Nielsen book. It was just a piece of paper with a pretty picture on it now, with no hint of the magic that had shimmered about it when it was being used as a gateway.

"I didn't even realize I had done that," Nick said. "I was surprised when the world started changing around me. I do remember trying to hang on to Cliff's desk. I guess I grabbed the book by mistake."

"And tore out the page," Lisa said, "and closed the gate. Which is another reason to find Count Berengar. It takes elvenkind to open a gateway; mortals can't do it. We don't just need his help to rescue Judith, Nick. We need his help to get us back again."

That information shocked Nick into silence for quite some time. For the rest of their tramp through the forest he did not speak. And when they emerged from the cool green shade of the forest to stand on the steep banks of the river Garron, just before sunset, his mouth fell open and he was quite unable to speak for a few minutes.

"Come on," Lisa said. "It's getting late." She nudged Nick and he awoke with a start from his brief trance.

"I—yes. Sorry. It's just . . ." Nick made a vague helpless gesture at the glory of sunset-tinged clouds and sparkling mist that filled the gorge, with a silver thread of river singing at the bottom of the cliff. "I never *saw* anything like that before!"

"I know," said Lisa more kindly. She supposed that after the dusty gray-green streets of Austin and the hills covered with dry thorny scrub, the sharp sweet clarity of this world must come as a perpetual joyous surprise to Nick. "It is beautiful. But it's getting dark, and Nick, we do not want to be outside after dark. Really. And Zahariel is impatient; it isn't used to the concept of doing favors, and it seems to get bored easily. We don't want it to fly off and leave us."

Nick looked up and down the long misty cliff once more. "Can't we find our own way from here? Didn't you say Berengar's keep was on the river?"

"Illusion-spells," Lisa said patiently. "Remember? You're standing in one now."

"You mean all this isn't real?"

"Oh, yes. It's real enough. But your desire to stand right here and watch the clouds changing color for the rest of your life—*that* isn't real. It's one of the traps the elvenkind put out to deter casual visitors. I can't tell you how many mortals get this close to an elflord's keep only to stare at the rainbows until they forget what they came for, and go home talking about the beautiful sights they saw on their day in the country."

"Why doesn't it affect you?"

"It does," Lisa said. *Oh, yes, it does; you'll never know how much.* "It's just that—"

"I suppose you had to fight it off when you were here before."

"You could say that," Lisa agreed. "But mostly it's that—I want to go home," she said. "I really do." It seemed to her that she'd been saying that all her life. But now, when it was impossible for her, she knew how much she meant it. "And these first traps only catch people who don't really need to see an elflord."

"Doesn't seem as if they'd be much use against an army, then." Nick tore his gaze away from the enchanting, ever-changing vista of clouds and water, and followed Lisa along the rocky path at the edge of the cliff. Ahead of her, Zahariel's flashing radiance made the sunset sky seem dim by comparison.

"You'd be surprised," Lisa called over her shoulder. "Many a baron has lost half his army, or more, in one of the longing-traps. The mercenaries, who'd follow anybody for the right pay; the small-holders who had to polish up grandfather's rusty armor and unhitch a plow-horse because they owe knight service when the lord calls for it; the allies who aren't entirely sure they care to go to war against the elvenkind. It's hard enough to keep an army together through a long boring siege as it is; elven spells just intensify the natural tendency to think of excuses to go home."

"Umm. I see your point. Even in modern armies, I don't suppose very many of the soldiers are there because they really want to fight a particular war. But . . ." Once again, Nick thought that Lisa seemed to know a lot about this world, more than one would expect her to pick up in the day and a night she'd spent here before.

"And another thing," Lisa went on hurriedly, "it's hard to keep your mind on besieging a castle that looks just like a piece of tree-covered hillside. The soldiers keep thinking, maybe it's really only a hill, maybe the real keep is somewhere else, maybe they're wasting their time."

Nick looked dubiously at the steep hill to his left. "You mean that could be the castle?"

"Exactly. And that could be an illusion set to keep you from walking through the open gate." Lisa pointed to one of the man-size boulders that swelled out of the hillside at intervals.

Nick paused and reached out a hand to touch the

rough, lichen-encrusted surface of the stone. "Very convincing illusion."

"They usually are," Lisa said calmly, "if you go at them slowly like that. You have to know that they are illusions, and walk right through them as if they didn't exist."

Nick backed off a few paces and stared at the boulder. It looked very solid and real indeed. "Well, if you say so . . ." He took three brisk paces forward, aiming at a point somewhere below the surface of the stone, and ran his knee and forehead into solid rock.

"Jesus!"

"I only said it *might* be an illusion," Lisa pointed out as she walked on. "This, on the other hand, really is an illusion."

Nick's head hurt and his knee was stiff and he had been following Lisa without really looking where he was going. Now he looked down and froze. An inch before his right foot, the solid rock of the path fell away into nothingness. Far, far below him he could see the silver thread of the river, and the jagged rocks that would break his falling body. He jerked back convulsively.

"Come *on!* It's getting dark!"

Lisa was standing in the middle of the empty air. Nick looked, swallowed, looked again and closed his eyes. If he didn't see the air beneath his feet, it wasn't quite so bad. He inched forward with an agonizingly cautious shuffle, hands before him.

Cool fingers clasped his right hand, and he found it a little easier to go on. "You can look now," Lisa's voice said, "we're past that illusion."

The ground was real and solid now—at least, Nick corrected himself, it *looked* real enough. The only thing he was sure of was Lisa, standing just before him and looking tired and impatient and thoroughly human. "Lisa," he said, "I think I love you." He threw his arms round her and hugged her. *This* was real: too thin, but a warm, breathing, part of his world.

"Enough!" Lisa gasped. "You're hurting me!"

"Sorry." Nick released her. "You understand, after crossing that particular illusion, I feel like kissing the ground—only I'm not sure that's real."

"So you thought you'd kiss me instead? As a substitute for the ground? Thanks for the compliment!"

Lisa spun round and marched up the path, stiff-backed and radiating righteous indignation. Far ahead, Zahariel was a golden glow against the deepening blue of the twilight. Nick followed, favoring his bruised knee slightly and feeling just a little happier than he had since this terrifying adventure had begun. Surprised, yes, but happy. The world was full of new and interesting possibilities. The path was broader here; he limped up to Lisa's side and took her hand. "I meant it, Lisa."

"No, you didn't," she said flatly. "You're just lost, and scared, and you think I'm going to be able to solve everything because I happen to know a little more about how this world works than you do, and you don't want to let me out of your sight. That's not love. That's just—finding me useful."

Nick blinked a little at this comprehensive rebuttal. But after a moment, he stopped feeling bruised on his own account and began to wonder what made Lisa so sure that she could only be useful, not lovable or desirable. "I have a feeling," he said eventually, "that I'm being tried for a crime somebody else committed."

"I don't know what you're talking about." Lisa pulled her hand free and marched on ahead of him. Nick thought he heard a faint sniffle, though, and that increased his faith in his guess.

"Maybe some other man, somewhere, pretended to love you because he wanted to use you," he hazarded. "That doesn't make it a universal rule. You shouldn't try me for that crime; I'm not guilty. I have an alibi. I was somewhere else at the time. I didn't even know you then. So you and I can start fresh."

Lisa stopped and turned to face him, so suddenly that he almost bumped into her. "No."

"What do you mean, no?" Nick protested. "It was a good argument."

"I can't. Start over. I made a bad mistake last time. I'm not going to do that again."

"You can't spend your entire life locked in a shell because you're afraid of getting hurt!"

"Don't you see, don't you *see*?" Lisa blazed at him. As if it responded to her feelings, the angel Zahariel whirred over her head in fiery circles, letting off sparks that snapped and danced in the darkening air. "It's not just a question of whether *I* get hurt. Last time a lot of other people got hurt too. That's what I can't risk again. I—oh, what's the use? You don't understand!"

"No," Nick agreed, "I don't. Maybe if you tried telling me about it—and I mean telling the truth, for a change—maybe we could find something to do about it."

"It's too late." Lisa walked on for a few paces beside Nick, staring at shapes only she could see in the thickening shadows. "Anyway, you didn't need to make that crack about telling the truth. When I told you about this world before, you didn't believe me. I only spun you that story about drug dealers and mobsters because it was what you wanted to hear."

"Oh, I didn't mean *that*," Nick said. "But I do think I had some reason for not quite believing your first story."

"You mean the inherent improbability of traveling into another world?" Lisa almost smiled. "How did that rock you walked into feel? Highly probable? One hundred percent likely?"

"I mean," Nick said, "that I had a sense you were leaving something out. Just as I did when Judith told me about how you'd come to work at the Center. Great portions of your life are shrouded in mystery, Lisa, and every time somebody tries to find out more you panic or pick a fight or change the subject."

"Ah. So because I don't choose to tell you my life story, what I do say must be untrue? Great reasoning. No wonder you can't make it as a lawyer."

"Who says I can't make it?"

"Well, I wouldn't call defending Arturo Ruiz from seven charges of drunk and disorderly exactly the pinnacle of success."

"I suppose you'd have more respect for me if I were some buttoned-down corporate lawyer bent on fleecing the public—" Nick stopped and shook his head. "Damn it, you're doing it again!"

"Doing what?"

"Picking a fight to avoid talking about yourself."

"Oh? *I* thought," Lisa said, too sweetly, "that I was just trying to get us to a place of safety before darkness falls. Which won't happen, Nick, if we stand here talking for hours and hours." She lengthened her stride and moved ahead of him. Nick caught up with her easily.

"We can walk and talk at the same time," he pointed out, "and changing the subject won't work, either. Your story just doesn't make sense, Lisa. There are too many unexplained gaps in it. To begin with—why does neither Judith nor anybody else have the least idea where you came from before you started working for the Center? To hear them tell it, you just appeared off the street one day, looking confused and in need of help, and Miss Penny gave you a job which you immediately filled like an experienced executive secretary."

"I was confused," Lisa said. "I had—some emotional problems. Which happen to be none of your damn business. I was referred to the Center for counseling. It just so happened that I needed a job more than I needed therapy; and Miss Penny needed someone to organize the place. Every little once in a while, Nick, people manage to help one another. I realize that in your highly successful legal practice you don't see much of that side of human nature, but there are a few of us out there who don't spend every Saturday night shooting up the town and getting drunk."

"Wrong order," Nick said, "Arturo got drunk first and then sprayed the Wal-Mart with a shotgun full of nails. It was closed, by the way, and no one was hurt. Please observe that your childish insults don't bother me in the least; I'm not going to be distracted again. Who referred you to the Center?"

Lisa shrugged. "Does it matter?"

"It matters," said Nick, "that you're being evasive about where you came from. Who referred you? Where were you born? Why don't you have a birth certificate or a social security number? Or even a driver's license?"

"I thought you had an explanation for that. I'm an illegal alien, right? A refugee from El Salvador or Sri Lanka or whatever third world country is exporting illegals this year."

"I suppose there are *some* blondes in El Salvador . . ."

"I bleach my hair," Lisa said, "so that I can pass among all you Anglos."

". . . but I can think of another explanation now," Nick went on as if she hadn't spoken. "You see, Lisa —or whatever your name is—when I met you, I had no idea that the United States was receiving refugees from any place off the known map of the world. I thought it had to be some place like Nicaragua. Despite your appearance. But now . . . You know a lot about this world, don't you? You know about the elvenkind and the standing stones and you're a regular expert on siege tactics and how to raise an eleventh-century feudal army. Rather an impressive fund of general knowledge from a girl who's never driven a car or seen a football game."

"Clearly my interests are more intellectual than yours."

"Someone who tumbled through a gateway from this world to mine," Nick mused aloud as though Lisa had not spoken, "would probably be quite confused, especially at first. She might wind up in the State Hospital, but these days they tend to encourage the harmlessly insane to go out and sleep on the streets. Some charitable soul might refer her to a place that does free counseling, though; I seem to remember that was one of Aunt Penny's plans for the Center, and I think she even got it on some semi-official lists of therapy centers before anybody found out the 'counselors' were crazier than most of their clients."

"Ginevra helped me a great deal," Lisa said coldly.

"I'm sure she did," Nick agreed, "and weren't you lucky you went to her? She's too far out in her own orbit even to notice little things like the fact that her client comes from another world. But somebody in this world put two and two together, didn't they? No wonder they're all convinced you are Sybille. It's the only explanation that makes sense."

"I can touch iron," Lisa said. "The elvenkind can't."

Nick shrugged. "So you say. But no one who was allergic to iron would last a day in our world—not in America, anyway. And I've only your word for it that the elves can't touch iron."

"Check it out with Count Berengar," Lisa suggested without breaking stride.

"I will. But anyway—oh, there are plenty of explanations. Maybe it's not a problem when you change worlds, maybe our iron is different, maybe you found a way around it the same way you learned to speak almost-perfect English."

"Almost?" Lisa was stung. "And what, pray tell, is wrong with my speech?"

"Hardly anything," Nick said soothingly, "but sometimes the words are a little stilted, as though you were thinking in one language and translating into another. Really nothing that anybody would notice— except for the other peculiarities in your behaviour."

"Nobody else thinks I'm peculiar!"

"You picked such a good place to hide," Nick said. "You blend right in with the other crackpots at the Center."

"Like your sister?"

"Judith is relatively sane," Nick allowed. "But any grown woman who reads those fairy tales for adults like Tolkien's books, and more than half believes them . . ."

"Yes. Believing that there might be a world in which magic works and elves are real—that's pretty crazy, isn't it?"

Nick was silent.

"And another thing," Lisa went on in her triumph, "you're wrong about me translating my thoughts into English. I don't know how it worked, but when I first came into your world, I found that my thoughts came out of my mouth in the language of the people around me. It wasn't until somebody used some of your peculiar concepts, like *washing machine* and *freeway* and *touchdown*, that I realized . . ."

For a long moment, the only sound was the crunching of their shoes on the rocky path and the rushing of the river Garron far below the cliffside path.

"I do," said Nick almost dreamily, "I do like a cooperative witness."

Lisa stared straight ahead.

"You wouldn't care to tell me a little more?" he

prodded. "Lisa? Are you there? Or should I just call you Sybille now?"

"I liked you better," Lisa said carefully, "when I first met you in Austin, before you believed any part of my story."

"I—Huh? But I had the impression you couldn't stand me then."

"That," said Lisa, "is absolutely correct. Here we are." She made an abrupt left turn and walked into a large boulder set between two tall green trees. The boulder shivered like mist around her, and through the outlines of rocks and trees and cliffside Nick could see a fantasy of gaily coloured towers and high pointing turrets.

"Wait for me!" The rock seemed to be closing again behind her; he pushed forward and was held by intangible nets, as fine and tangled as knots of human hair and as sticky as honey.

CHAPTER FOURTEEN

Imposito vino inebriabuntur mortales: et postposito coelo in terram respicient. Ab eis vultus avertent sidera, et solitum cursum confundent. Arebunt segetes his indignantibus, et humor convexi negabiture.

> —from the prophecies of Merlin in Geoffrey of Monmouth's *Historia Regum Britanniae*.

(Mortals shall be drunken on the wine that is given to them, and they shall neglect heaven to gaze at earth. The stars shall avert their countenance, and the accustomed paths of the heavens shall be disordered. The green corn shall dry up in the field, and the rains shall be forbidden to fall from heaven.)

It wasn't cold inside the circle of standing stones. Not really. Berengar had told her the nights were mild at this time of year, and he seemed to be right. But physical warmth wasn't everything, and Judith's perfectly adequate T-shirt and jeans did nothing at all to keep out the primitive shiver of fear that ran through her whenever she let herself be aware of the world outside this charmed circle. In here, Berengar had said, they would be safe from whatever beasts prowled this world by night. And Judith trusted him; and beyond that, she could almost feel the protective guardianship of the stones, like silent watchers in the night with invisible hands linked to protect the three who huddled together in the center and the nervous white horse that stood beside them.

But she could sense other things too—things not quite invisible, like a gathering blackness in the shadows, like the glow of eyes where no light should have been, like something breathing and snuffling around the circle of the stones. For what seemed to be hours she had lain still, half her body protected from the dew by Berengar's short cloak, telling herself that the breathing noises were only the wind in the trees and that the slight movements she sensed were only Fleurdevent shifting position on the grass behind them.

Then the urge to *look* had gotten the better of her. Both her companions were breathing slowly and evenly; Judith sat up in one quick motion, stared between two of the silent stones at the edge of the forest, and dared her imagination to do its worst.

Two glowing red eyes regarded her steadily from the far side of the clearing. A moment later they were joined by more red glowing spots, paired two and two and moving low to the ground, and where the bright red spots were thickest Judith had a feeling of transparent shapes squirming and pawing one another. Which was ridiculous. She could not possibly see anything in this darkness.

All the same she was seeing it. And the longer she looked at those things that weren't quite there, the more real and solid they grew, and the quiet snuffling sounds they made became quicker and more excited. Judith locked both arms around her knees and lowered her head and tried to suppress the quiet shivers running through her. *We're safe in the circle. Berengar said so. There's no point in waking him up just because I'm afraid.* Why she should trust him so utterly she did not know; but she did not doubt his word for an instant, and not only because he himself had lain down on the grass and gone to sleep as if he were in his own bed.

"All the same, I *wish* those things would go away," she whispered to her knees.

There was a stir and a rustle beside her, and two thin arms went around her body. "My lady? You see them too?"

"I thought you were asleep," Judith whispered to Giles.

The boy's whole body wriggled with something between a shudder and a laugh. "With *them* sniffing round, looking for a break in the circle?"

Judith thought of the chipped stone by which she'd recognized this place, and wished she hadn't. Surely a flaw that tiny wouldn't constitute a break by which those things could enter? But she didn't know this world, or the laws of this world; and in her own world, a change of one line in a massive piece of software could cause the whole program to crash.

It was hardly a comforting analogy.

"Never mind," she whispered to Giles. She sat up a little straighter and pulled him into the circle of her arms. It was comforting, in a way, to have somebody else to comfort.

"You're not scared, are you? I wish I was that brave."

"The count said we were safe in here," Judith replied obliquely. She, too, wished she were that brave. But it was a little better to be comforting someone else than to be arguing with her own fears.

"We've only to wait till morning, and—what else did he say before he went to sleep?"

"Don't leave the circle, whatever you may see and hear." Berengar sat up with the fluid grace that characterized all his movements.

"We woke you. I'm sorry."

Berengar shrugged. Even that unlovely gesture looked graceful when he performed it. "I had rested long enough. Dawn will come soon."

"Oh, do you think so?" Judith looked doubtfully at the velvety darkness above them. The pinpricks of light that dotted it in swirling clusters meant nothing to her; even the stars were different here. And she could see no streaks of light through the trees that surrounded them.

"The old tales say that *they* are at their strongest just before dawn." Berengar nodded towards the prowling shapes without actually looking at them.

"The old tales," Judith repeated. "You mean—you yourself don't know, then?" She wanted Berengar to say that she had misunderstood him, that these fluid, formless beasts were as common as roaches in Texas and that every elflord knew a dozen ways to squash the pests. When he shook his head slowly, she felt as if she had been cheated.

"Then how could you be so sure we were safe here?"

"No evil thing can come within one of the Places of Power," Berengar said simply. "It has always been so, even now when so much of the power has been drained from our land. The Wild Hunt has not roamed our land freely since long before my time or that of any one living, but since they have returned I have seen enough to know that they are the worst of evils. They take souls either directly, by maiming their victims and drawing them to ride after the Huntsman, or—worse—they make beasts of living men. Those who set you in the woods for a gift to the

Huntsman were ignorant peasants, Giles, scared and cruel in the manner of frightened, ignorant men. But it was an evil thing they did, and if it had worked and if they had continued, month after month, to sacrifice their own to the Dark God—well, I think that the Huntsman would be happy to have such willing servants on earth." He fell silent for a moment, and the heaviness of his voice kept Judith from voicing any of the doubts or fears that plagued her.

"Also," he said, raising his head, "I think they like to be spoken of, and to be feared. So let us speak of other things until the dawn."

Judith nodded, then shivered involuntarily as one of the translucent shapes raised what might have been its head, to stare directly at her with its red eyes. "I'm sorry," she apologized. "You're right. We should think of something else. Only—I've never been afraid of the dark—but I *do* hope the dawn comes soon!"

"Oh." Berengar sounded amused. "Would light help? That is easy enough. It will not even tire me. Forgive me; I thought you left the circle dark because you wished to sleep. I do tend to forget how limited you people are, with your dependence on flint and steel." His hand moved in the air, tracing a pattern that came alive as he spoke with a soft greenish glow. Slowly the complex lines of the pattern wavered, broadened, and dispersed in the air, like drops of green dye disappearing in water; and as the green dye left the water tinged with color, so the pattern of light left the air around them stained with a soft radiance in which Judith could see her companions quite clearly. The forest around them was still dark, and the shape-hounds still prowled round the boundaries of the circle, but now she found it easier to pretend that nothing was real except the three of them in the soft glow of the elf-light.

"Is that better? Good, now we shall tell old tales until dawn," Berengar said. He looked at Judith. "And perhaps we should begin with some newer stories. You have not yet told us how you came here, my lady."

"Don't call me that," said Judith. "I'm just a commoner like Giles here. A *mortal*. You can be as rude to me as you would be to anyone else."

"I beg your pardon," said Berengar rather stiffly, "a lord of Elfhame is trained in courtesy. I am rude to no one."

"Doubtless you don't notice it," Judith said, patting him on the knee. "A lot of racists aren't really aware of their bigotry."

"I do not understand these words."

"It takes time to grasp new concepts," Judith said kindly. "Never mind, I'll be happy to raise your consciousness as we go along."

Berengar shook his head slowly. "I *think* she's insulting me," he mumbled to himself. "No mortal woman would dare. Perhaps she is Sybille after all; who knows? She might have learned to handle iron without hurt in that dreadful world. She says she isn't Sybille. If she is Sybille and she doesn't want me to recognize her, I'd better not; a Lady of Elfhame strong enough to touch iron without hurt could probably turn me into a frog without thinking twice. But if she's mortal, I mustn't let her get away with talking to me like that; the others will get ideas. Ow!" He clutched at his silvery locks. "Woman, my head hurts. Mortal or faerie, I have never known anyone so confusing as you."

Judith thought it might be best not to pursue that argument for the moment, especially the part about turning people into frogs. Instead she launched into her story, beginning with Lisa's appearance at her houseboat on Lake Travis.

"So they only took you because Lisa came there?"

Berengar asked, almost absently. He rubbed his chin and stared into the greenish haze that surrounded them. "And—what was it, again, that their mage said about the Hounds?"

"That was . . . after we came through to this world," Judith said. She frowned, trying to remember. "After Giles threw the bees' nest at them—when we were running away. I wasn't listening properly—and it didn't make much sense anyway. Brother Hugh shouted something about making it rain."

"Making clouds," Giles piped up. "He said, 'If you were any kind of mage, you'd whistle a wind out of the north to becloud the sky, and then we'd have some help tracking the bitch.' " He mimicked Hugh's scratchy voice so well that Judith would have thought the Durandine leader was in the circle with them.

"And then Brother Alured said, 'Are you mad? They grow stronger each dark o' the moon, and it's all the full circle of us can do to hold them in check now.' And Hugh said, 'They'll obey me. I'm their master.' And then—" Giles screwed up his face. "Didn't hear no more. Too far away."

"That's marvelous, Giles!" Judith said warmly. "How ever did you remember all that? I was so busy trying to put one foot in front of the other that I didn't have any idea what they were saying—not that it would have made much sense to me anyway."

"Oh, it makes sense," Berengar said heavily. "It makes perfect sense—and perfect doom. For the elvenkind, anyway—you mortals may be spared, if you'll be content to live under Durandine rule."

He scowled at their blank faces. "Don't you understand? The Durandines are the ones who brought the Wild Hunt—"

There was a low growl from the darkness outside the stone circle, rising from nowhere and growing louder and stronger until it seemed to vibrate all around them. Berengar checked in midsentence and began again, choosing his words more carefully.

"Those whom we don't name," he said, "were strong in this world before, or so the tales say. In the days when all this land was forest, they hunted here unchecked, and the tribes that wandered the land made sacrifice of a woods-gift whenever they entered a new part of the forest."

Giles shuddered and Berengar put one hand out to ruffle the boy's black curls. "No more," he said, and Giles' tense shoulders relaxed. "Never on my land, boy, not while I am still Count of the Garronais. We speak of a past so distant that not the oldest elven scholar in Ys remembers it, nor do the scrolls of learning there record it. That time lives only in the memories of the peasants and in the tales they tell round the fire on winter nights. The tale as I had it from my mortal nurse was that long ago, when the Church and the Elvenkind were new-met, men and elves worked together to bind the One Who Rides. They could not banish him entirely, but they made him a shadow on this earth, without power to do more than frighten. And even that power was not entirely his, for mortal men might say the prayers taught by the church, and the elvenkind might call upon the powers of the Stones, and so they might be protected against that one."

"But those things are more than shadows," Judith protested, "and Lisa said they can kill, not just frighten."

"Now they can," Berengar said grimly. "For many ages the power of the Stones grew weaker in the Land, and the One Who Rides showed himself more and more often—but still without any corporeal existence. It has been a mystery to me how his beasts got claws and teeth, but now I think the mystery unravels somewhat. Elfhame is too weak now to hold the binding, and the other half of the bargain is undone. What the Church bound, the Church can unbind. Yes!" His fist crashed down into his palm. "Why did I not see it before? Oh, I have been blind—blind! Where the One who Rides looses his hunt, the peasants flee from the land, and who takes over the deserted lands? So often, and so conveniently, the lands have been sold to the Order of Saint Durand! Indeed, Master Map was right when he said that wherever those accursed monks go, they either find a desert or make one! He spoke only out of the promptings of malice, but his words were more true than he knew. They have unbound the One Who Rides, and the fools think to control him with no more than weak mortal magics of spells and chants and cantrips!"

"I take it," Judith said, "you don't think they can do it."

"Not for long, no. All the strength of Church and Elfhame together barely sufficed for the first binding at the Stones of Jura. If we could still call upon the Stones, perhaps the One Who Rides might be bound again; but their power was lost at the time when the Lady Sybille left us. Now—" Berengar spread his hands wide. "Saint Durand hated heretics, infidels, and all beings that did not acknowledge the Church. The Order which he founded has maintained the tradition of hatred, but most of all their enmity is directed at the elvenkind. They profess to fear for human kind if powers magical are held anywhere but in the calloused, ink-stained hands of some grubby monk who spends half his short life plowing like a peasant and the other half copying prayers—as if a mortal man would ever have time, in his miserable life span, to begin to understand the higher arts, even had he talent to use them!"

"We really must talk seriously about your racism," Judith said.

"What? Oh—my apologies, Lady Judith. I forget

that you are mortal; in truth you are fair enough to be sib to the Lady Alianora herself."

"Yes, and I'm cute when I'm mad—oh, never mind; it would take too long to explain. I don't know why, Berengar, but I think there's hope for you. Maybe you can learn not to be such a male chauvinist pig in a few hundred years."

"If you are really Sybille," said Berengar, "and you wish to turn me into a pig, by all means do so, if only you will afterwards restore the power of the Stones and bind those who watch us even now."

"I didn't mean—" Judith sighed again. "Skip it. I'm not Sybille. Honest. But *you're* an elf-lord, and you keep telling me how superior your people are. Why don't you go to the Stones and see if you can do anything about this menace? In fact, why don't you get all your people together there? Maybe together you could do something."

"Like what?"

"I don't know! There's got to be some alternative to sitting on your hands and waiting for the Durandines to exterminate you, though. At least you could go down fighting."

"It's no good," Berengar said again. "Do you think nobody's tried to revive the power of the Stones? They were failing even before the Catastrophe; since Sybille vanished, they have been dead to everything our wisest mages could attempt."

"That's true," Giles interjected. "It says so in the song."

"What, urchin! Do you know the ballad of Sybille and Joffroi?"

Giles threw his bony shoulders back and stuck out his scrawny chest. "I know all the ballads in the world," he boasted. "Didn't I used to sing 'em on holy days, t'keep the crowd happy while my master . . . um . . . well, anyway, I know the story."

"While your master cut a few purses here and

there?" Berengar teased. "No matter, lad. Whatever your past was, you're under my protection now. While I hold the Garronais, you have a place with me, for the service you have done to this lady. I fear," he added, "that is not much reward, as matters stand now. But it is all I have to give."

"Giles, would you sing the ballad now?" Judith asked. Perhaps it would distract Berengar from his gloomy thoughts. And in any case, she needed all the evidence she could get. Berengar was so sure their case was hopeless. Perhaps the human viewpoint on Lady Sybille's story would give her a fresh angle.

Giles wriggled and complained that he'd never been able to sing properly since his voice broke, but eventually Judith persuaded him into performing. His singing voice was a sweet husky tenor, quite adequate to the demands of a street ballad. Unfortunately, the song itself told Judith little that was new to her. It was basically the same story Lisa had told her, about the lord of Elfhame who had sought to draw the power of the stones unto himself, the mortal wizard's apprentice who had helped him, Lady Sybille's discovery of the evil pact and the price she'd paid to stop them. In the song, of course, all three died at the end; Berengar explained that Alianora had only recently formed the theory that Sybille had been forced through a gate to another world by the violence of the final shattering.

"Apart from that," Judith mused, "the only differences from the elven part of the story are matters of emphasis. Didn't you say that the power of the Stones was growing weaker even before Sybille's time?"

"So I have always been told."

"But that would only affect Elfhame. And this ballad was composed by a mortal; perhaps that explains why he doesn't mention it."

"The ballad was composed long after the Catastrophe," Berengar said dryly, "so I wouldn't waste too much energy hunting in it for clues if I were you. The poor mortal who made it up probably changed the story to fit the rhymes he could find. Can't blame him though; it's hard for mortals to be happy as poets or musicians. They should stick to things they've got a natural talent for, like fighting or sowing crops."

Judith closed her mouth firmly on the argument that was trying to get out. It was useless, really, to argue about things as hard to measure as musical talent; and they had more important things to think about. "The only other thing I noticed about the song," she said when she had control of her temper again, "was just a matter of emphasis. Your version of the story is mostly about Joffroi of Brittany trying to get the power of the Stones for himself, and failing, and destroying the Stones themselves in the process."

Berengar shrugged. "What else is there to say? It was the greatest single disaster that has befallen Elfhame; it may be the end of us all, now that the Durandines have brought the One Who Rides into being again. Do you mind if I prefer not to think about the details?"

"Yes, I do. One of those details just might have a clue that will save us. Unfortunately," Judith admitted, "the only one I've noticed is just a matter of the different viewpoint. I guess because a mortal composed it, he saw Alun's side of the story as being nearly as important as Joffroi's."

"Who?"

"The apprentice," Judith said with exaggerated restraint. "The wizard's apprentice. The mortal boy who was to have helped Joffroi. In case you didn't notice, nearly half the Song of Sybille is about how Joffroi lured the boy into cooperating by making him false promises of sharing the power of Elfhame with mortals."

"Aye, 'tis so," Giles chimed in eagerly. "There's even a separate song about him—popular with the crowds, it was; before my voice broke I always brought in a good hatful of coppers for 'Alun's Lament'." He sang a few verses half under his breath, coughed, apologized, and explained that 'Alun's Lament' was traditionally sung only by a young boy whose voice had not yet broken.

"Why?" Judith asked.

Giles shrugged.

"Well, never mind. Let me hear that last verse again," she requested.

Mortal turned to mortal's foe,
Elven power to mortal woe,
Too late I know my love betrayed,
too late I see the charm unmade.

Berengar snorted. "Tripe! It could be any one of a dozen of those sentimental mortal ballads about some girl nourishing a tragic love for an elf-lord. Probably came from one of them in the first case—nothing to do with Sybille and Joffroi."

"Yes, it is!" Giles argued. "Just listen to the last verse:

Elven lady, elven lord
Make and mar the ancient ward.
Lady, end the ancient strife,
A mortal pays with mortal life.

"You see? That's about Sybille and Joffroi—and about how Alun repented and paid with his life for his part in the plot."

"Oh, well, maybe so." Berengar dismissed this point without even looking up. "I suppose it may be as you say. Mortals do tend to overrate their part in great matters. Is it important?"

"Not unless—" Judith paused, frowning. "Berengar. Why did Joffroi need a mere mortal to help him concentrate the power of the Stones?"

"Nobody knows. Joffroi didn't say, and where he is

now—" Berengar smiled grimly to let Judith know this was supposed to be a jest—"he can hardly tell us."

"Mmm. Maybe you've got it backwards, Berengar. It's not that mortals overrate their part; it's that you elvenkind are such unconscious racists you don't even see us when we're standing right in front of you."

"I see *you*," Berengar pointed out. "I like seeing you. I should like to see much, much more of you when we have the time and opportunity. Did you know that unions between mortals and elves are not unlawful? The Church has been dithering about it for five hundred years now. They won't bless us, but you wouldn't be excommunicated for your involvement with me."

"Wonderful. Now do I fall into your arms with glad cries of joy? Or do I wait for you to crook your little finger first? Berengar, don't look so confused. It's all right, I know you're a sexist racist bigot and not terribly bright, but I like you anyway. But let's not discuss it now, okay? I am thinking."

Berengar shook his head and turned to Giles for enlightenment. "You're mortal. What did I do?"

"Don't ask me," said Giles. He was too delighted at meeting his first elflord, being rescued by his first elflord, and now being asked for advice by his hero. He truly hadn't found anything offensive in Berengar's manner. "She's a woman," he hazarded at last. "You never know about women, do you, my lord."

Berengar's face cleared and he nodded. "That must be it."

"What must be it?" Judith was not even looking at him.

"You're a woman."

"Mm-hm. I've noticed. You have too. That's nice, and I assure you, Berengar, I fully intend to do something about it when we have the time, but would you just shut up and let me think for a minute?"

"On the other hand," Berengar said, "although the Church has no formal objection, these involvements with mortals generally don't work out well. Look at Alianora—two mortal marriages in a row, and neither of them successful. Louis was bad enough, but Henry was a disaster."

"What?" This time he had rather more of Judith's attention. "Alianora? As in—we call her Eleanor, I think. Eleanor of *Aquitaine*? The one that married Henry the Second of England? Richard Coeur de Lion's mother?"

"He wasn't even king of England when she married him," Berengar said, "which only adds to the mystery of why she would lower herself. At least Louis was a king, but the Plantagenet—impossible!" He threw up his hands. "At least the children favored her. We do need more children in Elfhame, even half-bloods."

"Mm-hmm. There does seem to be a lot of correspondence between our worlds; I always suspected Richard Coeur de Lion was a fairy. But I do wish you wouldn't keep talking about these people as if they were still alive. It's rather confusing."

"They are. Well, not Henry, naturally. But Alianora is, believe me, very much alive." Berengar seemed to pale slightly, but perhaps it was the elf-light that made him look strained and apprehensive.

"Oh. Not that much correspondence. In my world they've been dead for nine hundred years." Judith frowned and muttered some figures. "Eight hundred? Twelfth century means eleven-something; oh, never mind; Berengar, you're distracting me again. I think I've got it. When was the last time the Church and the lords of Elfhame worked together on anything magical?"

"The binding of the One Who Rides, I suppose," Berengar said. "They haven't needed to since—anyway, it would probably be considered heresy for a priest to actually work with us. Even if we would have him."

"You don't do anything with mortals, do you?"

Berengar sighed. "I can think of something I'd like to do with at least one mortal—"

"Wait till we have privacy. And get serious for a moment."

"I am serious. My world is doomed, there is no salvation. The difference in our life spans won't matter if neither of us lives past the next dark of the moon. Can you think of a better way to pass the time?"

"Yes. How about saving the world? No, don't laugh, listen to me, Berengar! I may be a mere mortal, but I am used to thinking about things, and there's only one explanation for what you've told me so far." Judith raised one hand and ticked off the points on her outspread fingers. "First, the last time mortals and elvenkind worked magic together was so far back in history that even the elven scholars at Ys don't have records of it—but it was done at the Stones of Jura. Second, *since* that time, but *before* the catastrophe, Elfhame was suffering from losing the power of the Stones. Third, the catastrophe was precipitated by something unauthorized that Lord Joffroi of Brittany tried to do at the Stones, *for which he needed the aid of a mortal wizard*. And finally, none of the elvenkind, working alone, have been able to bring the power of the Stones back to your realm."

"They weren't working alone," Berengar objected, "all the best mages of Elfhame have shared their waning strength on . . . Ohh." He fell silent on one long-drawn breath, and his eyes sparkled like sun-dazzled sea. "My lady. My very intelligent lady. The power of the Stones can only be drawn back by mortals and elvenkind working together. That was what Joffroi was trying to do, not to bind the power unto himself. That was why he needed a mortal wizard's aid. That was why the strength of the Stones was dwindling in Elfhame before the catastrophe. Why did we never see it? You are brilliant!" He took Judith's hand and kissed her fingertips, one by one, and she decided not to say anything about unconscious racism.

"Not so brilliant," said Judith as calmly as she could, "but used to thinking things out rationally. Mortals are rather good at dull plodding logic." And all the logic in the world couldn't keep her from feeling short of breath and flushed and dizzy when Berengar kissed her fingers. She had the illusion that a rosy glow was replacing the dim greenish sphere of the elf-light.

No illusion; the sky above them was pink with dawn, and the shadowy figures that had prowled about the boundaries of the circle all night had vanished as silently as they came. Judith withdrew her hand from Berengar's and stood up. Her knees trembled slightly, but that might have been from sitting so long on the damp grass.

"We need to go."

"Yes." Berengar shifted position slightly and Judith realized that he couldn't stand up because Giles, at some point in the long discussion, had fallen asleep again on the elflord's knee. She helped Berengar lift the sleeping boy gently. Giles mumbled something that trailed off into a snore and flung out one hand, almost hitting Berengar in the face, but he was too tired to wake up. "Fleurdevent is rested, and so am I, but I think we'd best not use the elf-wind again unless necessary. We should be back at my keep before nightfall. Alianora will be coming there in a few days, with her counsellors from Poitiers. I had hoped that she might meet the Lady Sybille there; instead, she will find what may be of as much worth to Elfhame as the Lady herself. If your insight is correct, you have done us great service, Judith, and Elfhame will be indebted to you."

"Wait a minute." Judith felt unsteady, and hungry, and the thought of being taken to a safe place where there was food and proper beds was very appealing. But something about Berengar's calm, restful discussion of his plans made her feel uneasy. "You mean we're just going to go back to your—your keep, and sit there, and hope that your friends show up some time soon? And then what?"

Berengar looked startled. "Why, the council of the realm will have to discuss what is to be done. It's not something to be lightly undertaken—"

Judith nodded. "Look, Berengar. I don't know how Alianora's counselors operate, but I do know that it can take the Austin City Council three years to decide to pave one pothole. And there wasn't much of a moon last night. Didn't you say—that is, didn't one of the Durandine monks say that the One Who Rides and his beasts get stronger with each dark of the moon? I don't think we have time to sit in a nice safe castle and wait while the lords of Elfhame put it to the vote."

"We don't vote," Berengar corrected her. "Decisions are arrived at by common consent."

Judith groaned. "Even worse. We definitely don't have time to wait for a consensus."

"Well, what else would you propose? Do you think we should just set off for the Stones of Jura and test this half-baked notion of yours, by ourselves, without any proper planning or discussion?"

Judith blinked. "Why—yes. I suppose that is exactly what I think—at least, if the alternative is having the motion tied up in committee for God knows how long." Berengar started to ask a question and she hastily amended her words. "I mean, if we go back to your keep and wait for your friends, it seems that we might have to wait a very long time for them to decide what to do. And if those—things—are getting stronger all the time, I don't think we should wait at all. Do you?"

"When you put it like that, no." Berengar seemed slightly dazed. "You are right, of course. It is just that we of Elfhame usually do not move so quickly. We are used to having time enough to think out what is best. But—you're right," he repeated. "The One Who Rides may not give any of us that much time." Somehow, with the sleeping boy in his arms, he managed to sketch the outline of a courtly bow. "I had not guessed it would be so helpful to take counsel from a timebound one. Your people are always in such haste to accomplish all that you may in your short life spans. It's part of what makes you so dangerously attractive to us, that terrible doomed beauty of mortality. But in this case, mortal sight is clearer then elven wisdom."

Now that he had been nudged into action, Berengar was as quick and competent as Judith could have wished. "The Stones of Jura are less than a day's ride to the east. You and I can try our fortune there tonight, and if we fail we can always return to ask the advice of the council." He hoisted the sleepy Giles up on the saddle and walked beside him, holding the boy up with his good arm.

Despite the golden light now dancing in the treetops, Judith felt a shiver of fear when they stepped out of the protected circle of the stones. But nothing happened; nothing, that is, except that she saw a path where a moment ago she had seen only leaves and thick choking undergrowth of thorny vines. At first glance the path seemed too narrow for even one person, but by the time they reached the edge of the forest it was wide and straight enough for two people walking and a third on a horse, and Judith could not quite call to mind how it had looked before.

CHAPTER FIFTEEN

A certain rustic belonging to the village, going to see his friend, who resided in the neighbouring hamlet, was returning, a little intoxicated, late at night; when, behold, he heard, as it were, the voice of singing and revelling on an adjacent hillock, which I have often seen, and which is distant from the village only a few furlongs. Wondering who could be thus disturbing the silence of midnight with noisy mirth, he was ancious to investigate the matter more closely; and perceiving in the side of the hill an open door, he approached, and, looking in, he beheld a house, spacious and lighted up, filled with men and women, who were seated, as it were, at a solemn banquet.

—History of William of Newburgh

Berengar was not there.

The sentry who'd grudgingly allowed Nick to pass through the bespelled net, on Lisa's word that he was a friend, seemed rather pleased to be able to disappoint the two grubby mortals. Or so Nick thought. Just at that moment, staring bemused at the silver-haired guardian of the gates, he was not quite sure of anything. Zahariel had disappeared when they reached Berengar's keep; presumably he considered his debt to Lisa discharged. And apparently angels didn't bother with trivial small talk like saying goodbye.

"I think I want to go home now," he murmured to Lisa when, following the sentry's directions, they moved on down a pebbled path that wound between thick flowery hedges to reach the pleasure garden behind the castle. Some of the count's friends were gathered there, the man—no, the elf—had said; if the mortals did not wish to rest and take refreshment in the kitchens, they might as well join the party and ask there for what help they might get.

"Why now?"

"I'm not used to feeling short. Or clumsy. Or grubby." And the tall, bonelessly fluid sentry, with his cap of silver hair and his cool slanted eyes, was presumably not the most important of the elvenkind. "I can see why mortals and elvenkind don't get along."

"At least now you should also be able to see that I'm a mere human like yourself."

"If Berengar thought you might have cloaked yourself in mortal disguise," Nick retorted, "who am I to argue? Besides, you just *admitted*—"

"Hush!"

There was a flower-covered arch before them, and beyond the arch, a space of dark green grass set about with stone benches and tables. Over each table hung a delicate globe of tangled silken threads that shone with their own soft silver-blue light, and the translucent polished stone of the tabletops caught the blue lights and held their reflections deep below the surface. Men and women stood in small groups around the tables, talking in high bright voices that danced and rang like clusters of silver bells, and somewhere in the background the song of a flute rippled through the darkening garden.

"All right," Nick said fiercely under his breath. "It's the elvenworld equivalent of those society types in the theatre club, that's all. I'm a lawyer. I can convince a jury. I can work this crowd." And, with Lisa at his side, he strode under the flowered arch and into the blue-lit dusk of Elfhame.

The quality of the air was the first thing that shook him. It was as different, this side of the arch, as a tropical breeze is from a blue norther; soft and clear and calm and holding a gentle light that came from no particular place. In that light everything, near and far, small and large, stood forth with perfect clarity. The sculptured bells of tiny white flowers in the dark grass at his feet were as clear and bright to Nick as the silvery profile of the elflady nearest the arch, who turned to gaze at him with wide dark eyes and delicately arched brows. When her head moved, ten thousand silver ringlets danced like a halo of spun moonlight, and each of them gave off a faint ringing sound.

"At ilka tett of her horse's mane, Hung fifty silver bells and nine," Nick murmured, when he'd meant to say something quite different.

"Oh, no, mortal man," the elflady corrected him with a silvery laugh, "that song is about the Lady of Elfhame. You must not flatter me so!"

He wanted to move closer, to see if she was real, but something tangled around his feet like the nets that had caught him at the door. The air grew thick and heavy and pressed down all around him, making him feel, not bound exactly, but as if it would be unimaginably hard to move. He glanced at Lisa and saw that she was quite still, as though the same heavy air were holding her in place too.

"Just *like* a mortal," said an elflord who stood a

little apart from the nearest group, "can't tell the difference between young Vielle and the Queen herself! Who let these two within the bounds of Elfhame?"

"Make them pay a forfeit for trespassing!" suggested the delicate elflady who had first noticed Nick. "I do love games—although it's hard to find any that mortals play well!" Her tinkling laugh was like the music of her silver ringlets, light and gay and filled with subtle, unnerving discords.

"Don't play with them, Vielle," the elflord contradicted her suggestion. "I don't like your games. Just let them go. Think you Alianora will be pleased to find you toying with mortals when she arrives here?"

"Why not? If you recall, Yrthan, *she* has done more than toy with them!" Vielle snapped.

"Aye, but not even Alianora would admit them to grave councils of the realm." The elflord Yrthan turned slightly towards Nick and Lisa; the silvery glow of one of the lighted nets fell across his face, deepening the shadows and showing lines of fatigue. "That is not to say that I would have approved her decision. We can hardly afford to waste our scanty resources on opening Gates and chasing down faint trails that lead nowhere. But it's done now, and the least we can do is to pretend that we take her quest seriously. I don't know how these two wandered in here, but the usual measures will suffice. We'll put them out on the mountain and tell them it was all a pretty dream. *Now!*"

On the snap of the last word, Yrthan raised his right hand and brought it down sharply in a gesture that cut the dusky air, and Nick felt the invisible weights that had pressed around him flowing away like water running out of a pool.

"Wait a minute!" How long did he have before they threw him out. "We didn't just wander in here—

we came through that Gate you spoke of. You owe us a hearing."

"*Owe?*"

"Is there not justice in this world? How do you normally settle disputes between mortals and elven-kind?" Nick turned to Lisa for confirmation and she nodded slightly. He was on the right track. "Men of this world came through your Gate and took my sister away. We are friends of Lord Berengar's, and came here to ask his aid in rescuing her."

"Men, you say?"

"Monks of the Order of Saint Durand," Lisa amplified.

Yrthan relaxed slightly. "Then it is an affair between mortals and mortals, and not a matter of the elvenkind."

"If your people had not opened the Gate," Nick argued, "my sister would not have been taken."

"I always *knew* it was a mistake. Alianora should have consulted me first!" Yrthan muttered. "Oh, very well."

"You'll help?"

"My boy, we have grave matters of state to consider here. You can hardly expect the high councillors of Elfhame to abandon their deliberations on a mortal chase. If your sister is a good daughter of your mortal Church, then she will come to no harm in a house of holy men. If she is a heretic, then she should have thought of that before she got herself involved with the Durandines, who are hardly noted for tolerance. And besides," Yrthan added with fine irrelevance, "it was not by our counsel that this troublesome Gate was opened. You may wait, if you will, for the Queen of Elfhame to arrive, and when we have finished our own business you may put your case to her for judgment. Or you may wait for Lord Berengar to return, and if you are truly, as you say, friends of his, then perhaps he will be minded to help you. You may go now."

"I can't *believe* you people are so irresponsible!" Nick began.

"They are," Lisa said. She took his hand. "Let's find some place quiet to wait. It won't do us any good to argue with them."

"I will give you a path to the kitchens," Yrthan announced. He gestured again and spoke directly into the high dark-green hedges that surrounded the garden. The rows of small shining leaves parted and Nick saw a narrow path guarded on both sides by flowering shrubs with long sharp thorns.

"I—"

"Come *on*, Nick. It'll be worse if we make them angry!" Lisa whispered. She tugged at his hand. Nick stepped onto the narrow path and turned to say one last thing to Yrthan; but the hedge had silently closed behind them, and the glossy dark leaves and the long intertwined twigs and the waxen flowers grew as solidly together as if they had not been moved in a hundred years. They seemed to be moving slightly as he watched. He followed Lisa down the narrow path, and behind them the hedge continuously grew back together so that they could not take even one step back the way they had come.

"What now?"

"We wait. For Berengar."

"In the kitchen? Who tells us if he gets home? Where do we sleep?"

"I don't know," Lisa said. "Last time I was here I was in the celebrity suite. They thought I was . . ."

"Oh. Yeah." Bits of the wild story he had dismissed came back to Nick. "As Sybille, you'd be a VIP, right? Ummm . . . Want to try being Sybille now?"

"If I were Sybille," Lisa pointed out, "we wouldn't need Berengar's help."

There didn't seem to be any answer to that. Rather

glumly, Nick followed Lisa to an eight-sided stone building where fires blazed and a sweaty woman in a blue dress gave them a tray of something that looked like fruit and roasted birds and honey cakes. All the dishes tasted rather like unsalted oatmeal. Nick thought it must be his fatigue, but Lisa mumbled something about the weakening bonds of Elfhame and failing illusions. He fell asleep while she was trying to explain.

He woke before dawn, with a stiff neck and a cramp in one leg, in a greasy corner behind one of the large fireplaces. The fire was almost out. Someone had pillowed his head on a roll of rags.

Lisa was sitting on the large table, knees drawn up, hands clasped around her legs, watching him as silently as a cat. Her eyes looked unnaturally large in her pinched face. Nick wondered if she had slept at all.

"Berengar's back?" Even as he whispered the hopeful question, he knew he was kidding himself. There were snoring bodies on the kitchen floor, and all the fires were banked. Nick might not know much about medieval history, but he felt reasonably sure that if the lord of the manor had returned people would be running about and shouting and roasting cockantrices and garnishing peacocks and—whatever.

Lisa shook her head. "Not yet."

"We can't wait any longer." Nick uncoiled himself from the greasy floor, feeling new aches and pains pop out of his joints as he straightened. Damn, he was getting old. "I shouldn't have waited this long." Sleeping, while who knew what was happening to Judith?

"You were tired. We needed help." Lisa twisted her hands together, and Nick realized she was under as much strain as he was. "It seemed like a good idea at the time. Now . . ."

Nick nodded. "I know we need help. But I can't

sit here and wait forever. I have to find Judith. Even if it's just me . . ."

"Just us," Lisa corrected.

"You're coming with me?"

"Yes. But first, let's try and find some of the elvenkind. They might know when Berengar will be back. If the hedge will let us back there."

"And if they're willing to take the trouble."

"We will have to explain," Lisa said. "Slowly. And very politely."

There was a path open before them when they left the sleeping kitchen; Nick was not entirely sure it was the same path they'd followed the night before. But it was the only way to go, between the dark shining leaves and the thorny branches and the waxen white flowers.

"They don't understand about time," Lisa said as she walked. "The elvenkind live so much longer than we do, five or six hundred years usually. And even then, they don't die exactly, unless they are unlucky enough to run into an iron blade. They just get bored because they've seen everything so many times, and one day they ride away towards the ocean and are never seen again. To them, it must seem as if we are always in a hurry—and that we don't live long enough to understand anything properly—and that we couldn't understand anyway, not being equipped with superior elven senses and skills."

"And yet you came to them for help."

"Berengar is—different," Lisa said. "Young. He hasn't seen everything yet. He's rash, willing to take risks, impatient—and he seems to be a rather nice guy, too."

"Seems?"

"Well. I only met him that once," Lisa pointed out.

Nick sighed. "*Must* we continue this game? You've

already admitted that you came from this world originally."

"Yes, but not—" Lisa bit her lip and walked on, a little faster; the outflung flowers on the hedge brushed against her face and the tips of the sharp branches could hardly retract fast enough to keep from hurting her. "There is not," she said at last, "a great deal of social intercourse, in the ordinary way, between mortals and the elvenkind. I should think that much would have been clear to you by now."

"Sybille," said Nick softly, "is of the elvenkind."

Lisa whirled and stopped, so suddenly that Nick almost bumped into her. "For the last time!" she shouted, and her angry voice made the hedge quiver slightly and draw back all around them. "Take a good look at me! Do I *look* elven? Do I *act* like those conceited snobs? Have you noticed me casting illusions?"

"I don't know *what* you are," Nick shouted back, nose to nose with her. "I've seen you walk through a rock that I could have sworn was solid, and I've seen you find a bridge that looked like thin air to me, and Judith always said you could lock drawers by looking at them cross-eyed, and—" He swallowed down a rising lump in his throat. "I don't know what you are, Lisa, and I don't care. All I want is to find my sister—"

"My friend," Lisa interpolated quietly.

"—and all you've done so far is to lead me miles out of the way, to beg help from some people who don't seem much inclined to give it. I think I'd do better on my own. And the first step is to get out of here." Nick turned at right angles to the way the path had been growing and kicked at the hedge. To his surprise, the flowering bushes parted before him and their long thorns turned away from his body. He started down the new way that had opened and prayed this wasn't an example of elven humor, to send him wandering through an endless maze.

"Wait! Nick, wait!" Lisa ran after him. He ignored her and plodded on.

"This is what they want you to do," she said. "Damn you, don't you understand? Berengar would feel bound in honor to help us, I know he would, he's not like the rest of them. But if they can annoy you into going away of your own will before he returns, then he'll never know we were here and they can go on with their superior lives without troubling about us. Nick, don't leave the keep now, not this way! Nick—Nick!"

It wasn't a maze, or an elven joke. Nick's last step parted the hedge; before him were rocks and running water and the sky growing light to the east. And along the cliffside path, still blue-shadowed and half in the world of night, a silver-haired boy on a gleaming horse came towards them. Behind him two more horses followed, all pale silvery white, without saddles or bridles or leading-ropes, delicately picking their way along the stony path. "Is this your Berengar?"

"No." Lisa barely spared the boy a glance. "I never saw him before."

"Greetings, lady!" the boy called. "I am Lord Berengar's page. He regrets that he was not here to receive you, and sends these mounts that I may take you to him at once." He looked down at the path as he spoke, and Nick felt a little warmer to the elvenkind; evidently their children were as shy as mortals. And this boy was only a child, for all his formal speech and fine clothes.

"How did you—how did Berengar know we were waiting for him?" Lisa demanded.

The boy looked up, but did not meet her eyes; instead he addressed the tall flowering hedge behind her. "It is not for you to question the elvenkind," he said loftily. "What do mortals know of our ways of sending messages? I have been in realms that would chill the flesh from your bones, woman. It is nothing to me to bear you across the face of the world, if so it be my lord's will. Now will you mount, or shall I return and tell my lord that the mortals are too craven to save one of their own if it needs elven help to do so?"

"I'm with you," Nick said instantly. He stepped out of the arch in the hedge, dragging Lisa with him. The open archway closed behind him, one instant a seamless green wall of leaves and thorns, the next melting into a lichen-encrusted boulder like all the others in the hillside. He felt a moment's misgiving as the silvery horses moved forward, a sense of wrongness. Probably, he thought, it was just that one tended to forget how very large horses were. Nick hadn't ridden since he was a boy, and he had no idea what Lisa's skills were. "But I should warn you—I'm not used to riding. I don't know if I can control your master's horse."

"No need." The boy sounded amused. "In fact, it will not be possible. These horses cannot be mastered."

"Then how—?" Nick bit back his question. Presumably Berengar would not have sent unbroken, wild horses to carry a couple of clumsy mortals to him. Or would he? He had only Lisa's opinion that Berengar could be trusted, and he had seen the brittle elvish sense of humor for himself.

"They will bear you of their own accord to the place where you must go," the boy answered the unspoken question. "If you will lift up the lady, I will assist you to mount in your turn."

"Nick?" Lisa whispered. "Nick, I don't like this."

It was, Nick reminded himself, the first concrete offer of help they had received in this world—and from what he'd seen so far, it might well be the last one. It would not do to offend their only ally by complaining that he wanted a nice high Western-style saddle and a bridle on any horse he rode.

"Berengar is *your* friend," Nick said. He lifted Lisa onto the back of the first horse, and she sat as if she'd been riding bareback in the circus for half her life.

"Bravo!" the boy applauded. "Now you—"

He leaned down, reaching a hand to Nick, and Nick looked for the first time straight into the page's eyes.

There was nothing there.

The perfectly carved face and the silver hair framed two dark empty holes. No, not empty—there were stars wheeling in that darkness, and clouds, and a cold wind from nowhere—

Nick cried out incoherently, dizzy, and tried to pull free, but the boy was stronger than any mortal man. A tug that stretched his bones and muscles drew him up from the solid ground; he turned and twisted in the air, fighting nothing, and felt the cold flanks of a ghostly horse between his knees, and the wind that he'd sensed in the boy's eyes howled around his head.

When he looked down, the cliffside path and the forest and the peaked hills that concealed Berengar's keep were far, far below, dwindling into a child's toys that might be scattered in the wind that bore the three of them onward.

CHAPTER SIXTEEN

And many such have been taken away by the
sayd Spirits, for a fortnight or month together,
being carried by them in chariots through the
Air, over Hills, and Dales, Rocks and Precipices,
till at last they have been found lying in some
Meddow or Mountain bereaved of their sences,
and commonly of one of their Members to boot.

—Scot's Discoverie of Witchcraft

Clouds surrounded the path of the Wild Hunt,
and there were neither sun nor moon to light them
in that rush through the sky; only clammy air hanging on them like grave-clothes, and laughter and
wild cries from things behind them that he dared
not look at, and the haunting notes of a silver
horn urging the horse that carried him to greater
speed.

Lisa rode beside Nick, but they could not speak
over the hellish noises that surrounded them. He
looked at her once, and then looked away; a girl with
a deformed hip, pale as ice, was riding beside them,

and when she turned her head Nick saw that half of her throat was torn out.

At first Nick was afraid he would fall off the horse that was carrying him into the sky. Then, when he saw the company they kept, he tried to throw himself off; and after that he was afraid he would never be able to get off the horse, by falling or any other way. Was this what Lisa had been so afraid of? He tried to remember a story he'd only half listened to at the time, thinking it a fantasy like the ones in Judith's gaudy paperback books. She'd spoken of people maimed and killed by hunting hounds that came only out of the darkness, and of their bodies being taken to ride forever with the huntsman who was the master of those hounds. She had said nothing of living people being carried away by the Wild Hunt; nothing, at least, that he remembered.

But here they were, speeding through the misty air, surrounded by shrieking things out of nightmare. The only logical conclusion, Nick decided, was that they were no longer alive, and that this was Eternity.

Just as he decided this, the light from the rising sun pierced the gray mists that surrounded them. The Huntsman blew one long falling phrase on his horn, something sweet and piercing that embodied all the songs of retreat and death in battle that Nick had ever heard, and the ground came up to meet them too quickly. The horse's hooves hit rocks and dirt, a jar ran up Nick's spine to his head, he slithered backwards and found that the limestone plateau was every bit as hard as it looked, and falling off his horse was quite as easy as he'd always imagined it would be.

When he sat up, rubbing his head, the Hunt had become as translucent as raindrops against the light; and when he blinked and looked again, they were no longer there at all. There was only Lisa, rumpled and grubby and reassuringly mortal-looking despite her gaudy gold and scarlet dress; the gown had split where she'd come down hard on one elbow, and there was blood on the scraped skin.

"What happened? Where are we?"

Lisa shook her head. She scowled at the torn sleeve and as Nick watched, the edges clung together and slowly fused themselves into a seamless whole. Only the gold embroidered vine that danced down from shoulder to cuff was not quite right; there were two places, now, where the curlicued path of the vine was broken. It was chilly on this windswept plain, but that was not why Nick shivered. *Not so mortal, after all . . .*

"Was that the Wild Hunt?"

"We don't," said Lisa carefully, as though she had to think hard to bring out each individual word, "we do not usually speak the name aloud."

"Why not, for God's sake?"

"Do you come when you're called?"

"Sometimes—oh."

Lisa nodded and stood up, as slowly and carefully as she had spoken. Nick watched how she moved and decided that probably nothing was broken. She might be sore and bruised in a few places if she'd fallen off her horse as ungracefully as he had, but that wasn't the problem. It was the feeling of having been whisked into another realm, a world beyond time and understanding, that left you feeling as if something might break if you moved too fast. Nick could sympathize; he'd felt that way when they tumbled through the picture in Cliff Simmons' office and landed on the green grass of this world. Now, though, after that rough passage, and the further strangeness of Elfhame within this world already strange, he felt almost beyond shock. Perhaps later it would catch up with him.

Lisa was standing on tiptoes, almost sniffing the air in her concentration. Nick stood up too, and breathed

deeply. There was salt in the wind, and a hint of
flowers, and something else he could not name. It
troubled him, that something else; elusive, not quite
a scent or a taste, more like a trembling of the air
about them. Whatever it was, it made him want to
go away, very quickly.

"Do you know where we are?" he demanded.

Lisa nodded. "Somewhere close to the Stones of
Jura."

That name, at least, Nick remembered from Lisa's
fantastical story. Near here, then, was another circle
of standing stones, once the center of all power in
Elfhame; and in that circle, too long ago even for
elven memories, there had been a disaster that killed
mortals and elves alike and that left the power of
Elfhame slowly bleeding out of the land.

"I think I can find it," Lisa added. "It will take a
while . . ."

"Then why bother?" said Nick. "*I* want to find
Judith. We don't really have time for sightseeing."

His objections were practical, but the prickling
feeling on the back of his neck and the trembling he
sensed in the air had nothing to do with good sense
and necessary decisions. He wanted to get off this
barren, naked plateau. And he felt quite sure, without knowing how he knew, that whatever direction
the Stones of Jura were in, he wanted to go the other
way.

Lisa swallowed. She was very pale, and her fair
hair hung down in tangled points around her face.
"Because," she said almost inaudibly, "because I have
been running away from this place for a very long
time now, and because I think there must be a
reason that we have been brought here now. And
because if the evil that I brought into this land can
be corrected, then Judith will be safe; and if it can't,
then nobody will ever be safe again. Those who
brought us are not supposed to be able to take living

people, *ever*, even in the old tales. When I first came here they were stronger than ever before, and now they are even stronger. Today the sun stopped them, but not at first light. Do you want to live in a world where those things hunt freely by day?"

"I don't even want to live in a world where they get out once a year on Halloween," Nick said. He thought for a minute. "For that matter, I don't want to live in this world at all."

The shadow of a smile crossed Lisa's face. "Neither do I. And since the Gate is closed behind us, and the elvenkind have little interest in helping mortals out of mortal troubles, I think we had best go to the Stones for shelter, and—whatever else we may find there. Besides," she added practically, "it is a very long walk from here to the Remigius monastery. I d-don't think we could get there in time to do Judith much good."

Only on those last sensible words did Nick realize how much Lisa's voice was trembling, and that she must be feeling the compulsion to run away as strongly as he was—perhaps worse, since she was of this world. He took her hand; the palm was damp with sweat, and he could feel the smoothness of the new skin where Zahariel had healed her burn. She took burns and scrapes like any mortal, and she was just as scared as he was; if he closed his eyes for a minute, he could pretend she was a girl from his own world who needed help, nothing more.

"It's easier with my eyes closed," he said aloud, and Lisa's fingers shook within his grasp.

"You feel it too?"

"Feel what?"

Lisa sighed and withdrew her hand. Nick looked at her again. It didn't hurt. She looked pale and tired and dirty enough to be a normal person who'd been dragged through too many adventures, rather than a mysterious elf-queen who'd disappeared eons ago, who could walk through stones and mend dresses by scowling at them. And despite her bedraggled state, he still liked looking at her.

"We must have been talking about different things," she said at last. "I think I can find the Stones from here. We should go this way, I think."

She pointed inland and Nick squinted out over the barren, salty hills with their covering of low pale grass. He could see a very long way from this high plateau. "There's nothing there," he objected.

"Remember Berengar's castle?"

"Oh. More illusions. And I suppose to the elvenkind it's no trouble to see through elven illusions."

"I'm not elven!" Lisa snapped. "And for your information, I can't see through them any better than you. In the case of Berengar's castle, I had been there before, so I knew that the gap in the path and the rock were illusions. And in this case . . ."

"Yes?"

"The illusions here," Lisa said, "are more powerful; they were set by masters of elvenkind in the days when their power was strong in the land. And there's something else, something new, worse than the elven illusions . . ."

"Something that makes you afraid, without knowing why," Nick said, "that whimpers at you without making a sound, that makes your eyes want to look away and your legs want to run—"

"Yes. I don't know what it is; but we have to go into it. When I close my eyes, I can tell what direction it is coming from; can you?"

Nick covered his face for a moment. It was hard to make himself concentrate on the faint sensations of distaste and fear, but it seemed to him that they were all around him. "No."

"Probably . . . just as well," Lisa said, and now her voice was definitely shaking. "If I'm to walk blind, I'll need your help to guide me; all these little hummocks and tufts of salt-grass are real enough, and I'll fall down with every other step if I don't have help. And, Nick . . . I'm afraid."

So am I. That would probably be the least helpful thing he could say. "It will be all right," said Nick. He took Lisa's hand again. "Lead on."

The Remigius monastery was so far from the Stones of Jura that all Brother Alured's skill could bring forth only the faintest image of the travelers who stumbled and felt their way towards that oldest and greatest of the stone circles. Even that image, hardly more than a pattern of ripples upon the white liquid in the scrying-bowl, shook and all but dissolved when Hugh's raging disturbed his concentration.

"Why did the Hounds take them so far? I told you to have them brought here, to the Remigius, that our escaped elf-queen might know their lives forfeit for hers!"

"I have less control over the Hounds than at first," Brother Alured replied, "and—"

"Fool! Keep to your chant! We are losing her!" Furious steps paced up and down behind Alured's back, while he repeated the words of the finding-spell and dared neither look behind him nor answer Hugh's increasingly unanswerable questions.

"And where may Sybille be, now that you fools have let her slip?" The footsteps paused, and Brother Alured could feel the angry eyes behind him, looking over his shoulder at the image of Lisa stumbling forward with her eyes closed. "Pah! Much use your finding-spell is. It shows us only that one, who has proved herself to be mortal—"

"No. She has proved that she can touch cold iron without harm." This speaker's voice was full and calm, the voice of a man used to the reverence of those about him. Even Hugh, half-mad as he was, paused momentarily.

"It's the same thing," he snarled at last, and fell to pacing again.

"Is it? The elvenkind sought Sybille's trail among the stars, and this girl answered their call. We sent out a finding-spell along the same trail, and what do we see? The same girl. Sybille was the strongest of the elvenkind in her day. If she could cross between the worlds and cloak herself in mortal seeming, if she could live uncounted years in that world of iron-demons, perhaps she could also find some way to tolerate the touch of iron upon her person." The man who spoke bent over Brother Alured and gazed intently on the trembling image in the bowl, careful not to touch the mage-monk or to disturb his labored chanting. "The elvenkind called, and this girl answered. We sought, and found this girl. We sent the Hounds for her, and they carried her to the coast of Brittany—and now I believe she seeks the Stones of Jura, which we know are guarded by such spells that none but the elvenkind can see them truly from outside the circle itself."

The speaker straightened to his full height and bent a piercing glance on the monks assembled in the chapter house. "If Sybille has truly returned to our world, then this is she, and we were all wrong to dismiss her so quickly before. Forget the other woman; this is the one we want."

"Can we reach them before they find the Stones, and capture her again?"

"I do not think we should take the risk," the leader of the Durandincs replied. "True, that was our first plan, but that was when we thought Sybille would be weakened from her long stay in the world of the iron-demons. Instead— She has escaped us twice; somehow she made us think that she was of no account, probably by use of her demonic elven spells; and now she is very near to the Stones. I think that she is too dangerous to leave alive."

* * *

Judith and Berengar and Giles traveled nearly as quickly to the Stones of Jura as did Nick and Lisa, but they did not start so soon. Berengar was ashamed of his own weakness. A true elflord of the old days, he thought, would have been able to raise the elf-wind twice in two days without making such a pother about it—even if a night without sleep or food intervened; even if the ache of his iron-inflicted wound had grown through the night into such a throbbing torment that he could think of little else. A tough old count like Yrthan would probably be able to manage it even now. Yrthan was always hinting that Berengar was young and untried, too young to be trusted with the rule of his own lands along the Garron; and now, in the first real trial, Yrthan had been proved entirely right. Berengar had plunged into battle without thinking of anything but the need to save the very fair lady he saw so sorely beset. Now, tired from the previous day's exertions and troubled by his wound, he was in no case to save his lady or his realm. He could not even summon up enough power to take Fleurdevant more than an inch above the leaf-covered trail they followed. That scrawny boy, Giles the peddler, would probably be more use to her than anything he could do.

The cycle of self-recriminations and doubts and crushing despair occupied him so thoroughly that for some time he did little more than plod along beside Fleurdevent, too depressed even to lift his head and look at Judith perched on his horse in those amazing tight blue nether garments she still wore. In the first hour of their travels they exchanged no more than half a dozen sentences, all thoroughly practical: "Mind that branch," "I think the trail leads this way," "Look out for thorn-serpents under these rocks." Even Giles, who'd begun the day by skipping happily ahead of Fleurdevent with a high sense of adventure, grew

still and forgot to whistle in the apalling miasma of
Berengar's depression.

"Enough," said Judith when, for the third time in
a row, Berengar had absently missed a bend in the
trail to go plodding off among crackling leaves and
thorny underbrush.

He raised his head and looked at her with dull
eyes that hardly saw her. "You are tired? I am sorry—"

"I'm tired," said Judith, "of riding beside a zom-
bie. What's wrong? I thought you had discovered the
secret of the Hounds. I thought we were going to
save the world from the blessed brothers of the
blessed Durand."

"Sainted," Berengar corrected.

"Whatever. What's eating you, Berengar?"

She had to prod for a while longer before Berengar
could be brought to confess his failure, and then she
irritated both men—Berengar by her refusal to take
his failure seriously, Giles by her general lack of
respect for so important a personage as the elven
Count of the Garronais.

"Well, for pity's sake, of course you can't do magic
when you're tired and hurt and hungry!" Judith said
briskly. "I'm ravenous myself—would have mentioned it earlier, but I thought maybe you elven folk
supped on a drop of dew from the grass and wouldn't
want to be bothered with such coarse mortal con-
cerns. I can't do much about your wound, but surely
we can find something to eat and rest for an hour;
then, if you're feeling up to it, you can try to raise
the elf-wind again. And if not, we'll make better
speed for the rest and the food—and to tell the truth,
Berengar, I'd be just as happy if I never had to travel
in your peculiar fashion again."

Berengar smiled wanly at what he regarded as
Judith's little jest, but recovered enough to admit
that there might be a farmhouse at the northern
edge of the forest.

"Not my lands, though," he said glumly. "Under a mortal lord. Haimar of Odo."

"What difference does that make?"

"You'll see when we get there."

Thirty minutes later Judith came down from the top of the stone wall that bordered the stout farmhouse, somewhat hampered by Giles trying to climb her shoulders. Berengar stood in the gateway, pale and shaking with the effort of keeping the farmer's dogs confused by his illusions.

"You'd better come on down now," he said. "I don't know how much longer I can hold them." But he had enough energy left to spare an appreciative glance at Judith as she wriggled down from stone to stone and finally leapt to the ground. "Very practical garments, those," he said. "Wish our court ladies would take up something like—*no*, Black-spot!"

The white mastiff with black spots on its muzzle whimpered and began chasing its tail again, apparently under the illusion that it was hunting a particularly juicy rabbit. The other two dogs worried a stick with great enthusiasm. When Judith looked sideways at the stick she could just see the illusion of a meaty soup bone dancing around it like a ghostly halo.

"Who's there? Be off, you worthless beggars, or I'll—"

The stocky man in patched brown garments stopped at the kitchen door, mouth half open. "Oh, *no*," he said finally. "Isn't it bad enough I've got half the mortal beggars in Poitiers showing up here with their hands out, but now I've to deal with a tattered elfling as well? Let my dogs loose, you—"

"Man," Berengar snapped, "I am Count of the Garronais!"

"Oh, aye? And I suppose your dancing-girl there is Alianora of Poitiers? And what's the boy? Court jester?"

The stocky man stepped back half a pace before

the flash of light in Berengar's eyes, but the distraction had let the black and white mastiff free of the illusion that its tail was a rabbit. Berengar kicked the dog just before it sank its teeth into his leg, the farmer retreated another pace and began shouting for the scullion to bring his iron turnspits, and Giles slipped between the two men and began talking rapidly.

"Sir, you miscall us sadly, and your good lady will not thank you for turning away peddlers from the Land Beyond the Stars with marvellous goods to trade the like of which she has never seen before. . . ."

"And you with no packs!" the farmer sneered. "Show me these fine goods, then, or I'll set the dogs on all three of you and see which can jump highest."

Giles rolled his eyes at Judith. She stuck a hand into her hip pocket and pulled out whatever she found there, praying that it wasn't just used chewing gum and bent hairpins.

An hour later, they left the farmstead with a loaf of bread and several thick slices of ham to supplement the meal they'd just had of fresh-baked bread and milk warm from the cow. Judith's quick search of her back pockets had yielded a dollar and seventy-five cents in change, two hairpins and a black plastic comb with several teeth missing, two crumpled but unused tissues and a packet of matches from Cisco's Bakery. The farmer had rejected the money as obviously faked and not very well done at that, but his wife had seized upon the comb and spent the better part of an hour working it through her hair while Berengar, Giles and Judith ate steadily through the food she put out on the table. The tissues, straightened out between her work-roughened palms, had been marvelled at and admired by all the women of the household as the softest, finest faery weaving they'd ever been privileged to touch. Judith had prudently reserved the matches, thinking that in the next few days they might need another miracle out of her back pocket. And in leaving, to pay for the poultice of herbs and lard with which the farmwife dressed Berengar's wound, the bedraggled Count of the Garronais had laid an illusion over the wife's headdress that would cast the glow of youthful beauty over her face for at least a week.

"See there, Ivo," she'd told her husband as they were leaving, "and you always say the elvenfolk can't do aught of use to mortal men!"

"Hmmph. And what good's a pretty picture? Say this elflord casts illusion of a good harvest over t'fields, will that fill my barns?" Ivo demanded. But he gave over grumbling long enough to kiss his woman with her newly spring-fresh face, so Berengar did not feel entirely useless. And after an hour's nap in the shelter of farmer Ivo's barn, while Fleurdevent munched his fill of the farmer's oats, he pronounced himself fit enough to raise the elf-wind that should bring them almost to the Stones of Jura.

"Almost?"

"There are strong spells about the Stones," Berengar said. "Illusions set by the first lords of Faerie, and since the Catastrophe, another ring of protections— something like the spells about my keep, but where those just make people forget what they came for, these make you want to run away and hide." He gazed soberly at Judith. "It is a frightening place— worse, in some ways, than those who watched us last night. Are you sure you wish to essay this?"

"I don't see that we have much other choice," Judith said slowly. "There wasn't much of a moon last night. Tonight, or tomorrow night at best, it'll be dark . . . Do you think that we can do it?"

"I don't know. It's not been tried before—mortals and elvenkind working together at the Stones. For one thing . . ." Berengar thought better of what he'd been going to say: that most mortals couldn't be

tempted within a league of the place, even if an elf
had been willing to guide them.

"What?"

"Oh, nothing," Berengar lied. "I was just thinking.
We might need a mortal mage, and a stronger elf-
lord, to raise the Stones to their full power. But if we
can have any result at all—even a flicker of success—
well, then, maybe that will help our world get through
the next moon-dark. And maybe, with that evidence,
I can go to the Council and persuade them to link
our lords with mortal mages to raise the Stones again."

There was too much of 'maybe' and 'perhaps,' in
that to please Judith. But, as she'd said, what other
choice did they have? She wanted to get home.
Berengar wanted to stop the Wild Hunt before it
ravaged his entire world. And all Judith's previous
experiences with faculty meetings and computer stan-
dards councils had left her very, very wary of leaving
anything she really wanted to accomplish in the hands
of a committee.

"Are you ready?" Berengar had mounted Fleurdevent
while she tried to talk herself out of this journey. He
reached a hand down to her and lifted her up behind
him as easily as if she'd been no more weight than
Giles. The boy sprang up behind. Judith wondered
for a moment if she was the only person in this world
who couldn't mount a bareback horse from the ground.
Just one more reason to go home, to a world where
she had skills that counted for something. . . .

Then Berengar spoke the words that brought the
elf-wind whistling about her ears, and she wrapped
her arms around him and leaned her face against his
broad back and told herself it was no worse, really,
than riding a motorcycle, and probably much less
dangerous.

And after all, the anticipation was worse than the
reality. As they mounted into the clouds, Judith
remembered the wild elation of her first ride on

Fleurdevent, and she forgot to be afraid. They rode through thunder and crackling rain and sleet that stung her face, then broke into sunlight and danced in the blue and yellow of the clear sky. Fleurdevent arched his neck and curvetted in the air, Giles shouted with delight and Judith laughed aloud. For a few enchanted moments it didn't matter that she had lost the way home and that she was trapped on a besieged and dying world, or that the man before her was not quite human, or that the speed and freedom she enjoyed were his gift and nothing she could command on her own. All that mattered was sundazzle and sky and the high thin crystalline music that wove a hauntingly sweet song through the upper reaches of the sky.

"What was that music?" she called when they began to descend again, through mist and clouds, with the sound of the sea loud somewhere ahead and to the left.

"The music of the spheres." Berengar's voice was faint. "We went too high. But you took such joy in it."

Fleurdevent's hoofs rang out a harsher tune on the rocks where they came back to earth. "I thank you," Judith said gravely. The air was too thick here; she felt as though it must choke her. The mist had followed them down to the ground, too, so that she could see nothing beyond the foggy circle of grass and stones where they stood, and that troubled her; she had a sense of vague, inimical creatures watching at a distance, large shapeless things much more frightening than the hounds of the Wild Hunt. She could still hear the piercing sweetness of the spheres singing in her memory, though, and as long as she remembered that melody she felt a little safer. "If—whatever happens now, I am glad to have that to remember. I hope it did not cost too much of your strength."

Berengar leapt down from Fleurdevent's back and

stood facing her. He was very pale. "No. Not that. This place drains me—can't you feel it?"

Judith nodded. "Which way do we go?"

Berengar closed his eyes for a moment and then pointed into the mist, and at once Judith knew that the large shapes she feared were not around them in a circle; they were concentrated in the direction in which he pointed, and they *did not want* anybody coming closer. She swallowed and tried to force down the irrational fear that rose within her. "All right. But I think— Is Fleurdevent to stay here? Perhaps Giles had better stay to watch the horse?" The kid was hurt already, and he'd had as rough a night and morning as the rest of them. There didn't seem to be much point in dragging him to face whatever lay ahead.

Giles thought differently. "No. Old Flowery doesn't need watching, do you, old fellow?" He gave Fleurdevent a friendly slap on the flank. Berengar winced visibly at Giles' shortening of the horse's name. "I'm coming with you."

"Giles, you can't help us now," Judith protested, "and it's dangerous—"

"How do you know I can't? You don't know what's up ahead. Neither does he. And anyway—" Giles' street-sparrow cockiness faded. "I ain't staying here alone."

"Very well." Berengar stepped between Giles and Judith and took their hands. "Only, from here on, you must be guided by me. There are illusions set between us and the Stones, and there are also some very real dangers; mortal sight cannot distinguish between them."

"What about—" Judith hesitated. The fear that rolled towards her from the direction of the Stones was almost palpable, staining the air she breathed like an oil slick spreading its death over the waves. Would it grow stronger if she named it?

"Those who have been here since the Catastrophe," Berengar said, "tell us that all you can do about the feeling of repulsion is to ignore it."

At first, as they advanced into the clammy mist, Judith found this about as easy as ignoring the sound of squealing brakes or the dentist's drill or any other shrill warning of immediate danger. Then it got even worse. Her eyes told her that Berengar was glowing green and eight feet tall, and only his firm hold on her hand and his reassuring voice promised her that nothing had really changed; and after that, there was the illusion of a swampy lake filled with hissing snakes; and cleverly placed in the midst of all the illusory snakes, one real and very annoyed snake of a kind Judith had never seen before. She had just been admiring its gaudy colors and the artistic way the spellcaster had made it seem to writhe lazily in the mud, when one of those lazy writhing coils lashed out as fast as a whip and wrapped around Judith's waist. She screamed and Berengar gripped the squeezing coils in both hands and the pressure kept tightening until she had no breath to scream. Then, suddenly, the coil around her relaxed and the snake, or whatever it had been, slithered away into the mud and the mist.

Judith started to thank Berengar, but he shook his head. "Not me. I acted like a fool—when I saw it attacking you, I could not think. The strangledrakes are like shifting sands; the more you struggle against them, the more they use your own strength against you until you are crushed in their coils. Giles saved you. I don't know how he guessed that the strangledrakes cannot abide heat; maybe it was in one of those street ballads he sings."

Giles grinned and produced the remains of Judith's pack of matches.

"I—oh, good God," Judith said faintly. "Giles, in my own world I would have to talk to you about playing with matches, but here—How did you get those, anyway? And how did you know what to do with them?"

Giles reminded her that she'd lit one of the matches to impress farmer Ivo, and neatly evaded the question of how the matchbook had been transferred from Judith's pocket to the loose bag of his sleeve.

When they set their faces towards the Stones again, the spell of aversion was worse than ever, a crushing weight of despair and grief and guilt that was almost palpable.

"That means we're getting closer," said Berengar. He did not seem overjoyed at the prospect.

"Good!"

"Maybe."

"What's wrong now?"

"Do you have a feeling that we are not alone? Even I can't see very far in this mist, and what I do see is so mixed in with illusion that I cannot make much of it; but I keep thinking that I hear footsteps or voices."

"Another illusion-trap?"

"I hope so," said Berengar. The three of them clasped hands and moved on, but now Judith found that worrying about people she couldn't quite see or hear, somewhere out in the mist beyond their vision, was nearly as bad as trying to ignore the waves of aversion and fear that oozed out all around the Stones. Except it wasn't quite fear, she reflected. More like—

"Guilt," she said aloud. "Remorse, repentance— and it will never do any good, because it can never be undone, and the world will go down in chaos."

Berengar gave her a reproachful look. "You have captured the feeling of the Stones very well. Now would you mind not talking about it? It's hard enough to ignore without putting it into words." He sighed, and Judith saw that his forehead was damp with sweat. "If Sybille set these spells of aversion about the place—for it was not so, they say, before the Catastrophe—then she was a master mage with more power than any of the elvenkind now hold, and we shall never be able to undo what she has done."

"I think," said Judith, "that unreasoning despair must be a part of the spell, too. If you have to think like that, I'd prefer that you didn't talk about it either."

Berengar looked amused, the way he usually did when he noticed that a mortal was contradicting him. That, Judith thought, was a big improvement on despair. If it would keep his mind off the debilitating effects of the spell, she would be happy to contradict or insult him every few steps for the entire rest of the journey. She wondered what he would think of the Equal Rights Amendment; if she could explain the concept, his probable reactions should give her plenty of openings to insult him.

CHAPTER SEVENTEEN

The holy Durand was strenuous in discipline, and most severe to correct the failings of delinquents; wherefore was he much in demand to preach against the heretics in the South, where by the might of his words certain virgins who most obstinately adhered to the heresies of the Cathars and Bogomils were burned by the townsfolk rising in anger against them. Also he sent many good knights to perish in the body, that their souls might be saved, in wars against the heathen Wends of the Baltic regions and against the accursed Saracens of Outremer. But most of all was he zealous against the accursed demons called Elvenkind, against whose luxurious ways and sinful delights he raised up his Order. And in the fifty-third year of Alianora called Queen of the Middle Realm he went alone upon a mission to end the power of the elvenkind that they might acknowledge the strength of the One Way, and from that mission he never returned; wherefore we may know that Our Lord in pitifulness and mercy brought the blessed man directly to his bosom.

—Life of Saint Durand as recorded in the annals
of the Remigius Monastery

The rest of the journey was uneventful, if one didn't count such minor problems as a wailing voice off to the right, the appearance of a fiery chasm opening underfoot, and two more lazy strangledrakes who hissed and oozed off when Giles waved lighted matches at them. The only real problem was walking through the layers of invisible guilt and despair and repentance that lay deeper and deeper about them the closer they got. By the time Judith could make out the shapes of standing stones in the mist, she knew that everything bad that had ever happened to those she loved, from the death of her puppy when she was four to Nick's disappearance at the Stone-maidens, was eternally and irrevocably her fault, and that nothing she could ever do would make up for the one unidentified mistake that had doomed her and everyone she loved. She could barely remember that there was some reason why they had come here; head down, she pushed through waves of sorrow as palpable as cold sea tides, hardly aware of what she was doing. Berengar was holding her hand and talking steadily. She wanted to tell him to shut up; the sounds of the language he used grated on the inside of her head like the screech of tortured metal. But she couldn't even summon up the energy to snap at him until, between one step and the next, the waves of misery receded and she fell forward onto blessedly simple, plain, unadorned stony ground.

Berengar drew breath for another of those long grinding throat-stinging phrases.

"Stop," Judith begged. "*Please* stop. I don't know what you're saying, but it hurts my ears—and—we're here." All around them the stones reared into the sky like sentinels, and inside this great circle—at least three times bigger than that enclosed by the Stonemaidens—the mist and the illusions had vanished. The pale grass that grew in knots and tufts was blessedly real and clear to see, and when Judith lifted her head she could see blue sky overhead and hear a bird singing. It seemed forever since she had seen the sun, but she knew from looking at the sky that up above them was the golden and blue glory here they had flown on the elf-wind with Fleurdevent.

"Why, so we are," said Berengar, blinking and looking about him like one awakened from a dream. "And yet it seemed to me that we would never come here—that we were in a spiral that would never end." His voice sounded rusty, as if it was difficult to shift over from the magical language he had been using to fight the illusions into whatever he normally spoke; Judith had decided some time ago that none of them were speaking English, and had also decided not to worry over the implications of that. She was just grateful that she could talk to Berengar and the other people in this world. And now she was passionately grateful that they had reached the sanctuary of the Stones. Whatever evil had beaten at them outside, it could not touch them now.

Giles had thrown himself on the ground beside her, panting as though he'd just run all the way from Poitou. While he gasped in the cool, clean air of the circle, and while Berengar looked about him dazedly, Judith sat up and ran fingers through her tangled hair and wondered what would happen next. She did not feel nearly as concerned about it as she had a few minutes earlier; the calm blessing of these silent stones seeped into the ground and the air and even into her bones. The stones were part of the earth, and so was she; all things came right in the end; all things rested in the end. Judith breathed deeply, and listened to the bird singing overhead, and felt the aching sadness within her dissolving and vanishing like ripples dying out over a quiet pool.

Only one thing disturbed the symmetry of the circle; a pair of stones, as tall as the rest but somewhat rougher, leaned against each other as if they were about to step into the circle, hand in hand. Judith felt a flicker of disquiet whenever she looked at those two rough pillars, and so she very sensibly looked the other way, at the bluish stones behind Berengar's head.

"What do we do now?" she said when at last she felt that she had drunk her fill of the peace and quiet that filled this place like an unspoken blessing. She stood and laid one hand on the nearest stone. She could almost feel the power humming through it; but something stopped it, a break in the circle—perhaps the disturbing asymmetry of those two leaning stones on the far side. Judith hoped it was not that. She did not think the three of them could shift one of the stones an inch, let alone manhandling two such great pillars back into place. Besides, there was no place visible for those two stones; the circle of stones seemed to march on without a break behind them. Or maybe that was another illusion.

Berengar sighed and stood up. "I am not sure. By myself, I could barely bring the three of us through the illusion-traps and . . . the other things . . . that guarded this place. I do not know if I would have made it if you had not been with me."

"Then it didn't tire you out too much—protecting us?"

Berengar shook his head. "No, you lend me strength —or strength of will, at least. We of the elvenkind are too much inclined, when difficulties present themselves, to turn away and hope that matters will be easier on another day. You see, there always is another day; why suffer to no end? But how could I turn away, when you and Giles were so stubbornly determined to fight through to the circle?"

"Um. I thought it was the other way," Judith confessed. "I would have run for my life back there if you hadn't been holding my hand; or sat on the ground, convinced it was useless, and waited for a strangledrake to take me."

"I wonder," Berengar said slowly, "I wonder just how far the other elven lords came—those who tried before to lift the curse on the Stones. Many have returned, speaking of the illusion-traps and the crushing feelings that get worse the closer you come. I do not recall that anyone has ever mentioned that it gets better once you are actually in the circle." A slow smile, this time quite unforced, began to spread over his face. "I begin to suspect, my lady—my very fair and brave lady—that we are the first to have come this far since the Catastrophe." He gave her a vigorous one-armed hug. "Lady Judith, I salute you. With your help, I have done what no lord of Elfhame has attempted in all these dreary years."

Being so close to Berengar was dizzying; and now there was no elf-wind, no glory of sun and stars and clouds wheeling about them, to explain the way she felt.

"All the same," Judith said some moments later, wriggling free of Berengar's arm and trying not to look at Giles, "all the same, we *haven't* succeeded yet."

"No. Perhaps . . ." Berengar rubbed his chin and scowled at the silent stones. "There is a rite for calling the power of the Stones. I have read it in the scrolls at Ys."

"Marvellous. What did the scrolls say about it?"

"That since the Catastrophe it hasn't worked."

"Oh. Great."

"But," Berengar said cheerfully, "I strongly suspect that the scrolls didn't say everything. The others who've tried to raise the Stones probably never got this far, or they would have mentioned it. Instead, I'll wager they stood a good safe distance away from the Stones—about where we left Fleurdevent— and tried from there. We have two things helping us that they didn't have."

"We're in the circle," Judith agreed. "Maybe that's necessary? In any case, it should be easier to do magic here than out in the mist, with all the Stones' protections battering on us."

"Exactly. *And*," Berengar beamed at her, "they did not have the wit to invite mortal aid in their endeavor. You may be the key that unlocks the Stones to us."

"Um. Yes. Ah—what exactly do we do now?"

"We must find the keystone and link hands about . . ." Berengar fell silent. Judith followed the direction of his gaze. He was looking at the largest of the smooth bluish stones; at its base, rather, where something disturbed the smooth perfection of the turf.

"What's the matter?"

Berengar shook his head. "The Durandines were before us. They have chained the Stones. Look!"

"But aren't we going to unlock the power . . . Oh." Judith began to make sense of the irregular line of bumps and rounded curves that lay about the base of the keystone. "You weren't speaking metaphorically, were you?" She knelt and lifted the iron chain free of the grass that had grown over it. Each link was as thick as her wrist, and the ends of the chain were joined by a massive padlock, as large as a book, square and heavy and uncompromisingly solid. It was a mean-looking lock, the sort that said *You won't get the better of me*, the sort of lock that made one think of prisoners wasting away in dungeons until their bones slipped free of the iron bonds that held them to the wall. Judith did not like to touch it; she didn't even want to think of the effect this weight of iron could have on Berengar, whose elven flesh was scarred from a single brushing touch of a blade.

"We don't have to touch it?" she suggested, knowing as she said so that there would be something wrong with the suggestion.

Berengar shook his head. "So much iron—it will leach away the power even as we draw it to us. And I misdoubt me the rite will not succeed even so far; I cannot stand near that chain with a whole mind."

"We could try another stone?"

Again Berengar shook his head. "No other would do. This is the keystone of the Stones' power. As an arch has a keystone which is necessary to keep the other stones each in its place, so a circle of power has its keystone which holds the powers of the earth within the reach of elvenkind."

"How can you tell that it's this one?" Giles wanted to know.

"I dare not approach. But you may. Can't you feel it?"

Judith laid her cheek against the weathered surface of the stone and thought that she could indeed feel something. It was almost like a humming in the earth, vibrating through the stone and into her body. "Yes. The power is in it—it's almost alive. Giles, do stop fiddling with that chain and help me think of something to do!"

Giles was slumped on the ground, picking idly at the massive padlock. Judith couldn't bear to watch him. She stared out over the fog-enshrouded plain that surrounded them. Now that Berengar had pointed out the chain, every lump and hummock in the grassy expanse seemed to take on its own menacing secrets. A ripple in the grass could be a strangledrake waiting to catch them as they departed, the rounded mound just outside the circle could be . . .

"Berengar," she said quietly, "I think I know what happened to him."

"Who?"

"The man who set this chain about the keystone." Judith pointed, unwilling to step outside the protection of the circle. Berengar joined her and looked down where she pointed. Now that she knew what she was looking at, it was perfectly clear to Judith: the white rounded curve of bone, the empty eye-sockets filled with grass, the shreds of a gray robe blending with mud and dead grass.

"Aye," Berengar said softly. "Poor mortal. The Stones have their own power, and they would take their own revenge on the one who attempted to chain them." He shivered, and Judith remembered the crushing weight of despair that had beaten them down just before they stumbled into the circle. For the mortal man who put a chain about the keystone of Jura, the Stones might have been no refuge from that despair.

"I wonder if putting the chain on killed him, or if he just couldn't find the will to move once his task was accomplished?"

"We'll never know," Berengar said. "*I* wonder . . ."

"What?"

"Saint Durand is said to have met a martyr's death combating evil, by which he meant the elvenkind, but the tales of his death are vague and contradictory, and the Durandines have no relics of his body. I wonder . . ." he said again. "It would explain why no one knew that the Stones had been chained." He grimaced and ground his good fist into the surface of the stone. "Had I known, we might have brought a mortal smith with us . . . there are enough skilled metalworkers among my own serfs!"

"My lady?" Giles tugged at Judith's pants leg.

"Not now, Giles!" Judith snapped. Berengar was going into his Doom and Despair mode again, and she had to find some way to stop him; she couldn't take time to amuse the boy now.

"Thank you." Giles squatted on the ground again, happily fiddling with the iron chain. Judith remembered the flickering touch of fingers across her hip and patted her pocket. Last time he'd abstracted the matches; this time it was her hairpin he'd taken. Oh, well, whatever made him happy—

"There!" Giles grunted with satisfaction and stood up, staggering slightly under the weight of the iron chain. The ends of the chain trailed free, and the padlock lay open on the grass.

"Giles!" Judith's irritation vanished; she stooped down and hugged Giles. "How did you do it? You—you—"

"Picked the lock," Giles supplied while she kissed his cheek. "Gentlefolk," he said with a touch of scorn. "Don't *think*. Wasn't nothing to it, not for me as trained with Jacques the Finger."

Judith took the chain in both hands and heaved it out into the misty grass. It fell across the dead saint's bones with a grim clank. The padlock followed. The iron was only a few feet away now, but at least it was out of the circle, and she could see the color coming back into Berengar's face.

"Right," he said. "I am ashamed. Once again, a mortal has led the way. Link hands about the stone."

As quickly as that, he was back in command of the situation. "Natural born management material," Judith murmured, but she did as he said. The humming of the keystone was stronger now, almost as if it felt grateful to be freed of its iron bonds. When Berengar began speaking in that strange grating language, Judith felt a series of sharp, almost painful breaks in the humming noise. Giles squeaked in surprise and jumped back, breaking the contact.

"It *stung* me!" he apologized.

"No matter," Berengar said. "We will try again."

This time Giles held his place, but the jolts that went through the stone were fainter, and after a few seconds even the humming died away.

Berengar drew a deep breath and shook his head. "I can't do it. Maybe if you two learned the words and said them with me?"

"You haven't failed entirely," Judith said. "Look, the mist is lighter now. And I can almost see . . ."

She squinted into the white fog. There were outlines of running figures, men on foot, and men on horseback chasing them; she could see the dull glint of armor and hear the whistling sound of an ugly iron-studded ball on a chain as one of the men on horseback swung his weapon through the air. She gripped Berengar's arm. "What *is* that?"

Even as she spoke, the figures drew close enough for her to make out their features through the clinging mist. "Nick!" Judith ran out of the circle, and the fog engulfed her.

They'd had hard walking through the fog and illusions. Lisa, with her eyes closed, kept tripping over the low hummocks of salty grass. Nick tried to hold her hand and guide her as best he could, but he had problems of his own: he kept seeing things that weren't there. At least, he knew the sheet of flames that rose before him wasn't really there, because Lisa walked right through it without a singed hair; and he didn't really believe in the nest of snakes that turned into slithering rainbows when he stared hard at them; but he was never quite sure about another, larger snake that flicked its tongue at them and then, just as Lisa was about to step on it, turned and oozed off into the fog as if in search of better-tasting quarry.

All these little distractions kept Nick from guiding Lisa as well as he should. She stumbled and fell several times; once he was shielding his face from something that croaked like a frog and flew on long bat-wings, and another time he was staring at the rainbow snakes. And all the while, the weight of fear and sorrow and desolation that emanated from the Stones pressed heavier and heavier on both of them, so that it hardly seemed worth their while to speak. Nick was not even sure why they went on; except that having concentrated all his will in the effort to put one foot in front of the other, he was not able to change what remained of his mind.

Besides, Lisa would have gone on without him, and it was worse for her; he could tell that by looking at her. Her legs were scratched and scraped from falls, and there were tears running down from her closed eyes, but she kept stumbling ahead with one hand before her and the other clasping Nick's fingers, like a sleepwalker caught in an endless nightmare.

Why don't you leave her here? jeered the soft, smothering voices that came from the Stones. *You're no good to her. You let them take Judith, and you can't help Lisa—you're no good to anybody. Everything you have done has been a mistake and it is too late now to make it right.*

Nick admitted the indictment, pled guilty and waited for sentencing, but the trial went on and on in his head, and he had forgotten whatever words of law he might have used to defend himself. All he knew was that if he withdrew his hand from Lisa's cold fingers, she would be left alone in the nightmare; and nobody should be left alone here.

He never knew, afterwards, how long it took them to reach the Stones. It felt like days. The ache in his legs and the blister that was growing inside the worn spot on his sneakers told him that he'd been walking for half a day at least. And yet he had the feeling that if he looked back over his shoulder, if there were anything to mark the spot where the Wild Hunt had dropped them, if he could see through the fog, he would see that they had not come half a mile.

So he didn't look back.

He was bitterly tired, though, and he would have suggested to Lisa that they stop and rest if he'd thought she would have listened to him. He was relieved when she came to an abrupt halt, head up, sniffing the air again as though she could catch the

scent of the Stones in the muffling fog that surrounded them.

"Yes," Nick said. "It's about time for a rest." He
started to sit down on a low hummock of grass and
rocks, but Lisa tugged at his hand.

"Not *here*, you idiot! If you sit down, you'll start
wondering what's the point in going on, and then
you'll begin to wonder why you should get up again,
and then you'll stay here until you rot."

"How do you know that?"

Lisa opened her eyes and pointed over to the left.
Nick followed the direction of her finger and saw that
one of the low mounds he'd taken for grass-covered
rocks was actually composed of long yellowish bones.
And under the grass, he saw the rounded outline of a
skull.

"Oh." He swallowed. "That's, er, that's not an
illusion?"

"I can hear the man's death," Lisa said. "He sat
down to rest. He must have been mortal; his spirit is
lingering. I think it wants the bones to be taken away
for a Mass, and for burial in consecrated ground."

Nick looked suspiciously at the low mound of grass
where he'd been about to sit.

"It's all right," Lisa said. "That one's just grass . . . I
think."

"But it's not a good idea to stop."

"No . . ."

"Then why," asked Nick with the flickering rem-
nants of his reason, "why are we standing here?" Not
that he cared very much about the answer; he was
too tired to care. But whatever was left of his mind
still noticed incongruities.

"I thought I heard something." Lisa lifted her
shoulders a fraction of an inch and let them sag down
again, as if even shrugging was too much effort.
"Men calling . . . Probably another illusion."

Nick was about to agree, and wondering whether

it was worth the trouble to open his mouth, when he felt a shiver under his feet, as if the ground were stirring. Another, sharper jolt followed the first, and Nick had the illusion that he could see rents and fissures opening in the white wall of fog behind Lisa's head. And past those trembling cracks, there was a flickering image of tall stones standing against a blue sky.

"Look!" He grabbed Lisa's arm and pointed. "Is— is that the place?"

Even as he spoke, the image faded back into fog. But now it seemed to Nick that the mist was a little thinner, and that he could see the real bulk of the stones, bluish-gray shapes that stood unmoving no matter how the gauzy mist swirled about them.

"There they are!"

The shout came from behind them, the way they had come. Nick looked over his shoulder and saw a steel-clad man on horseback bearing down on them. Bushy dark eyebrows snarled together above a face full of hatred; the ground shook under the weight of his mailed horse. Behind them came more armed men, faceless in the mist, but all heading directly for Nick and Lisa with deadly intent.

Nick turned and ran into the thinning fog, heading straight for the place where he'd glimpsed that vision of the stones, dragging Lisa with him. How far? The stones had seemed close enough, but he could feel the pounding of hoofs just behind them. The illusions were thinner now, even Nick could see their nature. He and Lisa ran through a waterfall and across a chasm and stepped on a real, squirming scaled serpent with clawed legs, and kept on running. Behind them, a horse's hoof landed on the serpent's body. It screamed thinly, like a trapped rabbit, but only for a moment. Nick thought he could smell the sweat of their pursuers; he dared not pause to look over his shoulder. The tufts of long pale grass reached out devilish tendrils to snare their ankles; Nick could feel the saw-toothed blades cutting through his pants and the trickles of blood running down his legs. He didn't want to think of how the blades would be cutting Lisa's bare legs. She was sobbing for breath now; she could not go much farther. Something whizzed past Nick's head and he caught a bare glimpse of an ugly spiked ball on the end of a chain. The rider was coming up beside Lisa now; he aimed at her and Nick jerked her bodily out of the way of a swing that would have split her head in two.

Another flicker of light troubled the air, and Nick glimpsed the stones rising clear and tall like a promise of sanctuary. Too far away; the black-browed man on the horse would cut them off if they kept running.

Nick did not have time to think, but for once in his life his body did what he needed it to without planning or taking notes or preparing in advance. With one thrust he pushed Lisa ahead of him, towards the stones, and in the same motion he launched himself toward the horse's legs. He curled in a ball as he fell and wrapped his arms about his head and for a moment he thought it was going to work, that he would pass under the horse like a circus acrobat and come up unharmed on the other side. Then something struck the side of his head and the world exploded into a blackness of stars, very peaceful except for the pain in his head; the last thing he saw was another illusion, but one that let him go out smiling. It was good to see Judith again, even if he knew she couldn't really be there.

"What do we do now?" Lisa asked.

"I seem," said Judith almost inaudibly, "to have been asking that question for quite a long time. And I think we've all run out of answers."

They were sitting in the center of the Stones of

Jura. Nick's head was cradled in Lisa's lap; the faint
rise and fall of his chest showed that he still lived,
but the side of his head was a bloody concave mass of
crushed and splintered bone. Judith had seen him
fall, and she'd given up hope then; it was Lisa, tears
running down her face, who'd insisted that they drag
him into the circle of the Stones while Berengar's
illusions held the monks at bay.

All around them bluish-gray stones, smooth and
polished with centuries of sun and wind and rain,
kept watch; beyond the stones, the illusions that
Berengar was throwing at the armed Durandine monks
crackled and spat like burning ice. The bones of men
who'd died in the traps of the Stones rose again and
fought the Durandines, the little strangledrakes grew
wings of fire and screeched defiance, the horses reared
and snorted at the smells of fresh blood and old
bones. The monks shouted and turned on each other,
unable to tell friend from foe or reality from nightmare, until the call to retreat drew them back.
Berengar leaned against the tallest stone, the one he
had named the keystone, and tried to catch his breath.

"Will they be back?"

"Maybe. Probably. I don't know." Berengar made
an exhausted gesture. "I did not think the Durandines
were such doughty fighters. Their leader Hugh—
before, he seemed to prefer hanging back and leaving the fighting to others; what has turned him into
such a warrior?"

"It wasn't Hugh," Lisa said. With one hand she
kept smoothing the dark hair that fell over Nick's
forehead, and there were tears running down her
face, but she spoke as if she had not noticed them. "I
got a good look at the man in front. It was your
friend. Bishop Rotrou."

"Rotrou! But—" Berengar's instinctive gesture of
denial was checked almost before he had begun.
"Then . . . that explains much," he said, "that I had

wondered over. The Durandines keep the identity of their leader secret, ostensibly so that no king or baron can interfere with their right to free elections; now I see another advantage. I had always supposed that the leader of the Order must himself be a member of the Order; and at the same time, I wondered that a kindly and tolerant man like Rotrou should be so friendly with the Durandines, even to tolerating one of their number as his principal clerk. Now I understand. Hugh was useful to him to carry messages, for no one would wonder at the bishop's clerk visiting fellows of his own order; and Rotrou, as a secret Durandine, must have been most useful to them in their dealings with the world." He sighed and seemed to brace himself against an invisible pressure. "In that case, they will most certainly be back; Rotrou is a fighting bishop of the old type, and not one to be frightened off by ghosts and shadows."

"And you can't keep this up forever," Judith said. His face had gone from pale to greenish; the elf-bright hair was darkened and dampened with sweat, and from the awkward way he held his left arm she could guess that the iron-wound was paining him rather badly.

Berengar managed an exhausted smile. "My lady, I will continue to cast illusions as long as I may, but it would be well if we could bring other aid. Even the little attempt we made at wakening the Stones has roused them slightly; without them I could not have accomplished even so much as I have done."

"You want to try again? You were saying—if I could learn the words you were saying, would that help?"

"Yes. But I do not know if we should take the time." Berengar smiled again, and Judith felt her heart aching for him. It wasn't fair for a man to be so tired and despairing, to see his world going down about him, and still to smile at her so sweetly.

"It will not be necessary," Lisa said. Very gently, she lowered Nick's head to the ground. She frowned at the sight of his face turned sideways against the rough grass. One of the sleeves of her gown was hanging loose where the bishop's mace had slashed downward. She pulled it off, ignoring Berengar's and Judith's shocked gasps at the sight of her bruised and torn shoulder, and made a pillow of it for Nick's head. Then she turned to Berengar and met his eyes, lifting her chin slightly. "It will not be necessary to teach Judith the words of the rite," she said again. "I know them."

Berengar nodded slowly. "Then—you are Sybille, despite your mortal seeming? But we will still need the aid of a mortal to raise the stones, will we not?"

"You have it," said Lisa. There were still tears in her eyes, but her voice was almost gay, as if she were shedding an intolerable burden. "I keep *telling* you people I'm not Sybille; one of these days you're going to have to believe me."

"Then—who are you, who move between the worlds and know our ancient magic?" Berengar demanded.

Lisa smiled through her tears. "I should have thought you'd have guessed," she said. "I was the wizard's apprentice, of course. And all this is my fault; so if I can help now to redeem it, I will do whatever pleases you."

"The wizard's apprentice," Berengar said slowly. "The mortal boy—"

"That," said Lisa, "is one of the many errors that have crept into the story; I suppose because nobody could credit that a mere woman could be taught so much of magecraft as to be any use at all to a great elflord like Joffroi of Brittany." Her voice hardened. "Indeed, we would all have been better off if I had been a boy; maybe then I would not have been so beglamored by Joffroi's promises. But my father had only one plain, sickly girl-child, and what was a great wizard to do with a daughter too dull and plain to be well married, and no son to carry on his craft? He made me his apprentice, and in his pride he taught me more than any apprentice should know. It was rather a scandal at the time; strange how it should have been forgotten in the tales that remain. I suppose that is because the chronicles are mostly written by the elvenkind, and you think the details of mortal lives are hardly worth recording—we have such short lives anyway, like mayflies!" There was little humor in her dry laugh. "Isn't that strange, my lord Berengar, when here I am, a mere mortal, and yet I have lived longer than any of your elven lords? It seemed to me only the blink of an eye that I'd been out of this world, and yet I came back to find that everyone I knew was long dead and that even my great sinful story had been all but forgotten."

"We of the elvenkind have made many mistakes in our dealings with mortals," Berengar said quietly. "Mostly, I think, we underestimate your kind. That is one error I shall not make again."

"Don't worry," Lisa said, "it's nothing compared to my mistake. None of your errors stripped the world of magic and loosed the Wild Hunt upon men. I have the honor of having made the worst mistake of all this world's history."

"And that was?" Berengar prompted, as Lisa stared out beyond the blue pillars that surrounded them.

"Haven't you guessed? I told you that my training in magecraft was a scandal and a wonder in Poitou; even the elvenkind were interested, for once, in mortal doings, for it was said that there'd never been a mortal with such talent as I showed for magecraft— and I only a girl, and an apprentice! Oh, my father boasted mightily, and many were the days when an elven lord dined at our table and conversed with us, almost as if we were his equals, on the arts of magic. One of them," Lisa said, "one of them was Joffroi of

Brittany. And he was the only one who seemed to see *me*. The others saw, I don't know, a useful tool, a rarity, an oddity—a mortal freak, a girl with the talent and skills to be a wizard. Joffroi also saw a tool," she said, "but he knew that the tool had a face, and hands, and feelings. He talked to me about something other than magecraft; he pretended a concern about the bitterness between elves and mortals; he had grand plans to end the rift." She laughed again. "He and I were to join in marriage and magecraft, so he had it, and were to do something at the Stones of Jura that would free their power in the earth so that all might partake of it, elves and mortals alike."

"And you believed him? I do not think," said Berengar, "that was such a terrible mistake. It was a noble dream, even if the man who made it was a liar."

"No," Lisa said flatly. "I should have known he never meant to do it; there was evidence enough in the kind of questions he asked of my father and me, and I was warned by other elven lords that Joffroi had a bad name—oh, for dealings with women, mortal and elven, and for his lust after power. I didn't want to hear the warnings. I loved him, and I wanted him to be a man I should love, and I refused to see anything else."

"Until you came to the Stones of Jura," Berengar said.

"Yes. Even then I let him persuade me. I knew what we were doing; I knew that the words and signs we made between us were drawing all the power of the Stones into a single stream, something that one man—or one elflord—could hold between his two hands. He told me that was the only way to do it, that he would take the power of the Stones only so that he could give it back again to mortals and elvenkind equally. I wanted to believe him. Then

Sybille interrupted us—and he tried to kill her. Your people had more than illusion in those days, Berengar; the elf-fire he threw burned with real heat." Lisa pushed the long loose hair back from her face. There was a white scar on the left side of her forehead. "Sybille defended herself well enough, but—I was between them, and he knew I had no defense; he didn't mind if I was killed. And we had begun the rite, and all the power of the Stones was rushing past us like a stream, and I knew that he had used me and lied to me and that I was a fool who'd given over the world to him, and I—I just wanted it to stop, don't you see? And to get away. I was so ashamed. I don't know what I did, or how it worked; I threw myself into the stream of power and it carried me away."

"You wanted everything to stop," said Berengar, "and it did. You wanted to be someplace far away, and the Stones sent you out of this world. And—now I know what we've all been wading through to come to this place, what has kept both mortals and elvenkind away. I thought the aversion we felt was a spell set by Sybille. But it was just the Stones reflecting the last things you felt, guilt and shame and total misery."

Lisa nodded. "And cowardice. I didn't know what had happened here, and even if I had known how to come back, I think I would have been afraid to face it. But I swear to you, Berengar, I did not know it was this bad! I never dreamed that all the power of the Stones had gone out of the land!"

"I believe you," Berengar said. "And—it has not gone out of the land, I think. I think it became bound to you, rather than to Lord Joffroi, when you stepped out of the ritual he had devised."

Lisa looked at her empty hands. "To me? But—"

"You have been most amazingly lucky," Berengar said, "in this world and in that other one."

Judith spoke for the first time in a long while; her

voice was rough with the tears she had not shed for
Nick. "Drawers," she said unsteadily, "that lock by
themselves, and silver butterflies coming out of nowhere—"

"Angels of fire," Berengar added, "and a mortal
woman who can change the form of an elf-dress. I
should have suspected; but I thought you were Sybille.
Where *is* Sybille, then? And Joffroi?"

Lisa's eyes slid towards the two bluestone pillars
that seemed out of place. "I don't know," she said.
"That is—I'm not sure—oh, I don't want to think
about it! Do you think we can raise the Stones,
Berengar? Perhaps, if you're right, if I bound the
power to me, perhaps I can unbind it. Perhaps I can
undo everything, after all."

"We can try," Berengar said.

He and Lisa stood on opposite sides of the keystone and reached out their hands to make a circle.
Judith opened her mouth to tell them it wouldn't
work, that they would need her or Giles to complete
the circle; then she saw that their fingertips were
touching on both sides of the pillar, but whether it
had shrunk or they had grown she could not quite
tell. The words they spoke fitted together like sweet
chords of music, as if Lisa's voice complemented the
saw-edged words of Berengar's ritual and made them
whole again. And as their voices intertwined, Judith
felt the humming in the ground and saw the mist
around them thinning.

Nick was still breathing shallowly. If Lisa and
Berengar raised the Stones, could they heal him?
She did not dare ask for fear of disturbing their
concentration. Giles was huddled beside her, shiver-
ing; the wonders of the day had finally become too
much for a little street urchin from Paris. Judith put
her arm around the boy and they knelt together
beside Nick's unconscious body, two mortals watching an elf-lord and a girl who was no longer quite

mortal as they tried to raise forces neither of them fully understood.

Three times Berengar's voice faltered, and each time the humming died away, and on the third time his left arm dropped and he lost touch with Lisa's fingertips and a shock trembled through the earth.

"I'm sorry," he said. He was sweating again, and there were two bright red spots high on his cheek-bones. If elves could have infections and a raging fever, Judith thought, that was Berengar's trouble. "Perhaps later . . ."

He looked out into the mist. Judith had heard it too. There might be no *later*. The jingle of horses' gear and the rattle of mail sounded on every side of the stone circle. All Lisa's and Berengar's efforts had served only enough to lift the spells of illusion and repulsion about the Stones long enough for the monks of the Durandines to come closer.

"I'll have to try again."

"No!" Judith took his hand. "It's too dangerous. Don't you see, every time you and Lisa try to raise the Stones, the illusions lift for a moment; and the monks come closer. And . . . other things." Perhaps she'd been imagining the panting noise of shadowy things slinking close to the ground. But she did not think so. "We can't afford to try again."

Berengar shook his head. "You mean, we cannot afford to fail again." He glared at his wounded arm and spat out crackling phrases in the Old Tongue. "That I should be so weak, *now*, when for the first time there are others dependent on me! If only we had another of the elvenkind to lend me strength!"

He looked around the circle, and Judith thought that each of them weighed like another stone on his soul. Nick, wounded and near to death; Giles, look-ing up at Berengar with worship and fear mingled; Lisa, the bedraggled girl from another time and place, with her own bitter self-mocking strength to add to

Berengar's; and herself, bright enough to get them here but not clever enough to find a way out of the refuge that had turned into a trap. Four mortals, all of them dependent now on Berengar. "Do you hate us?" Judith asked. "For bringing you into this trap?"

Berengar smiled. "We are not trapped while hope is left, my dear lady. I will rest a moment and essay to raise the Stones once more." He squeezed her hand. "And even if I fail, you and the others should stand in no danger from Rotrou. The Durandines hate heretics, infidels, and the elvenkind. They have no quarrel with mortals who are good daughters of Mother Church. You must make a cross of something, and hold it before you, and—"

"And beg for mercy, and watch while they hack you down, or while the Wild Hunt takes you?"

"Oh, it need not come to that," said Berengar. "After all, if they enter the circle, Lisa and I will have failed; and if we failed to raise the Stones, then we are no danger to Rotrou's dreams of power. As for the One Who Rides, he must know that I have no soul to take."

Judith thought that Rotrou would not wish to leave any of them alive to identify him as the leader of the Durandines; and even if he were inclined to mercy, the Huntsman was there also in the mist that shut out sun and light.

Berengar leaned on the keystone and breathed slowly and deeply. With each breath he seemed to stand a little straighter, and his eyes sparkled. But his face was so pale that Judith imagined he was growing transparent, that she could see the weathered blue-gray surface of the stone through his white face. She dared not interrupt his concentration by asking what price he was paying for the strength that he seemed to breathe out of the air. What difference did it make? He would tell her that no price was too great. But she felt that he was consuming his own substance so that he might put forth one last effort to save them all, when he might yet have been able to use his elven powers to save himself; and she would have wept, but she had no tears left.

Lisa moved to stand beside her. "It may not be so bad as you think," she said in a low voice, not to break Berengar's concentration. "The—other ones you spoke of? They brought me here—me and Nick. I don't know why; but they did us no harm. They wanted me to come back to the Stones. I think they may mean us no ill."

Judith's head moved in a violent gesture of negation, but she stopped herself before she spoke. Lisa had seen the work of the Hounds; she had only seen their shadows and felt the fear and hopelessness that emanated from them. Lisa had more right than she to judge what they wanted.

Anyway, she thought, what difference did it make whether they were killed by a ghost-hound's teeth or the bishop's mace? Dead was dead. In a few minutes, as soon as Berengar tried and failed again, it would all be over for her, and she would no longer care that she could not go home again or that this world, which might have been so lovely, was to be given over entirely to the grim rule of the Durandines.

Judith stared at the blue pillar of the keystone, and blinked her eyes, and told herself that it was foolish to cry now when it was nearly over one way or the other. Then she blinked again, and rubbed her eyes, and tried not to begin hoping that what she imagined she saw meant some hope for them. The mist around the keystone was glowing with all the colors of sunrise, pink and lavender and opalescent reds and oranges. Had Berengar waked the stones after all, and were they coming from their long sleep now?

"Look!" she tried to say, but the word came out as an inelegant croak. She pointed, and the others turned their heads and stared as the sunrise glow moved, rose higher, and became a sparkle of light too bright to look at. The point of flame swooped above the keystone and darted down into their midst, and Judith, who would have been entranced by it at any other time, swallowed hard over her disappointment.

The light grew and diffused until Judith could see, bathed in a flickering cloak of fire, the form of a slender being with golden arms and legs and long streamers of golden hair and trailing wings of fire, with a face of such unearthly purity and beauty that it all but stopped her breath for a moment.

"Zahariel!" Lisa was knelt to the level of the fire-sprite, holding out her hands as if she welcomed an old friend; Judith could never imagine calling the creature behind that face *friend*. It was young-old, flawless, untouched by mortality; beside it, Berengar, who could bleed and suffer and make jokes in the face of death, seemed as human as she was herself.

Lisa cocked her head as if she could hear something in the dancing music that sparkled, bright and clear and heartless, around the fire-sprite's aurora of light. "What? No. No. *No*," she repeated a third time, so fiercely that Judith knew she must have been tempted by whatever the sprite offered. "I thank you, but—this is my trouble, you see, that I made a long time ago. I will not leave my friends now."

"It owes me a life," she said to the others. "It has helped me since then, but it keeps saying the debt is not paid until it can save my life in its turn; apparently it's been waiting for me to get into serious enough trouble to make it worthwhile to reappear."

"An angel," said Berengar slowly. He dropped to one knee beside Lisa and bowed his head in the blaze of cool fire that lit the entire circle now. "An angel of fire . . . I have read of such things; your Church speaks of them, but I know no one who has seen one before. And it will save you now?"

"No," said Lisa, calmer now. "I don't go without my friends," she told Zahariel. "Can't you save us all?"

I owe you one life, not many. The fire-angel's thought was so clear that Judith thought she could hear it inside her head; or maybe she was just filling in the blanks to match Lisa's half of the conversation.

"Well, then, one of these can go. It's not their fault; they were drawn in after me." Lisa turned to Berengar. "You are most at risk if the Durandines break through."

"I am a knight of the Middle Realm and Count of the Garronais," said Berengar, "and I do not abandon my people."

"Judith?"

Judith shook her head. "Where would I go in this world?" She had lost Nick. If the Stones could not be raised, she would lose her chance of going home, and she would also lose Berengar, which should have been trivial beside the other things, but somehow was not. Life was sweet, the damp salty mist she breathed was very sweet to taste, but— "Where would I go?" she repeated.

Giles did not even speak; he just clung to Judith's arm and tried to burrow into her lap. Judith tried to detach him, but he shook his head and would not be parted from her. And one last, insane, pointless hope came to Judith then.

"If none of us will go with Zahariel," she breathed, "could he—"

"It," Lisa corrected her. "Angels have no gender."

"Could it repay its debt in another way?" She looked at the fire-angel's beautiful, impossible presence, then at her brother with his crushed head pillowed on the torn sleeve of Lisa's green gown. Lisa was listening again.

"It says it can restore one life as payment of its debt," she reported, and sprang to her feet.

"Then—"

"No! Come with me, Zahariel!" Lisa thrust herself between Nick and the fire-sprite, and Judith gasped with horror. After all this, was Lisa going to betray them, to save herself and leave Nick to die with them? Even as Lisa ran across the grass to the far side of the circle, Judith began making excuses for her. What was the point of healing Nick, if they could neither raise the Stones nor escape the Durandines? At least, if Zahariel took Lisa away, one of them would live; wasn't that better than nothing?

But they were not leaving the circle. Lisa paused between the two stones that stood out of place and rested her hand on the nearest one. "I think it is this one," she said softly.

Zahariel circled the stone at the height of a man's head, and the humming that came from his fire-feathered wings was so high and sweet that Judith wanted to cover her ears, but at the same time she wanted to listen to it forever. The fire-music was the direct opposite of the silver hunting horn she had heard in the forest; where that music brought fear and a cold heart, this made her feel more alive than ever before, as if all that had passed before she heard the fire-angel had been only a waking dream. The very air seemed clear and bright where Zahariel passed; and the pillar—

The pillar of blue stone seemed to be quivering at the edges, as if the molecules of the stone were separating to release something long held within. The surface of the stone acquired flesh tones, began to show the rough modeling of a sculptor's first attempt at shaping a face. It was not quite clear yet, but it was going to be the head of a young man.

"No!" Lisa shrieked. "No! I made a mistake! Not that one!"

Zahariel's high sweet humming came to a discordant, jangling halt that left Judith feeling as though her nerves and muscles had been forcibly separated. She had been so intensely aware, living in and through the music, that there was nothing to shelter her from the discord. She staggered and fell back against Berengar, who barely managed to hold her up. She looked into his face and saw that the change in the music had hurt him too.

Giles had very sensibly curled himself into a ball and was trying to melt into the earth.

And Zahariel was circling the other pillar now, singing it into life, singing the stone into living, breathing softness until shapeless stone became a woman's face and the perfect folds of a long sweeping gown, until the face took on the shimmering pale tints of elven flesh and the folds of cloth glowed with green and lavender and hints of silver spray, until the cold perfection of the face awoke and the eyes as blue as Berengar's looked out on the world and the gown trembled.

Zahariel's song ended on a high triumphant note and he soard skyward, vanishing into the mist even as Sybille, Lady of Elfhame, stepped forth from the stone that had imprisoned her. "Who," she demanded of the world at large, "allowed these mortals within the circle?"

CHAPTER EIGHTEEN

Estivant nunc Dryades, colle sub umbroso
produnt Oreades, cetu glorioso,
Satyrorum concio psallit cum tripudio
Tempe per amena,
His alludens concinit, cum iocundi meminit
Veris, filomena.

—Ms. of Benedictbeuern

(The dryads are out for the summer; the mountain nymphs are free of their shady hill; the satyrs are playing and dancing their way to the valley. And to their dancing, remembering joy, sings the nightingale.)

Before any of them could answer, Sybille's eyes fixed on Lisa. "You. Mortal. Now I remember. You were conspiring to steal the power of the Stones. And I stopped you—I—" Sybille frowned. "I cannot quite remember. How came these others here? And what have you done with Lord Joffroi?"

Lisa looked at the other pillar, and Sybille turned her head a fraction of an inch to study the profile of a young man, beautiful and cold as any angel—and now Judith knew exactly what that meant, and in Joffroi's case it was true. As it was of Sybille. These two representatives of the older elvenkind had a cold unhuman purity that repelled her.

Finally Sybille gave a short, satisfied nod. "It is well," she said. "And now—can you think of any reason why I should not do the same to you, child?"

Berengar started forward. "Over my dead body!" He raised his good arm in a warding gesture, and the greenish glow of the elf-light encircled Lisa like a translucent wall.

"If you insist." Sybille looked at the elf-light and it died away, leaving Lisa somehow more vulnerable than she had been a moment before.

"My lady," Lisa said, "before you act, you should know that the world is not as it was. Many years have passed since the events you remember as happening only a few moments before, and Elfhame needs your aid far more than it needs any gestures of vengeance."

In a few sentences she sketched the history of this world since the Catastrophe, the lingering death of the elven powers, the growth of the Durandine order, the appearance of the Wild Hunt and the desperate decision of Alianora to send forth into another world for Sybille in the hope that she might be able to raise the Stones. As Lisa's story became clear, Sybille seemed to age imperceptibly. Her eyes closed for a moment and she was as still as the stone from which she had been freed.

"So," she said at last. "I dare not punish you as you deserve, mortal, because you think that the Stones can only be raised by the joint work of mortal and elvenkind. And if your tale is to be believed, you are the only mortal living who knows the rite in its entirety—so many hundreds of years having passed. A very convenient story for you."

"The lady speaks truth," Berengar said. "I, Berengar

of Garron, eleventh count of the Garronais, will so attest—"

"*Eleventh?*"

Sybille looked into Berengar's eyes for a long moment. "Yes. You are of the Garronais. I knew a Berengar once; he might not have been entirely ashamed to reckon you as his descendant. My Berengar," she said, seeming almost subdued for the first time since she had been freed from the stone, "my Berengar was also a Count of the Garronais. The ninth count."

"My grandsire," Berengar said softly.

"Yes . . ." For a moment Sybille seemed gentler, lost in dreams; then she shook her head and her high-piled braids of moonbeam hair quivered and she was again the great lady giving orders to her regrettably incompetent underlings. "Well, then, if that part of the tale is true, I suppose it all is; and if the current Count of the Garronais is almost as weak as a mortal, unable to heal himself of an iron-wound or to restore a few broken bones in a mortal's head, then I suppose I must do his work for him. Mortal girl, is it really necessary for me to touch your hands in this rite?"

"So Lord Joffroi believed," Lisa said, "and if you recall, his rite had every chance of succeeding—"

Sybille cut her off with an imperious nod. "I recall. It is not, however, necessary for us to have a cozy chat over the matter, as if I were one of your ale-drinking, gossiping mortal friends. You will speak when addressed and will confine your answers to the matter on which I question you. Also, do not look at me; you have grown presumptuous during your stay in this other world." She glanced at Judith. "Apparently the mortals of your world do not know their place. This boy is the only one who behaves appropriately."

Giles had uncurled from a ball long enough to see

Sybille emerging from the stone; ever since he had been face down on the grass, quivering slightly when she spoke.

Lisa rolled her eyes at Judith as she accompanied Sybille to the keystone.

Judith braced herself, expecting something like what had gone before; the chanting of strange syllables, the flickering of clear sight through the mists that surrounded the Stones, the shouts of the armed monks as they caught sight of their goal. But instead of the prolonged rite that Lisa and Berengar had strained to complete, what actually happened was clear and simple. The words of the Old Tongue in Sybille's mouth were like clean bright blades, not the jagged rusty sounds that Berengar had made of them. The words with which Lisa answered were like light dancing on the swords. There was a perfect match between mortal and elvenkind, between sound and sense, and for three breaths Judith actually imagined that she knew what they were singing and that it was the only story she would ever want to hear again. Then the humming of the Stones entered the song, beginning with the low bass rumble of the shifting earth and ending with Zahariel's high notes of fire and air, and in between those two there was a birdsong as liquid as trickling water and the mists dissolved, between one breath and the next, leaving all the actors in the drama suspended where they stood.

For just that moment all stood still, the pale translucent shapes of the Hounds and the glittering mailed figures of the mounted monks. Then Bishop Rotrou gave a shout of victory and drove forward into the circle, spurs striking blood from his horse's sides, the wicked morningstar swinging from its chain. Sybille held up one hand almost before the horse's foam-flecked nose, long fingers outspread in a fan, and spoke a single word that rang dully, like a cracked bell. The horse and the bishop were still and the morningstar hovered at the high point of its arc and the ringing sound went on and on, growing louder and louder, until the Stones of Jura joined in and the earth trembled under the singing stones. When it stopped, sharp as a broken stone, the bishop and the horse and the mailed men behind him remained frozen for one breath more; then there was nothing but their shapes in dust, and the soft air that now blew freely through the circle picked up the dust and stirred it into little troubled dust-devils that fell one by one, limply, into the earth from which they had sprung.

Judith let out one long-held breath and felt the sighing of the others around her.

"So that is the high Earth Magic," Berengar said shakily. "My lady Sybille, I think that the mortals of this world were right to hate and fear us in your day."

"The man willed death," Sybille said, as casually as if she were explaining the unimportance of a broken earthenware pot. "I did no more than turn his own will back upon him."

She looked at the shapes beyond the circle, and for the first time Judith saw what had assembled behind the Durandines, what even now longed to get into the circle of stones where they stood. The shadowy forms of red-eyed hunting hounds pressed against invisible boundaries. Beyond them was an army of the dead, from skeletons to fresh-killed, bleeding bodies, and beyond that, a dark shape of a rider at whom Judith could not quite look. Not directly. She knew that a silver hunting horn hung from his saddle, and that his eyes were very old within a young face; but she knew that without exactly seeing it, and she did not want to see any more.

The little group of mortals drew together in the center of the Stones, with Nick's unconscious body behind them and Berengar before them. One rider, not the Dark One, broke free from the massed army of the dead and spurred towards the circle, and Judith heard a sob from Berengar's throat as he looked at the pageboy with his elven-fair hair and his dark pools of empty eyes.

"Kieran?"

"My lord who was," the boy called, "I bear greetings from my lord who is. Herluin the Huntsman seeks right of passage."

Berengar turned to Sybille. "Do you know of what he speaks?"

"Do you know how these came here?" she replied. "They were driven out of our land long before my day. Who brought them back?"

"The monks of Durand chained my new lord to this earth," the boy Kieran called across the clear bright air, "and as they are now free, so would he be free."

"Don't!" Berengar caught Sybille by the arm as she moved forward. "My lady, you must not leave the circle. They seek to have you, and with you goes all our hope."

"One does not say *must* to the Lady of Elfhame." Sybille shook herself free and paced forward until she stood by the keystone. "Herluin," she called to the dark figure of shadow behind his army. "Herluin, there is no freedom for you in this world. The Stones are awake again."

The shadow huntsman set the silver horn to his lips and blew a long, intricate, sinking phrase of melody. While the music lasted, Judith thought that it answered all things; when it ended, she knew no more than before. But Sybille was smiling as though a riddle had been answered. "Then pass, Herluin, and ride the skies as a shadow again, without power to do good or ill to mortal men or elvenkind. Pass freely and do not return."

On her words, the shadow-tide of hounds and horses and dead poured through the gaps between the stones like a river in flood filling the valley; but this river filled nothing and went nowhere. Somewhere in the center of the circle the translucent shapes thinned out until they were the barest wisps of shadows, scarcely more than the memory of a shape sketched against the blue sky; and then they were gone; but there were always more to take their place. Only the boy once called Kieran lingered at the edge of the flowing pack, reaching forward as though he would take Berengar's hands, but that shadow could not touch flesh.

"Must you go?" Berengar entreated him.

"Do you want me to roam forever, finding peace only in taking others to become like me?" The boy's silver hair gleamed as if it were real, flashing in the sun as he shook his head. "Dear lord who was, I am dead, and so are these others. Let us find rest now, and let Herluin and his hounds be shadows of the sky as they were before."

The last of the translucent tide of shadows was pouring through the center of the circle now. Kieran turned away and ran into the sunlight there. "Wait for me—oh, wait!" he called, and then he was gone, and there was nothing but a few dried leaves rustling and floating in the soft breeze.

"I thought so," said Sybille with satisfaction. "If a renegade mage of the Durandines used his powers to bind the Huntsman into living flesh, that need not mean that Herluin welcomed the binding. As flesh on earth, the Hounds could not help but ravage; that was their nature. As shadows of the sky, they will again do no more than frighten mortal men; a little fear is good for mortals. It is all perfectly logical."

Judith looked at Berengar's ravaged face and entertained brief fantasies of hitting Sybille, whose perfect face showed no hint that her logical understanding made any room for loss and grief and other weakening emotions.

"And now," Sybille went on, "these others also should return to their place." She frowned at the group of mortals. "The child may stay; I can tell that he is of this world. Besides, he is the only one of you mortals with proper manners. You," she pointed at Judith, "should go back to your place, and this one with you." The pointed toe of her shoe indicated Nick.

"Lady, he will die if you do not help him," Lisa protested.

"And what is that to me?" Sybille's left hand moved slightly, and Judith remembered how Bishop Rotrou and all his armed monks had crumbled into dust. Lisa did not move.

"It was at my bidding," she said, staring into the ice crystals of Sybille's eyes, "that Zahariel freed you from the stone. You owe me a life."

Sybille laughed without amusement. "It was your folly that imprisoned me in the first place. And have I not saved you and your friends already? If—oh, never mind, never mind." The white hand that could deal out instant death waved Lisa into silence. "I see you are minded to argue, child, and I am too old for arguments. Let you take your lover back whole and sound, but at a price."

"Whatever it is," Lisa said, "I will gladly pay it."

"Will you?" Sybille laughed again as she knelt beside Nick and laid her long fingers over the depression in his skull. "The price I ask, mortal girl, is that you go back to the world of the iron-demons with these two whom you dragged into my world, and trouble me no more. I may have lived these hundreds of years as a stone," she said, "but there is an aching in my bones that I did not feel before, and I am much too old for such disturbances as turbulent mortals like you bring into my life. There, are you satisfied now?"

Nick moaned and stirred and his eyelids fluttered. Lisa knelt beside him and took his hands.

"What happened? Where—where did the army go?"

"Hush," Lisa whispered, "rest. I'll explain everything soon."

Judith dearly wanted to hear that explanation, but there was no time to linger. Where Sybille's fingers traced an arch in the center of the circle, there was a troubling of the air, and when she looked into the bright center Judith had a sense of sunlight reflecting off metal, machines buzzing about their tasks and impatient, hot, angry people with a terrible sense of haste about all they did.

It seemed impossibly foreign to her.

"First," Sybille said, "first, I think, I will send Joffroi of Brittany where he can work no more treasonous plots against the Middle Realm." She spoke directly at the other pillar, in three clear, sharp, rising notes, and with each word the form of the young man imprisoned in stone grew more and more distinct: taking on shape, taking on color, moving and drawing breath. He stared out at Sybille with angry eyes; but he was still partially of the stone, and he could not move out of the pillar.

"Joffroi of Brittany." Sybille was as arrogant and unpleasant as ever; but now there was something new in her voice, something that made Judith want to drop to her knees and bow her head. This was not just a spoiled, petulant elven lady; this was the Queen of the Middle Realm judging one of her subjects, and her voice carried an authority that could not be denied.

"Joffroi of Brittany," Sybille repeated, "you have committed high treason against the Queen's person and against the Lords of Elfhame and against the very fabric of the Middle Realm. Imprisoned in stone you could do no further harm, but I dare not return you to that state for fear some ignorant person—"she glanced at Lisa here, but Lisa did not notice her look —"might free you at some later date to do more damage to the realm. You may choose death or perpetual exile. Which shall it be?" And she gestured toward the archway where a hot, dusty street full of cars shimmered with the reflection of sun on metal hoods and fenders and bumpers.

"Exile, by your leave, my gracious queen."

"No!" Berengar started forward; Sybille waved him back with one long-fingered white hand. "My lady, if you intend to send him to that other world, you know it is no exile, but death for our kind—and death by torture, surrounded by so much iron. You must not—"

"Peace, child-lord," Sybille snapped.

"Little man, little man, one does not say *must* to princes," Judith quoted under her breath, thinking that Sybille was not so different from mortals as she had first seemed. She and that first Elizabeth of England might have dealt well together.

"I can so transform your nature, Joffroi of Brittany, that iron will have no more power to wound your flesh than it has over any mortal body. But the price of that transformation will be your own mortality. You may yet retain some of your elven powers, but not in their full strength, and what powers you have will work differently in that other world; how so, I cannot now say. You would be as a child among us, but as a prince in their world which knows not the elvenkind. Say now, will you die here a Lord of Elvendom, or live a few years as a prince among mortals?"

"Exile were sweeter to me than death," Joffroi replied. His voice was low and controlled, but the fury that raged behind his eyes made Judith feel weak at the knees.

"So be it." Sybille spoke just one more of those sharp, clear singing words, and the shell of the stone pillar crumbled away and Joffroi of Brittany walked free upon the earth of the Middle Realm for the last time. Judith thought that Sybille still held some compulsion over him, for he looked neither to left nor to right, but walked straight through the arch of shimmering air and faded to nothingness.

"Now you, mortals," Sybille said.

Nick was standing, albeit unsteadily. He looked at Lisa. "Do you wish to come back to our world?"

"Her wishes are of no account," Sybille said, "she has given her word to leave the Middle Realm, in exchange for your healing."

Nick looked straight at Sybille. "And if I do not choose to buy my life at such a price?"

"Your wishes also," said Sybille, "are of no interest to me. The bargain has been struck. Begone!"

Nick seemed as if he would linger still, but Lisa tugged him towards the arch. "Nick, for once, she is right. This is not my home. Everyone I knew is long dead. I want to go home," she said, staring into the image of a dusty street in Texas, "I want to go home!" And she and Nick passed through the arch and faded.

"You, mortal—hurry!" Sybille commanded Judith. "Do you think it is easy to open a Gate, especially with no door on the other side? Nor do I wish all the demons of your world to come pouring through to spoil ours. Enough trouble seems to have come through from this last ill-conceived Opening." She gave Berengar an icy look, but he was not watching her. He had taken Judith's hand and was looking at her with the intensity of an elflord who has just discovered how short time can be.

"Must you go with them?"

"I don't belong in this world," Judith said slowly.

"You belong with me."

"You—can't know that. Not so soon." Was it only yesterday that he'd come out of nowhere to ride down her enemies? It seemed a lifetime ago. The shiny, busy world beyond Sybille's Gate—was that really home?

"If you stay now, you stay forever, mortal woman!" Sybille called. "You, at least, have not deserved exile —but I do not mean to spend my time playing door-keeper for mortals."

"Don't listen to her," Berengar said. "Only stay a little while longer. The power of the Stones is back in the earth; can't you feel it? This world will begin anew. This is our springtime, my lady, and I would share it with you. If after a little while you still wish to go back to your world of iron-demons, a Gate will be made for you. Only give us ten or twenty years—"

It had been the wrong thing to say, and he knew it at once. Judith withdrew cold fingers from his. "Ten or twenty years," she repeated unsteadily. "Berengar, that is *my life*."

"Surely, even in your world, mortals are not so short-lived?"

"Berengar, *look* at me. I'm almost thirty. My body has already started to age. In ten years some of this blonde hair will be gray, and I'll be getting thick around the waist, and my teeth won't be so good," Judith said brutally. "In twenty years I'll have wrinkles. And you'll still be a bright young man beginning to learn his way around the world. You said it yourself, Berengar. These matches between mortals and elvenkind never work out well."

"I will not accept that," Berengar said. "*I will not accept it.*"

"The Gate is closing," Sybille said. Judith tore herself away with one last backward glance, and stepped through the bright arch of air and into a city street just one block from the New Age Center. Horns blared, tires screeched, and five Texas drivers leaned out their windows to curse the crazy people who were walking out of thin air, one after another. Judith reached the safety of the curb and turned for one last look at the world she had lost. For a moment it hovered there, green and cool above the smoky street; then it was gone as if it had never been.

But it had left its mark on their own world, Judith thought—or might yet. For Joffroi of Brittany was somewhere abroad in this world, now, an angry elf-lord with uncertain powers that he would surely not use for well. They would have to find him—or, she thought uneasily, would he make it his business to find them?

When she caught up with Nick and Lisa, on the steps of the Center, she decided not to trouble them with her speculations. Not that it would have mattered. Nick was playing his invalidism for all it was worth, reclining on the broad shady porch of the Center with his head in Lisa's lap while she told them the parts of the story that he had missed.

"So, you see," she finished, "there's no more magic about me, if there ever was. No more drawers that lock by themselves and dresses that change length to suit my moods. It was only a bit of the power of the Stones that clung to me and that I didn't even know how to use, and now it has been returned to the Stones where it belongs."

"Pity," said Nick lazily. "A wife who could alter her dresses by squinting at them would be a great help to a rising young lawyer with a regrettably small practice."

"A *what*? But—"

"I know, I know," Nick said. He rolled over and kissed Lisa's hand. "You don't even like me. Never mind; we'll work it out. You'll have to marry me first, though."

"And just why—"

"Because," Nick said, "even if your magic is gone

and the Durandines aren't going to send any more hit men after you, there are a few minor problems remaining in this world. You're still an undocumented alien. Marrying me will help to regularize your position; we'll work on creating you a paper history after that."

Judith rather thought that neither of them had noticed the cloud of green and silver butterflies that rose from Lisa's hair and circled above them in the gentle October sunshine. She filed that with her growing list of things not to trouble the children about, and went on into the Center to tell Aunt Penny that everything was as much back to normal as she could expect.